THE DECEIVER

BOOKS BY FREDERICK FORSYTH

The Biafra Story
The Day of the Jackal
The Odessa File
The Dogs of War
The Shepherd
The Devil's Alternative
No Comebacks
The Fourth Protocol
The Negotiator
The Deceiver

FREDERICK FORSYTH

THE DECEIVER

BANTAM BOOKS
NEW YORK • TORONTO • LONDON • SYDNEY • AUCKLAND

Grateful acknowledgment is made for permission to reprint the following: Excerpt from THOSE WERE THE DAYS, Words and Music by Gene Raskin. TRO—© Copyright 1962 (renewed) and 1968 Essex Music, Inc., New York, N.Y. Used by Permission. Excerpt from THE CARNIVAL IS OVER (Tom Springfield) © 1965 CHAPPELL MUSIC LTD. (PRS) All rights administered by CHAPPELL & CO. All rights reserved. Used by permission.

THE DECEIVER

A Bantam Book / October 1991

All rights reserved.
Copyright © 1991 by F.S.S. Partnership.
Book design by GDS/Jeffrey L. Ward
No part of this book may be reproduced or transmitted in any form or by any means, electronic or mechanical, including photocopying, recording, or by any information storage and retrieval system, without permission in writing from the publisher.
For information address: Bantam Books.

Library of Congress Cataloging-in-Publication Data
Forsyth, Frederick, 1938–
  The deceiver / Frederick Forsyth.
    p. cm.
  ISBN 0-553-07319-2
  I. Title.
PR6059.0699D43   1991
823'.914—dc20   91-13114
CIP

Published simultaneously in the United States and Canada

Bantam Books are published by Bantam Books, a division of Bantam Doubleday Dell Publishing Group, Inc. Its trademark, consisting of the words "Bantam Books" and the portrayal of a rooster, is Registered in U.S. Patent and Trademark Office and in other countries. Marca Registrada. Bantam Books, 666 Fifth Avenue, New York, New York 10103.

PRINTED IN THE UNITED STATES OF AMERICA

0 9 8 7 6 5 4 3 2 1

The Cold War lasted forty years. For the record, the West won it. But not without cost. This book is for those who spent so much of their lives in the shadowed places. Those were the days, my friends.

Contents

THE DECEIVER

Prologue

In the summer of 1983 the then Chief of the British Secret Intelligence Service sanctioned the formation, against a certain internal opposition, of a new desk.

The opposition came mainly from the established desks, almost all of which had territorial fiefdoms spread across the world, for the new desk was designed to have a wide-ranging jurisdiction that would span traditional frontiers.

The impetus behind the formation came from two sources. One was an ebullient mood in Westminster and Whitehall, and notably within the ruling Conservative government, following Britain's success in the Falklands war of the previous year. Despite the military success, the episode had left behind one of those messy and occasionally vituperative arguments over the issue: Why were we so taken by surprise when General Galtieri's Argentine forces landed at Port Stanley?

Between departments, the argument festered for over a year, reduced inevitably to charges and countercharges on the level of we-were-not-warned-yes-you-were. The Foreign Secretary, Lord Carrington, had felt obliged to resign. Several years later, the United States would be seized by a similar row following the destruction of the Pan American flight over

Lockerbie, with one agency claiming it had issued a warning and another claiming it had never received it.

The second impetus was the recent arrival at the seat of power, the General Secretaryship of the Communist Party of the Soviet Union, of Yuri V. Andropov, who had for fifteen years been Chairman of the KGB. Favoring his old agency, Andropov's reign instituted an upsurge of increasingly aggressive espionage and "active measures" by the KGB against the West. It was known that Andropov highly favored, among active measures, the use of disinformation—the spreading of despondency and demoralization by the use of lies, agents of influence, and character assassination, and by the sowing of discord among the Allies with planted untruths.

Mrs. Thatcher, then earning her Soviet-awarded title of the Iron Lady, took the view that two can play at that game and indicated she would not blanch at the notion of Britain's own intelligence agency offering the Soviets a little return match.

The new desk was given a ponderous title: Deception, Disinformation, and Psychological Operations. Of course, the title was at once reduced to Dee-Dee and Psy Ops, and thence simply to Dee-Dee.

A new desk head was appointed in November. Just as the man in charge of Equipment was known as the Quartermaster and the man in charge of the Legal Branch as the Lawyer, the new head of Dee-Dee was tagged by some wit in the canteen the Deceiver.

With hindsight—that precious gift so much more prevalent than its counterpart, foresight—the Chief, Sir Arthur, might have been criticized (and later was) for his choice: not a Head Office careerist accustomed to the prudence required of a true civil servant, but a former field agent, plucked from the East German desk.

The man was Sam McCready, and he ran the desk for seven years. But all good things come to an end. In the late spring of 1991 a conversation took place in the heart of Whitehall. . . .

The young aide rose from behind his desk in the outer office with a practiced smile. "Good morning, Sir Mark. The Permanent Under-Secretary asked that you be shown straight in."

He opened the door to the private office of the Permanent Under-Secretary of the Foreign and Commonwealth Office—the FCO—and ushered the visitor through it, closing the door behind him. The Permanent Under-Secretary, Sir Robert Inglis, rose with a welcoming smile.

"Mark, my dear chap, how good of you to come."

You do not become, however recently, Chief of the Secret Intelligence Service, or SIS, without developing a certain wariness when confronted by such warmth from a relative stranger who is clearly about to treat you as if you were blood brothers. Sir Mark steeled himself for a difficult meeting.

When he was seated, the country's senior Foreign Office civil servant opened the scarred red dispatch box lying on his desk and withdrew a buff file distinguished by the red diagonal cross running from corner to corner.

"You have done the rounds of your stations and will doubtless let me have your impressions?" he asked.

"Certainly, Robert—in due course."

Sir Robert Inglis followed the top-secret file with a red, paper-covered book secured at its spine by black plastic spiral binding.

"I have," he began, "read your proposals, 'SIS in the Nineties,' in conjunction with the Intelligence Co-Ordinator's latest shopping list. You seem to have met his requirements most thoroughly."

"Thank you, Robert," said the Chief. "Then may I count upon the Foreign Office's support?"

The diplomat's smile could have won prizes on an American game show.

"My dear Mark, we have no difficulties with the pitch of your proposals. But there are just a few points I would like to take up with you."

Here it comes, thought the Chief of the SIS.

"May I take it, for example, that these additional stations abroad that you propose have been agreed upon with the Treasury, and the necessary monies squirreled away in somebody's budget?"

Both men well knew that the budget for the running of the Secret Intelligence Service does not come wholly from the Foreign Office. Indeed, only a small part comes out of the FCO budget. The real cost of the almost-invisible SIS, which unlike the American CIA keeps an extremely low profile, is shared among all the spending ministries in the government. The spread is right across the board, including even the unlikely Ministry of Agriculture, Fisheries, and Food—perhaps on the grounds that they might one day wish to know how many cod the Icelanders are taking out of the North Atlantic.

Because its budget is spread so widely and hidden so well, the SIS cannot be "leaned upon" by the FCO with a threat of withholding funds if the FCO's wishes are not met.

Sir Mark nodded. "There's no problem there. The Co-Ordinator and I have seen the Treasury, explained the position (which we had cleared with the Cabinet Office), and Treasury has allocated the necessary cash, all tucked away in the research and development budgets of the least likely ministries."

"Excellent," beamed the Permanent Under-Secretary, whether he felt it was or not. "Then let us turn to something that *does* fall within my purview. I don't know what your staffing position is, but we are facing some difficulties with regard to staffing the expanded Service that will result from the end of the Cold War and the liberation of Central and Eastern Europe. You know what I mean?"

Sir Mark knew exactly what he meant. The virtual collapse of Communism over the previous two years was changing the diplomatic map of the globe, and rapidly. The Diplomatic Corps was looking to expanded opportunities right across Central Europe and the Balkans, possibly even miniembassies in Latvia, Lithuania, and Estonia if they secured independence from Moscow. By inference, he was suggesting that with the Cold War now laid out in the morgue, the position for his colleague in Secret Intelligence would be just the reverse: reduction of staff. Sir Mark was having none of it.

"Like you, we have no alternative but to recruit. Leaving recruitment to one side, the training alone is six months before we can bring a new man into Century House and release an experienced man for service abroad."

The diplomat dropped his smile and leaned forward earnestly. "My dear Mark, this is precisely the meat of the discussion I wished to have with you. Allocations of space in our embassies, and to whom."

Sir Mark groaned inwardly. The bastard was going for the groin. While the FCO cannot "get at" the SIS on budgetary grounds, it has one ace card always ready to play. The great majority of intelligence officers serving abroad do so under the cover of the embassy. That makes the embassy their host. No allocation of a "cover" job—no posting.

"And what is your general view for the future, Robert?" he asked.

"In future, I fear, we will simply not be able to offer positions to some of your more . . . colorful staffers. Officers whose cover is clearly blown. Brass-plate operators. In the Cold War it was acceptable; in the new Europe they would stick out like sore thumbs. Cause offense. I'm sure you can see that."

Both men knew that agents abroad fell into three categories. "Illegal" agents were not within the cover of the embassy and were not the concern of Sir Robert Inglis. Officers serving inside the embassy were either "declared" or "undeclared."

A declared officer, or brass-plate operator, was one whose real function was widely known. In the past, having such an intelligence officer in an embassy had worked like a dream. Throughout the Communist and Third Worlds, dissidents, malcontents, and anyone else who wished knew just whom to come to and pour out their woes as to a father confessor. It had led to rich harvests of information and some spectacular defectors.

What the senior diplomat was saying was that he wanted no more such officers any longer and would not offer them space. His dedication was to the maintenance of his department's fine tradition of appeasement of anyone not born British.

"I hear what you are saying, Robert, but I cannot and will not start my term as Chief of the SIS with a purge of senior officers who have served long, loyally, and well."

"Find other postings for them," suggested Sir Robert. "Central and South America, Africa . . ."

"And I cannot pack them off to Burundi until they come up for retirement."

"Desk jobs, then. Here at home."

"You mean what is called 'unattractive employments,' " said the Chief. "Most will not take them."

"Then they must go for early retirement," said the diplo-

mat smoothly. He leaned forward again. "Mark, my dear
chap, this is not negotiable. I will have the Five Wise Men
with me on this, be assured of it, seeing that I am one myself.
We will agree to handsome compensation, but . . ."

The Five Wise Men are the Permanent Under-Secretaries
of the Cabinet Office, the Foreign Office, the Home Office,
the Ministry of Defense, and the Treasury. Among them,
these five wield enormous power in the corridors of government. Among other things they appoint (or recommend to the
Prime Minister, almost the same thing) the Chief of the SIS
and the Director General of the Security Service, MI-5.

Sir Mark was deeply unhappy, but he knew the realities of
power well enough. He would have to concede. "Very well,
but I will need guidance on procedures."

What he meant was that, for his own position among his
own staff, he wanted to be visibly overruled. Sir Robert Inglis
was expansive; he could afford to be.

"Guidance will be forthcoming at once," he said. "I will
ask the other Wise Men for a hearing, and we will lay down
new rules for a new set of circumstances. What I propose is
that you instigate, under the new rules that will be handed
down, what the lawyers call 'a class action' and thus establish
specimen counts."

"Class action? Specimen counts? What are you talking
about?" asked Sir Mark.

"A precedent, my dear Mark. A single precedent that will
then operate for the whole group."

"A scapegoat?"

"An unpleasant word. Early retirement with generous pension rights can hardly be called victimization. You take one
officer whose early departure could be envisaged without
demur, hold a hearing, and thus set your precedent."

"One officer? Had you anyone in mind?"

Sir Robert steepled his fingers and gazed at the ceiling.

"Well, there is always Sam McCready."

Of course. The Deceiver. Ever since his latest display of
vigorous if unauthorized initiative in the Caribbean three
months earlier, Sir Mark had been aware that the Foreign
Office regarded him as a sort of unleashed Genghis Khan.
Odd, really. Such a . . . crumpled fellow.

*   *   *

Sir Mark was driven back across the Thames to his headquarters, Century House, in a deeply introspective mood. He
knew the senior civil servant in the Foreign Office had not
merely "proposed" the departure of Sam McCready—he was
insisting on it. From the Chief's point of view, he could not
have chosen a more difficult demand.

In 1983, when Sam McCready had been chosen to head up
the new desk, Sir Mark had been a Deputy Controller, a
contemporary of McCready and only one rank above him. He
liked the quirky, irreverent agent whom Sir Arthur had appointed to the new post—but then, so did just about everybody.

Shortly afterward, Sir Mark had been sent to the Far East
for three years (he was a fluent Mandarin-speaker) and had
returned in 1986 to be promoted to Deputy Chief. Sir Arthur
retired, and a new Chief sat in the hot seat. Sir Mark had
succeeded *him* the previous January.

Before leaving for China, Sir Mark had, like others, specu-
lated that Sam McCready would not last long. The Deceiver,
or so ran the received wisdom, was too rough a diamond to
cope easily with the in-house politics of Century House.

For one thing, he had thought at the time, none of the
regional desks would take kindly to the new man trying to
operate in their jealously guarded territories. There would be
turf wars that could only be handled by a consummate diplomat, and whatever else his talents, McCready had never been
seen as that. For another, the somewhat scruffy Sam would
hardly fit into the world of smoothly tailored senior officers,
most of whom were products of Britain's exclusive public
schools.

To his surprise Sir Mark, on his return, had found Sam
McCready flourishing like the proverbial green bay tree. He
seemed to be able to command an enviable and total loyalty
from his own staff while not offending even the most die-hard
territorial desk heads when asking for a favor.

He could talk the lingo with the other field agents when
they came home for furlough or a briefing, and from them he
seemed to amass an encyclopedia of information, much of
which, no doubt, should never have been divulged on a need-
to-know basis.

It was known he could share a beer with the technical

cadres, the nuts-and-bolts men and women—a camaraderie not always available to senior officers—and from them occasionally obtain a phone tap, mail intercept, or false passport while other desk heads were still filling out forms.

All this—and other irritating foibles like bending the rules and disappearing at will—hardly caused the Establishment to become enamored of him. But what kept him in place was simple—he delivered the goods, he provided the product, he ran an operation that kept the KGB fully stocked with indigestion tablets. So he had stayed . . . until now.

Sir Mark sighed, climbed out of his Jaguar in the underground car park of Century House, and took the lift to his top-floor office. For the moment he need do nothing. Sir Robert Inglis would confer with his colleagues and produce the "new set of rules," the "guidance" that would enable the troubled Chief to say, truthfully but with a heavy heart, "I have no alternative."

It was not until early June that the "guidance"—or in reality the edict—came down from the Foreign and Commonwealth Office and enabled Sir Mark to summon his two Deputies to his office.

"That's a bit bloody stiff," said Basil Gray. "Can't you fight it?"

"Not this time," said the Chief. "Inglis has got the bit between his teeth, and as you see, he has the other four Wise Men with him."

The paper he had given his two Deputies to study was a model of clarity and impeccable logic. It pointed out that by October 3, East Germany—once the toughest and most effective of Eastern European Communist states—would literally have ceased to exist. There would be no embassy in East Berlin, the Wall was already a farce, the formidable secret police, the SSD, or *Stasi,* were in full retreat, and the Soviet forces were pulling out. An area that had once demanded a large operation by the SIS in London would become a sideshow, if any show at all.

Moreover, the paper went on, that nice Mr. Vaclav Havel was taking over in Czechoslovakia, and *their* spy service, the StB, would soon be teaching Sunday school. Add to that the collapse of Communist rule in Poland, Hungary, and Romania, its coming disintegration in Bulgaria, and one could grasp the approximate shape of the future.

"Well," sighed Timothy Edwards, "one has to concede we won't have the operations we used to have in Eastern Europe, or need the manpower there. They have a point."

"How kind of you to say so," smiled the Chief.

Basil Gray he had promoted himself, his first act on being appointed Chief in January. Timothy Edwards he had inherited. He knew Edwards was hungry to succeed him in three years' time; knew also that he had not the slightest intention of recommending him. Not that Edwards was stupid. Far from it; he was brilliant, but . . .

"They don't mention the other hazards," grumbled Gray. "Not a word about international terrorism, the rise of the drug cartels, the private armies—and not a word about proliferation."

In his own paper, "SIS in the Nineties," which Sir Robert Inglis had read and apparently approved, Sir Mark had laid stress on the shifting rather than the diminishing of the global threats. At the top of these had been proliferation—the steady acquisition by dictators, some of them wildly unstable, of vast arsenals of weapons; not war-surplus pieces such as in the old days, but high-tech modern equipment, rocketry, chemical and bacteriological warheads, even nuclear access. But the paper before him now had treacherously skimmed over these matters.

"So what happens now?" asked Timothy Edwards.

"What happens," said the Chief mildly, "is that we envisage a shift of population—our population. Back from Eastern Europe to the home base."

He meant that the old Cold War warriors, the veterans who had run their operations, their active measures, their networks of local agents out of the embassies east of the Iron Curtain, would come home—to no jobs. They would be replaced, of course, but by younger men whose true profession would not be known and who would blend into the embassy staffs unperceived, so as not to give offense to the emergent democracies beyond the Berlin Wall. Recruitment would go on, of course—the Chief had a Service to run. But that left the problem of the veterans. Where to put them? There was only one answer—out to pasture.

"We will have to set a precedent," said Sir Mark. "One precedent that will clear the way for the smooth passage into early retirement for the rest."

"Anyone in mind?" asked Gray.

"Sir Robert Inglis does. Sam McCready."

Basil Gray stared across with his mouth open. "Chief, you can't fire Sam."

"No one's firing Sam," said Sir Mark. He echoed Robert Inglis's words. "Early retirement with generous compensation is hardly victimization."

He wondered how heavy those thirty pieces of silver had felt when the Romans handed them over.

"It's sad, of course, because we all like Sam," said Edwards predictably. "But the Chief does have a Service to run."

"Precisely. Thank you," said Sir Mark.

As he sat there he realized for the first time exactly why he would not be recommending Timothy Edwards to succeed him one day. He, the Chief, would do what had to be done because it had to be done, and he would hate it. Edwards would do it because it would advance his career.

"We'll have to offer him three alternative employments," Gray pointed out. "Perhaps he'll take one." Privately, he sincerely hoped so.

"Possibly," Sir Mark grunted.

"What have you in mind, Chief?" asked Edwards.

Sir Mark opened a folder, its contents the result of a conference with the Director of Personnel.

"Those available are the Commandant of the Training School, the Head of Administration/Accounts, and the Head of Central Registry."

Edwards smiled thinly. That should do the trick, he thought.

Two weeks later the subject of all these conferences prowled around his office while his deputy, Denis Gaunt, stared gloomily at the sheet in front of him.

"It's not all that bad, Sam," he said. "They want you to stay on. It's just the question of the job."

"Someone wants me out," said McCready flatly.

London flagged under a heat wave that summer. The office

window was open, and both men had removed their jackets. Gaunt was in a smart pale-blue shirt from Turnbull and Asser; McCready had a confection from Viyella that had turned woolly from much washing. Moreover, the buttons had not been inserted into the right buttonholes so that it rode up on one side. By the lunch hour, Gaunt suspected, some secretary would have spotted the error and put it right with much tut-tutting. The women around Century House always seemed to want to do something for Sam McCready.

It baffled Gaunt, the matter of McCready and the ladies. It baffled everyone, for that matter. He, Denis Gaunt, at six feet, topped his boss by two inches. He was blond, good-looking, and as a bachelor no shrinking violet when it came to the ladies.

His desk chief was of medium height, medium build with thinning brown hair, usually awry, and clothes that always looked as if he had slept in them. He knew McCready had been widowed for some years, but he had never remarried, preferring apparently to live alone in his little flat in Kensington.

There must be somebody, Gaunt mused, to clean his flat, wash up, and do the laundry. A charlady, perhaps. But no one ever asked, and no one was ever told.

"Surely you could take one of the jobs," said Gaunt. "It would cut the ground right out from under their feet."

"Denis," replied McCready gently, "I am not a school-teacher, I am not an accountant, and I am not a bloody librarian. I'm going to make the bastards give me a hearing."

"That might swing it," agreed Gaunt. "The board won't necessarily want to go along with this."

The hearing inside Century House began as always on a Monday morning, and it was held in the conference room one floor down from the Chief's office.

In the chair was the Deputy Chief, Timothy Edwards, immaculate as ever in a dark Blades suit and college tie, the man the Chief had picked to ensure the required verdict. He was flanked by the Controller of Domestic Operations and the Controller for Western Hemisphere. To one side of the room sat the Director of Personnel, next to a young clerk from Records who had a large pile of folders in front of him.

Sam McCready entered last and sat in the chair facing the table. At fifty-one, he was still lean and looked fit. Otherwise, he was the sort of man who could pass unnoticed. That was what had made him in his day so good, so damned good. That, and what he had in his head.

They all knew the rules. Turn down three "unattractive employments," and they had the right to require you to take premature retirement. But he had the right to a hearing, to argue for a variation.

He brought with him to speak on his behalf Denis Gaunt, ten years his junior, whom he had raised over five years to the number-two slot under himself. Denis, he reckoned, with his brilliant smile and public school tie, would be able to handle them better than he could.

All the men in the room knew each other and were on first-name terms, even the clerk from Records. It is a tradition of Century House, perhaps because it is such a closed world, that everyone may call everyone by first names except the Chief who is called "Sir" or "Chief" to his face and "the Master" or other things behind his back. The door was closed, and Edwards coughed for silence. He would.

"All right. We are here to study Sam's application for a variation of a Head Office order, not amounting to redress of grievance. Agreed?"

Everyone agreed. It was established Sam McCready had no grievance, inasmuch as the rules had been abided by.

"Denis, I believe you are going to speak for Sam?"

"Yes, Timothy."

The SIS was founded in its present form by an admiral, Sir Mansfield Cumming, and many of its in-house traditions (though not the familiarity) still have a vaguely nautical flavor. One of these is the right of a man before a hearing to have a fellow officer speak for him, a right that is often invoked.

The Director of Personnel's statement was brief and to the point. The powers-that-be had decided they wished to transfer Sam McCready from Dee-Dee to fresh duties. He had declined to accept any of the three on offer. That was tantamount to electing early retirement. McCready was asking, if he could not continue as Head of Dee-Dee, for a return to the field or to a desk that handled field operations. Such a posting was not on offer. QED.

Denis Gaunt rose.

"Look, we all know the rules. And we all know the realities. It's true Sam has asked not to be assigned to the training school, or the accounts, or the files because he is a field man by training and instinct. And one of the best, if not the best."

"No dispute," murmured the Controller for Western Hemisphere. Edwards shot him a warning look.

"The point is," suggested Gaunt, "that if it really wanted to, the Service could probably find a place for Sam. Russia, Eastern Europe, North America, France, Germany, Italy. I am suggesting the Service ought to make that effort, because . . ."

He approached the man from Records and took a file.

"Because he has four years to go to retire at fifty-five on full pension."

"Ample compensation has been offered," Edwards cut in. "Some might say extremely generous."

"Because," resumed Gaunt, "of years of service, loyal, often very uncomfortable, and sometimes extremely dangerous. It's not a question of the money, it's a question of whether the Service is prepared to make the effort for one of its own."

He had, of course, no idea of the conversation that had taken place the previous month between Sir Mark and Sir Robert Inglis at the Foreign Office.

"I would like us to consider a few cases handled by Sam over the previous six years. Starting with this one."

The man of whom they were speaking stared impassively from his chair at the rear of the room. None present could guess at the anger, even despair, beneath that weathered face.

Timothy Edwards glanced at his watch. He had hoped this affair could be terminated within the day. Now he doubted it could.

"I think we all recall it," said Gaunt. "The matter concerning the late Soviet general, Yevgeni Pankratin. . . ."

PRIDE AND
EXTREME PREJUDICE

Chapter 1

May 1983

The Russian colonel stepped out of the shadows slowly and carefully, even though he had seen and recognized the signal. All meetings with his British controller were dangerous and to be avoided if possible. But this one he had asked for himself. He had things to say, to demand, that could not be put in a message in a dead-letter box. A loose sheet of metal on the roof of a shed down the railway line flapped and creaked in a puff of predawn May wind of that year, 1983. He turned, established the source of the noise, and stared again at the patch of darkness near the locomotive turntable.

"Sam?" he called softly.

Sam McCready had also been watching. He had been there for an hour in the darkness of the abandoned railway yard in the outer suburbs of East Berlin. He had seen, or rather heard, the Russian arrive, and still he had waited to ensure that no other feet were moving amidst the dust and the rubble. However many times you did it, the knotted ball in the base of the stomach never went away.

At the appointed hour, satisfied they were alone and unac-

companied, he had flicked the match with his thumbnail, so
that it had flared once, briefly, and died away. The Russian
had seen it and emerged from behind the old maintenance
hut. Both men had reason to prefer the gloom, for one was a
traitor and the other a spy.

McCready moved out of the darkness to let the Russian see
him, paused to establish that he too was alone, and went
forward.

"Yevgeni. It's been a long time, my friend."

At five paces they could see each other clearly, establish
that there had been no substitution, no trickery. That was
always the danger in a face-to-face. The Russian might have
been taken and then broken in the interrogation rooms, allow-
ing the KGB and the East German SSD to set up a trap for a
top British intelligence officer. Or the Russian's message
might have been intercepted, and it might be he was moving
into the trap, thence to the long dark night of the interrogators
and the final bullet in the nape of the neck. Mother Russia had
no mercy for her traitorous elite.

McCready did not embrace or even shake hands. Some
assets needed that: the personal touch, the comfort of contact. But Yevgeni Pankratin, Colonel of the Red Army, on
attachment to the GSFG, was a cold one: aloof, self-con-
tained, confident in his arrogance.

He had first been spotted in Moscow in 1980 by a sharp-
eyed attaché at the British Embassy. It was a diplomatic
function—polite, banal conversation, then the sudden tart
remark by the Russian about his own society. The diplomat
had given no sign, said nothing. But he had noted and reported. A possible. Two months later a first tentative approach had been made. Colonel Pankratin had been noncom-
mital but had not rebuffed it. That ranked as positive. Then
he had been posted to Potsdam, to the Group of Soviet Forces
Germany, the GSFG, the 330,000-man, twenty-two-division
army that kept the East Germans in thrall, the puppet Honecker in power, the West Berliners in fear, and NATO on the
alert for a crushing break-out across the Central German
Plain.

McCready had taken over; it was his patch. In 1981 he
made his own approach, and Pankratin was recruited. No

fuss, no outpourings of inner feelings to be listened to and agreed with—just a straight demand for money.

People betray the lands of their fathers for many reasons: resentment, ideology, lack of promotion, hatred of a single superior, shame for their bizarre sexual preferences, fear of being summoned home in disgrace. With Russians, it was usually a deep disillusionment with the corruption, the lies, and the nepotism they saw all around them. But Pankratin was the true mercenary—he just wanted money. One day he would come out, he said, but when he did, he intended to be rich. He had called the dawn meeting in East Berlin to raise the stakes.

Pankratin reached inside his trenchcoat and produced a bulky brown envelope, which he extended toward McCready. Without emotion he described what was inside the envelope as McCready secreted the package inside his duffle coat. Names, places, timings, divisional readiness, operational orders, movements, postings, weaponry upgrades. The key, of course, was what Pankratin had to say about the SS-20, the terrible Soviet mobile-launched medium-range missile, with each of its independently guided triple-nuke warheads targeted on a British or European city. According to Pankratin, they were moving into the forests of Saxony and Thuringia, closer to the border, able to range in an arc from Oslo through Dublin to Palermo. In the West huge columns of sincere, naïve people were on the march behind socialist banners demanding that their own governments strip themselves of their defenses as a gesture of goodwill for peace.

"There is a price, of course," said the Russian.

"Of course."

"Two hundred thousand pounds sterling."

"Agreed." It had not been agreed, but McCready knew his government would find it somewhere.

"There is more. I understand I am being slated for promotion. To Major-General. And a transfer back to Moscow."

"Congratulations. As what, Yevgeni?"

Pankratin paused to let it sink in. "Deputy Director, Joint Planning Staff, Defense Ministry."

McCready was impressed. To have a man in the heart of 19 Frunze Street, Moscow, would be incomparable.

"And when I come out, I want an apartment block. In

California. Deeds in my name. Santa Barbara, perhaps. I have heard it is beautiful there.''

"It is," agreed McCready. "You wouldn't like to settle in Britain? We would look after you."

"No, I want the sun. Of California. And one million dollars, U.S., in my account there."

"An apartment can be arranged," said McCready. "And a million dollars—if the product is right."

"Not an apartment, Sam. A block of apartments. To live off the rents."

"Yevgeni, you are asking for between five and eight million American dollars. I don't think my people have that kind of money, even for your product."

The Russian's teeth gleamed beneath his military moustache in a brief smile. "When I am in Moscow, the product I will bring you will be beyond your wildest expectations. You will find the money."

"Let's wait till you have your promotion first, Yevgeni. Then we will talk about an apartment block in California."

They parted five minutes later, the Russian to return, in uniform, to his desk at Potsdam, the Englishman to slip back through the Wall to the stadium in West Berlin. He would be searched at Checkpoint Charlie. The package would cross the Wall by another safer but slower route. Only when it joined him in the West would he fly back to London.

October 1983

Bruno Morenz knocked on the door and entered in response to the jovial "*Herein.*" His superior was alone in the office, in his important revolving leather chair behind his important desk. He was delicately stirring his first cup of real coffee of the day in the bone china cup, deposited by the attentive Fräulein Keppel, the neat spinster who waited upon his every legitimate need.

Like Morenz, the Herr Direktor was of the generation that could recall the end of the war and the years thereafter, when Germans made do with chicory extract and only the American occupiers and occasionally the British could get hold of real coffee. No longer. Dieter Aust appreciated his Colombian coffee in the morning. He did not offer Morenz any.

Both men were nudging fifty, but there the similarity ended. Aust was short, plump, beautifully barbered and tailored, and the director of the entire Cologne Station. Morenz was taller, burly, gray-haired. But he stooped and appeared to shamble as he walked, chunky and untidy in his tweed suit. Moreover, he was a low-to-medium-rank civil servant who would never aspire to the title of Director, nor have his own important office with Fräulein Keppel to bring him Colombian coffee in bone china before he started the day's work.

The scene of a senior man summoning a low-level staffer to his office for a talk was probably being enacted in many offices all over Germany that morning, but the area of employment of these two men would not have been mirrored in many other places. Nor indeed would the conversation that followed. For Dieter Aust was the Director of the Cologne outstation of the West German Secret Intelligence Service, the BND.

The BND is actually headquartered in a substantial walled compound just outside the small village of Pullach, some six miles south of Munich, on the River Isar in the south of Bavaria. This might seem an odd choice bearing in mind that the national capital since 1949 has been in Bonn, hundreds of miles away on the Rhine. The reason is historical. It was the Americans who, just after the war, set up a West German spy service to counteract the efforts of the new enemy, the USSR. They chose for the head of the new service the former wartime German spy chief Reinhard Gehlen, and at first it was simply known as the Gehlen Organization. The Americans wanted Gehlen within their own zone of occupation, which happened to be Bavaria and the south.

The Mayor of Cologne, Konrad Adenauer, was then a fairly obscure politician. When the Allies founded the Federal German Republic in 1949, Adenauer, as its first Chancellor, established its unlikely capital in his hometown of Bonn, fifteen miles along the Rhine from Cologne. Almost every federal institution was encouraged to establish there, but Gehlen held out and the newly named BND remained at Pullach, where it sits to this day. But the BND maintains outstations in each of the *Land* or provincial capitals of the Federal Republic, and one of the most important of these is the Cologne Station. For although Cologne is not the capital city of North Rhine—Westphalia, which is Düsseldorf, it is the closest to Bonn, and as the capital of the republic, Bonn is the nerve center of government. It is also full of foreigners, and the BND is concerned with foreign intelligence.

Morenz accepted Aust's invitation to sit, and he wondered what, if anything, he had done wrong. The answer was, nothing.

"My dear Morenz, I won't beat about the bush." Aust delicately wiped his lips on a fresh linen handkershief. "Next week our colleague Dorn retires. You know, of course. His duties will be taken over by his successor. But he is a much younger man, going places—mark my words. There is, however, one duty that requires a man of more mature years. I would like you to take it over."

Morenz nodded as if he understood. He did not. Aust steepled his plump fingers and gazed out the window, folding his features into an expression of regret at the vagaries of his fellow man. He chose his words carefully.

"Now and again, this country has visitors, foreign dignitaries, who, at the end of a day of negotiations or official meetings, feel in need of distraction . . . entertainment. Of course, our various ministries are happy to arrange visits to fine restaurants, the concert, the opera, the ballet. You understand?"

Morenz nodded again. It was as clear as mud.

"Unfortunately, there are some—usually from Arab countries or Africa, occasionally Europe—who indicate quite strongly that they would prefer to enjoy female company. Paid-for female company."

"Call girls," said Morenz.

"In a word, yes. Well, rather than have important foreign visitors accosting hotel porters or taxi drivers, or haunting the red-lit windows of the Hornstrasse or getting into trouble in bars and nightclubs, the government prefers to suggest a certain telephone number. Believe me, my dear Morenz, this is done in every capital of the world. We are no exception."

"We run call girls?" asked Morenz.

Aust was shocked. "Run? Certainly not. We do not run them. We do not pay them. The client does that. Nor, I must stress, do we use any material we might get concerning the habits of some of our visiting dignitaries. The so-called 'honey trap.' Our constitutional rules and regulations are quite clear and not to be infringed. We leave honey traps to the Russians and"—he sniffed—"the French.''

He took three slim folders from his desk and handed them to Morenz.

"There are three girls. Different physical types. I am asking you to take this over because you are a mature married man. Just keep an avuncular, supervisory eye on them. Make sure they have regular medicals, keep themselves presentable. See if they are away, or unwell, or on holiday. In short, if they are available.

"Now, finally. You may on occasion be rung by a Herr Jakobsen. Never mind if the voice on the phone changes—it will always be Herr Jakobsen. According to the visitor's tastes, which Jakobsen will tell you, choose one of the three, establish the time for a visit, and ensure that she is available. Jakobsen will ring you back for the time and place, which he will then pass on to the visitor. After that, we leave it up to the call girl and her client. Not a burdensome task, really. It should not interfere with your other duties.''

Morenz lumbered to his feet with the files. Great, he thought as he left the office. Thirty years' loyal work for the Service, five years to retirement, and I get to baby-sitting hookers for foreigners who want a night on the town.

Early the following month, Sam McCready sat in a darkened room deep in the subbasement of Century House in London, headquarters of the British Secret Intelligence Service, or SIS—usually miscalled by the press MI-6; referred to by insiders as "the Firm.'' He was watching a flickering screen upon which the massed might (or a part of it) of the USSR rolled endlessly over Red Square. The Soviet Union likes to hold two vast parades each year in that square: one for May Day, and the other to celebrate the Great October Socialist Revolution. The latter is held on November 7, and today was the eighth. The camera left the vista of rumbling tanks and panned across the row of faces atop Lenin's mausoleum.

"Slow down," said McCready. The technician at his side moved a hand over the controls, and the pan-shot slowed. President Reagan's "evil empire'' (he would use the phrase later) looked more like a home for geriatrics. In the chill wind the sagging, aged faces had almost disappeared into the collars of their coats, whose upturned edges reached to meet the gray trilbies or fur *shapkas* above.

The General Secretary himself was not even there. Yuri V. Andropov, Chairman of the KGB from 1963 to 1978, who had taken the power in late 1982 following the too-long delayed death of Leonid Brezhnev, was himself dying by inches out at the Politburo Clinic at Kuntsevo. He had not been seen in public since the previous August, nor ever would he be again.

Chernenko (who would succeed Andropov in a few months) was up there, with Gromyko, Kirilenko, Tikhonov and the hatchet-faced Party theoretician Suslov. The Minister of Defense, Ustinov, was muffled in his marshal's greatcoat with enough medals to act as a windbreak from chin to waist. There were a few young enough to be competent—Grishin, the Moscow Party Chief, and Romanov, the boss of Leningrad. To one side was the youngest of them all, still an outsider, a chunky man called Gorbachev.

The camera lifted to bring into focus the group of officers behind Marshal Ustinov.

"Hold it," said McCready. The picture froze. "That one, third from the left. Can you enhance? Bring it closer?"

The technician studied his console and fine-tuned carefully. The group of officers came closer and closer. Some passed out of eyeshot. The one McCready had indicated was moving too far to the right. The technician ran back three or four frames until he was full center, and kept closing. The officer was half hidden by a full general of the Strategic Rocket Forces, but it was the moustache, unusual among Soviet officers, that clinched it. The shoulder boards on the greatcoat said Major-General.

"Bloody hell," whispered McCready, "he's done it. He's there." He turned to the impassive technician. "Jimmy, how the hell do we get hold of an apartment block in California?"

"Well, the short answer, my dear Sam," said Timothy Edwards two days later, "is that we don't. We can't. I know it's tough, but I've run it past the Chief and the money boys, and the answer is he's too rich for us."

"But his product is priceless," protested McCready. "This

man's beyond just gold. He's a mother lode of pure platinum."

"No dispute," Edwards said smoothly. He was younger than McCready by a decade, a high-flyer with a good degree and private wealth. Barely out of his thirties and already an Assistant Chief. Most men his age were happy to head up a foreign station, delighted to command a desk, yearning to rise to Controller rank. And Edwards was just under the top floor.

"Look," he said, "the Chief's been in Washington. He mentioned your man, just in case he got his promotion. Our Cousins have always had his product since you brought him in. They've always been delighted with it. Now it seems they'll be happy to take him over, money and all."

"He's tetchy, prickly. He knows me. He might not work for anyone else."

"Come now, Sam. You're the first to agree he's a mercenary. He'll go where the money is. And we'll get the product. Please ensure there's a smooth handover."

He paused and flashed his most winning smile.

"By the way, the Chief wants to see you. Tomorrow morning, ten A.M. I don't think I'm out of order in telling you he has in mind a new assignment. A step up, Sam. Let's face it— things sometimes work out for the best. Pankratin's back in Moscow, which makes him harder for you to get at; you've covered East Germany for an awful long time. The Cousins are prepared to take over, and you get a well-deserved promotion. A desk, perhaps."

"I'm a field man," said McCready.

"Why don't you listen to what the Chief has to say," suggested Edwards.

Twenty-four hours later, Sam McCready was made Head of Dee-Dee and Psy Ops. The CIA took over the handling, running, and paying of General Yevgeni Pankratin.

It was hot in Cologne that August. Those who could had sent the wives and children away to the lakes, the mountains, the forests, or even their villas in the Mediterranean and would join them later. Bruno Morenz had no holiday home. He soldiered on at his job. His salary was not large and was not likely to increase, for with three years to retirement when he turned fifty-five, a further promotion was extremely unlikely.

He sat at an open-air terrace café and sipped a tall glass of
keg beer, his tie undone and jacket draped over the back of
his chair. No one gave him a passing glance. He had dispensed
with his winter tweeds in favor of a seersucker suit that was,
if anything, even more shapeless. He sat hunched over his
beer and occasionally ran a hand through his thick gray hair
until it was awry. He was a man who had no vanity in the area
of personal appearances, or he would have put a comb
through his hair, shaved a bit closer, used a decent cologne
(after all, he was in the city that had invented it), and bought
a well-tailored suit. He would have thrown out the shirt with
the slightly frayed cuffs and straightened his shoulders. Then
he would have appeared quite an authoritative figure. He had
no personal vanity.

But he did have his dreams. Or rather, he had had his
dreams, once, long ago. And they had not been fulfilled. At
the age of fifty-two, married, the father of two grown-up
children, Bruno Morenz stared gloomily at the passersby on
the street. Had he known it, he was suffering from what the
German call *Türschlusspanik*. It is a word that exists in no
other language but means the panic of closing doors.

Behind the facade of the big amiable man who did his job,
took his modest salary at the end of the month, and went
home each night to the bosom of his family, Bruno Morenz
was a deeply unhappy man.

He was locked into a loveless marriage to his wife Irmtraut,
a woman of quite bovine stupidity and potatolike contours
who had, as the years ebbed away, even stopped complaining
of his lowly salary and lack of promotion. Of his job she knew
only that he worked for one of the government agencies
concerned with the civil service and couldn't have cared less
which one. If he was unkempt with frayed cuffs and a baggy
suit, it was in part because Irmtraut had ceased to care about
that, either. She kept their small apartment in a featureless
street in the suburb of Porz more or less neat and tidy, and
his evening meal would be on the table ten minutes after he
arrived home, semicongealed if he was late.

His daughter Ute had turned her back on both parents
almost as soon as she left school, espoused various left-wing
causes (he had had to undergo a positive vetting at the office
because of Ute's politics), and was living in a squat in Düssel-

dorf with various guitar-strumming hippies—Bruno could never work out with which. His son Lutz was still at home, slumped forever in front of the television set. A pimply youth who had flunked every exam he had ever taken, he now resented education and the world that set store by it, preferring to adopt a punk hairstyle and clothes as his personal protest against society but stopping well short of actually accepting any job that society might be prepared to offer him.

Bruno had tried; well, he reckoned he had tried. He had done his best, such as it was. Worked hard, paid his taxes, kept his family as best he could, and had little enough fun in life. In three years—just thirty-six-months—they would pension him off. There would be a small party in the office, Aust would make a speech, they would clink glasses of sparkling wine, and he would be gone. To what? He would have his pension and the savings from his "other work" that he had carefully hoarded in a variety of medium-to-small accounts around Germany under a variety of pseudonyms. There would be enough there, more than anyone thought or suspected; enough to buy a retirement home and do what he *really* wanted. . . .

Behind his amiable facade, Bruno Morenz was also a very secretive man. He had never told Aust or anyone else in the Service about his "other work"—in any case, it was strictly forbidden and would have led to instant dismissal. He had never told Irmtraut about *any* of his work, or his secret savings. But that was not his real problem—as he saw it.

His real problem was that he wanted to be free. He wanted to start again, and as if on cue he could see how. For Bruno Morenz, well into middle age, had fallen in love. Head over heels, deeply in love. And the good part was that Renate, the stunning, lovely, youthful Renate, was as much in love with him as he was with her.

There, in that café on that summer afternoon, Bruno finally made up his mind. He would do it; he would tell her. He would tell her he intended to leave Irmtraut well provided for, take early retirement, quit the job, and take her away to a new life with him in the dream home they would have up in his native north by the coast.

Bruno Morenz's real problem, as he did *not* see it, was that he was not heading for, but was well into, a truly massive midlife crisis. Because he did not see it and because he was a professional dissimulator, no one else saw it, either.

Renate Heimendorf was twenty-six, at five feet seven inches a tall and handsomely proportioned brunette. At the age of eighteen she had become the mistress and plaything of a wealthy businessman three times her age, a relationship that had lasted five years. When the man dropped dead of a heart attack, probably brought on by a surfeit of food, drink, cigars, and Renate, he had inconsiderately failed to make provision for her in his will, something his vengeful widow was not about to rectify.

The girl had managed to pillage their expensively furnished love-nest of its contents, which, together with the jewelry and trinkets he had given her over the years, fetched at sale a tidy sum.

But not enough to retire on; not enough to permit her to continue the life-style to which she had become accustomed and had no intention of quitting for a secretarial job and a tiny salary. She decided to go into business. Skilled at coaxing a form of arousal from overweight, out-of-condition, middle-aged men, there was really only one business into which she could go.

She bought a long lease on an apartment in quiet and respectable Hahnwald, a leafy and staid suburb of Cologne. The houses there were of good solid brick or stone construction, in some cases converted into apartments, like the one in which she lived and worked. It was a four-story stone building with one apartment on each floor. Hers was on the second. After moving in, she had carried out some structural refurbishment.

The flat had a sitting room, kitchen, bathroom, two bedrooms, and an entry hall and passageway. The sitting room was to the left of the entry hall, the kitchen next to it. Beyond them, to the left of the passage that turned to the right from the hall, were one bedroom and the bathroom. The larger bedroom was at the end of the passage, so that the bathroom was between the two sleeping rooms. Just before the door of the larger bedroom, built into the wall on the left, was a two-yard-wide coat-closet that borrowed space off the bathroom.

She slept in the smaller bedroom, using the larger one at

the end of the passage as her working room. Apart from building the coat-closet, her refurbishment had included the soundproofing of the master bedroom, with cork blocks lining the inside walls, papered and decorated to hide their presence, double-glazed windows, and thick padding on the inside of the door. Few sounds from inside the room could penetrate outside to disturb or alarm the neighbors, which was just as well. The room, with its unusual decor and accoutrements, was always kept locked.

The closet in the passage contained only normal winter wear and raincoats. Other closets inside the working room provided an extensive array of exotic lingerie, a range of outfits running from schoolgirl, maid, bride, and waitress to nanny, nurse, governess, schoolmistress, air hostess, police-woman, Nazi Bund *Mädchen*, campguard,. and Scout leader, along with the usual leather and PVC gear, thigh boots, capes, and masks.

A chest of drawers yielded a smaller array of vestments for clients who had brought nothing with them, such as Boy Scout, schoolboy, and Roman slave apparel. Tucked in a corner were the punishment stool and stocks, while a trunk contained the chains, cuffs, straps, and riding crops needed for the bondage and discipline scene.

She was a good whore; successful, anyway. Many of her clients returned regularly. Part actress—all whores have to be part actress—she could enter into her client's desired fantasy with complete conviction. Yet part of her mind would always remain detached—observing, noting, despising. Nothing of her job touched her—in any case, her personal tastes were *quite* different.

She had been in the game for three years and in two more intended to retire, clean up just once in a rather major way, and live on her investments in luxury somewhere far away.

That afternoon, there was a ring at her doorbell. She rose late and was still in a negligée and housecoat. She frowned; a client would only come by appointment. A glance through the peephole in her front door revealed, as in a goldfish bowl, the rumpled gray hair of Bruno Morenz, her minder from the Foreign Ministry. She sighed, put a radiant smile of ecstatic welcome on her beautiful face, and opened the door.

"Bruno, daaaaarling . . ."

*   *   *

Two days later Timothy Edwards took Sam McCready out to
lunch at Brooks's Club in St. James, London. Of the several
gentlemen's clubs of which Edwards was a member, Brooks's
was his favorite for lunch. There was always a good chance
one could bump into and have a few courteous words with
Robert Armstrong, the Cabinet Secretary, deemed to be
possibly the most influential man in England and certainly the
chairman of the Five Wise Men who would one day select the
new Chief of the SIS for the Prime Minister's approval.

It was over coffee in the library, beneath the portraits of
that group of Regency bucks, the Dilettantes, that Edwards
broached specifics.

"As I said downstairs, Sam, everyone's very pleased, very
pleased indeed. But there is a new era coming, Sam. An era
whose leitmotif may well have to be the phrase 'by the book.'
A question of some of the old ways, the rule-bending, having
to become, how shall I put it . . . restrained?"

"*Restrained* is a very good word," agreed Sam.

"Excellent. Now, a riffle through the records shows that
you still retain, admittedly on an ad hoc basis, certain assets
who really have passed their usefulness. Old friends, perhaps.
No problem, unless they are in delicate positions . . . unless
their discovery by their own employers might cause the Firm
real problems."

"Such as?" asked McCready. That was the trouble with
records—they were always there, on file. As soon as you paid
someone to run an errand, a record of payment was created.
Edwards dropped his vague manner.

"Poltergeist. Sam, I don't know how it was overlooked so
long. Poltergeist is a full-time staffer of the BND. There'd be
all hell let loose if Pullach ever discovered he moonlighted for
you. It's absolutely against all the rules. We do not, repeat do
not, 'run' employees of friendly agencies. It's way out of
court. Get rid of him, Sam. Stop the retainer. Forthwith."

"He's a mate," said McCready. "We go back a long way.
To the Berlin Wall going up. He did well then, ran dangerous
jobs for us when we needed people like that. We were caught
by surprise. We hadn't got anyone, or not enough, who would
and could go across like that."

"It's not negotiable, Sam."

"I trust him. He trusts me. He wouldn't let me down. You can't buy that sort of thing. It takes years. A small retainer is a tiny price."

Edwards rose, took his handkerchief from his sleeve and dabbed the port from his lips.

"Get rid of him, Sam. I'm afraid I have to make that an order. Poltergeist goes."

At the end of that week, Major Ludmilla Vanavskaya sighed, stretched and leaned back in her chair. She was tired. It had been a long haul. She reached for her packet of Soviet-made Marlboros, noticed the full ashtray, and pressed a bell on her desk.

A young corporal entered from the outer office. She did not address him, just pointed to the ashtray with her fingertip. He quickly removed it, left the office, and returned it cleaned a few seconds later. She nodded. He left again and closed the door.

There had been no talk, no banter. Major Vanavskaya had that effect on people. In earlier years some of the young bucks had noticed the shining short-cropped blond hair above the crisp service shirt and slim green skirt and had tried their luck. No dice. At twenty-five she had married a colonel—a career move—and divorced him three years later. His career had stalled, hers taken off. At thirty-five she wore no more uniforms, just the severe tailored charcoal-gray suit over the white blouse with the floppy bow at the neck.

Some still thought she was beddable, until they caught a salvo from those freezing blue eyes. In the KGB, not an organization of liberals, Major Vanavskaya had a reputation as a fanatic. Fanatics intimidate.

The Major's fanaticism was her work—and traitors. An utterly dedicated Communist, ideologically pure of any doubts, she had devoted herself to her self-arrogated pursuit of traitors. She hated them with a cold passion. She had wangled a transfer from the Second Chief Directorate, where the targets were the occasional seditious poet or complaining worker, to the independent Third Directorate, also called the Armed Forces Directorate. Here the traitors, if traitors there were, would be higher-ranking, more dangerous.

The move to the Third Directorate—arranged by her colo-

nel-husband in the last days of their marriage, when he was
still desperately trying to please her—had brought her to this
anonymous office block just off the Sadovaya Spasskaya,
Moscow's ring road, and to this desk, and to the file that now
lay open in front of her.

Two years of work had gone into that file, although she had
had to squeeze that work in between other duties until people
higher up began to believe her. Two years of checking and
cross-checking, begging for cooperation from other departments, always fighting the obfuscation of those bastards in the
army who always sided with one another; two years of corre-
lating tiny fragments of information until a picture began to
emerge.

Major Ludmilla Vanavskaya's job and vocation was tracking down backsliders, subversives, or, occasionally, full-
blown traitors inside the army, navy, or air force. Loss of
valuable state equipment through gross negligence was bad
enough; lack of vigor in the pursuit of the Afghan war was
worse; but the file on her desk told her a different story. She
was convinced that somewhere in the army there was a
deliberate leak. And he was high, damned high.

There was a list of eight names on the top sheet of the file
before her. Five were crossed out. Two had question marks.
But her eye always came back to the eighth. She lifted a
phone and was put through to the male secretary of General
Shaliapin, head of the Third Directorate.

"Yes, Major. A personal interview? No one else? I see. . . .
The problem is, the Comrade General is in the Far East. . . .
Not until next Tuesday. Very well then, next Tuesday."

Major Vanavskaya put down the phone and scowled. Four
days. Well, she had already waited two years—she could wait
four more days.

"I think I've clinched it," Bruno told Renate with childlike
delight the following Sunday morning. "I've just got enough
for the freehold purchase and some more left over for decorating and equipping it. It's a wonderful little bar."

They were in bed in her own bedroom—it was a favor she
sometimes allowed him because he hated the "working"
bedroom as much as he hated her job.

"Tell me again," she cooed. "I love to hear about it."

He grinned. He had seen it just once but fallen for it completely. It was what he had always wanted and right where he wanted it—by the open sea, where the brisk winds from the north would keep the air crisp and fresh. Cold in winter, of course, but there was central heating, which would need fixing.

"Okay. It's called the Lantern Bar, and the sign is an old ship's lantern. It stands on the open quay right on the Bremerhaven dock front. From the upper windows you can see as far as Mellum Island—we could get a sailboat if things go well and sail there in summer.

"There's an old-fashioned brass-topped bar—we'll be behind that serving the drinks—and a nice snug apartment upstairs. Not as large as this, but comfy once we've fixed it up. I've agreed on the price and paid the deposit. Completion is at the end of September. Then I can take you away from all this."

She could hardly keep herself from laughing out loud. "I can't wait, my darling. It will be a wonderful life. . . . Do you want to try again? Perhaps it will work this time."

If Renate had been a different person, she would have let the older man down gently, explaining that she had no intention of being taken away from "all this," least of all to a bleak and windswept quay in Bremerhaven. But it amused her to prolong his delusion so that his eventual misery would be all the greater.

An hour after Bruno and Renate's conversation in Cologne, a black Jaguar sedan swept off the M3 motorway and sought the quieter lanes of Hampshire, not far from the village of Dummer. It was Timothy Edwards's personal car, and his Service driver was at the wheel. In the back was Sam McCready, who had been summoned from his habitual Sunday pleasures at his apartment in Abingdon Villas, Kensington, by a telephoned appeal from the Assistant Chief.

"Without the option, I'm afraid, Sam. It's urgent."

He had been enjoying a long, deep, hot bath when the call came, with Vivaldi on the stereo and the Sunday newspapers strewn gloriously all over the sitting-room floor. He had had time to throw on a sports shirt, corduroy trousers, and jacket by the time John, who had picked up the Jaguar at the motor pool, was at the door.

The sedan swept into the graveled forecourt of a substantial Georgian country house and came to a halt. John came around the car to open the rear passenger door, but McCready beat him to it. He hated being fussed over.

"I was told to say they will be round the back, sir, on the terrace," said John.

McCready surveyed the mansion. Timothy Edwards, ten years earlier, had married the daughter of a duke, who had been considerate enough to drop off his perch in early middle age and leave a substantial estate to his two offspring, the new duke and Lady Margaret. She had collected about three million pounds. McCready estimated that about half of that was now invested in a prime piece of Hampshire real estate. He wandered round the side of the house to the colonnaded patio at the back.

There were four easy cane chairs in a group. Three were occupied. Farther on, a white cast-iron table was set for lunch for three. Lady Margaret would doubtless be staying inside, not lunching. Neither would he. The two men in the rattan chairs rose.

"Ah, Sam," said Edwards. "Glad you could make it."

That's a bit rich, thought McCready. No bloody option was what I was given.

Edwards looked at McCready and wondered, not for the first time, why his extremely talented colleague insisted on coming to a Hampshire country house party looking as if he had just been gardening, even if he was not staying long. Edwards himself was in brilliant brogues, razor-creased tan slacks, and a blazer over a silk shirt and neckerchief.

McCready stared back and wondered why Edwards always insisted on keeping his handkerchief up his left sleeve. It was an army habit, started in the cavalry regiments because on dining-in nights cavalry officers wore trousers so tight that a bunched handkerchief in the pocket might give the ladies the impression they had put on a touch too much perfume. But Edwards had never been in the cavalry, nor in any regiment. He had come to the Service directly from Oxford.

"I don't think you know Chris Appleyard," said Edwards, as the tall American held out his hand. He had the leathery

look of a Texan cowhand. In fact, he was a Bostonian. The
leathery look came from the Camels he chain-smoked. His
face was not suntanned, just medium rare. That was why they
were lunching outside, Sam mused. Edwards would not want
the Canalettos covered in nicotine.

"Guess not," said Appleyard. "Nice to meet you, Sam.
Know your reputation."

McCready knew who he was from the name and from
photographs: Deputy Head, European Division, CIA. The
woman in the third chair leaned forward and held out a hand.

"Hi, Sam, how're you doing these days?"

Claudia Stuart, still at forty a great-looking woman. She
held his gaze and his hand a mite longer than necessary.

"Fine, thanks, Claudia. Just fine."

Her eyes said she did not believe him. No woman likes to
think a man with whom she once offered to share her bed has
ever completely recovered from the experience.

Years earlier, in Berlin, Claudia had had a serious crush on
Sam McCready. It had puzzled and frustrated her that she
had gotten nowhere. She had not then known about Sam's
wife, May.

Claudia had been with the CIA's West Berlin Station; he
had been visiting. He had never told her what he was doing
there. Actually, he was recruiting the then Colonel Pankratin,
she learned later. It was she who had taken him over.

Edwards had not missed the body language. He wondered
what was behind it and guessed aright. It never ceased to
amaze him that women seemed to like Sam. He was so . . .
rumpled. There was talk that several of the women at Century
House would like to straighten his tie, sew on a button, or
more. He found it inexplicable.

"Sorry to hear about May," said Claudia.

"Thank you," said McCready. May. Sweet, loving, and
much-loved May, his wife. Three years since she had died.
May, who had waited through all the long nights in the early
days, always been there when he came home from across the
Curtain, never asking, never complaining. Multiple sclerosis
can act fast or slow. With May, it had been fast. In one year
she was in a wheelchair and two years later gone. He had
lived alone in the Kensington apartment since then. Thank

God their son had been at college, just summoned home for
the funeral. He had not seen the pain or his father's despair.

A butler—there would have to be a butler, thought Mc-
Cready—appeared with an extra flute of champagne on a
salver. McCready raised an eyebrow. Edwards whispered in
the butler's ear, and he came back with a tankard of beer.
McCready sipped. They watched him. Lager. Designer beer.
Foreign label. He sighed. He would have preferred bitter ale,
room temperature, redolent of Scottish malt and Kentish
hops.

"We have a problem, Sam," said Appleyard. "Claudia,
you tell him."

"Pankratin," said Claudia. "Remember him?"

McCready studied his beer and nodded.

"In Moscow we've run him mainly through drops. Arm's
length. Very little contact. Fantastic product, and very pricey
payments. But hardly any personal meets. Now he has sent a
message. An urgent message."

There was silence. McCready raised his eyes and stared at
Claudia.

"He says he's got hold of an unregistered copy of the
Soviet Army War Book. The entire Order of Battle. For the
whole of the Western front. We want it, Sam. We want it very
badly."

"So go get it," said Sam.

"This time he won't use a dead-letter box. Says it's too
bulky. Won't fit. Too noticeable. He will only hand it over to
someone he knows and trusts. He wants you."

"In *Moscow*?"

"No, in East Germany. He begins a tour of inspection
soon. Lasts a week. He wants to make the hand-over in the
deep south of Thuringia, up near the Bavarian border. His
swing will take him south and west through Cottbus, Dresden,
Karl-Marx-Stadt, and on to Gera and Erfurt. Then back to
Berlin on Wednesday night. He wants to make the pass
Tuesday or Wednesday morning. He doesn't know the area.
He wants to use lay-bys—road pull-offs. Other than that, he
has it all planned how he'll get away and do it."

Sam sipped his beer and glanced up at Edwards. "Have
you explained, Timothy?"

"Touched on it," said Edwards, then turned to his guests.

"Look, I have to make it clear that Sam actually can't go. I've mentioned it to the Chief, and he agrees. Sam's been black-flagged by the SSD."

Claudia raised an eyebrow.

"It means that if they catch me again over there, there'll be no cozy exchange at the border."

"They'll interrogate him and shoot him," added Edwards unnecessarily. Appleyard whistled.

"Boy, that's against the rules. You must have really shaken them up."

"One does one's best," said Sam sadly. "By the way, if I can't go, there is one man who could. Timothy and I were discussing him last week at the club."

Edwards nearly choked on his flute of Krug. "Poltergeist? Pankratin says he'll only make the pass to someone he knows."

"He knows Poltergeist. Remember I told you how he had helped me in the early days? Back in '81, when I brought him in, Poltergeist had to baby-sit him till I could get there. Actually, he liked Poltergeist. He'd recognize him again and make the pass. He's no fool."

Edwards straightened the silk at his neck.

"Very well, Sam. One last time."

"It's dangerous, and the stakes are high. I want a reward for him. Ten thousand pounds."

"Agreed," said Appleyard without hesitation. He took a sheet of paper from his pocket. "Here are the details Pankratin has provided for the method of the pass. Two alternate venues are needed. A first and a back-up. Can you let us know in twenty-four hours the lay-bys you've picked? We'll get it to him."

"I can't force Poltergeist to go," McCready warned. "He's a free-lance, not a staffer."

"Try, Sam, please try," said Claudia. Sam rose.

"By the way, this 'Tuesday'—which one is it?"

"A week from the day after tomorrow," said Appleyard. "Eight days away."

"Jesus Christ," said McCready.

Chapter 2

Sam McCready spent most of the next day, Monday, poring over large-scale maps and photographs. He went back to his old friends still on the East German desk and asked a few favors. They were protective of their territory but complied—he had the authority—and they knew better than to ask the Head of Deception and Disinformation what he was up to.

By midafternoon he had two locations that would suit. One was a sheltered lay-by just off East Germany's Highway Seven, which runs in an east-west line parallel to Autobahn E40. The smaller road links the industrial city of Jena to the more pastoral town of Weimar and thence to the sprawl of Erfurt. The first lay-by he chose was just west of Jena. The second was on the same road, but halfway between Weimar and Erfurt, not three miles from the Soviet base at Nohra.

If the Russian general was anywhere between Jena and Erfurt on his tour of inspection the following Tuesday and Wednesday, he would only have a short run to either rendezvous. At five, McCready proposed his choices to Claudia Stuart at the American Embassy in Grosvenor Square. A coded message went to CIA headquarters, Langley, Virginia; they approved and passed the message to Pankratin's designated controller in Moscow. The information went into a dead-letter box behind a loose brick in Novodevichi Cemetery in the early morning of the next day, and General Pankratin picked it up on his way to the Ministry four hours later.

Before sundown on Monday, McCready sent a coded message to the head of the SIS station in Bonn, who read it, destroyed it, picked up the telephone, and made a local call.

Bruno Morenz returned home at seven that evening. He was halfway through his supper when his wife remembered something.

"Your dentist called. Dr. Fischer."

Morenz raised his head and stared at the congealed mess in front of him.

"Uh-uh."

"Says he should look at that filling again. Tomorrow. Could you come to his office at six."

She returned to her absorption in the evening game show on television. Bruno hoped she had gotten the message exactly right. His dentist was not Dr. Fischer, and there were two bars where McCready might want to meet him. One was called "office," the other "clinic." And "six" meant midday, during the lunch hour.

On Tuesday morning, McCready had Denis Gaunt drive him to Heathrow for the breakfast-hour flight to Cologne.

"I'll be back tomorrow night," he said. "Mind the shop for me."

At Cologne, with only a briefcase, he moved swiftly through passport and customs controls, took a taxi, and was dropped off outside the opera house just after eleven. For forty minutes he wandered around the square, down the Kreuzgasse and into the busy pedestrian mall of Schildergasse. He paused at many shop windows, doubled suddenly back, and entered a store by the front and left by the back. At five to twelve, satisfied he had not grown a tail, he turned into the narrow Krebsgasse and headed for the old-style, half-timbered bar with the gold Gothic lettering. The small tinted windows made the interior dim. He sat in a booth in the far corner, ordered a stein of Rhine beer, and waited. The bulky figure of Bruno Morenz slid into the chair opposite him five minutes later.

"It's been a long time, old friend," said McCready.

Morenz nodded and sipped his beer.

"What do you want, Sam?"

Sam told him. It took ten minutes. Morenz shook his head.

"Sam, I'm fifty-two. Soon I retire. I have plans. In the old days it was different, exciting. Now, frankly, those guys over there frighten me."

"They frighten me too, Bruno. But I'd go in spite of it, if I could. I'm black-flagged. You're clean. It's a quick one—go over in the morning, back by nightfall. Even if the first pass doesn't work, you'll be back the next day, midafternoon. They're offering ten thousand pounds, cash."

Morenz stared at him.

"That's a lot. There must be others who would take it. Why me?"

"He knows you. He likes you. He'll see it isn't me, but he won't back off. I hate to ask you this way, but this is really for me. The last time, I swear it. For old times' sake."

Bruno finished his beer and rose.

"I must get back. . . . All right, Sam. For you. For old times' sake. But then, I swear, I'm out. For good."

"You have my word, Bruno—never again. Trust me. I won't let you down."

They agreed on the next rendezvous, for the following Monday at dawn. Bruno returned to his office. McCready waited ten minutes, strolled up to the taxi stand on Tunistrasse, and hailed a cab for Bonn. He spent the rest of the day and Wednesday discussing his needs with Bonn Station. There was a lot to do, and not much time to do it.

Across two time zones, in Moscow, Major Ludmilla Vanavskaya had her interview with General Shaliapin just after lunch. He sat behind his desk, a shaven-headed, brooding Siberian peasant who exuded power and cunning, and read her file carefully. When he had finished, he pushed it back toward her.

"Circumstantial," he said. He liked to make his subordinates defend their assertions. In the old days—and General Shaliapin went right back to the old days—what he had in front of him would have sufficed. The Lubyanka always had room for one more. But times had changed and were still changing.

"So far, Comrade General," Vanavskaya conceded. "But a *lot* of circumstances. Those SS-20 rockets in East Germany two years ago—the Yanks *knew* too quickly."

"East Germany is crawling with spies and traitors. The Americans have satellites, RORSATS—"

"The movements of the Red Banner fleet out of the northern ports. Those bastards in NATO always seem to know."

Shaliapin smiled at the young woman's passion. He never disparaged vigilance in his staff—it was what they were there for. "There may be a leak," he admitted, "or several. Negligence, loose talk, an array of small agents. But you think it's one man . . ."

"This man." She leaned forward and tapped the photo on top of the file.

"Why? Why him?"

"Because he's always there."

"Nearby," he corrected.

"Nearby. In the vicinity, in the same theater. Always available."

General Shaliapin had survived a long time, and he intended to survive some more. Back in March, he had spotted that things were going to change. Mikhail Gorbachev had been rapidly and unanimously elected General Secretary on the death of yet another geriatric, Chernenko. He was young and vigorous. He could last a long time. He wanted reform. Already, he had started to purge the Party of its more obvious deadwood.

Shaliapin knew the rules. Even a General Secretary could antagonize only one of the three pillars of the Soviet state at a time. If he took on the Party old guard, he would have to keep the KGB and the Army sweet. He leaned over the desk and jabbed a stubby forefinger at the flushed major.

"I cannot order the arrest of a senior staff officer within the Ministry on the basis of this. Not yet. Something hard—I need something hard. Just one tiny thing."

"Let me put him under surveillance," urged Vanaskaya.

"Discreet surveillance."

"All right, Comrade General. Discreet surveillance."

"Then I agree, Major. I'll make the staff available."

*   *   *

"Just a few days, Herr Direktor. A short break in lieu of a full summer vacation. I would like to take my wife and son away for a few days. The weekend, plus Monday, Tuesday, and Wednesday."

It was Wednesday morning, and Dieter Aust was in an expansive mood. Besides, as a good civil servant, he knew his staff were entitled to their summer vacations. He was always surprised that Morenz took so few holidays. Perhaps he could not afford many.

"My dear Morenz, our duties in the Service are onerous. The Service is always generous with its staff holidays. Five days is not a problem. Perhaps if you had given us a bit more forewarning—but yes, all right, I will ask Fraülein Keppel to rearrange the rosters."

That evening, at home, Bruno Morenz told his wife he would have to leave on business for five days.

"Just the weekend, plus the next Monday, Tuesday, and Wednesday," he said. "Herr Direktor Aust wants me to accompany him on a trip."

"That's nice," she said, engrossed in the TV.

Morenz in fact planned to spend a long, self-indulgent, and romantic weekend with Renate, give Monday to Sam Mc-Cready and the day-long briefing, and make his run across the East German border on Tuesday. Even if he had to spend the night in East Germany for the second rendezvous, he would be back in the West by Wednesday evening and could drive through the night to be home in time for work on Thursday. Then he would hand in his notice, work it out through the month of September, make his break with his wife, and leave with Renate for Bremerhaven. He doubted if Irmtraut would care—she hardly noticed whether he was there or not.

On Thursday, Major Vanavskaya suffered her first serious setback, let out a very unladylike expletive, and slammed the phone down. She had her surveillance team in place, ready to begin shadowing her military target. But first she had needed to know roughly what his routines and usual daily movements were. To find this out, she had contacted one of the several KGB Third Directorate spies inside the military intelligence organization, the GRU.

Although the KGB and its military counterpart, the GRU,

were often at daggers-drawn, there is little doubt which is the dog and which the tail. The KGB was far more powerful, with a supremacy that has been strengthened since the early sixties, when a GRU colonel called Oleg Penkovsky had blown away so many Soviet secrets as to rank as the most damaging turncoat the USSR had ever had. Since then, the Politburo had permitted the KGB to infiltrate scores of its own people into the GRU. Although they wore military uniform and mingled day and night with the military, they were KGB through and through. The real GRU officers knew who they were and tried to keep them as ostracized as possible, which was not always an easy task.

"I'm sorry, Major," the young KGB man inside the GRU had told her on the phone. "The movement order is here in front of me. Your man leaves tomorrow for a tour of our principal garrisons in Germany. Yes, I have his schedule here."

He had dictated it to her before she put the phone down. She remained for a while deep in thought, then put in her own application for permission to visit the Third Directorate staff at the KGB headquarters in East Berlin. It took two days to ratify the paperwork. She would leave for the Potsdam military airfield on Saturday morning.

Bruno made a point of getting through his chores as fast as he could on Friday and escaping from the office early. As he knew he would be handing in his notice as soon as he returned in the middle of the following week, he even cleared out some of his drawers. His last chore was his small office safe. The paperwork he handled was of such low-level classification that he hardly used the safe. The drawers of his desk could be locked, his office door was always locked at night, and the building was securely guarded. Nevertheless, he sorted out the few papers in his safe. At the bottom, beneath them all, was his service-issue automatic.

The Walther PPK was filthy. He had never used it since the statutory test-firing on the range at Pullach years before. But it was so dusty, he thought he ought to clean it before handing it back next week. His cleaning kit was at home in Porz. At ten to five he put it in the side pocket of his seersucker suit and left.

In the elevator on the way down to the street level, it banged so badly against his hip that he stuck it into his waistband and buttoned his jacket over it. He grinned as he thought this would be the first time he had ever shown it to Renate. Perhaps then she would believe how important his job was. Not that it mattered. She loved him anyway.

He shopped in the center of town before driving out to Hahnwald—some good veal, fresh vegetables, a bottle of real French claret. He would make them a cozy supper at home; he enjoyed being in the kitchen. His final purchase was a large bunch of flowers.

He parked his Opel Kadett round the corner from her street—he always did—and walked the rest of the way. He had not used the car phone to tell her he was coming. He would surprise her. With the flowers. She would like that. There was a lady coming out of the building as he approached the door, so he did not even have to ring the front bell and alert Renate. Better and better—a real surprise. He had his own key to her apartment door.

He let himself in quietly to make the surprise even nicer. The hall was quiet. He opened his mouth to call "Renate, darling, it's me," when he heard a peal of her laughter. He smiled. She would be watching the cartoons on television. He peeked into the sitting room. It was empty. The laughter came again, from down the passage toward the bathroom. He realized with a start at his own foolishness that she might have a client. He had not called to check. Then he realized that with a client she would be in the "working" bedroom with the door closed, and that the door was soundproofed. He was about to call again when someone else laughed. It was a man. Morenz stepped from the hall into the passageway.

The master bedroom door was open a few inches, the gap partly obscured by the fact that the big closet doors were also open, with overcoats strewn on the floor.

"What an arsehole," said the man's voice. "He really thinks you're going to marry him?"

"Head over heels, besotted. Stupid bastard! Just look at him." Her voice.

Morenz put down the flowers and the groceries and moved down the passage to the bedroom door. He was puzzled. He eased the closet doors closed to get past them and nudged the bedroom door open with the tip of his shoe.

Renate was sitting on the edge of the king-sized bed with the black sheets, smoking a joint. The air was redolent of cannabis. Lounging on the bed was a man Morenz had never seen before—lean, young, tough, in jeans and a leather motorcycle jacket. They both saw the movement of the door and jumped off the bed, the man in a single bound that brought him to his feet behind Renate. He had a mean face and dirty blond hair. In her private life Renate liked what is known as "rough trade," and this one, her regular boyfriend, was as rough as they came.

Morenz's eyes were still fixed on the video flickering on the TV set beyond the end of the bed. No middle-aged man looks very dignified when making love, even less so when it is not happening for him. Morenz watched his own image on the TV with a growing sense of shame and despair. Renate was with him in the film, occasionally looking over his back to make gestures of disdain at the camera. That was apparently what had caused all the laughter.

In front of him now, Renate was almost naked, but she recovered from her surprise quickly enough. Her face flushed with anger. When she spoke, it was not in the tones he knew, but the screech of a fishwife.

"What the fuck are you doing here?"

"I wanted to surprise you," he mumbled.

"Yeah, well you've fucking surprised me. Now bug off. Go home to your stupid potato sack in Porz."

Morenz took a deep breath.

"What really hurts," he said, "is that you could have told me. You didn't need to let me make such a fool of myself. Because I really did love you."

Her face was quite contorted. She spat the words.

"*Let* you? You don't need any help. You *are* a fool. A fat old fool. In bed and out. Now bug off."

That was when he hit her. Not a punch—an open-handed slap to the side of the face. Something snapped in him, and he hit her. It caught her off balance. He was a big man, and the blow knocked her to the floor.

What the blond man was thinking of, Morenz later could never decide. Morenz was about to leave when the pimp

reached inside his jacket. It seemed he was armed. Morenz
pulled his PPK from his waistband. He thought the safety
catch was on. It should have been. He wanted to scare the
pimp into raising his arms and letting him go. But the pimp
went on pulling his pistol out. Morenz squeezed the trigger.
Dusty it may have been, but the Walther went off.

On the shooting range Morenz could not have hit a barn
door. And he hadn't been on the range for years. Real
marksmen practice almost daily. It was beginner's luck. The
single bullet hit the pimp right in the heart at fifteen feet. The
man jerked, an expression of disbelief on his face. But nervous reaction or not, his right arm kept coming up, clutching
his Beretta. Morenz fired again. Renate chose that moment to
rise from the floor. The second slug caught her in the back of
the head. The padded door had swung shut during the alter-
cation; not a sound had left the room.

Morenz stood for several minutes looking at the two bodies.
He felt numb, slightly dizzy. Eventually, he left the room and
pulled the door closed behind him. He did not lock it. He was
about to step over the winter clothes in the hall when it
occurred to him, even in his bemused state, to wonder why
they were there at this time of year. He looked into the coat
closet and noticed that the rear panel of the closet appeared
to be loose. He pulled the loose panel toward him. . . .

Bruno Morenz spent another fifteen minutes in the apartment, then left. He took with him the videotape of himself,
the groceries, the flowers, and a black canvas grip that did not
belong to him. He could not later explain why he had done
that. Two miles from Hahnwald he dropped the groceries,
wine, and flowers into separate garbage cans by the roadside.
Then he drove for almost an hour, threw the videotape of
himself and his gun into the Rhine from the Severin Bridge,
turned out of Cologne, deposited the canvas grip, and finally
made his way home to Porz. When he entered the sitting room
at half-past nine, his wife made no comment.

"My trip with the Herr Direktor has been postponed," he
said. "I'll be leaving very early on Monday morning instead."

"Oh, that's nice." she said.

He sometimes thought he could come in from the office of
an evening and say, "Today I popped down to Bonn and shot
Chancellor Kohl," and she would still say, "Oh, that's nice."

She eventually prepared him a meal. It was uneatable, so he did not eat it.

"I'm going out for a drink," he said. She took another chocolate, offered one to Lutz, and they both went on watching television.

He got drunk that night. Drinking alone. He noticed that his hands were shaking and that he kept breaking out in sweat. He thought he had a summer cold coming on. Or the flu. He was not a psychiatrist, and there was none available to him. So no one told him he was heading for a complete nervous breakdown.

That Saturday, Major Vanavskaya arrived at Berlin-Schönefeld and was driven in an unmarked car to KGB headquarters, East Berlin. She checked at once on the whereabouts of the man she was stalking. He was in Cottbus, heading for Dresden, surrounded by army men, moving in a military convoy and out of her reach. On Sunday he would reach Karl-Marx-Stadt, Monday Zwickau, and Tuesday Jena. Her surveillance mandate did not cover East Germany. It could be extended, but that would require paperwork. Always the damned paperwork, she thought angrily.

The following day, Sam McCready arrived back in Germany and spent the morning conferring with the head of Bonn Station. In the evening he took delivery of the BMW car and the paperwork and drove to Cologne. He lodged at the Holiday Inn out at the airport, where he took and prepaid a room for two nights.

Before dawn on Monday, Bruno Morenz rose, long before his family, and left quietly. He arrived at the Holiday Inn about seven on that bright, early September morning and joined McCready in his room. The Englishman ordered breakfast for both from room service, and when the waiter had gone, he spread out a huge motoring map of Germany, West and East.

"We'll do the route first," he said. "Tomorrow morning you leave here at four A.M. It's a long drive, so take it easy, in stages. Take the E35 here past Bonn, Limburg, and Frankfurt. It links to the E41 and E45, past Würzburg and Nuremburg. North of Nuremburg, pull left on the E51 past Bayreuth

and up to the border. That's your crossing point, near Hof.
The Saale Bridge border station. It's no more than a six-hour
drive. You want to be there about eleven. I'll be there ahead
of you, watching from cover. Are you feeling all right?''

Morenz was sweating, even with his jacket off.

"It's hot in here," he said. McCready turned up the air
conditioning.

"After the border, drive straight north to the Hermsdorfer
Kreuz. Turn left onto the E40 heading back toward the West.
At Mellingen, leave the Autobahn and head into Weimar.
Inside the town, find Highway Seven and head west again.
Four miles west of the town, on the right of the road, is a lay-
by.''

McCready produced a large blown-up photograph of that
section of the road, taken from a high-flying aircraft, but at an
angle, for the aircraft had been inside Bavarian airspace.
Morenz could see the small lay-by—some cottages, even the
trees that shaded the patch of gravel designated as his first
rendezvous. Carefully and meticulously, McCready ran him
through the procedure he should follow and, if the first pass
aborted, how and where he should spend the night and where
and when to attend the second, backup rendezvous with
Pankratin. At midmorning they broke for coffee.

At nine that morning, Frau Popovic arrived for work at the
apartment in Hahnwald. She was the cleaning lady, a Yugo-
slav immigrant worker who came every day from nine until
eleven. She had her own keys to the front door and the
apartment door. She knew Fräulein Heimendorf liked to sleep
late, so she always let herself in and started with the rooms
other than the bedroom so that her employer could rise at
half-past ten. Then she would tidy the lady's bedroom. The
locked room at the end of the passage, she never entered. She
had been told—and had accepted—that it was a small room
used for storing furniture. She had no idea what her employer
did for a living.

That morning, she started with the kitchen, then did the
hall and the passage. She was vacuum-cleaning the passage
right up to the door at the end when she noticed what she
thought was a brown silk slip lying on the floor at the base of
the locked door. She tried to pick it up, but it was not a silk

slip. It was a large brown stain, quite dry and hard, that seemed to have come from under the door. She tut-tutted at the extra work she would have to scrub it off, then went to get a bucket of water and a brush. She was working on her hands and knees when she kicked the door. To her surprise it moved. She tried the handle and found it was not locked.

The stain was still resisting her attempts to scrub it off, and she thought it might happen again, so she opened the door to see what might be leaking. Seconds later, she was running screaming down the stairs to hammer at the door of the ground-floor apartment and arouse the bewildered retired bookseller who lived there. He did not go upstairs, but he did call the 110 emergency number and ask for the police.

The call was logged in the Police *Präsidium* on the Waid-markt at 9:51. The first to arrive, according to the unvarying routine of all German police forces, was a *Streifenwagen*, or stripe-car, with two uniformed policemen. Their job was to establish whether an offense had indeed been committed, into which category it fell, and then to alert the appropriate departments. One of the men stayed downstairs with Frau Popovic, who was being comforted by the bookseller's elderly wife, and the other went up. He touched nothing, just went down the passage and looked through the half-open door, gave a whistle of amazement, and came back down to use the bookseller's phone. He did not have to be Sherlock Holmes to work out that this one was for Homicide.

According to procedure, he first called the emergency doctor—in Germany, always supplied by the fire brigade. Then he called the Police *Präsidium* and asked for the *Leidstelle*, the Violent Crime switchboard. He told the operator where he was and what he had found and asked for two more uniformed men. The message went up to the *Mordkommission* or Murder Squad, always known as "First K" on the tenth and eleventh floors of the ugly, functional, green-concrete building covering all of one side of the Waidmarkt square. The Director of First K assigned a commissar and two assistants. Records showed later that they arrived at the Hahnwald apartment at 10:40 A.M., just as the doctor was leaving.

He had taken a closer look than the uniformed officer, felt for signs of life, touched nothing else, and left to make his

formal report. The commissar, whose name was Peter Schiller, met him on the steps. Schiller knew him.

"What have we got?" he asked. It was not the doctor's job
to do a post-mortem, simply to establish the fact of death.

"Two bodies. One male, one female. One clothed, one
naked."

"Cause of death?" asked Schiller.

"Gunshot wounds, I'd say. The paramedic will tell you."

"Time?"

"I'm not the pathologist. Oh, one to three days, I would
say. Rigor mortis is well established. That's unofficial, by the
way. I've done my job. I'm off."

Schiller went upstairs with one assistant. The other stayed
below to try and get statements from Frau Popovic and the
bookseller. Neighbors began to gather up and down the street.
There were now three official cars outside the apartment
house.

Like his uniformed colleague, Schiller gave a low whistle
when he saw the contents of the master bedroom. Renate
Heimendorf and her pimp were still where they had fallen,
the head of the near-naked woman lying close to the door,
under whose sill the blood had leaked outside. The pimp was
across the room, slumped with his back to the TV set, the
expression of surprise still on his face. The TV set was off.
The bed with the black silk sheets still bore the indentations
of two bodies that had once lain there.

Treading carefully, Schiller flipped open a number of the
closets and drawers.

"A hooker," he said. "Call girl, whatever. Wonder if they
knew downstairs. We'll ask. In fact, we'll need all the tenants.
Start to get a list of names."

The assistant commissar, Wiechert, was about to go when
he said, "I've seen the man somewhere before. . . . Hoppe.
Bernhard Hoppe. Bank robbery, I think. A hard man."

"Oh, good," said Schiller ironically, "that's all we need. A
gangland killing."

There were two telephone extensions in the flat, but Schiller, even with gloved hands, used neither. They might have
prints. He went down and borrowed the bookseller's phone.
Before that, he posted two uniformed men at the door of the

house, another in the hall, and the fourth outside the apartment door.

He called his superior, Rainer Hartwig, Director of the Murder Squad, and told him there might be gangland ramifications. Hartwig decided he had better tell his own superior, the president of the Crime Office, the *Kriminalamt*, known as the KA. If Wiechert was right and the body on the floor was a gangster, then experts from other divisions besides Murder Squad—robbery and racketeering, for example—would have to be consulted.

In the interim Hartwig sent down the *Erkennungsdienst*, the forensic team, one photographer and four fingerprint men. The apartment would be theirs and theirs alone for hours to come; until, in fact, every last print and scraping, every fiber and particle that could be of interest, had been removed for analysis. Hartwig also detached eight more men from their duties. There was a lot of door-knocking to be done, the search for witnesses who had seen a man or men come or go.

The log would later show that the forensic men arrived at 11:31 A.M. and stayed for almost eight hours.

At that hour Sam McCready put down his second cup of coffee and folded up the map. He had taken Morenz carefully through both rendezvous with Pankratin in the East, shown him the latest photograph of the Soviet general, and explained that the man would be in the baggy fatigues of a Russian army corporal with a forage cap shading his face and driving a GAZ jeep. That was the way the Russian had set it up.

"Unfortunately, he thinks he will be meeting me. We must just hope he recognizes you from Berlin and makes the pass anyway. Now, to the car. It's down there in the parking lot. We'll go for a drive after lunch, let you get used to it.

"It's a BMW sedan, black, with Würzburg registration plates. That's because you're a Rhinelander by birth, but now live and work in Würzburg. I'll give you your full cover story and backup papers later. The car with those number plates actually exists. It *is* a black BMW sedan.

"But this one is the Firm's car. It has made several crossings of the Saale Bridge border point, so hopefully they'll be accustomed to it. The drivers have always been different because it's a Company car. It has always driven to Jena, apparently to visit the Zeiss works there. And it has always been clean. But this time there is a difference. Under the battery shelf there is a flat compartment, just about invisible unless you really look for it. It is big enough to take the book you will receive from Smolensk."

(On a need-to-know basis, Morenz had never known Pankratin's real name. He did not even know the man had risen to Major-General or was now based in Moscow. The last time he had seen him, Pankratin was a colonel in East Berlin, codename Smolensk.)

"Let's have lunch," said McCready.

During the meal, from room service, Morenz drank wine greedily and his hands shook.

"Are you sure you're all right?" asked McCready.

"Sure. This damned summer cold, you know? And a bit nervous. That's natural."

McCready nodded. Nerves were normal—with actors before going onstage. With soldiers before combat. With agents before an illegal run into the Sovbloc. Still, he did not like the shape Morenz was in. He had seldom seen a case of nerves like this. But with Pankratin unreachable and twenty-four hours to the first contact, he had no choice.

"Let's go down to the car," he said.

Not much happens in Germany today that the press does not hear about, and it was the same in 1985, when Germany was West Germany. The veteran and ace crime reporter of Cologne was and remains Guenther Braun of the *Kölner Stadt-Anzeiger*. He was lunching with a police contact who mentioned that there was a flap going on in Hahnwald. Braun arrived outside the house with his photographer, Walter Schiestel, just before three. He tried to get to Commissar Schiller, but he was upstairs, sent word he was busy, and referred Braun to the *Präsidium* press office. Fat chance. Braun would get the sanitized police communiqué later. He began to ask around. Then he made some phone calls. By early evening, well in time for the first editions, he had got his story. It was a good one, too. Of course, radio and TV would be ahead of him with the broad outlines, but he knew he had an inside track.

Upstairs, the forensic team had finished with the bodies.

The photographer, Schiestel, had snapped the corpses from every conceivable angle, plus the decor of the room, the bed, the huge mirror behind the headboard, and the equipment in the closets and chests. Lines were drawn around the bodies, then the cadavers were bagged and removed to the city morgue, where the forensic pathologist went to work. The detectives needed the time of death and those bullets—urgently.

The entire apartment had yielded nineteen sets or partial sets of fingerprints. Three were eliminated; they belonged to the two deceased and to Frau Popovic, now down at the *Präsidium* with her prints carefully on file. That left sixteen.

"Probably clients," muttered Schiller.

"But one set the killer's?" suggested Wiechert.

"I doubt it. It looks pretty pro to me. He probably wore gloves."

The major problem, mused Schiller, was not lack of motive but too many. Was the call girl the intended victim? Was the murderer an outraged client, a former husband, a vengeful wife, a business rival, an enraged former pimp? Or was she incidental, and her pimp the real target? He had been confirmed as Bernhard Hoppe, ex-con, bank robber, gangster, very nasty, and a real low-life. A settling of accounts, a drug deal that went sour, rival protection-racketeers? Schiller suspected it was going to be a tough one.

The tenants' statements and those of the neighbors indicated no one knew of Renate Heimendorf's secret profession. There had been gentlemen callers, but always respectable. No late-night parties, blaring music.

As the forensic team finished with each area of the flat, Schiller could move around more and disturb things. He went to the bathroom. There was something odd about the bathroom, but he could not figure out what it was. Just after seven, the forensic team finished and called to him that they were off. He spent an hour puttering about the gutted flat while Wiechert complained that he wanted his dinner. At ten past eight, Schiller shrugged and called it a day. He would resume the case tomorrow up at headquarters. He sealed the flat, left one uniformed man in the hallway in case someone returned to the scene of the crime—it had happened—and went home.

There was still something that bothered him about that flat. He was a very intelligent and perceptive young detective.

McCready spent the afternoon finalizing the briefing of Bruno Morenz.

"You are Hans Grauber, aged fifty-one, married, three children. Like all proud family men you carry pictures of your family. Here they are, on holiday: Heidi, your wife, along with Hans Junior, Lotte, and Ursula, known as Uschi. You work for BKI Optical Glassware in Würzburg—they exist, and the car is theirs. Fortunately, you once did work in optical glassware, so you can use the jargon if you have to.

"You have an appointment with the director of foreign sales at the Zeiss works in Jena. Here is his letter. The paper is real; so is the man. The signature looks like his, but it is ours. The appointment is for three P.M. tomorrow. If all goes well, you can agree to place an order for Zeiss precision lenses and return to the West the same evening. If you need further discussions, you may have to overnight. That's just if the border guards ask you for such a mass of detail.

"It's extremely unlikely the border guards would check with Zeiss. The SSD would, but there are enough Western businessmen dealing with Zeiss for one more not to be a cause for suspicion. So here are your passport, letters from your wife, a used ticket from the Würzburg Opera House, credit cards, driving license, a bunch of keys including the ignition key of the BMW. The baggy raincoat—the lot.

"You'll only need the attaché case and the overnight bag. Study the attaché case and its contents. The security lock opens to the numbers of your fictional birthday, fifth April '34, or 5434. The papers all concern your desire to purchase Zeiss products for your firm. Your signature is Hans Grauber in your own handwriting. The clothes and washkit are all genuine Würzburg purchases, laundered and used, with Würzburg laundry tags. Now, old friend, let's have some dinner."

Dieter Aust, Director of Cologne's BND out-station, missed the evening TV news. He was out to dinner. He would regret it later.

*   *   *

At midnight, McCready was collected in a Range Rover by Kit Johnson, a communications man from the SIS Bonn Station. They drove off together to be at the Saale River in northern Bavaria before Morenz.

Bruno Morenz stayed in McCready's room, ordered whiskey from room service, and drank too much. He slept badly for two hours and rose when the bedside alarm went off at three. At four that Tuesday morning, he left the Holiday Inn, started the BMW, and headed through the darkness toward the Autobahn south.

At the same hour Peter Schiller awakened in Cologne beside his sleeping wife and realized what it was about the Hahnwald apartment that had puzzled him. He telephoned and awoke an outraged Wiechert and told him to meet him at the Hahnwald house at seven. German police officers have to be accompanied on an investigation.

Bruno Morenz was slightly ahead of time. Just south of the border, he killed twenty-five minutes at the Frankenwald service area restaurant. He did not drink liquor; he drank coffee. But he filled his hip flask.

At five to eleven that Tuesday morning Sam McCready, with Kit Johnson beside him, was concealed amid pine trees on a hill south of the Saale River. The Range Rover was parked out of sight in the forest. From the treeline they could see the West German border post below and half a mile in front of them. Beyond it was a gap in the hills, and through the gap, the roofs of the East German border post, half a mile farther on.

Because the East Germans had built their controls well inside their own territory, a driver would be inside East Germany as soon as he left the West German post. Then came a two-lane highway between high chain-link fencing. Behind the fencing were the watchtowers. From the trees, using powerful binoculars, McCready could see the border guards behind the windows with their own field glasses, watching the West. He could also see the machine guns. The reason for the half-mile corridor inside East Germany was so that anyone bursting through the eastern border post could be cut to pieces between the chain-link fencing before reaching the West.

At two minutes to eleven, McCready picked out the black BMW moving sedately through the cursory West German controls. Then it purred forward into the corridor, heading for the land controlled by the East's most professional and dreaded secret police, the *Stasi*.

Chapter 3

"It's the bathroom, it has to be the bathroom," said Commissar Schiller just after seven A.M. as he led a sleepy and reluctant Wiechert back into the flat.

"It looks all right to me," grumbled Wiechert. "Anyway, the forensic boys cleaned it out."

"They were looking for prints, not measurements," said Schiller. "Look at this closet in the passage. It's two yards wide, right?"

"About that."

"The far end is flush with the door to the call girl's bedroom. The door is flush with the wall and the mirror above the headboard. Now, as the bathroom door is beyond the built-in wall closet, what do you deduce?"

"That I'm hungry," said Wiechert.

"Shut up. Look, when you enter the bathroom and turn to your right, there should be two yards to the bathroom wall. The width of the cupboard outside, right? Try it."

Wiechert entered the bathroom and looked to his right. "One yard," he said.

"Exactly. That's what puzzled me. Between the mirror

behind the washbasin and the mirror behind the headboard, there's a yard of space missing.''

Poking around in the hall closet, it took Schiller thirty minutes to find the door catch, a cunningly concealed knothole in the pine planking. When the rear of the closet swung open, Schiller could dimly discern a light switch inside. He used a pencil to flick the switch, and the inner light came on, a single bulb hanging from the ceiling.

"I'll be damned," said Wiechert, looking over his shoulder. The secret compartment was ten feet long, the same length as the bathroom, but it was only three feet wide. But wide enough. To their right was the rear side of the mirror above the headboard next door, a one-way mirror that exposed the whole bedroom. On a tripod at the center of the mirror, facing into the bedroom, was a video camera, a state-of-the-art high-tech piece of equipment that would certainly provide clear-definition film despite shooting through the glass and into subdued lighting. The sound-recording equipment was also of the best. The entire far end of the narrow passageway was ceiling-to-floor shelving, and each shelf held a row of video-cassette cases. On the spine of each was a label, and each label had a number. Schiller backed out.

The phone was usable, since the forensic men had cleaned it of prints the previous day. He called the *Präsidium* and got straight through to Rainer Hartwig, Director of First K.

"Oh shit," said Hartwig when he had the details. "Well done. Stay there. I'll get two fingerprint men down to you."

It was eight-fifteen. Dieter Aust was shaving. In the bedroom the morning show was on television. The news roundup. He could hear it from the bathroom. He thought little of the item about a double murder in Hahnwald until the newscaster said, "One of the victims, high-class call girl Renate Heimendorf . . ."

That was when the Director of the Cologne BND cut himself quite badly on his pink cheek. In ten minutes he was in his car and driving fast to his office, where he arrived almost an hour early. This much disconcerted Fräulein Keppel, who was always in an hour ahead of him.

"That number," said Aust, "the vacation contact number Morenz gave us. Let me have it, would you?"

When he tried it, he got the "disconnected" tone. He checked with the operator down in the Black Forest, a popular vacation area, but she told him it appeared to be out of order. He did not know that one of McCready's men had rented a vacation chalet, then locked it after taking the phone off the hook. As a long shot Aust tried Morenz's home number in Porz, and to his amazement he found himself speaking to Frau Morenz. They must have come home early.

"Could I speak to your husband please? This is Director Aust speaking, from the office."

"But he's with you, Herr Direktor," she explained patiently. "Out of town. On a trip. Back late tomorrow night."

"Ah, yes, I see. Thank you, Frau Morenz."

He put the phone down, worried. Morenz had lied. What was he up to? A weekend with a girlfriend in the Black Forest? Possible, but he did not like it. He put through a secure-line call to Pullach and spoke to the Deputy Director of the Operations Directorate, the division they both worked for. Dr. Lothar Herrmann was frosty. But he listened intently.

"The murdered call girl, and her pimp. How were they killed?" Herrmann asked.

Aust consulted the *Stadt-Anzeiger* lying on his desk.

"They were shot."

"Does Morenz have a personal sidearm?" asked the voice from Pullach.

"I, er—believe so."

"Where was it issued, by whom, and when?" asked Dr. Herrmann. Then he added, "No matter, it must have been here. Stay there, I will call you back."

He was back on the phone in ten minutes.

"He has a Walther PPK, Service issue. From here. It was tested on the range and in the lab before we gave it to him. Ten years ago. Where is it now?"

"It should be in his personal safe," said Aust.

"Is it?" asked Herrmann coldly.

"I will find out and call you back," said the badly flustered Aust. He had the master key for all the safes in the department. Five minutes later, he was talking to Herrmann again.

"It's gone," he said. "He might have taken it home, of course."

"That is strictly forbidden. So is lying to a superior officer, whatever the cause. I think I had better come to Cologne. Please meet me off the next plane from Munich. Whichever it is, I will be on it.''

Before leaving Pullach, Dr. Herrmann made three phone calls. As a result, Black Forest policemen would visit the designated vacation home, let themselves in with the landlord's key, and establish that the phone was off the hook but the bed had not been slept in. At all. That was what they would report. Dr. Herrmann landed at Cologne at five to twelve.

Bruno Morenz cruised the BMW into the complex of concrete buildings that made up the East German border control and was waved into an inspection bay. A green-uniformed guard appeared at the driver's side window.

''*Aussteigen, bitte. Ihre Papiere.*''

He climbed out and offered his passport. Other guards began to surround the car, all quite normal.

''Hood open, please, and trunk.''

He opened both; they began the search. A mirror on a trolley went under the car. A man pored over the engine bay. Morenz forced himself not to look as the guard studied the battery.

''The purpose of your journey to the German Democratic Republic?''

He brought his eyes back to the man in front of him. Blue eyes behind rimless glasses stared at him. He explained he was going to Jena, to discuss purchases of optical lenses from Zeiss; that if all went well, he might be able to return that same evening; if not he would have to have a second meeting with the foreign sales director in the morning. Impassive faces. They waved him into the Custom Hall.

It's all just normal, he told himself. Let them find the papers themselves, McCready had said. Don't offer *too* much. They went through his attaché case, studied the letters exchanged between Zeiss and BKI in Würzburg. Morenz prayed the stamps and postmarks were perfect. They were. His bags were closed. He took them back to the car. The inspection of the car was finished. A guard with a huge Alsatian stood nearby. Behind windows, two men in civilian clothes watched. Secret police.

"Enjoy your visit to the German Democratic Republic," said the senior border guard. He did not look as if he meant it.

At that moment there was a scream and several shouts from the column of cars across the concrete dividing reservation, the column trying to get out. Everyone spun around to look. Morenz was back behind the wheel. He stared in horror.

There was a blue Combi minivan at the head of the column. West German plates. Two guards were dragging a young girl out of the back, where they had discovered her hiding under the floor in a recess built for the purpose. She was screaming. The girlfriend of the West German youth driving the van. He was hauled out in a circle of straining dogs' muzzles and submachine gun barrels. He threw his hands up, bone white.

"Leave her alone, you assholes," he shouted. Someone hit him in the stomach. He doubled over.

"*Los*. Go," snapped the guard beside Morenz. He let the clutch in, and the BMW surged forward. He cleared the barriers and stopped at the People's Bank to change Deutschmarks into worthless Ostmarks at one-for-one and get his currency declaration stamped. The bank teller was subdued. Morenz's hands were shaking. Back in his car he looked in the rearview mirror and saw the youth and the girl being hauled into a concrete building, still screaming.

He drove north, sweating profusely, his nerve completely gone, a burnt-out case. The only thing that held him together was his years of training—and his conviction that he would not let his friend McCready down.

Though he knew drinking and driving was utterly forbidden in the GDR, he reached for his hip flask and took a swig. Better. Much better. He drove on steadily. Not too fast, not too slow. He checked his watch. He had time. Midday. Rendezvous at four P.M. Two hours' drive away. But the fear, the gnawing fear of an agent on a black mission facing ten years in a slave labor camp if caught, was still working on a nervous system already reduced to ruins.

McCready had watched him enter the corridor between the two border posts, then lost sight of him. He had not seen the incident of the girl and the youth. The curve of the hill meant he could see only the roofs on the East German side and the great flag with the hammer, compasses, and wheatsheaf flut-

tering above them. Just before twelve, far in the distance, he
made out the black BMW driving away into Thuringia.

In the back of the Range Rover, Johnson had what looked
like a suitcase. Inside was a portable telephone, with a difference. The set could send out or receive messages in clear
talk, but scrambled, from the British Government Communication Headquarters, or GCHQ, near Cheltenham in England,
or Century House in London, or SIS Bonn Station. The
handset looked like an ordinary portable phone, with numbered buttons for dialing. McCready had asked that it be
brought along so he could stay in touch with his own base and
inform them when Poltergeist came safely home.

"He's through," McCready remarked to Johnson. "Now
we just wait."

"Want to tell Bonn or London?" asked Johnson.

McCready shook his head. "There's nothing they can do,"
he said. "Nothing anyone can do now. It's up to Poltergeist."

At the flat in Hahnwald, the two fingerprint men had finished
with the secret compartment and were on their way. They
had lifted three sets of prints from inside the room.

"Are they among the ones you got yesterday?" asked
Schiller.

"I don't know," said the senior print-man. "I'll have to
check back at the lab. Let you know. Anyway, you can go in
there now."

Schiller entered and surveyed the racks of cassette boxes
at the back. There was nothing to indicate what was in them,
just numbers on the spine. He took one at random, went into
the master bedroom, and slotted it into the video. With the
remote control he switched both TV and video on, then hit
the "play" button. He sat on the edge of the stripped bed.
Two minutes later, he stood up and switched the set off, a
rather shaken young man.

"*Donnerwetter nochmal!*" whispered Wiechert, standing
in the doorway munching a pizza.

The senator from Baden-Württemberg may only have been
a provincial politician, but he was well known nationally for
his frequent appearances on national television, calling for a
return to earlier moral values and a ban on pornography. His
constituents had seen him photographed in many poses—

patting children's heads, kissing babies, opening church fétes, addressing the conservative ladies. But they probably had not seen him crawling naked around a room in a spiked dog collar attached to a leash held by a young woman in stiletto heels brandishing a riding crop.

"Stay here," said Schiller. "Don't leave, don't even move. I'm going back to the *Präsidium*."

It was two o'clock.

Morenz checked his watch. He was well west of the Hermsdorfer Kreuz, the major crossroad where the north-south Autobahn from Berlin to the Saale River border crosses the east-west highway from Dresden to Erfurt. He was ahead of time. He wanted to be at the lay-by for the rendezvous with Smolensk at ten to four—no earlier or it would look suspicious, being parked there for so long in a West German car.

In fact, to stop at all would invite curiosity. West German businessmen tended to go straight to their destination, do their business, and drive back out again. Better to keep driving. He decided to go past Jena and Weimar to the Erfurt pull-off, go right around the roundabout, and come back toward Weimar. That would kill time. A green and white Wartburg People's Police car came past him in the overtaking lane, adorned with two blue lights and an outsize bullhorn on the roof. The two uniformed highway patrolmen stared at him with expressionless faces.

He held the wheel steady, fighting down the rising panic. "They know," a small treacherous voice inside him kept saying. "It's all a trap. Smolensk has been blown. You're going to be set up. They'll be waiting for you. They're just checking because you've overshot the turnoff."

"Don't be silly," his cogent mind urged. Then he thought of Renate, and the black despair joined hands with the fear, and the fear was winning.

"Listen, you fool," said his mind, "you did something stupid. But you didn't mean to do it. Then you kept your head. The bodies won't be discovered for weeks. By then, you'll be out of the Service, out of the country, with your savings, in a land where they'll leave you alone. In peace. That's all you want now—peace. To be left alone. And they'll leave you alone because of the tapes."

The People's Police, or VOPO, car slowed and studied him. He began to sweat. The fear was rising and still winning. He could not know that the young policemen were car buffs and had not seen the new BMW sedan before.

Commissar Schiller spent thirty minutes with the Director of First K, the Murder Squad, explaining what he had found. Hartwig bit his lip.

"It's going to be a bastard," he said. "Had she started blackmailing already, or was this to be her retirement fund? We don't know."

He lifted the phone and was put through to the forensic lab.

"I want the photographs of the recovered bullets and the prints—the nineteen of yesterday and the three of this morning—in my office in one hour." Then he rose and turned to Schiller.

"Come on. We're going back. I want to see this place for myself."

It was actually Director Hartwig who found the notebook. Why anyone should be so secretive as to hide a notebook in a room that was already so well hidden, he could not imagine. But it was taped under the lowest shelf where the videos were stored.

The list was, they would discover, in Renate Heimendorf's handwriting. Clearly she had been a very clever woman, and this was her operation—from the skillful refurbishment of the original apartment to the harmless-looking remote control that could turn the camera behind the mirror on or off. The forensic boys had seen it in the bedroom but had thought it was a spare for the TV.

Hartwig ran through the names in the notebook, which corresponded with the numbers on the spines of the video-cassettes. Some he recognized, some not. The ones he did not know, he reckoned would be men from out of state, but important men. The ones he recognized included two senators, a parliamentarian (government party), a financier, a banker (local), three industrialists, the heir to a major brewery, a judge, a famous surgeon, and a nationally known television personality. Eight names appeared to be Anglo-Saxon (British? American? Canadian?), and two French. He counted the rest.

"Eighty-one names," he said. "Eighty-one tapes. Christ, if the names I do recognize are anything to go by, there must be enough here to bring down several state governments, maybe Bonn itself."

"That's odd," said Schiller. "There are only sixty-one tapes."

They both counted them. Sixty-one.

"You say there were three sets of prints lifted here?"

"Yes, sir."

"Assuming two were from Heimendorf and Hoppe, the third is probably the killer. And I have a horrible feeling he's taken twenty tapes with him. Come on—I'm going to the President with this. It's got beyond a murder, way beyond."

Dr. Herrmann was finishing lunch with his subordinate, Aust.

"My dear Aust, we know nothing as yet. We simply have reason for concern. The police may quickly arrest and charge a gangster, and Morenz may return on schedule after a sinful weekend with a girlfriend at someplace other than the Black Forest. I have to say that his immediate retirement with loss of pension is beyond a doubt. But for the moment, I just want you to try and trace him. I want a female operative to move in with his wife in case he calls. Use any excuse you like. I will attempt to find out just what is the state of the police investigation. You know my hotel. Contact me if there is news of him."

Sam McCready sat on the tailgate of the Range Rover in warm sunshine high above the Saale River and sipped coffee from a flask. Johnson put down his handset. He had been speaking to Cheltenham, the huge national listening station in the west of England.

"Nothing," he said. "All normal. No extra radio traffic in any sector—Russian, SSD, or People's Police. Just routine."

McCready checked his watch. Ten to four. Bruno should be moving toward the lay-by west of Weimar about now. He had told him to be five minutes early and allow no more than twenty-five minutes if Smolensk failed to show up. That would count as an abort. He kept calm in front of Johnson, but he hated the waiting. It was always the worst part, waiting for an agent across the border. The imagination played tricks, creating a whole range of things that could have happened to him but probably had not. For the hundredth time, he calculated the schedule. Five minutes at the lay-by; the Russian hands it over; ten minutes to let the Russian get away. Four-fifteen departure. Five minutes to switch the manual from inside his jacket to the compartment under the battery; one hour and forty-five minutes of driving—he should be coming into view about six . . . another cup of coffee.

The Police President of Cologne, Arnim von Starnberg, listened gravely to the young commissar's report. He was flanked by Hartwig of the Murder Squad and Horst Fraenkel, Director of the whole *Kriminalamt*. Both senior officers had felt it right to come straight to him. When he heard the details, he agreed they were correct. This thing was not only bigger than a murder; it was bigger than Cologne. He already intended to take it higher. The young Schiller finished.

"You will remain completely silent about this, Herr Schiller," said von Starnberg. "You and your colleague, Assistant Commissar Wiechert. Your careers depend on it, you understand?" He turned to Hartwig. "The same applies to those two fingerprint men who saw the camera room."

He dismissed Schiller and turned to the other detectives.

"How far exactly have you got?"

Fraenkel nodded to Hartwig, who produced a number of large high-definition photographs.

"Well, Herr President, we now have the bullets that killed the call girl and her friend. We need to find the gun that fired those bullets." He tapped two photographs. "Just two bullets, one in each body. Second, the fingerprints. There were three sets in the camera room. Two came from the call girl and her pimp. We believe the third set must belong to the killer. We also believe it was he who stole the twenty missing cassettes."

None of the three men could know there were actually twenty-one missing cassettes. Morenz had thrown the twenty-first, the one of himself, into the Rhine on Friday evening. He was not listed in the notebook because he had never been a major blackmail prospect—just fun.

"Where are the other sixty-one tapes?" asked von Starnberg.

"In my personal safe," said Fraenkel.

"Please have them brought straight up here. No one must view them."

When he was alone, President von Starnberg began telephoning. That afternoon, the responsibility for the affair went up the official hierarchy faster than a monkey up a tree. Cologne passed the affair to the Provincial *Kriminalamt* in the provincial capital, Düsseldorf. That office passed it at once to the Federal *Kriminalamt* in Wiesbaden. Guarded limousines with the sixty-one tapes and the notebook sped from city to city. At Wiesbaden, it stopped for a while as senior civil servants worked out how to tell the Justice Minister in Bonn— he was the next up the ladder. By this time all sixty-one sexual athletes had been identified. Half were merely wealthy; the other half were both rich and firmly Establishment figures. Worse, six senators and parliamentarians of the ruling party were involved, plus two from the other parties, two senior civil servants, and an army general. That was only the Germans. There were two foreign diplomats based in Bonn (one from a NATO ally), two foreign politicians who had been visiting, and a White House staffer close to Ronald Reagan.

But even worse was the now-identified list of the twenty whose recorded frolics were missing. They included a senior member of the West German ruling party parliamentary caucus, another parliamentarian (federal), a judge (appeals court), another senior armed forces officer (air force, this time), the beer magnate spotted by Hartwig, and a rising junior minister. That was apart from some of the proud cream of commerce and industry.

"Naughty businessmen can be laughed off," commented a senior detective in the Federal Criminal Office in Wiesbaden. "If they are ruined, it's their own fault. But this bitch specialized in the Establishment."

In the later afternoon, simply for procedural reasons, the country's internal security service, the BfV, was informed. Not of all the names, just the history of the investigation and its state of progress. Ironically, the BfV is headquartered in Cologne, back where it all started. The interdepartmental memorandum on the case landed on the desk of a senior officer in counterintelligence called Johann Prinz.

*   *   *

Bruno Morenz rolled slowly west along Highway Seven. He was four miles west of Weimar and one mile from the big white-walled Soviet barracks at Nohra. He came to a curve, and there was the lay-by, just where McCready had said it would be. He checked his watch; eight minutes to four. The road was empty. He slowed and pulled into the lay-by.

According to instructions, he climbed out, released the trunk, and removed the toolkit. This he opened and laid beside the front offside wheel, where it would be visible to a passerby. Then he flicked the catch and raised the hood. His stomach began to churn. There were bushes and trees behind the lay-by and across the road. In his mind's eye he saw crouching agents from the SSD waiting to make a double arrest. His mouth was dry, but the sweat ran in rivulets down his back. His fragile reserve was close to snapping like an overstretched rubber band.

He took a wrench, the right size for the job, and bent his head inside the engine bay. McCready had showed him how to loosen the nut connecting the water pipe to the radiator. A trickle of water escaped. He changed the wrench for one clearly the wrong size and tried vainly to tighten the nut again.

The minutes ticked by. Inside the engine bay he tinkered vainly away. He glanced at his watch. Six minutes past four. Where the hell are you? he asked. Almost at once there was a slight crunch of gravel under wheels as a vehicle came to a halt. He kept his head down. The Russian would come up to him and say in his accented German, "If you are having trouble, perhaps I have a better set of tools," and offer him the flat wooden toolbox from the jeep. The Soviet Army War Book would be under the wrenches in a red plastic cover.

The dropping sun was blocked by the shadow of someone approaching. Boots crunched on gravel. The man was beside and behind him. He said nothing. Morenz straightened. An East German police car was parked five yards away. One green-uniformed policeman stood by the open driver's door. The other was beside Morenz, gazing down into the BMW's open engine bay.

Morenz wanted to vomit. His stomach pumped out acid. He felt his knees becoming weak. He tried to straighten up and nearly stumbled.

The policeman met his gaze. "*Was ist los?*" he asked.

Of course it was a ploy, a courtesy to mask the triumph. The inquiry if anything was wrong was to precede the screams and shouts and the arrest. Morenz's tongue felt as if it were stuck to the roof of his mouth.

"I thought I was losing water," he said. The policeman put his head into the engine bay and studied the radiator. He removed the wrench from Morenz's hand, stooped, and came up with another one.

"This one will fit," he said. Morenz used it and retightened the nut. The trickle stopped.

"Wrong wrench," said the cop. He gazed at the BMW engine. He seemed to be staring straight at the battery. "*Schöner Wagen,*" he said. Nice car. "Where are you staying?"

"In Jena," said Morenz. "I have to see the foreign sales director at Zeiss tomorrow morning. To buy products for my company."

The policeman nodded approvingly.

"We have many fine products in the GDR," he said. It was not true. East Germany had one single factory that produced Western-standard equipment, the Zeiss works.

"What are you doing out here?"

"I wished to see Weimar . . . the Goethe memorial."

"You are heading in the wrong direction. Weimar is that way."

The policeman pointed down the road behind Morenz. A gray-green Soviet GAZ jeep rolled past. The driver, eyes shaded by a forage cap, gazed at Morenz, met his eyes for a second, took in the parked VOPO car, and rolled on. An abort. Smolensk would not approach now.

"Yes. I took a wrong turn out of town. I was looking for a place to turn when I saw the water gauge misbehaving."

The VOPOs supervised his U-turn and followed him back to Weimar. They peeled off at the entry to the town. Morenz drove on to Jena and checked into the Black Bear Hotel.

At eight, on his hill above the Saale River, Sam McCready put down his binoculars. The gathering dusk made it impossible to see the East German border post and the road behind it. He felt tired, drained. Something had gone wrong up there behind the minefields and the razor-wire. It might be nothing

of importance, a blown-out tire, a traffic jam. . . . Unlikely.
Perhaps his man was even now motoring south toward the
border. Perhaps Pankratin had not shown up at the first meet,
unable to get a jeep, unable to get away. . . . Waiting was
always the worst, the waiting and the not knowing what had
gone wrong.

"We'll go back down to the road," he told Johnson. "Can't
see anything here anyway."

He installed Johnson in the parking area of the Frankenwald
service station, on the southbound side but facing north
toward the border. Johnson would sit there all night, watching
for the BMW to appear. McCready found a truck driver
heading south, explained that his car had broken down, and
hitched a lift six miles south. He got off at the Münchberg
junction, walked the mile into the small town, and checked
into the Braunschweiger Hof. He had his portable phone in a
totebag if Johnson wanted to call him. He ordered a cab for
six A.M.

Dr. Herrmann had a contact in the BfV. The two men had met
and collaborated years earlier, working on the Guenther Guil-
laume scandal, when the private secretary of Chancellor Willy
Brandt had been revealed as an East German agent. That
evening at six, Dr. Herrmann had rung the BfV in Cologne
and asked to be put through.

"Johann? This is Lothar Herrmann. . . . No, I'm not. I'm
here in Cologne. . . . Oh, routine, you know. I was hoping I
could offer you dinner. . . . Excellent. Well, look, I'm at the
Dom Hotel. Why don't you join me in the bar? About eight?
I look forward to it."

Johann Prinz put the phone down and wondered what had
brought Herrmann to Cologne. Visiting the troops?
Possibly. . . .

Two hours later, they sat at the corner dining table and
ordered. For a while, they fenced gently. How are things?
Fine. . . . Over the crab cocktail, Herrmann moved a little
closer.

"I suppose they've told you about the call girl affair?" he
asked.

Prinz was surprised. When had the BND learned of it? He

had only seen the file at five. Herrmann had telephoned at six, and he was already in Cologne.

"Yes," he said. "Got the file this afternoon."

Now Herrmann was surprised. Why would a double murder in Cologne have been passed to counterintelligence? He had expected to have to explain it to Prinz before asking for his favor. "Nasty affair," he murmured as the steak arrived.

"And getting worse," agreed Prinz. "Bonn won't like those sex tapes floating around."

Herrmann kept his face impassive, but his stomach turned over. Sex tapes? Dear God, *what* sex tapes? He affected mild surprise and poured more wine.

"Got that far, has it? I must have been out of the office when the latest details arrived. Mind filling me in?"

Prinz did so. Herrmann lost all his appetite. The odor in his nostrils was not so much of the claret as of a scandal of cataclysmic proportions.

"And still no clues," he murmured sorrowfully.

"Not a lot," agreed Prinz. "First K have been told to pull every man off every case and put them onto this one. The search, of course, is for the gun and the owner of the finger-prints."

Lothar Herrmann sighed. "I wonder if the culprit could be a foreigner?" he suggested.

Prinz scooped up the last of his ice cream and put down his spoon. He grinned. "Ah, now I see. Our external intelligence service has an interest?"

Herrmann shrugged dismissively. "My dear friend, we both accomplish much the same task. Protecting our political mas-ters."

Like all senior civil servants, both of these men had a view of their political masters that wisely was seldom shared with the politicians themselves.

"We do, of course, have some records of our own," said Herrmann. "Fingerprints of foreigners who have come to our attention. . . . Alas, we haven't got copies of the prints our friends in the KA are seeking."

"You could ask officially," Prinz pointed out.

"Yes, but then why start a hare that will probably lead nowhere? Now, unofficially—"

"I don't like the word *unofficial,*" said Prinz.

"No more do I, my friend, but . . . now and again—for old times' sake. You have my word, if I turn anything up, it comes straight back to you. A joint effort by the two services. My word on it. If nothing turns up, then no harm done."

Prinz rose. "All right, for old times' sake. Just this once."

As he left the hotel, he wondered what the hell Herrmann knew, or suspected, that he did not.

In the Braunschweiger Hof in Münchberg, Sam McCready sat at the bar. He drank alone and stared at the dark paneling. He was worried, deeply so. Again and again he wondered if he should have sent Morenz over.

There was something wrong about the man. A summer cold? More like the flu. But that doesn't make you nervous. His old friend had seemed very nervous. Was his nerve gone? No, not old Bruno. He had done it many times before. And he was "clean"—as far as McCready knew.

McCready tried to justify sending Bruno. He had had no time to find a younger man. And Pankratin would not "show" for a strange face. It was Pankratin's life on the line, too. If he'd refused to send Morenz, they'd have lost the Soviet War Book. He had had no choice . . . but he could not stop worrying.

Seventy miles north, Bruno Morenz was in the bar of the Black Bear Hotel in Jena. He too drank, and alone, and too much.

Across the street he could see the main entrance to the centuries-old Schiller University. Outside was a bust of Karl Marx. A plaque revealed that Marx had taught in the philosophy faculty there in 1841. Morenz wished the bearded philosopher had dropped dead while doing it. Then he would never have gone to London and written *Das Kapital,* and Morenz would not now be going through his misery so far from home.

At one A.M. Wednesday, a sealed brown envelope arrived at the Dom Hotel for Dr. Herrmann. He was still up. The envelope contained three large photographs: two of various 9mm slugs, one of a set of thumb, finger, and palm prints. He resolved not to wire them down to Pullach but to take them himself that morning. If the tiny scratches along the sides of the bullets, and the prints, matched up with his expectations, he was going to face a very major quandary. Whom to tell, and how much. If only that bastard Morenz would show up. . . . At nine A.M. he caught the first flight back to Munich.

At ten Major Vanavskaya in Berlin checked again on the whereabouts of the man she was tracking. He was with the garrison outside Erfurt, she was told. He leaves at six tonight for Potsdam. Tomorrow he flies back to Moscow.

"And I'll be with you, you bastard," she thought.

At half past eleven, Morenz rose from the table in the coffee bar where he had been killing time and made for the car. He felt hung over. His tie was undone, and he could not face his razor that morning. Gray stubble covered his cheeks and chin. He did not look like a businessman about to discuss optical lenses in the boardroom at the Zeiss works. He drove carefully out of town, heading west toward Weimar. The lay-by was three miles away.

It was bigger than the lay-by of yesterday, shaded by leafy beech trees that flanked the road on both sides. Set into the trees across from the lay-by was the Mühltalperle coffee house. No one seemed to be about. It was not seething with guests. He pulled into the lay-by at five to twelve, got out his toolkit, and opened the hood again. At two minutes after twelve, the GAZ jeep rolled onto the gravel and stopped. The man who got out wore baggy cotton fatigues and knee-boots. He had corporal's insignia and a forage cap pulled over his eyes. He strolled toward the BMW.

"If you are having trouble, perhaps I have a better toolbox," he said. He swung his wooden toolbox into the engine bay and laid it on the cylinder block. A grubby thumbnail flicked open the catch. There was a clutter of wrenches inside.

"So, Poltergeist, how are you these days?" he murmured.

Morenz's mouth was dry again. "Fine," he whispered back. He pulled the wrenches to one side. The red-plastic-covered manual lay underneath. The Russian took a wrench and tightened the loose nut. Morenz removed the book and stuffed it inside his light raincoat, jamming it with his left arm under his armpit. The Russian replaced his wrenches and closed the toolbox.

"I must go," he muttered. "Give me ten minutes to get clear. And show gratitude. Someone might be watching."

He straightened up, waved his right arm, and walked back to his jeep. The engine was still running. Morenz stood up and waved after him. "*Danke,*" he called. The jeep drove away, back toward Erfurt. Morenz felt weak. He wanted to get out of there. He needed a drink. He would pull over later and stash the manual in the compartment beneath the battery. Right now he needed a drink. Keeping the manual pinned beneath his armpit, he dropped the engine cover, tossed his tools into the trunk, closed it, and climbed into the car. The hip flask was in the glove compartment. He got it out and took a deep, satisfying pull. Five minutes later, his confidence restored, he turned the car back to Jena. He had spotted another lay-by, beyond Jena, just before the link road to the Autobahn back to the border. He would pause there to stash the manual.

The crash was not even his fault. South of Jena, in the suburb of Stadtroda, when he was driving between the huge and hideous apartment blocks of the housing estate, a Trabant came bucketing out of a side road. He nearly stopped in time, but his reflexes were poor. The much-stronger BMW crunched the rear of the East German mini.

Morenz began to panic almost at once. Was it a trap? Was the Trabant driver really the SSD? The man climbed out of his car, stared at his crushed rear, and stormed up to the BMW. He had a pinched, mean face and angry eyes.

"What the hell do you think you're doing?" he yelled. "Damned Westerners, think you can drive like maniacs!"

He had the small round badge of the Socialist Unity Party in his jacket lapel. The Communists. A Party member. Morenz jammed his left arm tight to his body to hold the manual in place, climbed out, and reached for a wad of Marks. Ostmarks, of course; he couldn't offer Deutschmarks—that was another offense. People began to stroll toward the scene.

"Look, I'm sorry," he said. "I'll pay for the damage. This must be more than enough. But I really am very late."

The angry East German looked at the money. It really was a very large wad.

"That's not the point," he said. "I had to wait four years for this car."

"It'll repair," said another man standing nearby.

"No, it damn well won't," said the aggrieved one. "It'll have to go back to the factory."

The crowd now numbered twenty. Life was boring on an industrial housing estate, and a BMW was worth looking at. That was when the police car arrived. Routine patrol, but Morenz began to shake. The policemen got out. One looked at the damage.

"It can be fixed," he said. "Do you want to prefer charges?"

The Trabant driver was backing off. "Well . . ."

The other policeman approached Morenz. "*Ausweis, bitte,*" he said. Morenz used his right hand to bring out his passport. The hand was trembling. The cop looked at the hand, the bleary eyes, the unshaven chin.

"You've been drinking," he said. He sniffed and confirmed it. "Right. Down to the station. Come on, into the car."

He began to hustle Morenz toward the police car, whose engine was still running. The driver's door was open. That was when Bruno Morenz finally disintegrated. He still had the manual under his arm. At the police station it would be found anyway. He swung his one free arm violently back, hit the policeman under his nose, breaking it, and knocked the man down. Then he leaped into the police car, slammed it into gear, and drove off. He was facing the wrong way, north toward Jena.

The other policeman, stunned, managed to fire off four shots from his sidearm. Three missed. The VOPO car, swerving wildly, disappeared around a corner. It was leaking gasoline from the fourth bullet, which had drilled a hole in the tank.

Chapter 4

The two VOPOs were so stunned by what had happened that they reacted slowly. Nothing in their training or previous experience as People's Police had accustomed them to this kind of civil disobedience. They had been publicly assaulted and humiliated in front of a crowd of people, and they were beside themselves with rage. A fair amount of shouting took place before they worked out what to do.

The uninjured officer left his broken-nosed colleague on the scene while he headed back to the police station. They had no personal communicators because they were accustomed to using the car radio to report to HQ. Appeals to the crowd for a telephone had met with shrugs. Working-class people did not have telephones in the GDR.

The Party member with the battered Trabant asked if he could leave and was promptly arrested at gunpoint by Broken Nose, who was prepared to believe that anyone could have been part of the conspiracy.

His colleague, marching up the road toward Jena, saw a Wartburg coming toward him, flagged it down (also at gunpoint), and ordered the driver to take him straight to the police station in central Jena. A mile farther on, they saw a police patrol car coming toward them. The VOPO in the civilian Wartburg frantically waved his colleagues to a stop and explained what had happened. Using the patrol car's radio, they checked in, explained the nature of the several crimes that had been committed, and were told to report immediately to police HQ. Meanwile, backup prowl cars were sent to the crash scene.

The call to Jena Central was logged at 12:35. It was also logged many miles away, high in the Harz Mountains on the other side of the border by a British listening post code-named Archimedes.

At one P.M. Dr. Lothar Herrmann, back at his desk in Pullach, lifted his phone and took the awaited call from the BND ballistics laboratory in a neighboring building. The lab was situated adjacent to the armory and firing range. It had the shrewd practice, when issuing a sidearm to an operative, not simply to note the serial number of the gun and get it signed for, but to fire two rounds into a sealed chamber, then to retrieve and keep the slugs.

In a perfect world, the technician would have preferred the actual bullets from the cadavers in Cologne, but he made do with the photographs. All rifle barrels are different from one another in minute respects, and when firing a bullet, each barrel leaves miniscule scratches, called lands, on the discharged slug. They are like fingerprints. The technician had compared the lands on the two sample slugs he still retained from a Walther PPK issued ten years ago with the photographs he had been given and about whose origin he had no idea at all.

"A perfect match? I see. Thank you," said Dr. Herrmann. He called the fingerprint section—the BND keeps a full set of prints of its own staffers, apart from others who come to its attention—and received the same reply. He exhaled deeply and reached for the phone again. There was nothing for it; this had to go to the Director General himself.

What followed was one of the most difficult interviews of Dr. Herrmann's career. The DG was obsessive about the efficiency of his agency and its image, both in the corridors of power in Bonn and within the Western intelligence community. The news Herrmann brought was like a body blow to

him. He toyed with the idea of "losing" the sample slugs and
Morenz's fingerprints but quickly dismissed the idea. Morenz
would be caught by the police sooner or later, the lab technicians would be subpoenaed—it would only make the scandal
worse.

The BND in Germany is answerable only to the Chancellor's Office, and the DG knew that sooner or later, and
probably sooner, he would have to take news of the scandal
there. He did not relish the prospect.

"Find him," he ordered Herrmann. "Find him quickly, and
get those tapes back." As Herrmann turned to leave, the DG,
who spoke English fluently, added another remark.

"Dr. Herrmann, the English have a saying that I recommend to you. 'Thou shalt not kill, yet need not strive/offi-
ciously to keep alive.' "

He had given the rhyming quotation in English. Dr. Herrmann understood it but was puzzled by the word *officiously*.
Back in his office, he consulted a dictionary and decided the
word *unnötig*—unnecessarily—was probably the best translation. In a lifetime's career in the BND, it was the broadest
hint he had ever been given. He rang the central registry in
the Personnel Office.

"Send me the curriculum vitae of one of our staff officers,
Bruno Morenz," he ordered.

At two o'clock Sam McCready was still on the hillside where
he and Johnson had been since seven. Though he suspected
the first meet outside Weimar had aborted, one never knew;
Morenz could have motored over at dawn. But he hadn't.
Again, McCready ran through his timings: rendezvous at
twelve, departure twelve-ten, an hour and three-quarters driving—Morenz should be appearing at almost any time. He
raised his binoculars again to the distant road across the
border.

Johnson was reading a local newspaper he had bought at
the Frankenwald service station when his phone trilled discreetly. He picked it up, listened, and offered the handset to
McCready.

"GCHQ," he said. "They want to speak to you."

It was a friend of McCready, speaking from Cheltenham.

"Look, Sam," said the voice, "I think I know where you

are. There's been a lot of radio traffic suddenly broken out not far from you. Perhaps you should call Archimedes. They have more than we do."

The line went dead.

"Get me Archimedes," McCready said to Johnson. "Duty officer, East German Section." Johnson began to punch in the numbers.

In the mid-1950s the British government, acting through the British Army of the Rhine, had bought a dilapidated old castle high in the Harz Mountains, not far from the pretty and historic little town of Goslar. The Harz are a range of densely wooded uplands through which the East German border ran in twisting curves, sometimes across the flank of a hill, sometimes along a rocky ravine. It was a favorite area for potential East German escapers to try their luck.

Schloss Löwenstein had been refurbished by the British, ostensibly as a retreat for military bands to practice their art. This ruse was maintained by the continuous sounds of band practice issuing from the castle with the aid of tape recorders and amplifiers. But in repairing the roof, engineers from Cheltenham had installed some very sophisticated antennae, upgraded with better technology through the years. Although local German dignitaries were occasionally invited to a real concert of chamber and military music by a band flown in for the occasion, Löwenstein was really an out-station of Cheltenham, code-named Archimedes. Its job was to listen to the endless babble of East German and Russian radio chit-chat from across the border. Hence the value of the mountains; the height gave perfect reception.

"Yes, we've just passed it down the line to Cheltenham," said the duty officer when McCready had established his credentials. "They said you might call direct."

He talked for several minutes, and when McCready put the phone down, he was pale.

"The police in Jena District are going apeshit," he told Johnson. "Apparently there's been a crash outside Jena. Southern side. A West German car, make unknown, hit a Trabant. The West German slugged one of the VOPOs who attended the crash and drove off—in the VOPO car, of all things. Of course, it might not be our man."

Johnson looked sympathetic, but he no more believed it than McCready.

"What do we do?" he asked.

McCready sat on the tailgate of the Range Rover, his head in his hands.

"We wait," he said. "There's nothing else we can do. Archimedes will call back if more comes through."

At that hour the black BMW was being driven into the compound of the Jena police headquarters. No one was think-ing of fingerprints—they knew who they wanted to arrest. The VOPO with the damaged nose had been patched up and was making a long statement, his colleague likewise. The Trabant driver was being detained and questioned, as were a dozen onlookers. On the desk of the precinct commandant lay the passport in the name of Hans Grauber, picked up from the street where the broken-nosed VOPO had dropped it. Other detectives were going through every item in the attaché case and overnight bag. The foreign sales director of Zeiss was brought in, protesting that he had never heard of Hans Grauber, but yes, he had done business in the past with BKI of Würzburg. When confronted with his forged signature on the introduction letters, he claimed it looked like his signature but could not be. His nightmare was just beginning.

Because the passport was West German, the People's Police Commandant made a routine call to the local SSD office. Ten minutes later they were back. We want that car taken on a low-loader to our main garage in Erfurt, they said. Stop putting fingerprints all over it. Also, deliver all items retrieved from the car to us. And copies of all statements from wit-nesses. Now.

The VOPO colonel knew who was really in charge. When the *Stasi* gave an order, you obeyed. The black BMW arrived at the SSD main garage in Erfurt on its trailer at four-thirty and the secret police mechanics went to work. The VOPO colonel had to admit the SSD was right. Nothing made sense. The West German would probably have faced a hefty fine for drunk-driving—East Germany always needed the hard cur-rency. Now he faced years in prison. Why had he run? Anyway, whatever the *Stasi* wanted with the car, his job was to find the man. He ordered every police car and foot patrol for miles around to keep an eye open for Grauber and the stolen police car. The description of both was passed by radio to all units—up to Apolda north of Jena and west to Weimar. No press appeals were made for assistance from the general public. Public help for the police in a police state is a rare luxury. But all the frantic radio traffic was heard by Archimedes.

At four P.M., Dr. Herrmann called Dieter Aust in Cologne. He did not tell him the result of the lab tests, or even what he had received the previous night from Johann Prinz. Aust had no need to know.

"I want you to interview Frau Morenz personally," he said. "You have a woman operative with her? Good, keep her there. If the police come to interview Frau Morenz, do not impede, but let me know. Try and get from her any clue as to where he might go, any vacation home, any girlfriend's apartment, any relative's house—anything at all. Use your entire staff to follow up any lead she gives you. Report back anything to me."

"He hasn't got any relatives in Germany," said Aust, who had already been through Morenz's past life as revealed in the personnel files, "other than his wife, son, and daughter. I believe his daughter is a hippie, lives in a squat in Düsseldorf. I'll have it visited, just in case."

"Do that," said Herrmann, and he put down the phone. Based on something he had seen in Morenz's file, he then sent a *blitz*-category-coded signal to Wolfgang Fietzau, the BND agent on the staff of the German Embassy, Belgrave Square, London.

At five o'clock, the phone set on the tailgate of the Range Rover trilled. McCready picked it up. He thought it would be London or Archimedes. The voice was thin, tinny, as if the speaker were choking.

"Sam? Is that you Sam?"

McCready stiffened. "Yes," he snapped, "it's me."

"I'm sorry, Sam. I'm so sorry. I messed it up."

"Are you okay?" said McCready urgently. Morenz was wasting vital seconds.

" 'Kay. Yeah, *k* as in *kaput*. I'm finished, Sam. I didn't mean to kill her. I loved her, Sam. I loved her."

McCready slammed down the phone, severing the connection. No one could make a phone call to the West from an East German phone booth. All contact was forbidden by the East Germans. But the SIS maintained a safe house in the Leipzig area, occupied by an East German agent-in-place who worked for London. A call to that number, dialed from inside East Germany, would run through pass-on equipment that would throw the call up to a satellite and back into the West.

But calls had to be four seconds long, no more, to prevent the East Germans triangulating onto the source of the call and locating the safe house. Morenz had babbled on for nine seconds. Although McCready could not know it, the SSD listening watch had already got as far as the Leipzig area when the connection was severed. Another six seconds, and they would have had the safe house and its occupant. Morenz had been told to use the number only in dire emergency and very briefly.

"He's cracked up," said Johnson. "Gone to pieces."

"For Christ's sake, he was crying like a child," snapped McCready. "He's had a complete nervous breakdown. Tell me something I don't know. What the hell did he mean—'I didn't mean to kill her.' "

Johnson was pensive. "He comes from Cologne?"

"You know that."

Actually, Johnson did not know that. He only knew he had picked up McCready from the Cologne airport Holiday Inn. He had never seen Poltergeist. No need to. He took the local newspaper and pointed out the second lead story on the front page. It was Guenther Braun's story from his Cologne newspaper, picked up and reprinted by the *Nordbayrischer Kurier*, the north Bavarian paper printed in Bayreuth. The story was datelined Cologne and the headline read, CALL GIRL/PIMP SLAUGHTERED IN LOVE-NEST SHOOT-OUT. McCready read it, put it down, and stared across toward the north.

"Oh, Bruno, my poor friend. What the hell have you done?"

Five minutes later Archimedes phoned.

"We heard that," said the duty officer. "So, I imagine, did everyone else. I'm sorry. He's gone, hasn't he?"

"What's the latest?" asked Sam.

"They are using the name Hans Grauber," said Archimedes. "There's an all-points watch out for him all over southern Thuringia. Drink, assasult, and theft of a police car. The car he drove was a black BMW, right? They've taken it to the SSD main garage at Erfurt. Seems all the rest of his gear has been impounded and handed over to the *Stasi*."

"What time exactly was the crash?" asked Sam.

The duty officer conferred with someone.

"The first call to the Jena police was from a passing patrol car. The speaker was apparently the VOPO who had not been punched. He used the phrase 'five minutes ago.' Logged at twelve thirty-five."

"Thank you," said McCready.

At eight o'clock in the Erfurt garage, one of the mechanics found the cavity beneath the battery. Around him three other mechanics labored over what remained of the BMW. Its seats and upholstery were all over the floor, its wheels off and its tires inside-out. Only the frame remained, and it was there that the cavity was discovered. The mechanic called over a man in civilian clothes, a major of the SSD. They both examined the cavity, and the major nodded.

"*Ein Spionwagen,*" he said. A spy car. Work continued, though there was little more to do. The major went upstairs and called Lichtenberg, the East Berlin headquarters of the SSD. The major knew where to place the call; it went straight to Abteilung II, the Counterespionage Department of the service. There the matter was taken in hand by the Director of the Abteilung himself, Colonel Otto Voss. His first command was for absolutely everything connected with the case to be brought to East Berlin; his second was for everyone who had even glimpsed the BMW or its occupant since it entered the country, starting with the border guards at the Saale River, to be brought in and questioned minutely. That would later include the staff of the Black Bear Hotel, the patrolmen who had studied the BMW as they cruised alongside it on the Autobahn—especially the two who had caused the first rendezvous to abort—and the ones who had had their patrol car stolen.

Voss's third order was for an absolute end to any mention of the matter on radios or on nonsecure telephone lines. When he had done that, he picked up his internal phone and was connected with Abteilung VI, Crossing Points and Airports.

At ten P.M. Archimedes phoned McCready for the last time.

"I'm afraid it's over," said the duty officer. "No, they haven't got him yet, but they will. They must have discovered something in the Erfurt garage. Heavy radio traffic, coded, between Erfurt and East Berlin. A total shutdown of loose chit-chat on the airwaves. Oh, and all border points are on full alert—guards doubled, searchlights on the border working overtime. The lot. Sorry."

Even from where he stood on the hillside, McCready could see that over the past hour the headlights of cars coming out of East Germany were very few and far between. They must be holding them for hours under the arc lights a mile away as they searched every car and truck until a mouse could not escape detection.

At ten-thirty, Timothy Edwards came on the line.

"Look, we're all very sorry, but it's over," he said. "Come back to London at once, Sam."

"They haven't got him yet. I should stay here. I may be able to help. It's not over yet."

"Bar the shouting, it is," insisted Edwards.

"There are things here we have to discuss—the loss of the package being not the least of them. Our American Cousins are not a happy group, to say the least. Please be on the first plane out of Munich or Frankfurt, whichever is the first of the day."

It turned out to be Frankfurt. Johnson drove him through the night to the airport, then took the Range Rover and its equipment back to Bonn, a very tired young man. McCready grabbed a few hours' sleep at the airport's Sheraton and was on the first flight for Heathrow the next day, landing, with the one-hour time difference, just after eight o'clock. Denis Gaunt met him and drove him straight to Century House. He read the file of radio intercepts in the car.

Major Ludmilla Vanavskaya rose early that Thursday, and for lack of a gymnasium did her sit-ups in her own room at the KGB barracks. Her flight was not till midday, but she intended to pass by the KGB headquarters for a last check on the itinerary of the man she hunted.

She knew he had returned from Erfurt to Potsdam in convoy the previous evening and spent the night in the officers' quarters there. They were both due to take the same flight back from Potsdam to Moscow at noon. He would sit up front in the seats reserved, even on military flights, for the *vlasti*, the privileged ones. She was posing as a humble stenographer from the huge Soviet Embassy on Unter den Linden, the real seat of power in East Germany. They would not meet—he would not even notice her; but as soon as they entered Soviet air space, he would be under surveillance.

At eight she walked into the KGB headquarters building half a mile from the embassy and made her way to the Communications Office. They would be able to call Potsdam and confirm that the flight schedule was unchanged. While waiting for her information, she took coffee and shared a table with a young lieutenant who was plainly very tired and yawned often.

"Up all night?" she asked.

"Yep. Night shift. The krauts have been in a flap the whole time."

He did not use her title because she was in plain clothes, and the word he used for the East Germans was uncomplimentary. The Russians all did that.

"Why?" she asked.

"Oh, they intercepted a West German car and found a secret cavity in it. Reckon it was being used by one of their agents."

"Here in Berlin?"

"No, down at Jena."

"Where is Jena, exactly?"

"Look, love, my shift's over. I'm off to get some sleep."

She smiled sweetly, opened her purse, and flashed her red-covered ID card. The Lieutenant stopped yawning and went pale. A full major of the Third Directorate was very bad news indeed. He showed her—on the wall map at the end of the canteen. She let him go and stayed looking at the map. Zwickau, Gera, Jena, Weimar, Erfurt—all in a line, a line followed by the convoy of the man she hunted. Yesterday . . .

Erfurt. And Jena fourteen miles away. Close, too damned close.

Ten minutes later, a Soviet Major was briefing her on the way the East Germans worked.

"By now, it will be with their Abteilung II," he said. "That's Colonel Voss, Otto Voss. He'll be in charge."

She used his office phone, pulled some rank, and secured an interview at the Lichtenberg headquarters at the SSD with Colonel Voss. Ten o'clock.

At nine, London time, McCready took his seat at the table in the conference room one floor below the Chief's office at Century House. Claudia Stuart was opposite, looking at him reproachfully. Chris Appleyard, who had flown to London to escort the Soviet War Book personally back to Langley, smoked and stared at the ceiling. His attitude seemed to be: This is a limey affair. You screwed it up, you sort it out. Timothy Edwards took the chair at the head, a sort of arbitrator. There was only one unspoken agenda: damage assessment. Damage limitation, if any was possible, would come later. No one needed to be briefed as to what had happened; they had all read the file of intercepts and the situation reports.

"All right," said Edwards. "It appears your man Poltergeist has come apart at the seams and blown the mission away. Let's see if there's anything we can salvage from the mess."

"Why the hell did you send him, Sam?" asked Claudia in exasperation.

"You know why. Because you wanted a job done," said McCready. "Because you couldn't do it yourselves. Because it was a rush job. Because I was stopped from going myself. Because Pankratin insisted on me personally. Because Poltergeist would be the only acceptable substitute. Because he agreed to go."

"But now it appears," drawled Appleyard, "that he had just killed his hooker girlfriend and was already at the end of his tether. You didn't spot anything?"

"No. He appeared nervous but under control. Nerves are normal—up to a point. He didn't tell me about his personal mess, and I'm not clairvoyant."

"The damned thing is," said Claudia, "he's seen Pankratin. When the *Stasi* get him and go to work, he'll talk. We've lost Pankratin as well, and God knows how much damage his interrogation in the Lubyanka will do."

"Where is Pankratin now?" asked Edwards.

"According to his schedule, he's boarding a military flight from Potsdam to Moscow right about now."

"Can't you get to him and warn him?"

"No, dammit. When he lands, he's taking a week's furlough. With army friends in the countryside. We can't get our emergency warning code to him till he gets back to Moscow—if he ever does."

"What about the War Book?" asked Edwards.

"I think Poltergeist's got it on him," said McCready.

He got their undivided attention. Appleyard stopped smoking.

"Why?"

"Timing," said McCready. "The rendezvous was at twelve. Assume he quit the lay-by at about twelve-twenty. The crash was at twelve-thirty, ten minutes and five miles away, on the other side of Jena. I think if he had had the manual stashed in the compartment beneath the battery, even in his state he'd have taken the drunk-driving rap, spent the night in the cells, and paid his fine. Chances are the VOPOs would never have given the car a rigorous search.

"If the manual was lying in the BMW, I think some hint of the elation of the police would have come through on the intercepts. The SSD would have been called in within ten minutes, not two hours. I think he had it on him—under his jacket, maybe. That's why he couldn't go to the police station. For a blood test, they'd have taken his jacket off. So he ran for it."

There was silence for several minutes.

"It all comes back to Poltergeist," said Edwards. Even though everyone now knew the agent's real name, they preferred his operational code-name. "He must be somewhere. Where would he go? Has he friends near there? A safe house? Anything?"

McCready shook his head. "There's a safe house in East Berlin. He knows it from the old days. I've tried it—no contact. In the south, he knows nobody. Never even been there.''

''Could he hide out in the forests?'' asked Claudia.

''It's not that kind of area. Not like the Harz with its dense forests. Open rolling farmland, towns, villages, hamlets, farms.''

''No place for a middle-aged fugitive who's lost his marbles,'' commented Appleyard.

''Then we've lost him,'' said Claudia. ''Him, the War Book, and Pankratin. The whole deal.''

''I'm afraid it looks so,'' said Edwards. ''The People's Police will use saturation tactics. Roadblocks on every street and lane. Without sanctuary, I fear they'll have him by midday.''

The meeting ended on that gloomy note. When the Americans had gone, Edwards detained McCready at the door.

''Sam, I know it's hopeless, but stay with it, will you? I've asked Cheltenham, East German Section, to step up the listening watch and let you know the instant they hear anything. When they get Poltergeist—and they must—I want to know at once. We're going to have to placate our Cousins somehow, though God knows how.''

Back in his office, McCready threw himself into his chair in deep dejection. He took the phone off the cradle and stared at the wall.

If he had been a drinker, he would have reached for the bottle. Had he not given up cigarettes years earlier, he would have reached for a pack. He had failed, and he knew it. Whatever he might tell Claudia of the pressures they had put on him, it had, finally, been his decision to send in Morenz. And it had been a wrong one.

He had lost the War Book and probably blown away Pankratin. It would have surprised him to know that he was the only man in the building to hold these losses as secondary to another failure.

For him, the worst was that he had sent a friend to certain capture, interrogation, and death because he had failed to note the warning signs that now—too late—were so blazingly clear. Morenz had been in no state to go. He had gone rather than let down his friend Sam McCready.

The Deceiver knew now—again, too late—that for the rest

of his days, in the wee hours when sleep refuses to come, he would see the haggard face of Bruno Morenz in that hotel room. . . .

He tried to drive his guilt away and turned his mind to wondering what happens inside a man's head when he undergoes a complete nervous breakdown. Personally, he had never seen that phenomenon. What was Bruno Morenz like now? How would he react to his situation? Logically? Crazily? He put through a call to the Service's consultant psychiatrist, an eminent doctor known irreverently as "the Shrink." He traced Dr. Alan Carr to his office in Wimpole Street. Dr. Carr said he was busy through the morning but would be happy to join McCready for lunch and an ad hoc consultation. McCready made a date for the Montcalm Hotel at one o'clock.

Punctually at ten, Major Ludmilla Vanavskaya entered the main doors of the SSD headquarters building at 22 Normannenstrasse and was shown up to the fourth floor, the floor occupied by the Counterespionage Department. Colonel Voss was waiting for her. He conducted her into his private office and offered her the chair facing his desk. He took his seat and ordered coffee. When the steward left, he asked politely, "What can I do for you, Comrade Major?"

He was curious as to what had brought about this visit on what would for him undoubtedly be an extremely busy day. But the request had come from the commanding general at KGB headquarters, and Colonel Voss was well aware who really ruled the roost in the German Democratic Republic.

"You are handling a case in the Jena area," said Vanavskaya. "A West German agent who ran off after a crash and left his car behind. Could you let me have the details so far?"

Voss filled in the details not included in the situation report that the Russian had already seen.

"Let us assume," said Vanavskaya when he was finished, "that this agent, Grauber, had come to collect or deliver something. . . . Was anything found in the car or in the secret cavity that could be what he either brought in or was trying to take out?"

"No, nothing. All his private papers were merely his cover story. The cavity was empty. If he brought something in, he had already delivered. If he sought to take something out, he had not collected.''

"Or it was still on his person.''

"Possibly, yes. We will know when we interrogate him. May I ask the reason for your interest in the case?''

Vanavskaya chose her words carefully.

"There is a possibility, just a chance, that a case upon which I am working overlaps your own.''

Behind his impassive face, Otto Voss was amused. So this handsome Russian ferret suspected the West German might have been in the East to make contact with a *Russian* source, not an East German traitor. Interesting.

"Have you any reason to know, Colonel, whether Grauber was to make a personal contact or just administer a dead-letter box?''

"We believe he was here to make a personal meet,'' said Voss. "Although the crash was at twelve-thirty yesterday, he actually came through the border at eleven on Tuesday. If he simply had to drop off a package or pick one up from a dead-letter box, it would not have taken over twenty-four hours. He could have done it by nightfall on Tuesday. As it was, he spent Tuesday night at the Black Bear in Jena. We believe it was a personal pass that he came for.''

Vanavskaya's heart sang. A personal meet, somewhere in the Jena-Weimar area, along a road probably, a road traveled by the man she hunted at almost exactly the same time. It was you he came to meet, you bastard! she thought.

"Have you identified Grauber?'' she asked. "That is certainly not his real name.''

Concealing his triumph, Voss opened a file and passed her an artist's impression. It had been drawn with help from two policemen at Jena, two patrolmen who had helped Grauber tighten a nut west of Weimar, and the staff of the Black Bear. It was very good. Without a word Voss then passed her a large photograph. The two were identical.

"His name is Morenz,'' said Voss. "Bruno Morenz. A full-time career officer of the BND, based in Cologne.''

Vanavskaya was surprised. So it was a West German operation. She had always suspected that her man was working for the CIA or the British.

"You haven't got him yet?''

"No, Major. I confess I am surprised at the delay. But we will. The police car was found abandoned, late last night. The reports state its gasoline tank had a bullet hole through it. It would have run for only ten to fifteen minutes after being stolen. It was found here, near Apolda, just north of Jena. So our man is on foot. We have a perfect description—tall, burly, gray-haired, in a rumpled raincoat. He has no papers, a Rhineland accent, physically not in good shape. He will stick out like a sore thumb."

"I want to be present at the interrogation," said Vanavskaya. She was not squeamish. She had seen them before.

"If that is an official request from the KGB, I will of course comply."

"It will be," said Vanavskaya.

"Then don't be far away, Major. We will have him, probably by midday."

Major Vanavskaya returned to the KGB building, cancelled her flight from Potsdam, and used a secure line to contact General Shaliapin. He agreed.

At twelve noon, an Antonov 32 transport of the Soviet Air Force lifted off from Potsdam for Moscow. General Pankratin and other senior Army and Air Force officers returning to Moscow were on board. Some junior officers were farther back, with the mail sacks. There was no dark-suited "secretary" from the embassy sharing the lift home.

"He will be," said Dr. Carr over the melon and avocado hors d'oeuvre, "in what we call a dissociated, or twilight, or fugue state."

He had listened carefully to McCready's description of a nameless man who had apparently suffered a massive nervous breakdown. He had not learned, or asked, anything about the mission the man had been on, or where this breakdown had occurred, save that it was in hostile territory. The empty plates were removed and the sole prepared, off the bone.

"Dissociated from what?" asked McCready.

"From reality, of course," said Dr. Carr. "It is one of the classic symptoms of this kind of syndrome. He may already have been showing signs of self-deception before the final crackup."

And how, thought McCready, Morenz had been kidding

himself that a stunning hooker had really fallen for him, that he could get away with a double murder.

"Fugue," Dr. Carr pursued as he speared a forkful of tender sole meunière, "means flight. Flight from reality, especially harsh, unpleasant reality. I think your man will by now be in a really bad way."

"What will he actually do?" asked McCready. "Where will he go?"

"He will go to a sanctuary, somewhere he feels safe, somewhere he can hide, where all the problems will go away and people will leave him alone. He may even return to a childlike state. I had a patient once who, overcome by problems, retired to his bed, curled into the fetal position, stuck his thumb in his mouth, and stayed there. Wouldn't come out. Childhood, you see. Safety, security. No problems. Excellent sole, by the way. Yes, a little more Meursault. . . . Thank you."

Which is all very fine, thought McCready, but Bruno Morenz has no sanctuaries to run to. Born and raised in Hamburg, stationed in Berlin, Munich, and Cologne, he could have no place to hide near Jena or Weimar. He poured more wine and asked, "Supposing he has no sanctuary to head for?"

"Then I'm afraid he will just wander about in a confused state, unable to help himself. In my experience, if he had a destination he could act logically to get there. Without one"— the doctor shrugged—"they will get him. Probably got him by now. At latest by nightfall."

But they didn't. Through the afternoon Colonel Voss's rage and frustration rose. It had been over twenty-four hours, coming up on thirty hours; police and secret police were at every street corner and roadblock in the region of Apolda-Jena-Weimar; and the big, shambling, ill, confused, disoriented West German had simply vaporized.

Voss paced his office at Normannenstrasse through the night; Vanavskaya sat on the edge of her cot in the female bachelors' quarters of the KGB barracks; men sat hunched over radio sets at Schloss Löwenstein and Cheltenham; vehicles were waved to a halt by torchlight on every road and lane in southern Thuringia; McCready drank a steady stream of black coffees in his office at Century House. And . . . nothing. Bruno Morenz had disappeared.

Chapter 5

Major Vanavskaya could not sleep. She tried, but she just lay awake in the darkness wondering how on earth the East Germans, reputedly so efficient in their control of their own population, could lose a man like Morenz within an area twenty miles by twenty miles. Had he hitched a lift? Stolen a bicycle? Was he still crouched in a ditch? What on earth were the VOPOs doing down there?

By three in the morning, she had convinced herself there was something missing, some little part of the puzzle of how a half-crazed man on the run in a small area teeming with People's Police could escape detection.

At four, she rose and returned to the KGB offices, perturbing the night staff with her demand for a secure line to SSD headquarters. When she had it, she spoke to Colonel Voss. He had not left his office at all.

"That picture of Morenz," she said. "Was it recent?"

"About a year ago," said Voss, puzzled.

"Where did you get it?"

"The HVA," said Voss. Vanavskaya thanked him and put down the phone.

Of course, the HVA, the Haupt Verwaltung Aufklärung,

East Germany's foreign intelligence arm, which for obvious linguistic reasons, specialized in running networks inside West Germany. Its Head was the legendary Colonel-General Marcus Wolf. Even the KGB, notoriously contemptuous of satellite intelligence services, held him in considerable respect. Marcus "Mischa" Wolf had perpetrated some brilliant coups against the West Germans, notably the "running" of Chancellor Brandt's private secretary.

Vanavskaya called and awoke the local head of the Third Directorate and made her request, citing General Shaliapin's name. That did the trick. The Colonel said he would see what he could do. He called back in half an hour. It seemed that General Wolf was an early bird, he said; she would have a meeting with him in his office at six.

At five that morning the cryptography department at GCHQ Cheltenham finished decoding the last of the mass of low-level paperwork that had built up in the previous twenty-four hours. In its in-clear form it would be transmitted down a series of very secure land lines to a variety of recipients—some for the SIS at Century House, some for MI-5 at Curzon Street, some for the Ministry of Defense in Whitehall. Much would be "copied" as of possible interest to two or even all three. Urgent intelligence was handled much more quickly, but the small hours of the morning was a good time to send the low-level stuff to London; the lines were not so busy.

Among the material was a signal on Wednesday evening from Pullach to the BND staffer at the West German Embassy in London. Germany, of course, was and remains a valued and respected ally of Britain. There was nothing personal in Cheltenham intercepting and decoding a confidential message from an ally to its own embassy. The code had been quietly broken sometime before. Nothing offensive, just routine. This particular message went to MI-5 and to the NATO desk in Century House, which handled all intelligence liaison with Britain's allies except the CIA, which had its own designated liaison desk.

It was the head of the NATO desk who had first drawn Edwards's attention to the embarrassment of McCready running an officer of the allied BND as his personal agent. Still, the NATO desk chief remained a friend of McCready's. When he saw the German cable at ten that morning, he resolved to bring it to his friend Sam's attention. Just in case. . . . But he did not have time until midday.

At six, Major Vanavskaya was shown into Marcus Wolf's office, two floors above that of Colonel Voss. The East German spymaster disliked uniforms and was in a well-cut dark suit. He also preferred tea to coffee and had a particularly fine blend sent to him from Fortnum and Mason in London. He offered the Soviet major a cup.

"Comrade General, that recent picture of Bruno Morenz. It came from you."

Mischa Wolf regarded her steadily over the rim of his cup. If he had sources, assets, inside the West German establishment, which he did, he was not going to confirm it to this stranger.

"Could you possibly get hold of a copy of Morenz's curriculum vitae?" she asked.

Marcus Wolf considered the request. "Why would you want it?" he asked softly.

She explained. In detail. Breaking a few rules.

"I know it's only a suspicion," she said. "Nothing concrete. A feeling there is a piece missing. Maybe something in his past."

Wolf approved. He liked lateral thinking. Some of his best successes had stemmed from a gut feeling, a suspicion that the enemy had an Achilles' heel somewhere, if only he could find it. He rose, went to a filing cabinet, and withdrew a sheaf of eight sheets without saying a word. It was Bruno Morenz's life story. From Pullach, the same one Lothar Herrmann had studied on Wednesday afternoon. Vanavskaya exhaled in admiration. Wolf smiled.

If Marcus Wolf had a specialty in the espionage world, it was not so much in suborning and traducing high-ranking West Germans, though that could sometimes be done, as in placing prim spinster secretaries of impeccable life-style and security clearance at the elbows of such bigwigs. He knew that a confidential secretary saw everything her master saw and sometimes more.

Over the years, West Germany had been rocked by a series of scandals as private secretaries to ministers, civil servants,

and defense contractors had either been arrested by the BfV
or had slipped quietly away back to the East. One day, he
knew, he would pull Fräulein Erdmute Keppel out of the
Cologne BND and back to her beloved German Democratic
Republic. Until then, she would continue to arrive at the office
an hour ahead of Dieter Aust and copy anything of interest,
including the personnel records of the entire staff. She would
continue, in summer, to take her lunch in the quiet park eating
her salad sandwiches with prim precision, feeding the pigeons
with a few neat crumbs, and finally placing the empty sandwich bag in a nearby trash can. There it would be retrieved a
few moments later by the gentleman walking his dog. In
winter she would lunch instead in the warm café and drop her
newspaper into the garbage container near the door, whence
it would be rescued by the street cleaner.

When she came east, Fräulein Keppel would arrive to a
state reception, a personal greeting from Security Minister
Erich Mielke or possibly Party boss Erich Honecker himself,
a medal, a state pension, and a snug retirement home by the
lakes of Fürstenwalde.

Of course, not even Marcus Wolf was clairvoyant. He could
not know that by 1990 East Germany would have ceased to
exist, that Mielke and Honecker would be ousted and disgraced, that he would be retired and writing his memoirs for
a fat fee, or that Erdmute Keppel would be spending her
declining years in West Germany in a place of seclusion rather
less comfortable than her designated flat at Fürstenwalde.

Major Vanavskaya looked up.

"He has a sister," she said.

"Yes," said Wolf. "You think she may know something?"

"It's a long shot," said the Russian. "If I could go and see
her . . ."

"If you can get permission from your superiors," Wolf
prompted her gently. "You do not, alas, work for me."

"But if I could, I would need a cover. Not Russian, not
East German."

Wolf shrugged self-depracatingly. "I have certain 'legends,'
ready for use. Of course. It is part of our strange trade."

There was a Polish Airline flight to London LOT 104, staged
through Berlin-Schönefeld airport at ten A.M. It was held for

ten minutes to enable Ludmilla Vanavskaya to board. As Wolf had pointed out, her German was adequate but not good enough to pass. Few people in London that she would meet spoke Polish. She had papers of a Polish schoolteacher visiting a relative. That would be plausible since Poland had a much more liberal regime.

The Polish airliner landed in London at eleven, gaining an hour due to time difference. Major Vanavskaya passed through passport and customs control inside thirty minutes, made two phone calls from a public booth in Terminal Two concourse, and took a taxi to a district of London called Primrose Hill.

The phone on Sam McCready's desk trilled at midday. He had just put the phone down after talking again to Cheltenham. The answer was—still nothing. Forty-eight hours, and Morenz was still on the run. The new caller was the man from the NATO desk downstairs.

"There's a chit came through in the morning bag," he said. "It may be nothing; if so, throw it away. Anyway, I'm sending it up by messenger."

The chit arrived five minutes later. When he saw it, and the timing on it, McCready swore loudly.

Normally, the need-to-know rule in the covert world works admirably. Those who do not need to know something in order to fulfill their functions are not told about it. That way, if there is a leak—either deliberate or through sloppy talk— the damage is reasonably limited. But sometimes it works the other way around. Sometimes a piece of information that might have changed events is not passed on because no one thought it was necessary.

The Archimedes listening station in the Harz Mountains and the East Germany–listeners at Cheltenham had been told to pass to McCready without delay anything they got. The words *Grauber* or *Morenz* were particular triggers for an instant pass-on. But no one had thought to alert those who listen to *Allied* diplomatic and military traffic to pass what they picked up to McCready.

The message he held was timed at 4:22 P.M. on Wednesday evening. It said:

Ex—Herrmann
Pro—Fietzau.
Top urgent. Contact Mrs. A. Farquarson, nee Morenz,
believed living London stop Ask if she has seen or heard
of or from her brother in last four days endit.

He never told me he had a sister in London. Never told me he
had a sister at all, thought McCready. He began to wonder
what else his friend Bruno had not told him about his past.
He dragged a telephone directory from a shelf and looked
under the name of Farquarson.

Fortunately, it was not a terribly common name. Smith
would have been a different matter entirely. There were
fourteen Farquarsons, but no "Mrs. A." He began to ring
them in sequence. Of the first seven, five said there was no
Mrs. A. Farquarson to their knowledge. Two failed to answer.
He was lucky at the eighth; the listing was for Robert Farquarson. A woman answered.

"Yes, this is Mrs. Farquarson."

A hint of German accent?

"Would that be Mrs. A. Farquarson?"

"Yes." She seemed defensive.

"Forgive my ringing you, Mrs. Farquarson. I am from the
Immigration Department at Heathrow. Would you by chance
have a brother named Bruno Morenz?"

A long pause.

"Is he there? At Heathrow?"

"I'm not at liberty to say, madam. Unless you are his
sister."

"Yes, I am Adelheid Farquarson. Bruno Morenz is my
brother. Could I speak to him?"

"Not at the moment, I'm afraid. Will you be at that address
in, say, fifteen minutes? It's rather important."

"Yes, I will be here."

McCready called for a car and driver from the motor pool
and raced downstairs.

It was a large studio apartment at the top of a solidly built
Edwardian villa, tucked behind Regent's Park Road. He
walked up and rang the bell. Mrs. Farquarson greeted him in
a painter's smock and showed him into a cluttered studio with
paintings on easels and sketches strewn on the floor.

She was a handsome woman, gray-haired like her brother. McCready put her in her late fifties, older than Bruno. She cleared a space, offered him a seat, and met his gaze levelly. McCready noticed two coffee mugs standing on a nearby table. Both were empty. He contrived to touch one while Mrs. Farquarson sat down. The mug was warm.

"What can I do for you, Mr. . . . "

"Jones. I would like to ask you about your brother, Herr Bruno Morenz?"

"Why?"

"It's an Immigration matter."

"You are lying to me, Mr. Jones."

"Am I?"

"Yes. My brother is not coming here. And if he wished to, he would not have problems with British Immigration. He is a West German citizen. You are a policeman?"

"No, Mrs. Farquarson. But I am a friend of Bruno. Over many years. We go back a long way together. I ask you to believe that because that *is* true."

"He is in trouble, isn't he?"

"Yes, I'm afraid so. I'm trying to help him, if I can. It's not easy."

"What has he done?"

"It looks as if he has killed his mistress in Cologne. And he has run away. He got a message to me. He said he didn't mean to do it. Then he disappeared."

She rose and walked to the window, staring out at the late summer foliage of Primrose Hill Park.

"Oh, Bruno. You fool. Poor, frightened Bruno."

She turned and faced him.

"There was a man from the German Embassy here yesterday morning. He had called before, on Wednesday evening while I was out. He did not tell me what you have—just asked if Bruno had been in touch. He hasn't. I can't help you, either, Mr. Jones. You probably know more than I do, if he got a message to you. Do you know where he has gone?"

"That's the problem. I think he has crossed the border. Gone into East Germany. Somewhere in the Weimar area. Perhaps to stay with friends. But so far as I know, he's never been near Weimar in his life."

She looked puzzled. "What do you mean? He lived there for two years."

McCready kept a straight face, but he was stunned. "I'm sorry. I didn't know. He never told me."

"No, he wouldn't. He hated it there. They were the unhappiest two years of his life. He never talked about it."

"I thought your family was Hamburg, born and raised."

"We were, until 1943. That was when Hamburg was destroyed by the RAF. The great Fire Storm bombing. You have heard of it?"

McCready nodded. The Royal Air Force had bombed the center of Hamburg with such intensity that raging fires started. The fires had sucked oxygen in from the outer suburbs until a raging inferno was created in which temperatures rose so high that steel ran like water and concrete exploded like bombs. The inferno had swept through the city, vaporizing everything in its path.

"Bruno and I were orphaned that night." She paused and stared, not at McCready but past him, seeing again the flames raging through the city where she had been born, consuming to cinders her parents, her friends, her schoolmates, the landmarks of her life. After several seconds she snapped out of her reverie and resumed talking in that quiet voice with the remaining hint of an original German accent.

"When it was over, the authorities took charge of us and we were evacuated. I was fifteen, Bruno was ten. We were split up. I was billeted with a family outside Göttingen. Bruno was sent to stay with a farmer near Weimar. After the war, I searched for him, and the Red Cross helped to reunite us. We returned to Hamburg. I looked after him. But he hardly ever talked about Weimar. I began to work in the British NAAFI canteen, to keep Bruno. Times were very hard, you know."

McCready nodded. "Yes, I'm sorry."

She shrugged. "It was the war. Anyway, in 1947 I met a British sergeant. Robert Farquarson. We married and came to live here. He died eight years ago. When Robert and I left Hamburg in 1948, Bruno secured a residential apprenticeship with a firm of optical lens makers. I have only seen him three or four times since then, and not in the past ten years."

"You told that to the man from the embassy?"

"Herr Fietzau? No, he did not ask about Bruno's child-hood. But I told the lady."

"The lady?"

"She left only an hour ago. The one from the Pensions Department."

"Pensions?"

"Yes. She said Bruno still worked in optical glassware, for a firm called BKI in Würzburg. But it seems BKI is owned by Pilkington Glass of Britain, and with Bruno's retirement ap-proaching, she needed details of his life to assess his full entitlement. She was not from Bruno's employers?"

"I doubt it. Probably West German police. I'm afraid they are looking for Bruno, too, but not to help him."

"I'm sorry. I seem to have been very foolish."

"You weren't to know, Mrs. Farquarson. She spoke good English?"

"Yes, perfect. Slight accent—Polish, perhaps."

McCready had little doubt where the lady had come from. There were other hunters out for Bruno Morenz, many of them, but only McCready and one other group knew about BKI of Würzburg. He rose.

"Try hard to think what little he said in those years after the war. Is there anyone, anyone at all, to whom he might go in his hour of need for sanctuary?"

She thought long and hard.

"There was one name he mentioned, someone who had been nice to him. His primary-school teacher. Fräulein . . . dammit . . . Fräulein Neuberg. No, I remember now, Fräulein Neumann. That was it. Neumann. Of course, she's probably dead by now. It was forty years ago."

"One last thing, Mrs. Farquarson. Did you tell this to the lady from the glass company?"

"No, I've only just remembered it. I just told her Bruno had once spent two years as an evacuee on a farm not ten miles from Weimar."

Back at Century House, McCready borrowed a Weimar tele-phone directory from the East German desk. There were several Neumanns listed, but just one with *Frl*, short for *Fräulein*, in front of it. A spinster. A teenager would not have her own apartment and phone, not in East Germany. A

mature spinster, a professional woman, might. It was a long
shot, very long. He could have one of the East German desk's
agents-in-place across the Wall place a call. But the *Stasi*
were everywhere, bugging everything. The mere question—
"Were you once the schoolteacher of a small boy called
Morenz and has he showed up?"—that could blow it all away.

His next visit was to the section inside Century House
whose specialty is the preparation of very untrue identity
cards.

He rang British Airways, who were unable to help. But
Lufthansa was. They had a flight at five-fifteen to Hanover.
He asked Denis Gaunt to drive him to Heathrow again.

The best-laid plans of mice and men, as the Scottish poet
might have said, sometimes end up looking like a dog's
breakfast. The Polish Airlines flight from London back to
Warsaw via East Berlin was due for takeoff at three-thirty.
But when the pilot switched on his flight systems, a red
warning light glowed. It turned out to be just a faulty solenoid,
but it delayed the takeoff until six. In the departures lounge,
Major Ludmilla Vanavskaya glanced at the televised departure
information, noted the delay "for operational reasons,"
cursed silently, and returned to her book.

McCready was leaving the office when the phone rang. He
debated whether to answer it and decided he ought to. It
could be important. It was Edwards.

"Sam, someone in Funny Paper has been on to me. Now
look, Sam, you are not—as in absolutely not—getting my
permission to go into East Germany. Is that clear?"

"Absolutely, Timothy. Couldn't be clearer."

"Good," said the Assistant Chief, and put the phone down.

Gaunt had heard the voice at the other end of the phone
and what it had said. McCready was beginning to like Gaunt.
He had joined the desk only six months earlier, but he was
showing he was bright, trustworthy, and could keep his mouth
shut.

As he negotiated Hogarth Roundabout, cutting a lot of
corners in the dense Friday-afternoon commuter traffic on the
Heathrow road, Gaunt chose to open it.

"Sam, I know you've been in more tight places than a

shepherd's right arm, but you've been black-flagged in East Germany and the boss has forbidden you to go back.''

"Forbidding is one thing," said McCready. "Preventing is another."

As he strode through the departure lounge of Terminal Two to catch the Lufthansa flight to Hanover, he cast not a glance at the trim young woman with the shiny blond hair and piercing blue eyes who sat reading two yards from him. And she did not look up at the medium-built, rather rumpled man with thinning brown hair in a gray raincoat as he walked past.

McCready's flight took off on time, and he landed at Hanover at eight, local time. Major Vanavskaya got away at six and landed at Berlin-Schönefeld at nine. McCready rented a car and drove past Hildesheim and Salzgitter to his destination in the forests outside Goslar. Vanavskaya was met by a KGB car and driven to Normannenstrasse 22. She had to wait an hour to see Colonel Otto Voss, who was closeted with State Security Minister Erich Mielke.

McCready had telephoned his host from London; he was expected. The man met him at the front door of his substantial home, a beautifully converted hunting lodge set on a sweep of hillside with a view, in daylight, far across a long valley clothed in conifers. Only five miles away, the lights of Goslar twinkled in the gloom. Had the day not already faded, Mc-Cready might have seen, far to the east on a distant peak of the Harz, the roof of a high tower. One might have mistaken it for a hunting tower, but it wasn't. Its purpose was the hunting not of wild boar but of men and women. The man McCready had come to visit had chosen to spend his comfortable retirement within sight of the very border that had once made his fortune.

His host had changed over the years, thought McCready as he was shown into a wood-paneled sitting room hung with the heads of boars and the antlers of stags. A bright fire crackled in a stone hearth; even in early September it was chilly at night in the high hills.

The man who greeted him had put on weight; the once-lean physique was now fleshed out. He was still short, of course, and the round pink face topped by white candy-floss hair made him look even more harmless than ever. Until you looked into his eyes. Cunning eyes, wily eyes that had seen too much and made many deals about life and death and that had lived in the sewers and survived. A malign child of the Cold War who had once been the uncrowned underworld king of Berlin.

For twenty years, from the building of the Berlin Wall in 1961 until his retirement in 1981, Andre Kurzlinger had been a *Grenzgänger*; literally, a border-goer, a border-crosser. It was the Wall that had made his fortune. Prior to its construction, East Germans wishing to escape to the West simply had to go to East Berlin and walk into West Berlin. But during the night of August 21, 1961, the great concrete blocks had been slammed into place, and Berlin became the divided city. Many tried to jump the Wall; some succeeded. Others were hauled back screaming and sent to long terms of jail. Others were machine-gunned on the wire and hung there like stoats until cut down. For most, crossing the Wall was a one-time exploit. For Kurzlinger, who until then had been just a Berlin black marketeer and gangster, it became a profession.

He brought people out—for money. He went across in a variety of disguises, or sent emissaries, and negotiated the price. Some paid in Ostmarks—a lot of Ostmarks. With these, Kurzlinger would buy the three products in East Berlin that *were* good: Hungarian pigskin luggage, Czech classical LPs, and Cuban corona coronas. They were so cheap that, even with the cost of smuggling them west, Kurzlinger could make a huge profit.

Other refugees agreed to pay him in Deutschmarks once they had reached the West and gotten a job. Few reneged. Kurzlinger was meticulous about collecting debts; he employed several large associates to ensure he was not cheated.

There were rumors he worked for Western intelligence. They were not true, though he occasionally brought out someone on contract to the CIA or SIS. There were rumors he was hand-in-glove with the SSD or the KGB; that was unlikely, as he did East Germany too much damage. Certainly he had bribed more border guards and Communist officials than he could remember. It was said he could smell a bribable official at a hundred paces.

Although Berlin was his bailiwick, he also ran lines through the East German–West German border, which ran from the Baltic to Czechoslovakia. When he retired finally with a handsome fortune he chose to settle in West Germany, not in West Berlin. But he still could not drag himself away from that border. His manor was only five miles from it, high in the Harz Mountains.

"So, Herr McCready, Sam my friend, it has been a long time."

He stood with his back to the fire, a retired gentleman in a velvet smoking jacket, a long way from the animal-eyed alley-kid who had crawled out of the rubble in 1945 to start selling girls to GIs for Lucky Strikes. "You are retired also now?" he asked.

"No, Andre, I still have to work for my crust. Not as clever as you, you see."

Kurzlinger liked that. He pressed a bell, and a manservant brought crisp Mosel wine in crystal glasses.

"Then," asked Kurzlinger as he surveyed the flames through the wine, "what can an old man do for the mighty *Spionage* service of Her Majesty?"

McCready told him. The older man continued staring at the fire, but he pursed his lips and shook his head.

"I am out of it, Sam. Retired. Now they leave me alone. Both sides. But you know, they have warned me, as I think they have warned you. If I start again, they will come for me. A quick operation, across the border, and back before dawn. They will have me, right here in my own home. They mean it. In my time I did them a lot of damage you know."

"I know," said McCready."

"Also, things change. Once, in Berlin, yes, I could get you across. Even in the countryside I had my rabbit runs. But they were all discovered eventually. Closed down. The mines I had disconnected were replaced. The guards I had bribed were transferred. You know they never keep guards on this border for long. Constantly switch them around. My contacts have all gone cold. It is too late."

"I have to go over," said McCready slowly, "because we have a man over there. He is sick, very sick. But if I can bring him out, it will probably break the career of the one who now heads Abteilung II. Otto Voss."

Kurzlinger did not move, but his eyes went very cold. Years ago, as McCready knew, he had had a friend. A very close friend indeed, probably the closest he had ever had. The man had been caught crossing the Wall. Talk was, later, that he had raised his hands. But Voss had shot him all the same. Through both kneecaps first, then both elbows and both shoulders. Finally in the stomach. Soft-nosed slugs.

"Come," said Kurzlinger, "we will eat. I will introduce you to my son."

The handsome young blond man of about thirty who joined them at table was not actually Kurzlinger's son, of course. But he had formally adopted him. Occasionally, the older man would smile at him, and the adopted son would look back adoringly.

"I brought Siegfried out of the East," said Kurzlinger, as if making conversation. "He had nowhere to go, so . . . now he lives here with me."

McCready continued eating. He suspected there was more.

"Have you ever heard," said Kurzlinger over the grapes, "of the *Arbeitsgruppe Grenzen?*"

McCready had. The Borders Working Group. Deep within the SSD, apart from all the Abteilungen with their Roman-numeral designations, was a small unit with a most bizarre specialty.

Most times, if Marcus Wolf wanted to spirit an agent into the West, he could do it by passing through a neutral country, the agent adopting his new legend during the stopover. But sometimes the SSD or the HVA wanted to put a man across the border on a "black" operation. For this to happen, the East Germans would actually cut a rabbit run through their own defenses from East to West. Most rabbit runs were cut from West to East to bring out people who were not supposed to leave. When the SSD wanted a rabbit run cut for its own purposes, it used the experts of the *Arbeitsgruppe Grenzen* for the job. These engineers, working at dead of night (for the West German Frontier Service *also* watched the border), would burrow under the razor-wire, cut a thin line through the minefield, and leave no trace of where they had been.

That still left the two-hundred-yard-wide plowed strip, the shooting ground, where a real refugee would probably be caught in the searchlights and machine-gunned. Finally, on the Western side, there was the fence. The *Arbeitsgruppe Grenzen* would leave that intact, cut a hole for the agent as he went through, and lace it up again after him. The searchlights, on the nights they ran someone westward, would be facing the other way, and the plowed strip was usually thick with grass, especially in late summer. By morning, the grass would have straightened itself, obliterating all traces of the running feet.

When the East Germans did it, they had the cooperation of their own border guards. But breaking in was another matter; there would be no East German cooperation.

"Siegfried used to work for the ACG," said Kurzlinger. "Until he used one of his own rabbit runs. Of course, the *Stasi* closed that one down immediately. Siegfried, our friend here needs to go across. Can you help?"

McCready thought that he had judged his man aright. Kurzlinger hated Voss for what he had done, and the man's grief for his murdered love was not to be underestimated.

Siegfried thought for a while.

"There used to be one," he said at length. "I cut it myself. I was going to use it, so I did not file the report. In the event, I came out a different way."

"Where is it?" asked McCready.

"Not far from here," said Siegfried. "Between Bad Sachsa and Ellrich."

He fetched a map and pointed out the two small towns in the southern Harz, Bad Sachsa in West Germany and Ellrich in the East.

"May I see the papers you intend to use?" asked Kurzlinger. McCready passed them over. Siegfried studied them. "They are good," he said.

"What is the best time to go?" asked McCready.

"Four o'clock. Before dawn. The light is darkest, and the guards are tired. They sweep the plowed strip less frequently. We will need camouflage smocks in case we are caught by the lights. The camouflage may save us."

They discussed details for another hour.

"You understand, Herr McCready," said Siegfried, "it has been five years. I may not be able to recall where it was. I left a fishing line on the ground where I cut the path through the minefield. I may not be able to find it. If I cannot, we will come back. To go into the minefield not knowing the path I cut is death. Or my former colleagues may have found it and closed it down. In that case we come back—if we still can.''

"I understand," said McCready. "I'm very grateful."

They left, Siegfried and McCready, at one o'clock for the slow two-hour drive through the mountains. Kurzlinger stood on the doorstep.

"Look after my boy," he said. "I only do this for another boy Voss took from me long ago."

"If you get through," said Siegfried as they drove, "walk the six miles into Nordhausen. Avoid the village of Ellrich—there are guards there, and the dogs will bark. Take the train from Nordhausen south to Erfurt, and the bus to Weimar. There will be workers on both."

They drove quietly through the sleeping town of Bad Sachsa and parked at the outskirts. Siegfried stood in the darkness with a compass and a penlight. When he had his bearing, he plunged into the pine forest, heading east. McCready followed him.

Four hours earlier, Major Vanavskaya had confronted Colonel Voss in his office.

"According to his sister, there is one place he could go to hide in the Weimar area."

She explained about Bruno Morenz's evacuation during the war.

"A farm?" said Voss. "Which farm? There are hundreds in that area."

"She didn't know the name. Just that it was not ten miles from Weimar itself. Draw your ring, Colonel. Bring in troops. Within the day you will have him."

Colonel Voss called Abteilung XIII, the intelligence and security service of the National People's Army, the NVA. Phones rang in the NVA headquarters out at Karlshorst, and before dawn trucks began to roll south toward Weimar.

"The ring is formed," said Voss at midnight. "The troops will move outward from Weimar town, sweeping by sectors, outward toward the ring. They will search every farm, barn, store, cowshed, and pigsty until they reach the ten-miles ring.

I only hope you are right, Major Vanavskaya. There are now a lot of men involved.''

In the small hours he left in his personal car for the south. Major Vanavskaya accompanied him. The sweep was due to start at dawn.

Chapter 6

Siegfried lay on his belly at the edge of the treeline and studied the dark contours of the forest three hundred yards away that marked East Germany. McCready lay beside him. It was three A.M. on Saturday.

Five years earlier, also in darkness, Siegfried had cut his rabbit run from the base of a particularly tall pine tree on the eastern side, in the direction of a gleaming white rock high on the hill slope on the Western side. His problem now was, he had always thought he would see the rock from the east, gleaming palely in the dim light before dawn. He had not foreseen that he would ever have to head the other way. Now the rock was high above him, screened by the trees. It would become visible only from a position far out in No Man's Land. He judged the line as best he could, crawled forward the last ten yards of West Germany, and began to snip quietly at the chain-link fence.

When Siegfried had his hole, McCready saw his arm rise in a beckoning motion. He crawled out of cover toward the wire. He had spent the five minutes studying the watchtowers of the East German border guards and the sweep of their search-lights. Siegfried had chosen his spot well—halfway between two of the watchtowers. An added bonus was that the tree-growth of summer had caused some of the pine branches across the minefield to extend outward by several feet; one searchlight, at least, was being partially blocked by this extra growth. In autumn, tree surgeons would come to prune back the branches, but they had not done so yet.

The other searchlight had a clear view of their intended path, but the man behind it must have been tired or bored, for it sent off for minutes on end. When it came on again, it was always pointing the other way. Then it would make its sweep toward them, sweep back, and go out. If the operator kept up this pattern, they would have a few seconds' warning.

Siegfried jerked his head and crawled through the hole. McCready followed, dragging his gunny sack. The German turned and pushed the cut mesh back into place. It would not be noticed except at close range, and the guards never crossed the strip to check the wire unless they had already noticed a break. They did not like minefields, either.

It was tempting to run across the hundred yards of plowed strip, now thickly grassed with extra-tall dock, thistle, and nettle growing at intervals in the grass. But there could be tripwires linked to sound-alarms. It was safer to crawl. They crawled. At the halfway point they were shaded by trees from the searchlight to their left, but then the one to their right came on. Both men froze in their green smocks and lay face down. They had blackened their faces and hands, Siegfried with boot polish, McCready with burnt cork that would wash off more easily on the other side.

The pale light splashed over them, hesitated, moved back, and went off again. Ten yards farther on, Siegfried found a tripwire and gestured McCready to crawl around it. Another forty yards, and they reached the minefield. Here the thistles and grasses were chest-high. No one tried to plow up the minefield.

The German looked back. High above the trees, McCready could see the white rock, a patch of paleness against the darkness of the pine forest. Siegfried swiveled his head and checked the giant tree against the rock. He was ten yards to the right of his line. He crawled again, down the edge of the minefield. When he stopped, he began to feel tenderly in the long grass. After two minutes McCready heard his breath hiss out in triumph. He held a fine strand of fishing line between finger and thumb. He pulled gently. If it was loose at the other end, the mission was over. It went tight and held.

"Follow the fishing line," Siegfried whispered. "It will take you through the minefield to the tunnel under the wire. The path is only two feet wide. When do you come back?"

"Twenty-four hours," said McCready. "Or forty-eight. After that, forget it. I will not be coming. I will use my pencil light from the base of the big tree just before I make the run. Hold the fence open for me."

He disappeared on his belly into the minefield, not quite hidden by the tall grass and weeds. Siegfried waited for the searchlight to wash over him one last time, then crawled back to the West.

McCready went forward through the mines, following the nylon line. Occasionally he tested it to make sure it was still straight. He knew he would not see any mines. These were not big plate-mines that could throw a truck in the air. They were small antipersonnel mines made of plastic, not responsive to metal detectors, which had been tried by escapers and had not worked. The mines were buried, pressure-operated. They would not explode for a rabbit or a fox, but they were sensitive enough for a human body. And vicious enough to blow away a leg or the entrails, or to tear out the chest cavity. Often they did not kill quickly but left the would-be escaper screaming through the night until the guards came after sunrise, with guides, to retrieve the body.

McCready saw the rolling waves of razor-wire looming ahead of him, the end of the minefield. The fishing line led him to a shallow scrape under the wire. He rolled on his back, pushed the wire upward with his totebag, and kicked with his heels. Inch by inch, he slid beneath the entanglement. Above him he could see the glittering razors that made this kind of wire so much more painful than barbed wire.

There were ten yards of it, but piled eight feet high above him. When he came out on the Eastern side, he found the nylon strand attached to a small peg that was almost out of the ground. Another tug, and it would have come loose, aborting the whole crossing. He covered the peg with a mat of thick pine needles, noted its position directly in front of the outsize pine tree, held his compass in front of him, and crawled away.

He crawled on a heading of 90 degrees until he came to a track. There he stripped off his smock, bundled it around his compass, and hid them beneath more pine needles ten yards inside the forest. If any dogs came down the track, they would not be able to smell the buried clothing. At the edge of the track he broke off a branch above head height and left it hanging by a thread of bark. No one else would notice it, but he would.

On his return he would have to find the track and the broken branch and recover his smock and compass. A heading of 270 degrees would bring him back to the giant pine. He turned and walked away toward the east. As he walked, he noted every marker—fallen trees, piles of logs, twists and turns. After a mile, he came out on a road and saw the spire of the Lutheran church of Ellrich village ahead of him.

He skirted it, as briefed, walking through fields of cut wheat until he intercepted the road to Nordhausen, five miles farther on. It was just five o'clock. He stayed by the side of the road, prepared to dive into a ditch if a vehicle appeared from either direction. Farther south, he hoped his scuffed reefer jacket, corduroy trousers, boots, and forage cap, worn by so many German farm workers, would escape scrutiny. But here the community was so small that everyone would know everyone else. He did not need to be asked where he was going, even less where he had come from. Behind him, there was nowhere he could have come from but Ellrich village or the border.

Outside Nordhausen he had a lucky break. Over the picket fence of a darkened house, a bicycle was propped against a tree. It was rusty but usable. He weighed the risks of taking it against its usefulness in covering distance faster than a pair of legs. If its loss remained undiscovered for thirty minutes, it was worth it. He took it, walked for a hundred yards, then mounted it and rode to the railway station. It was five to six. The first train to Erfurt was due in fifteen minutes.

There were several dozen working men on the platform waiting to head south to work. He presented some money, was issued a ticket, and the train steamed in, an old-fashioned steam locomotive but on time. Accustomed to British Rail Commuter services, he was grateful for that. He consigned his bicycle to the luggage van and took his place on the wooden seats. The train stopped again at Sondershausen, Greussen, and Straussfurt before rolling into Erfurt at 6:41. He retrieved his bicycle and pedaled away through the streets toward the eastern outskirts of the city and the start of Highway Seven to Weimar.

Just after half past seven, a few miles east of the city, a tractor came up behind him. It had a flat trailer behind it, and an old man was at the wheel. It had been delivering sugar beet to Erfurt and was heading back to the farm. The old man slowed and stopped.

"Steig mal rauf," he called above the snarl of the dilapidated engine, which belched rich black smoke. McCready waved his gratitude, hurled the bicycle onto the flatbed, and climbed on. The noise of the tractor engine prevented conversation, which was just as well, for McCready, fluent in German, did not possess that strange accent of Lower Thuringia. Anyway, the old farmer was happy to suck on his empty pipe and drive.

Ten miles out of Weimar, McCready saw the wall of soldiers.

They were on the road, several dozen, spread out across the fields to left and right. He could see their helmeted heads among the maize stalks. There was a farm track off to the right. He glanced down it. Soldiers lined it, ten yards apart, facing toward Weimar.

The tractor slowed for the roadblock and stopped. A sergeant shouted up to the driver, telling him to switch off his engine.

The old man shouted back in German, "If I do I probably won't start it again. Will your men give me a push?"

The sergeant considered, shrugged, and gestured for the old man's papers. He looked at them, gave them back, and came down to where McCready sat.

"Papiere," he said. McCready handed over his ID card. It said he was Martin Hahn, farm worker, and had been issued by the Weimar administrative district. The sergeant, who was a townsman from Schwerin up in the north, sniffed.

"What's that?" he asked.

"Sugar beets," said McCready. He did not volunteer that he was a hitchhiker on the tractor, and no one asked.

Nor did he point out that before carrying the sugar beets, the trailer had borne a much fruitier cargo. The sergeant wrinkled his nose, gave back the papers, and waved the tractor on. A more interesting truck was coming toward them out of Weimar, and he had been told to concentrate on people—or a man with gray hair and a Rhineland accent—trying to get *out* of the ring, not a smelly tractor trying to get in. The tractor went to a track three miles from the town and turned off. McCready jumped down, pulled his bicycle to the ground, waved his thanks at the old farmer, and pedaled into town.

From the outskirts on, he stayed close to the curb to avoid the trucks disgorging troops in the gray-green uniforms of the National People's Army, the NVA. There was a fair sprinkling of the brighter-green uniforms of the People's Police, the VOPOs. Knots of Weimar citizens stood on streetcorners staring in curiosity. Someone suggested it was a military exercise; no one disagreed. Maneuvers normally happened in the military, though not usually in the center of a town.

McCready would have liked a town map, but he could not afford to be seen studying one. He was not a tourist. He had memorized his route from the map he borrowed from the East German desk in London, which he had studied on the plane to Hanover. Coming into town on the Erfurterstrasse, he rode straight on toward the ancient town center and saw the National Theater looming up in front of him. The paved road became cobbles. He rode left into Heinrich Heinestrasse and on toward Karl Marx Platz. There he dismounted and began to push the bicycle, his head down, as the VOPO cars rushed by him in both directions.

At Rhathenau Platz he looked for Brennerstrasse and found it on the far side of the square. According to his recall, Bockstrasse should lie to the right. It did. Number fourteen was an old building, long in need of repair, like just about everything else in Herr Honecker's paradise. The paint and plaster were peeling and the names on the eight bell-pushes were faded. But he could make out, against flat number three, the single name, Neumann. He pushed his bicycle through the large front door, left it in the stone-flagged hall, and walked up. There were two apartments on each floor. Number three was on the second floor. He took off his cap, straightened his jacket, and rang the bell. It was ten to nine.

Nothing happened for a while. After two minutes there was a shuffling sound, and the door opened slowly. Fräulein Neumann was very old, in a black dress, white-haired, and she supported herself on two canes. McCready judged her to be in her late eighties. She looked up at him and said, *"Ja?"*

He smiled broadly as if in recognition.

"Yes, it is you, Fräulein. You have changed. But not more than me. You won't remember me. Martin Kroll. You taught me at primary school forty years ago."

She stared at him levelly, bright blue eyes behind gold-rimmed glasses.

"I happened to be in Weimar today. From Berlin, you know. I live there now. And I wondered if you were still here. The telephone directory listed you. I just came on the off chance. May I come in?"

She stood aside, and he entered. A dark hall, musty with age. She led the way, hobbling on arthritic knees and ankles, into her sitting room, whose windows looked down on the street. He waited for her to sit, then took a chair.

"So I taught you once, in the old primary school on Heinrich Heinestrasse. When was that?"

"Well, it must have been '43 and '44. We were bombed out. From Berlin. I was evacuated here with others. Must have been the summer of '43. I was in a class with . . . *ach*, the names—well, I recall Bruno Morenz. He was my buddy."

She stared at him for a while, then pulled herself to her feet. He rose. She hobbled to the window and looked down. A truck full of VOPOs rumbled past. They all sat upright, their Hungarian AP9 pistols holstered on their belts.

"Always the uniforms," she said softly as if talking to herself. "First the Nazis, now the Communists. And always the uniforms and the guns. First the Gestapo, and now the SSD. Oh, Germany, what did we do to deserve you both?"

She turned from the window. "You are British, aren't you? Please sit down."

McCready was glad to do so. He realized that despite her age, she still had a mind like a razor.

"Why do you say such an extraordinary thing?" he asked indignantly. She was not fazed by his show of anger.

"Three reasons. I remember every boy I ever taught at that school during the war and afterward, and there was no Martin Kroll among them. And second, the school was not on Heinrich Heinestrasse. Heine was Jewish, and the Nazis had erased his name from all streets and monuments."

McCready could have kicked himself. He should have known that the name of Heine, one of Germany's greatest writers, was restored only after the war.

"If you scream or raise the alarm," he said quietly, "I will not harm you. But they will come for me and take me away and shoot me. The choice is yours."

She hobbled to her seat and sat down. In the manner of the very old, she began to reminisce.

"In 1934 I was a professor at the Humboldt University in Berlin. The youngest, and the only woman. The Nazis came to power. I despised them. I said so. I suppose I was lucky—I could have been sent to a camp. But they were lenient; I was sent here, to teach primary school to the children of farm laborers.

"After the war I did not go back to the Humboldt. Partly because I felt the children here had as much right to the teaching I could give them as the smart youth of Berlin; partly because I would not teach the Communist version of lies, either. So, Mr. Spy, I will not raise the alarm."

"And if they capture me anyway, and I tell them about you?"

She smiled for the first time.

"Young man, when you are eighty-eight, there is nothing they can do to you that the good Lord is not going to do quite soon now. Why did you come?"

"Bruno Morenz. You do remember him?"

"Oh, yes, I remember him. Is he in trouble?"

"Yes, Fräulein, bad trouble. He is here, not far away. He came on a mission—for me. He fell ill, sick, in the head. A complete breakdown. He is hiding out there somewhere. He needs help."

"The police, all those soldiers—they are for Bruno?"

"Yes. If I can get to him first, I may be able to help. Get him away in time."

"Why did you come to me?"

"His sister in London, she said he had told her very little

of his two years here during the war. Just that he had been very unhappy, and his only friend had been his schoolteacher, Fräulein Neumann.''

She rocked backward and forward for some time.

"Poor Bruno," she said at length. "Poor, frightened Bruno. Always so frightened. Of the shouting and the pain."

"Why was he frightened, Fräulein Neumann?"

"He came from a Social Democrat family in Hamburg. His father was dead, in the bombing, but he must have made some uncomplimentary remark about Hitler in his home before he died. Bruno was billeted with a farmer outside the town, a brutal man who drank much. Also, an ardent Nazi. One evening Bruno must have said something he learned from his father. The farmer took his belt to him and whipped him. Hard. After that, he did it many times. Bruno used to run away."

"Where did he hide, Fräulein? Please, where?"

"In the barn. He showed me once. I had gone to the farm to remonstrate with the farmer. There was a barn at the far end of the hay meadow, away from the house and the other barns. He made a hole in the hay bales up in the loft. He used to crawl in there and wait until the farmer had fallen into his usual drunken sleep."

"Where, exactly, was the farm?"

"The hamlet is called Marionhain. I think it is still there. Just four farms in a group. All collectivized now. It lies between the villages of Ober and Nieder Grünstedt. Take the road out toward Erfurt. Four miles out, turn left down a track. There is a signpost. The farm was called Müller's Farm, but that will be changed now. It probably just has a number. But if it is still there, look for a barn set two hundred yards away from the group, at the end of the meadow. Do you think you can help him?"

McCready rose.

"If he is there, Fräulein, I will try. I swear I will try. Thank you for your help."

He turned at the door.

"You said there were three reasons you thought I was English, but you gave me only two."

"Oh, yes. You are dressed as a farm worker, but you said you came from Berlin. There are no farms in Berlin. So you are a spy. Either working for them"—she jerked her head toward the window, where another truck rumbled past—"or for the other side."

"I could have been an agent for the SSD."

She smiled again. "No, Mister Englander. I remember the British officers from 1945, for a short while before the Russians came. You are much too polite to be SSD."

The track off the main road was where she had said it would be, to the left, toward the tract of rich farmland that lies between Highway Seven and the Autobahn E40. A small sign said OBER GRÜNSTEDT. He cycled down the track to a junction a mile farther on. The road split. To his left lay Nieder Grünstedt. He could see a wall of green uniforms surrounding it. On either side of him lay fields of uncut maize, five feet high. He crouched low over the handlebars and pedaled away to his right. He skirted Ober Grünstedt and saw an even narrower track. Half a mile down it, he could make out the roofs of a group of farmhouses and barns, built in the Thuringian style with steeply sloped tiles, towering peaks, and tall wide doors to admit the hay wains to the hollow square yards inside. Marionhain.

He did not want to pass through the hamlet. There might be farm workers there who would clearly spot him as a stranger. He hid his bicycle in the maize and climbed a gate to get a better view. To his right he saw a single tall barn, of brick and black-tarred timbers, set away from the main group. Crouching inside the maize, he began to work his way around the hamlet toward it. On the horizon the tide of green uniforms began to move out of Nieder Grünstedt.

Dr. Lothar Herrmann was also working that Saturday morning. Since he sent the cable to Fietzau at the German Embassy in London that had elicited a reply which brought his investigation no further forward, the trail of the missing Bruno Morenz had gone cold. He did not usually work on Saturdays, but he needed something to take his mind off his predicament. The previous evening he had had dinner with the Director General. It had not been an easy meal.

No arrest had been made in the case of the Heimendorf slayings. The police had not even issued a wanted notice for a particular person whom they wished to interview. They seemed to be up against a brick wall on the issue of one set of fingerprints and two used pistol bullets.

A number of very respectable gentlemen in both the private and the public sector had been discreetly questioned and had finished the interviews puce with embarrassment. But each had cooperated to the limit. Fingerprints had been given, handguns turned in for testing, alibis checked. The result was . . . nothing.

The Director General had been regretful but adamant. The Service's lack of cooperation had gone on long enough. On Monday morning he, the DG, was going to go to the Chancellor's office for an interview with the State Secretary who had responsibility, at the political level, for the BND. It would be a very difficult interview, and he, the DG, was not pleased. Not pleased at all.

Now Dr. Herrmann opened the thick file dealing with cross-border radio traffic covering the period of Wednesday to Friday. He noted that there seemed to be an awful lot of it. Some kind of flap among the VOPOs in the Jena area. Then his eye caught a phrase used in a conversation between a VOPO patrol car and Jena Central: *"Big, gray-haired, Rhineland accent."* He became pensive. That rang a bell. . . .

An aide entered and placed a message in front of his boss. If the Herr Doktor insisted on working on Saturday morning, he might as well get the traffic as it came in. The message was a complimentary pass-on from the internal security service, the BfV. It simply said that a sharp-eyed operative at Hanover airport had noted a face entering Germany on a London flight under the name of Maitland. Being an alert fellow, the BfV man had checked his files and passed his identification on to the Head Office in Cologne. Cologne had passed it on to Pullach. The man Maitland was Mr. Samuel McCready.

Dr. Herrmann was affronted. It was most discourteous of a senior officer in an allied NATO service to enter the country unannounced. And unusual. Unless . . . He looked at the intercepts from Jena and the message from Hanover. He wouldn't dare, he thought. Then another part of his mind said: Yes, he damned well would. Dr. Herrmann lifted a phone and began to make his dispositions.

*   *   *

McCready left the cover of the maize, glanced to the left and the right, and crossed the few yards of grass to the barn. The door creaked on rusty hinges as he let himself in. Light streaked into the gloom from a dozen splits in the woodwork, making motes of dust dance in the air and revealing the huddled shapes of old carts and barrels, horse-tackle and rusting troughs. He glanced up. The upper floor, reached by a vertical ladder, was piled with hay. He went up the ladder and called softly, "Bruno."

There was no reply. He walked past the piled hay looking for recent signs of disturbance. At the end of the barn he saw a fragment of raincoat fabric between two bales. He gently lifted one of the bales away.

Bruno Morenz lay in his sanctuary on his side. His eyes were open, but he made no movement. As the light entered his hiding place, he winced.

"Bruno, it's me. Sam. Your friend. Look at me, Bruno."

Morenz swiveled his gaze toward McCready. He was gray-faced and unshaven. He had not eaten for three days and had drunk only stagnant water from a barrel. His eyes appeared unfocused. They tried to register as he looked at McCready.

"Sam?"

"Yes, Sam. Sam McCready."

"Don't tell them I'm here, Sam. They won't find me if you don't tell them."

"I won't tell them, Bruno. Never."

Through a crack in the planking he saw the line of green uniforms moving across the maize fields toward Ober Grünstedt.

"Try and sit up, Bruno."

He helped Morenz into a sitting position, his back against the hay bales.

"We must hurry, Bruno. I'm going to try to get you out of here."

Morenz shook his head dully. "Stay here, Sam. It's safe here. No one could ever find me here."

No, thought McCready, a drunken farmer never could. But five hundred soldiers could and would. He tried to get Morenz to his feet, but it was hopeless. The weight of the man was too much. His legs would not work. He clutched his hands across his chest. There was something bulging under his left arm. McCready let him slump back into the hay. Morenz curled up again. McCready knew he would never get him back to the border near Ellrich, under the wire, and across the minefield. It was over.

Through the crack, across the maize cobs bright in the sun, the green uniforms were swarming over the farms and barns of Ober Grünstedt. Marionhain would be next.

"I've been to see Fräulein Neumann. You remember Fräulein Neumann? She's nice."

"Yes, nice. She might know I'm here, but she won't tell them."

"Never, Bruno. Never. She said you have your homework for her. She needs to mark it."

Morenz unbuttoned his raincoat and eased out a fat red manual. Its cover bore a gold hammer and sickle. Morenz's tie was off and his shirt open. A key hung on a piece of twine around his neck. McCready took the manual.

"I'm thirsty, Sam."

McCready held out a small silver hip flask that he had taken from his back pocket. Morenz drank the whiskey greedily. McCready looked through the crack. The soldiers had finished with Ober Grünstedt. Some were coming down the track, while others fanned out through the fields.

"I'm going to stay here, Sam," said Morenz.

"Yes," said McCready, "so you are. Good-bye, old friend. Sleep well. No one will ever hurt you again."

"Never again," murmured the man, and slept.

McCready was about to rise when he saw the glint of the key against Morenz's chest. He eased the twine from around his neck, stowed the manual in his totebag, slithered down the ladder, and slipped away into the maize. The ring closed two minutes later. It was midday.

It took him twelve hours to get back to the giant pine tree on the border near Ellrich village. He changed into his smock and waited beneath the trees until half-past three. Then he flashed his pencil light three times toward the white rock across the border and crawled under the wire, through the minefield, and across the plowed strip. Siegfried was waiting for him at the fence.

On the drive back to Goslar, he flicked over the key he had taken from Bruno Morenz. It was made of steel, and engraved on the back were the words *Flughafen Köln*. Cologne airport. Sam bade farewell to Kurzlinger and Siegfried after a sustaining breakfast and drove southwest instead of north to Hanover.

At one o'clock on that Saturday afternoon, the soldiers made contact with Colonel Voss, who arrived in a staff car with a woman in a civilian suit. They went up the ladder and examined the body in the hay. A thorough search was made, the barn was almost torn apart, but no sign was found of any written material, least of all a thick manual. But then, they did not know what they were looking for anyway.

A soldier pried a small silver flask from the dead man's hand and passed it to Colonel Voss. He sniffed it and muttered, "Cyanide." Major Vanavskaya took it and turned it over. On the back was written HARRODS, LONDON. She used a very unladylike expression. Although his command of Russian was basic, Colonel Voss thought it sounded like "You Motherfucker."

At noon on Sunday, McCready entered Cologne airport, well in time for the one o'clock flight. He changed his Hanover-to-London ticket for a Cologne-London one, checked in, and wandered toward the steel luggage lockers to one side of the concourse. He took the steel key and inserted it into locker 47. Inside was a black canvas grip. He withdrew it.

"I think I will take the bag, thank you, Herr McCready."

He turned. The Deputy Head of the Operations Directorate of the BND was standing ten feet away. Two large gentlemen hovered farther on. One studied his fingernails, the other the ceiling, as if looking for cracks.

"Why, Dr. Herrmann. How nice to see you again. And what brings you to Cologne?"

"The bag . . . if you please, Mr. McCready."

It was handed over. Herrmann passed it to one of his team. He could afford to be genial.

"Come, Mr. McCready, we Germans are a hospitable people. Let me escort you to your plane. You would not wish to miss it."

They walked toward passport control.

"A certain colleague of mine . . ." suggested Herrmann.

"He will not be coming back, Dr. Herrmann."

"Ah, poor man. But just as well, perhaps."

They arrived at passport control. Dr. Herrmann produced a card and flashed it at the immigration officers, and they were ushered through. When the flight boarded, McCready was escorted to the aircraft door.

"Mr. McCready."

He turned in the doorway. Herrmann smiled at last.

"We also know how to listen to cross-border radio chit-chat. Good journey, Mr. McCready. My regards to London."

The news came to Langley a week later. General Pankratin had been transferred. In future, he would command a military detention complex of prison camps in Kazakhstan.

Claudia Stuart learned the news from her man in the Moscow Embassy. At the time, she was still basking in the plaudits that rained down from on high as the military analysts studied the complete Soviet Order of Battle. She was prepared to be philosophical about her Soviet general. As she remarked to Chris Appleyard in the commissary, "He keeps his skin and his rank. Better than the lead mines of Yakutsia. As for us—well, it's cheaper than an apartment block in Santa Barbara."

Interlude

The hearing resumed on the following morning, Tuesday. Timothy Edwards remained formal courtesy itself, while privately hoping the entire affair could be wound up with the minimum delay. He, like the two Controllers who flanked him, had work to do.

"Thank you for reminding us of the events of 1985," he said, "though I feel one might point out that in intelligence terms, that year now constitutes a different and even a vanished age."

Denis Gaunt was having none of it. He knew he was entitled to recall any episode he wished from the career of his desk chief in an attempt to persuade the board to recommend to the Chief a variation of decision. He also knew there was scant chance of Timothy Edwards making that recommendation, but it would be a majority choice at the end of the hearing, and it was to the two Controllers that he wished to appeal. He rose and crossed to the clerk from Records to ask him for another file.

Sam McCready was hot and becoming bored. Unlike Gaunt, he knew his chances were as slim as a dipstick. He had insisted on the hearing mainly out of contrariness. He leaned back and allowed his attention to wander. Whatever Denis Gaunt would say, he knew it already.

It had been so long, thirty years, that he had lived in the small world of Century House and the Secret Intelligence Service—just about all his working life. If he was ousted now, he wondered where he would go. He even wondered, not for the first time, how he had gotten into that strange, shadowed world in the first place. Nothing about his working-class birth could ever have predicted that one day he would be a senior officer of the SIS.

He had been born in the spring of 1939, the same year the second World War broke out, the son of a milkman in south London. Only vaguely, in one or two frozen flashback memories, could he recall his father.

As a baby, along with his mother, he had been evacuated from London after the fall of France in 1940, when the Luftwaffe began its long hot summer of raids on the British capital. He remembered none of it. His mother told him later that they had returned in the autumn of 1940 to the small terraced house in poor but neat Norbury Street, but by then his father had gone to the war.

There was a picture of his parents on their wedding day— he remembered that very clearly. She was in white, with a posy, and the big man beside her was very stiff and proper in a dark suit with a carnation in his buttonhole. It stood on the mantle shelf above the fireplace, in a silver frame, and she polished it every day. Later, another picture took its place at the other end of the shelf, of a big smiling man in uniform with a sergeant's stripes on his sleeve.

His mother went out every day, leaving him in the care of Auntie Vi, who ran the sweet shop down the road. She caught the bus to Croydon, where she scrubbed the steps and hall-ways of the prosperous middle-class people who lived there. She took in washing, too; he could just recall how the tiny kitchen was always full of steam as she worked through the night to have it ready by morning.

Once—it must have been 1944—the big smiling man came home and picked him up and held him high in the air as he squealed. Then he went away again to join the forces landing on the Normandy beaches and to die in the assault on Caen. Sam remembered his mother crying a lot that summer, and that he tried to say something to her but did not know what to say, so he just cried as well, even though he did not really know why.

The next January, he started at a play school. He thought that was a pity because Auntie Vi used to let him lick his finger and dip it into the sherbet jar. It was the same spring that the German V-1 rockets, the doodlebugs, began to rain down on London, launched from their ramps in the Low Countries.

He remembered very clearly the day, just before his sixth birthday, when the man in the air raid warden's uniform had come to the play school, his tin hat on his head and his gas mask swinging at his side.

There had been an air raid, and the children had spent the morning in the cellar, which was much more fun than lessons. After the all-clear sounded, they had gone back to class.

The man had a whispered conversation with the headmistress, and she took him out of class and led him by the hand to her own parlor behind the schoolroom, where she fed him seed cake. He waited there, very small and bewildered, until the nice man from Dr. Barnardo's came to take him away to the orphanage. Later they told him there was no more silver-framed picture and no more photo of the big smiling man with the sergeant's stripes.

He did well at Barnardo's and passed all his exams, and he left to join the army as a boy soldier. When he was eighteen, they posted him to Malaya, where the undeclared war was going on between the British and the Communist terrorists in the jungle. He was seconded to the Intelligence Corps as a clerk.

One day he went to his Colonel and made a suggestion. The Colonel, a career officer, promptly said, "Put it in writing," so he did.

The counterintelligence people had captured a leading terrorist with the help of some local Malay Chinese. McCready proposed that information be leaked through the Chinese community that the man was singing like a canary and was to be moved down from Ipoh to Singapore in a convoy on a certain day.

When the terrorists attacked the convoy, the van turned out to be armored inside and to contain slits hiding machine guns on tripods. When the ambush was over, there were sixteen Communist Chinese dead in the bush, twelve more badly injured, and the Malay Scouts cleaned up the rest. Sam McCready remained at his duties in Kuala Lumpur for another year, then left the army and returned to England. The proposal he had written for his Colonel was certainly filed away, but someone somewhere must have seen it.

He was waiting in line at the Labour Exchange—they did not call them Job Centers in those days—when he felt a tap on his arm, and a middle-aged man in a tweed jacket and brown trilby suggested he come to the nearby pub for a drink. Two weeks and three more interviews later, he was recruited into the Firm. Since then, for thirty years, the Firm had constituted the only family he had ever had.

He heard his name mentioned and snapped out of his reverie. Might as well pay attention, he reminded himself; it's my career they're talking about.

It was Denis Gaunt, with a bulky file in his hands.

"I think, gentlemen, we might with advantage consider a series of events in 1986 that alone might justify a reconsideration in the case of the early retirement of Sam McCready. Events that started, at least as far as we are concerned, on a spring morning on Salisbury Plain. . . ."

THE PRICE
OF THE BRIDE

Chapter 1

There was still a hint of fog hanging, away to their right, over the stretch of woodland known as Fox Covert, presaging a warm clear day to come.

On the knoll that dominated the rolling stretch of ground known to generations of soldiers as Frog Hill, the group of mixed military officers took their station to observe the forthcoming army maneuvers that would simulate a battle at battalion strength between two matched sets of opponents. Both groups would be British soldiers, divided for the sake of diplomacy not into "the Brits" and "the enemy" but into the Blues and the Greens. Even the usual designation of one group as "the Reds" had been changed, in deference to the composition of the officers on the knoll.

Across the stretch of open country at the northern edge of Salisbury Plain, so beloved by the British Army as a perfect maneuver ground much resembling the Central German Plain, over which it had been assumed the Third World War might have to be fought, umpires were scattered who would award points that would eventually decide the outcome of the battle. Men would not die that day; they would just prepare to.

Behind the officer group were the vehicles that had brought

them there: several staff cars and a greater number of less comfortable Land-Rovers in camouflage stripes or dull green. Orderlies from the Catering Corps set up field kitchens to provide the succession of mugs of steaming tea and coffee that would be demanded throughout the day and began to unpack a cold collation of snacks.

The officers milled about or stood stationary in the poses and activities of observing officers anywhere in the world. Some studied maps protected by plastic sheeting, on which notations in chinagraph pencils would later be made and erased. Others studied the distant terrain through powerful field glasses. Others conferred gravely among each other.

At the center of the group was the senior British general, the commanding officer of Southern Command. Beside him stood his personal guest, the senior ranking general of the visitors. Between and slightly behind them stood a bright young Subaltern fresh out of language school, who murmured a running translation into the ears of both men.

The British group of officers was the larger, just over thirty men. They all wore an air of gravity, as if well aware of both the unusualness and the importance of the occasion. They also seemed somewhat wary, as if unable quite to shake off the habit of years. For this was the first year of *perestroika*, and although Soviet officers had been invited to watch British maneuvers in Germany, this was the first time they had come to the heart of England as guests of the British Army. Old habits die hard.

The Russians were as grave as the British, or more so. There were seventeen of them, and each had been carefully picked and screened. Several spoke passable English and admitted it; five spoke perfect English and pretended not to.

The speaking of English had not, however, been the first priority in their selection. Expertise was the first consideration. Each Soviet officer was an expert in his field and well acquainted with British equipment, tactics, and structures. Their instructions were not simply to listen to what they were told, even less to accept it; but to study hard, miss nothing, and report back exactly how good the Brits were, what equipment they used, how they used it, and if at all, where their weak points lay.

They had arrived the previous evening after a day in London, much of it spent at their own embassy. The first dinner at the Officers' Mess at Tidworth Army Base had been fairly formal, even a trifle strained, but without incident. The jokes and the songs would come later, perhaps on their second or third evening. The Russians were aware that among the seventeen of them, there had to be five at least who were watching the rest, and probably each other as well.

No one mentioned this to the British group, nor did the British see fit to point out that among their own thirty members there were four who were actually from Counterintelligence, the watchers. At least the British watchers were only there to watch the Russians and not their fellow countrymen.

The Russian group comprised two generals, one whose insignia showed him to be from Motorized Rifles, the other from the Armored Corps; a General Staff full colonel; from Military Intelligence one colonel, one major, and one captain, all "declared," meaning they admitted they really were from Military Intelligence; a colonel of the Airborne Forces at whose open-necked combat blouse could be seen a triangle of blue-white-striped singlet, the insignia of Spetsnaz, or Special Forces; a colonel and a captain from Infantry and the same from Armored. In addition there was a half-colonel from Ops Staff, plus a major and two captains; and a colonel and major from Signals.

The Soviet Military Intelligence Corps is known as the GRU, and the three "declared" GRU men wore their proper insignia. They alone knew that the Signals major and one of the captains from Ops Staff were also GRU but undeclared. Neither the remainder of the Russians nor the British knew this.

The British, for their part, had not felt it necessary to tell the Russians that twenty operatives from the Security Service were posted around the officers' mess at Tidworth and would remain until the Soviet delegation departed for London and the Moscow flight on the morning of the third day. These watchers were now tending the lawns and flower beds, waiting table, or polishing bits of brass. Through the night they would "spell" each other, taking turns to keep the mess building under observation from vantage points scattered in a wider ring. As the Chief of General Staff had mentioned to the OC

Southern Command at a ministry briefing several days earlier, "One really would prefer not to lose one of the buggers."

The war game began on schedule at nine o'clock and proceeded throughout the day. The paratroop drop by Second Battalion, Parachute Regiment, took place just after lunch. A major of Two Para found himself standing next to the Soviet Airborne Colonel, who was watching with the keenest interest.

"I see," observed the Russian, "that you still favor the two-inch company mortar."

"A useful tool," agreed the Britisher. "Effective and still reliable."

"I agree," said the Russian in slow, accented English. "I used them in Afghanistan."

"Indeed. I used them in the Falklands," said the major from Two Para. He thought, but did not say, "And the difference is, we won in short order in the Falklands, and you are losing badly in Afghanistan."

The Russian permitted himself a grim smile. The Britisher smiled back. "Bastard," thought the Russian. "He's thinking how badly we are doing in Afghanistan."

Both men kept smiling. Neither could have known that in two years the remarkable new General Secretary in Moscow would order the entire Soviet Army to withdrawn from the Afghan adventure. It was early days, and old habits die hard.

That evening the dinner at Tidworth barracks was more relaxed. The wine flowed; vodka, which the British Army rarely drinks, was in evidence. Across the language barrier an element of jocularity raised its head. The Russians took their cue from their senior general, the Motorized Rifles one. He seemed to be beaming at the translated conversation from the British general, so they relaxed. The major from Ops Staff listened to a British tank man tell a joke and nearly burst out laughing before realizing he was not supposed to understand any English and had to wait for the translation.

The major from Two Para found himself next to the declared major from Soviet Military Intelligence, the GRU. He thought he would practice his smattering of Russian.

"Govoritya-vi pa-Angleeski?" he asked.

The Russian was delighted. *"Ochen malinko,"* he replied,

then dropped into halting English. "Very little, I am afraid. I try with books at home, but it is not so good."

"Better than my Russian, I'm sure," said the paratrooper. "By the way, I'm Paul Sinclair."

"Please, I am so sorry," said the Russian. He reached around and held out his hand. "Pavel Kuchenko."

It was a good dinner and ended with songs in the bar before the two groups of officers trooped off to their rooms at eleven o'clock. A number of them would appreciate that the following morning would permit a lie-in—the orderlies were instructed to appear with cups of tea at seven o'clock.

In fact, Major Kuchenko was up at five and spent two hours seated quietly behind the lace curtains that covered the windows of his bachelor bedroom. He sat with all his lights out and studied the road that ran past the front of the officers' mess toward the main gate leading to the Tidworth road. He spotted or thought he spotted three men in the half-gloom of very early morning who might be watchers.

He also spotted, precisely at six o'clock, Colonel Arbuthnot appear from the main doors of the mess almost beneath him and depart on what was apparently his regular morning jogging run. He had reason to believe it was a regular habit—he had seen the elderly colonel do exactly the same the previous morning.

Colonel Arbuthnot was not a difficult man to spot, for his left arm was missing. He had lost it years earlier while on patrol with his levies in that strange half-forgotten war in the hills of Dhofar, a campaign fought by British Special Forces and Omani levies to prevent a Communist revolution from toppling the Sultan of Oman and taking control of the Straits of Hormuz. A sentimental Army board had permitted him to stay on in the Army, and he was by then the catering officer at Tidworth officers' mess. Every morning he kept in trim with a five-mile jog down the road and back, an accepted figure in white tracksuit with cowl hood and blue piping, the loose left sleeve neatly pinned to the fabric by his side. For the second morning, Major Kuchenko watched him thoughtfully.

The second day of war games passed without incident, and finally all the officers of both nationalities agreed the umpires had done a good job in awarding a technical victory to the

Greens, who had finally dislodged the Blues from their positions on Frog Hill and secured Fox Covert from counterat-
tack. The third dinner was very jolly, with copious toasts and
later a much-applauded rendering of "Malinka" from the
young Russian Ops Staff captain, who was not a spy but had
a fine baritone voice. The Russian group was due to congre-
gate in the main lobby after breakfast at nine A.M. the next
morning to board the coach for Heathrow. The coach would
come from London with two embassy staff on board to see
them through the airport. During the singing of "Malinka,"
no one noticed that Colonel Arbuthnot's room, which was not
locked, was entered by someone who left sixty seconds later
as quietly as he had come and who later rejoined the group at
the bar, coming from the direction of the men's toilet.

At ten minutes to six the next morning a figure in white-
cowled tracksuit with blue piping, the empty left sleeve pinned
to the side, trotted down the steps of the mess and turned
toward Main Gate. The figure was spotted by a watcher behind
the glass of a window in an upper room of another building
two hundred yards away. He made a note but took no action.

At the gate the Corporal of the Guard came out of the
guardroom and threw up a salute to the figure as it ducked
under the barrier. The runner, not wearing a cap, was unable
to return the salute but raised a hand in salutation, then
turned in the usual direction and jogged toward Tidworth.

At ten past six the corporal glanced up, stared, then turned
to his sergeant.

"I've just seen Colonel Arbuthnot go past," he said.

"So?" asked the sergeant.

"Twice," said the corporal. The sergeant was tired. They
would both be relieved in twenty minutes. Breakfast awaited.
He shrugged.

"Must have forgotten something," he said. He would regret
that remark—later, at the disciplinary hearing.

Major Kuchenko ducked into some trees beside the road
after half a mile and slipped out of the stolen white tracksuit
and hid it in deep undergrowth. When he went back to the
road he was in gray flannel slacks and tweed jacket over a
shirt and tie. Only his Adidas runnning shoes were at odds
with the outfit. He suspected but could not be sure that a mile

behind him jogged an annoyed Colonel Arbuthnot, who had wasted ten fruitless minutes searching for his regular tracksuit before coming to the conclusion that his orderly must have taken it for laundering and not returned it. He was wearing his spare, and he had not yet noticed he was also missing a shirt, tie, jacket, slacks, and a pair of running shoes.

Kuchenko could easily have stayed ahead of the British colonel until Arbuthnot turned around to make his way back, but he was saved the trouble by a car that came from behind him and stopped at his wave. Kuchenko leaned toward the window on the passenger side.

"I'm awfully sorry," he said, "but my car seems to have broken down. Back there. I was wondering whether I could get some help from a garage in North Tidworth?"

"Bit early," said the driver, "but I can run you up there. Jump in."

The paratroops major would have been amazed at Kuchenko's sudden mastery of English. But the foreign accent was still there.

"Not from these parts, are you?" asked the driver by way of conversation. Kuchenko laughed.

"No. I am from Norway. Touring your British cathedrals."

Kuchenko was dropped by the kindly driver in the center of the sleepy town of North Tidworth at ten minutes to seven. The driver drove on toward Marlborough. He would never see any reason to mention the incident again, nor would anyone ever ask him.

In the town center Kuchenko found a phone booth and at exactly one minute to seven dialed a London number, punching in a fifty-pence piece to start the call. It was answered at the fifth ring.

"I'd like to speak to Mr. Roth, Mr. Joe Roth," said Kuchenko.

"Yeah, this is Joe Roth speaking," said the voice at the other end.

"Pity," said Kuchenko. "You see, I really hoped I might talk to Chris Hayes."

In his small but elegant Mayfair apartment, Joe Roth stiffened, and all his professional antennae went onto red alert. He had only been awake for twenty minutes, still in pajamas, unshaven, running a bath, and preparing his first coffee of the

day. He had been crossing the sitting room from the kitchen,
juice in one hand, coffee in the other, when the phone rang.
It was early, even for him, and he was not a late riser, even
though his job as Assistant Public Affairs officer at the American Embassy just a quarter of a mile away in Grosvenor
Square did not require him to check in until ten.

Joe Roth was CIA, but he was not the Company's Head of
London Station. That honor went to William Carver, and
Carver was with Western Hemisphere Division, as all station
heads would be. As such, Carver was "declared," which
meant that just about everyone who mattered knew what he
was and what job he did. Carver would sit, ex officio, on the
British Joint Intelligence Committee, the official representative of the Company in London.

Roth came from the Office of Special Projects, a bureau
formed only six years ago to handle, as its name implied,
projects and active measures that Langley regarded as suffi-
ciently sensitive to merit the station Heads later being able to
claim innocence, even to America's allies.

All CIA officers, of whatever department they come from,
have a real name and an operational or professional name.
The real name, in friendly embassies, actually is real; Joe
Roth really was Joe Roth and was listed as such in the
Diplomatic List. But unlike Carver, Joe was undeclared,
except to a tiny caucus of three or four British counterparts
in the Secret Intelligence Service. And his professional name
was equally known to only that same few, plus some of his
colleagues back in America. To have it thrown at him down a
phone line at seven A.M., and in a voice with a non-British
accent, was like a warning buzzer.

"I'm sorry," he said carefully, "You've got Joe Roth here.
Who is that speaking?"

"Listen carefully, Mr. Roth, or Mr. Hayes. My name is
Pyotr Alexandrovitch Orlov. I am a full colonel of the KGB."

"Look, if this is a joke—"

"Mr. Roth, my calling you by your operational name is no
joke for you. My defection to the U.S.A. is no joke for me.
And that is what I am offering to do. I want to get to
America—fast. Very soon now, it will be impossible for me to
go back to my own side. No excuse will be accepted. I have
an enormous amount of information of great value to your

Agency, Mr. Roth. You must make your decision quickly, or
I go back while there is time."

Roth was scribbling rapidly on a jotting pad he had clawed
off his sitting-room coffee table. The pad still had the scores
from the poker game he had concluded late the previous
evening with Sam McCready. He recalled later thinking, "Jesus, if Sam could hear this now, he'd go apeshit." He cut in.

"Where exactly are you now, Colonel?"

"In a phone booth in a small town near Salisbury Plain,"
said the voice. Grammatically, the English was near perfect.
Only the accent was clearly foreign. Roth had been trained to
discern accents, place them. This one was Slavic, probably
Russian. He still wondered whether this would turn out to be
one of Sam McCready's crazy jokes, whether he would suddenly hear peals of laughter coming down the phone at him.
Dammit, it wasn't even April Fool's Day. It was the third.

"For three days," said the voice, "I have been with a group
of Soviet officers attending British military maneuvers on
Salisbury Plain. Staying at Tidworth barracks. My cover there
was as Major Pavel Kuchenko of the GRU. I walked out one
hour ago. If I am not back within one hour, I cannot go back
at all. It will take me half an hour to get back. You have thirty
minutes to give me your decision, Mr. Roth."

"Okay, Colonel. I'll go with it—so far. I want you to call
me back in fifteen minutes. The line will be clear. You will
have your answer."

"Fifteen minutes. Then I walk back," said the voice, and
the phone went down.

Roth's mind was racing. He was thirty-nine, and he had
spent twelve years in the Agency. Nothing like this had ever
happened to him before. But then, many men spent their
entire working lives in the Agency and never smelled a Soviet
defector. But he knew about them, they all knew about them;
all field operatives were briefed and lectured and trained to be
aware of the constant possibility of a Soviet defection.

Most, he knew, came after initial, tentative approaches.
Usually, they came after long thought and some preparation
by the defector. Messages were passed to the known Agency
men in the area: "I want to meet, I want to discuss terms."
Usually the potential defector was asked to stay in place and
provide a stream of information before finally "coming over."

If he refused, he was urged at least to come with a bagful of documents. The amount he could send out before coming over or bring with him would affect his standing, his rewards, his life-style. In the trade, it was called the bride-price.

Occasionally, just occasionally, you got what is called a "walk-in." The defector simply appeared, having burned his boats behind him, unable to go back. That left little choice; you either accepted the man or cast him back into a refugee camp. The latter was rarely done, not even in the case of a rather useless, low-level defector like a merchant seaman or a private soldier with nothing to offer. It was usually done only if lie-detector tests at the point of defection proved the man was a disinformation agent. Then America would refuse to accept him. When that happened, the Russians just bit the bullet, got their agent out of the refugee camp, and took him home.

On one occasion, to Roth's knowledge, the KGB had traced a turned-down defector to a refugee camp and liquidated him because he had failed the polygraph test, even though he had been telling the truth. The machine had interpreted his nervousness as lies. Damned bad luck. Of course, that was in the old days; the lie detectors were better now.

And here was a man claiming to be a full colonel of the KGB who wanted just to walk in. No forewarning. No haggling. No suitcase full of documents fresh from the KGB *Rezidentsia* of his latest posting. And defecting right in the heart of England of all places, not the Middle East or Latin America. And to the Americans, not the Brits. Or had he already approached the Brits? Been turned down? Roth's mind raced across the possibilities, and the minutes ticked away.

Five past seven—five past two in Washington. Everyone asleep. He ought to call Calvin Bailey, head of Special Projects, his boss. Now no doubt fast asleep in Georgetown. But the time—there wasn't time. He flipped open a wall cabinet to reveal his private computer. Swiftly, he tapped himself into the mainframe deep beneath the embassy in Grosvenor Square. He put the computer into encrypted mode and asked the mainframe to consider senior KGB officers known to the West. Then he asked: Who is Pyotr Alexandrovitch Orlov?

One of the strange things about the covert world is the

almost clublike atmosphere that can exist within it. Pilots share the same sort of camaraderie, but they are allowed to. Paratroopers have it also, and Special Forces. Professionals tend to respect each other, even across the barriers of rivalry, opposition, or outright hostility. In the Second World War the fighter pilots of the Luftwaffe and the RAF seldom hated each other, leaving such sentiments to the zealots and civilians. Professionals serve their political masters and bureaucrats loyally, but would usually prefer to sink a pint of beer with others of their own arcane skills, even the opposition.

In the covert world, careful note is taken of just whom the opposition is putting up at bat this week. Promotions and transfers in allied, rival, or enemy agencies are carefully noted and filed. In any capital city the KGB *Rezident* will probably know who the British and American stations heads are, and vice versa. In Dar-es-Salaam once, the KGB chief at a cock-tail party came up to the British SIS station head with a whiskey and soda.

"Mr. Child," he announced solemnly, "you know who I am, and I know who you are. Ours is a difficult profession. We should not ignore each other." They drank to that.

The CIA mainframe computer in London is linked straight through to Langley, Virginia. In response to Roth's question, little circuits began to run through lists of KGB officers known to the CIA. There were hundreds of "confirmed" and thou-sands of "suspected." Mostly this knowledge came from defectors themselves, for one of the areas that debriefing officers are always keen to explore with a newly arrived defector is that of who is who these days, who has been transferred, who demoted or promoted. The knowledge grows with each new defector.

Roth knew that over the past four years, the British had been more than helpful in this regard, providing hundreds of names—many of them new, others confirmations of suspi-cions. The Brits attributed their knowledge in part to inter-cepts, in part to smart analysis, and in part to defectors like Vladimir Kuzichkin, the Illegals Directorate man they had spirited out of Beirut. Wherever Langley's databank had got its original information, it did not waste time. Letters in green began to flash up on Roth's small screen.

PYOTR ALEXANDROVITCH ORLOV. KGB. FULL COLO-
NEL. PAST FOUR YEARS BELIEVED IN THIRD DIRECTOR-
ATE. BELIEVED MASQUERADING AS GRU MAJOR IN-
SIDE RED ARMY JOINT PLANNING STAFF MOSCOW.
PREVIOUS POSTINGS KNOWN AS OPS PLANNING MOS-
COW CENTER AND FIRST CHIEF DIRECTORATE (ILLE-
GALS DIRECTORATE) YAZENEVO.

Roth whistled as the machine ended its knowledge of a man
called Orlov, and he shut it down. What the voice on the
phone had said made sense. The Third or Armed Forces
Directorate of the KGB was that department tasked to keep a
constant eye on the loyalty of the Armed Forces. As such, it
was deeply resented but tolerated. AFD officers usually infiltrated the Armed Forces disguised as GRU or Military Intelligence officers. This would explain their being anywhere and
everywhere, and asking questions, and keeping up surveillance. If Orlov had really been for four years posing as a GRU
major on the Joint Planning Staff of the Soviet Defense
Ministry, he would be a walking encyclopedia. It would also
account for his being in the group of Soviet officers invited
under the recent NATO–Warsaw Pact agreement to Salisbury
Plain to watch the British war games.

He checked his watch. Seven-fourteen. No time to call
Langley. He had sixty seconds to decide. Too risky—tell him
to go back to the officers' mess, slip into his room, and accept
a nice cup of tea from a British steward. Then back to
Heathrow and Moscow. Try and persuade him to do his run
at Heathrow, give me time to contact Calvin Bailey in Washington. The phone rang.

"Mr. Roth, there is a bus outside the phone booth. The first
of the morning. I think it is taking civilian cleaning staff to
Tidworth barracks. I can just get back in time, if I have to."

Roth took a deep breath. Career on the line, boy, right on
the line.

"Okay, Colonel Orlov, we'll take you. I'll contact my
British colleagues—they'll have you safe within thirty minutes."

"No." The voice was harsh, brooking no opposition. "I
come to the Americans only. I want out of here and into
America fast. That is the deal, Mr. Roth. No other deal."

"Now look, Colonel—"

"No, Mr. Roth, I want you to pick me up yourself. In two hours. The forecourt of the Andover railway station. Then to Upper Heyford USAF base. You get me on a transport to America. It's the only deal I will take."

"All right, Colonel. You got it. I'll be there."

It took Roth ten minutes to throw on street clothes, grab a passport, CIA identification, money, and car keys, and head downstairs for his car in the basement garage.

Fifteen minutes after putting down the phone, he eased his way into Park Lane and headed north for Marble Arch and the Bayswater Road, preferring that route to the scramble through Knightsbridge and Kensington.

By eight, he was past Heathrow and had turned south on the M25 then southwest along the M3, linking to the A303 to Andover. He entered the forecourt of the railway station at ten past nine. There was a stream of cars sweeping in to deposit travelers and leaving the forecourt within seconds. The travelers hurried into the station concourse. Only one man was not moving. He leaned against a wall in a tweed jacket, gray trousers, and running shoes and scanned a morning paper. Roth approached him.

"I think you must be the man I have come to meet," he said softly. The reader looked up, calm gray eyes, a hard face in its midforties.

"That depends if you have identification," said the man. It was the same voice as the one on the phone. Roth tendered his CIA pass. Orlov studied it and nodded. Roth gestured to his car, engine still running, blocking several behind it. Orlov looked around as if saying good-bye for the last time to a world he had known. Without a word, he stepped into the car.

Roth had told the Embassy Duty Officer to alert Upper Heyford that he would be coming with a guest. It took nearly two hours more to cut across country to the Oxfordshire base of the USAF. Roth drove straight to the Base Commander's office. There were two calls to Washington; then Langley cleared it with the Pentagon, who instructed the Base Commander. A communications flight out of Upper Heyford to Andrews Air Force Base, in Maryland, that afternoon at three P.M. had two extra passengers.

That was five hours after everything had hit the fan from Tidworth to London and back. Long before takeoff, there was a most imperial row going on among the British Army, the Defense Ministry, the Security Service, and the Russian Embassy.

The Soviet group had assembled for breakfast around eight o'clock in the officers' mess dining hall, by now chatting relaxedly to their British counterparts. There were sixteen of them by eight-twenty. The absence of Major Kuchenko was noted, but not with any sense of alarm.

About ten minutes before nine, the sixteen Russians reassembled in the main lobby with their baggage, and again the absence of Major Kuchenko was noted. A steward was dispatched to his room to ask him to hurry up. The coach stood outside the door.

The steward returned to say the major's room was empty, but his gear was still there. A delegation of two British officers and two Russians went up to look for him. They established that the bed had been slept in, that the bath towel was damp, and that *all* Kuchenko's clothes were apparently present, indicating he must be somewhere nearby. A search was made of the bathroom down the corridor (only the two Russian generals had been accorded private bathrooms), but the search drew a blank. Toilets were also checked, but they were empty. By now the faces of the two Russians, including the GRU colonel, had lost all trace of bonhomie.

The British were also becoming worried. A complete search of the mess building was made, but to no avail. A British Intelligence captain slipped out to talk to the invisible watchers from the Security Service. Their log showed that two officers in tracksuits had gone jogging that morning but only one had returned. A frantic call was made to Main Gate. The night log showed only that Colonel Arbuthnot had left and that he had returned.

To solve the problem, the Corporal of the Guard was summoned from his bed. He related the double departure of Colonel Arbuthnot, who was confronted and hotly denied he had ever left Main Gate, returned, and left again. A search of his room revealed that he was missing a white tracksuit, plus a jacket, shirt, tie, and slacks. The Intelligence captain had a hurried and whispered conversation with the senior British general, who became extremely grave and asked the senior Russian to accompany him to his office.

When the Russian general emerged, he was white with anger and demanded an immediate staff car to take him to his embassy in London. Word spread among the other fifteen Russians, who became frosty and unapproachable. It was ten o'clock. The telephoning began.

The British general raised the Chief of Staff in London and gave him a complete situation report. Another sitrep went from the senior watcher to his superiors in the Security Service headquarters at Curzon Street, London. There it went right up to the Deputy Director General, who at once suspected the hand of TSAR, the friendly acronym by which the Security Service sometimes refers to the Secret Intelligence Service. It stands for: Those Shits Across the River.

South of the Thames in Century House, Assistant Chief Timothy Edwards took a call from Curzon Street but was able to deny that the SIS had had anything to do with it. As he put the phone down he pressed a buzzer on his desk and barked: "Ask Sam McCready to step up here at once, would you?"

By noon, the Russian general, accompanied by the GRU colonel, was closeted in the Soviet Embassy in Kensington Palace Gardens with the Soviet Defense attaché, who was posing as a Major-General of Infantry but actually held the same rank in the GRU. None of the three knew that Major Kuchenko was actually Colonel Orlov of the KGB—a knowledge confined to a very few senior officers on the Joint Planning Staff in Moscow. In fact, all three men would have been deeply relieved to know—few things please Russian Army men as much as the KGB with egg all over its face. In London, they thought that they had lost a GRU major and were deeply unhappy at Moscow's expected reaction.

At Cheltenham, the Government Communications Headquarters, the nation's listening post, noted and reported a sudden frantic increase in Soviet radio traffic between the embassy and Moscow, in both the diplomatic and the military codes.

During the lunch hour the Soviet Ambassador, Leonid Zamyatin, lodged a vigorous protest with the British Foreign Office, alleging kidnapping, and demanded immediate access to Major Kuchenko. The protest bounced straight back down from the Foreign Office to all the covert agencies, who in unison held up their lily-white hands and replied, "But we haven't got him."

Long before midday, the rage of the Russians was being matched by the puzzlement of the British. The manner in which Kuchenko (they were still calling him that) had made his escape was bizarre, to put it mildly. Defectors did not simply defect in order to go to a bar for a beer; they headed for sanctuary, usually one that had been prepared in advance. If Kuchenko had bolted into a police station—it had been known—the Wiltshire police would have notified London at once. With all the British agencies protesting their innocence, that left the possibility of other agencies based on British soil.

Bill Carver, the CIA station head in London, was in an impossible position. Roth had been forced to contact Langley from the air base to get clearance on the USAF flight, and Langley had informed Carver. Carver knew the rules of the Anglo-American agreement on such matters—it would be taken as deeply offensive for the Americans to spirit a Russian out of England under the nose of the Brits without telling them. But Carver was warned to delay until the military flight cleared British airspace. He took refuge in the ruse of being unavailable all morning, then asked for an urgent meeting with Timothy Edwards at three P.M., which was granted.

Carver was late—he had sat three blocks away in his car until he learned on the car phone that the flight was airborne. By the time he saw Edwards, it was ten past three and the American jet was clear of the Bristol Channel and south of Ireland, next stop Maryland.

By the time Edwards confronted him, Carver had already received a full report from Roth, brought by a USAF dispatch rider from the air base to London. Roth explained that he had been given no choice but to take Kuchenko/Orlov at zero notice or let him go back, and that Orlov would absolutely come only to the Americans.

Carver used this to try to take the sting out of the insult to the British. Edwards had long since checked with McCready and knew exactly who Orlov was—the American databank consulted by Roth just after seven A.M. had come from the SIS in the first place. Privately, Edwards knew that he too would have acted exactly as Roth had, given the opportunity of such a prize, but he remained cool and offended. Having formally received Carver's report, he at once informed his own Defense Ministry, Foreign Office, and sister service, Security. Kuchenko (he saw no need to tell everyone that the man's real name was Orlov—yet) was on American sovereign territory and out of any British control.

An hour later, Ambassador Zamyatin arrived at the Foreign Office in King Charles Street and was shown straight to the office of the Foreign Secretary himself. Though he purported to receive the explanation with skepticism, he was privately prepared to believe Sir Geoffrey Howe, whom he knew to be a very honorable man. With a show of continuing outrage, the Russian went back to the embassy and told Moscow. The Soviet military delegation flew home late that night, deeply dejected at the prospect of the endless interrogations that were in store for them.

In Moscow itself, a blazing row had been raging between the KGB, which accused the GRU of not exercising sufficient vigilance, and the GRU, which accused the KGB of having treasonous officers on its staff. Orlov's wife, deeply distraught and protesting her innocence, was being interrogated, as were all Orlov's colleagues, superiors, friends, and contacts.

In Washington, the Director of Central Intelligence took an angry phone call from the Secretary of State, who had received a deeply pained telgram from Sir Geoffrey Howe over the handling of the matter. As he put the phone down, the DCI looked across his desk at two men: the Deputy Director (Operations) and the Head of Special Projects, Calvin Bailey. It was to the latter that he spoke.

"Your young Mr. Roth. He certainly stirred up a hornets' nest on this one. You say he acted on his own authority?"

"He did. As I understand it, the Russian gave him no time to go through channels. It was take it or leave it."

Bailey was a thin, astringent man, not given to making close personal friendships in the Agency. People found him aloof, chilly. But he was good at his job.

"We've upset the Brits pretty badly. Would you have taken the same risk?" asked the DCI.

"I don't know," said Bailey. "We won't know until we talk to Orlov. Really talk."

The DCI nodded. In the covert world, as in all others, the rule was simple. If you took a gamble and it paid rich dividends, you were a smart fellow, destined for the highest office. If the gamble failed, there was always early retirement. The DCI wanted to pin it down.

"You taking responsibility for Roth? For better, for worse?"

"Yes," said Bailey, "I will. It's done now. We have to see what we've got."

When the military flight landed at Andrews just after six P.M. Washington time, there were five Agency cars waiting on the tarmac. Before the service personnel could disembark, the two men whom none of them recognized or would ever see again were escorted off the plane and enveloped by the dark-windowed sedans waiting below. Bailey met Orlov, nodded coolly, and saw the Russian ensconced in the second car. He turned to Roth.

"I'm giving him to you, Joe. You brought him out, you debrief him."

"I'm not an interrogator," said Roth. "It's not my specialty."

Bailey shrugged. "He asked for you. You brought him out. He owes you. Maybe he'll be more relaxed with you. You'll have all the backup—translators, analysts, specialists in every area he touches on. And the polygraph, of course. Start with the polygraph. Take him to the Ranch—they're expecting you. And Joe—I want it all. As it comes, at once, my eyes only, by hand. Okay?"

Roth nodded.

Seventeen hours earlier, when he donned a white tracksuit in a bedroom in England, Pyotr Orlov, alias Pavel Kuchenko, had been a trusted Soviet officer with a home, a wife, a career, and a motherland. Now he was a bundle, a package, huddled in the back of a sedan in a strange land, destined to be squeezed for every last drop of juice, and certainly feeling, as they all do, the first pangs of doubt and maybe panic.

Roth turned to climb into the car beside the Russian.

"One last thing, Joe," said Bailey. "If Orlov, who is now code-named Minstrel, turns out to be a no-no, the Director is going to have my ass. About thirty seconds after I have yours. Good luck."

The Ranch was and remains a CIA safe house, a genuine farm in the horse-raising country of southern Virginia. Not too far from Washington, it is buried in deep woodland, railed and fenced, approached by a long driveway, and guarded by teams of very fit young men who have all passed the unarmed combat and weapons training courses at Quantico.

Orlov was shown to a comfortable two-room suite in restful colors and with the usual appurtenances of a good hotel—television, video, tape player, easy chairs, small dining table. Food was served—his first meal in America—and Joe Roth ate with him. On the flight over, the two men had agreed they would call each other Peter and Joe. Now it appeared their acquaintance was going to be extended.

"It won't always be easy, Peter," said Roth as he watched the Russian dealing with a large hamburger. He might have been thinking of the bulletproof windows that would not open, the one-way mirrors in all the rooms, the recording of every word spoken in the suite. And the rigorous debriefing to come.

The Russian nodded.

"Tomorrow we have to start, Peter. We have to talk, really talk. You have to take a polygraph test. If you pass that, you have to tell me . . . many things. Everything, in fact. Everything you know or suspect. Over and over again."

Orlov put down his fork and smiled.

"Joe, we are men who have lived our lives in this strange world. You do not have to"—he searched for the phrase—"mince the words. I have to justify the risk you have taken for me, to get me out. What you call the price of the bride, yes?"

Roth laughed.

"Yes, Peter, that's what we need to have now. The price of the bride."

In London, the Secret Intelligence Service had not been entirely inactive. Timothy Edwards had quickly learned the name of the missing man from the Ministry of Defense—Pavel Kuchenko. His own databank had quickly revealed that that was the cover-name of Colonel Pyotr Orlov of the KGB Third Directorate. That was when he summoned Sam McCready.

"I've screwed our American Cousins as hard as I can. Deep offense taken, outrage at all levels—that sort of thing. Bill Carver is deeply mortified—he sees his own position here as damaged. Anyway, he will press Langley to give us the lot, as and when it comes. I want to form a small group to have a look at the Orlov product when it reaches us. I'd like you to be in charge—under me.''

"Thank you," said The Deceiver. "But I'd go for more. I'd ask for access. It could be that Orlov knows things that are specific to us. Those things won't be high on Langley's list. I'd like access, personal access.''

"That might be hard," mused Edwards. "They've probably got him stashed in Virginia somewhere. But I can ask.''

"You've got the right," insisted McCready. "We've been giving them a hell of a lot of product recently.''

The thought hung in the air. They both knew where most of the product had been coming from these past four years. And there was the Soviet Army War Book, handed over to Langley the previous year.

"Another thing," said Sam. "I'd like to check on Orlov with Keepsake.''

Edwards stared hard at McCready. Keepsake was a British "asset," a Russian working for the SIS. He was so highly placed and so sensitive that only four men in Century House were aware who he was, and less than a dozen knew that he existed at all. Those who knew his identity were the Chief himself, Edwards, the Controller Sovbloc, and McCready, his case officer, the man who "ran" him.

"Is that wise?" asked Edwards.

"I think it is justified.''

"Be careful.''

The black car, the following morning, was clearly parked on a double yellow line, and the traffic warden had no hesitation in writing out a ticket. He had just finished and slipped the polythene envelope under the windshield wiper when a slim, well-dressed man in a gray suit emerged from a nearby shop, spotted the ticket, and began to protest. It was such an everyday scene that no one noticed, even on a London street.

From afar, an onlooker would have seen the normal gesticulations from the driver and the impervious shrugs from the traffic warden. Tugging at the warden's sleeve, the driver urged the official to come to the back of the car and look at the plates. When he did, the warden saw the telltale CD plate of the Diplomatic Corps next to the registration plate. He had clearly missed it, but was unimpressed. Foreign diplomatic staff might be immune from the fine, but not from the ticket. He began to move off.

The driver snatched the ticket off the windshield and waved it under the warden's nose. The warden asked a question. To prove he really was a diplomat, the driver delved into his pocket and produced an identity card, which he forced the warden to look at. The warden glanced, shrugged again, and moved away. In a rage the driver screwed up the parking ticket and hurled it into the car before climbing in and driving off.

What the onlooker would not have seen was the paper stuck inside the ID card saying: "Reading Room, British Museum, tomorrow, two P.M." Nor would he have noticed the driver a mile later smooth out the crumpled ticket and read on the reverse side: "Colonel Pyotr Alexandrovich Orlov has defected to the Americans. Do you know anything about him?"

The Deceiver had just contacted Keepsake.

Chapter 2

The treatment, or "handling," of a defector varies widely from case to case, according to the emotional state of the defector or to the usages of the host agency undertaking the debriefing. The only common factor is that it is always a sensitive and complicated business.

The defector must first be housed in an environment that does not appear menacing but that precludes his escape, often for his own good. Two years before Orlov, the Americans had made a mistake with Vitali Urchenko, another walk-in. Attempting to create an air of normality, they had taken him to dinner in a Georgetown, Washington, restaurant. The man changed his mind, escaped through the men's room window, walked back to the Soviet Embassy, and gave himself up. It did him no good; he was flown back to Moscow, brutally interrogated, and shot.

Apart from the defector's possible self-destructive tendencies, he must be protected from possible reprisals. The USSR—and notably the KGB—are notoriously unforgiving toward those they regard as traitors and have been wont to hunt them down and liquidate them if possible. The higher the defector's rank, the worse the treason, and a senior KGB

154

officer is regarded as the highest of all. For the KGB are the cream of the cream, afforded every privilege and luxury in a nation where most live hungry and cold. To reject this life-style, the most cosseted the USSR has to offer, is to show ingratitude worthy of death itself.

The Ranch offered, apparently, security against reprisals as well as self-destruction.

The principal complicating factor is the mental state of the defector himself. After the first, adrenaline-packed rush into the West, many develop rethink symptoms. The full enormity of the step they have taken sinks in, the realization of never again seeing wife, family, friends, or homeland. This can lead to depression, like the down after the high of a drug-taker.

To counteract this, many debriefings start with a leisurely survey of the defector's past life, a complete curriculum vitae from birth and childhood onward. The narration of the early years—description of mother and father, schoolday friends, skating in the park in winter, walks in the country in sum-mer—instead of producing more nostalgia and depression, usually has a calming effect. And everything, every last detail and gesture, is noted.

One thing that debriefers are always keenly interested in is motivation. Why did you decide to come over? (The word *defect* is never used. It implies disloyalty rather than a reason-able decision to change one's views.)

Sometimes the defector lies about his reasons. He may say he became utterly disillusioned by the corruption, cynicism, and nepotism of the system he served and left behind. For many, this is the genuine reason; in fact, it is by far the most common reason. But it is not always true. It may be that the defector had his hand in the cashbox and knew he faced harsh punishment from the KGB. Or he may have been on the threshold of recall to Moscow to face discipline for a tangled love life. A demotion, or a hatred of a certain superior, may have been the real reason. The host agency may be well aware of why the man *really* defected. The excuses are nonetheless listened to carefully and sympathetically, even though they are known to be false. And they are noted. The man may lie as to his motivations out of vanity, but he does not necessarily lie about real secret intelligence. Or does he . . .?

Others tell untruths out of vainglory, seeking to embellish

their own importance in their earlier life, to impress their hosts. Everything will be checked out; sooner or later, the hosts will know the real reason, the real status. For the moment, everything is listened to very sympathetically. The real cross-examination will come later, as in court.

When the area of secret intelligence is finally broached, pitfalls are set. Many, many questions are asked to which the debriefing officers already know the answers. Or if they do not, the analysts, working through the nights on the tapes, will soon find out by collating and cross-checking. There have, after all, been many defectors, and the Western agencies have a huge volume of knowledge of the KGB, the GRU, the Soviet Army, Navy, and Air Force, even of the Kremlin, on which to draw.

If the defector is seen to lie about things that, according to his declared postings, he ought to know the truth of, he immediately becomes suspect. He may be lying out of bravado, to impress; or because he was never privy to that information but seeks to claim he was; or because he has forgotten; or . . .

It is not easy to lie to a host agency during a long and arduous debriefing. The questioning can take months, even years, depending on the amount of things the defector claims that do not seem to check out.

If something a new defector says is at variance with the believed truth, it could be that the believed truth was wrong. So the analysts check out the original source of their information again. It may be that they have been wrong all the time, and the new defector is right. The subject is dropped while checks are made, and returned to later. Again and again.

Often the defector does not realize the significance of some small piece of information he provides and to which he assigns no particular importance. But for his hosts, that seeming bagatelle may be the one missing piece of a jigsaw puzzle that has eluded them for a long time.

In among the questions to which the answers are already known are the questions to which true answers are *really* valuable. This is the pay dirt. Can this new defector tell the host agency anything it doesn't already know, and if so, how important?

In the case of Colonel Pyotr Alexandrovitch Orlov, the CIA came to the view within four weeks that it had fortuitously tapped into a mother lode of pure gold. The man's "product" was fantastic.

For one thing, he was very cool and calm from the start. He narrated to Joe Roth the story of his life from birth in a humble shack near Minsk just after the war to the day he decided, six months earlier in Moscow, that he could tolerate no more of a society and regime that he had come to despise. He never denied retaining a deep love for his motherland of Russia, and he showed the normal emotion at the knowledge he had left it behind forever.

He declared that his marriage to Gaia, a successful theater director in Moscow, had been over in all but name for three years, and he admitted with expectable anger her several affairs with handsome young actors.

He passed three separate lie-detector tests concerning his background, career, private life, and political change of heart. And he began to reveal information of the first order.

For one thing, his career had been very varied. From his four years with the Third or Armed Forces Directorate, working inside the Joint Planning Staff at Army headquarters while posing as GRU Major Kuchenko, he had a wide knowledge of the personalities of a range of senior military officers, of the dispositions of divisions of the Soviet Army and Air Force, and of the Navy's ships at sea and in the yards.

He provided fascinating insights into the defeats suffered by the Red Army in Afghanistan, told of the unsuspected demoralization of the Soviet troops there and of Moscow's growing disillusion with Afghan puppet dictator Babrak Kamal.

Prior to working in the Third Directorate, Orlov had been with the Illegals Directorate, that department inside the First Chief Directorate responsible for the running of "illegal" agents worldwide. The "illegals" are the most secret of all agents who spy against their own country (if they are nationals of it) or who live in the foreign country under deep cover. These are the agents who have no diplomatic cover, for whom exposure and capture does not entail the merely embarrassing penalty of being declared persona non grata and expelled, but the more painful therapy of arrest, harsh interrogation, and sometimes execution.

Although his knowledge was four years out of date, Orlov seemed to have an encyclopedic memory and began to blow away the very networks he had once helped establish and run, mainly in Central and South America, which had been his previous area.

When a defector arrives whose information turns out to be controversial, there usually appear among the officers of the host agency two camps: those who believe and support the new defector, and those who doubt and oppose him. In the history of the CIA the most notorious such case was that of Golytsin and Nosenko.

In 1960, Anatoli Golytsin defected and made it his business to warn the CIA that the KGB had been behind just about everything that had gone wrong in the world since the end of the Second World War. For Golytsin, there was no infamy to which the KGB would not stoop or was not even then preparing. This was music to the ears of a hardline faction in the CIA headed by counterintelligence chief James Jesus Angleton, who had been warning his superiors of much the same thing for years. Golytsin became a much-prized star.

In November 1963, President Kennedy was assassinated, apparently by a left-winger, with a Russian wife, called Lee Harvey Oswald, who had once defected to the USSR and lived there for over a year. In January 1964, Yuri Nosenko defected. He declared he had been Oswald's case officer in Russia and that the KGB had found Oswald to be a pain in the neck, had severed all contact with him, and had had nothing to do with the Kennedy slaying.

Golytsin, supported by Angleton, at once denounced his fellow Russian, who was interrogated extremely harshly but refused to change his story. The dispute tore the Agency into two camps for years and rumbled on for two decades. Depending on the outcome of the question of who was right and who was wrong, careers were made and broken, for it is axiomatic that the careers of those behind a major success will start to rise.

In the case of Pyotr Orlov, there was no such hostile action to be found, and the glory fell upon Calvin Bailey, the head of Special Projects, the office that had brought him in.

The day after Joe Roth began to share his life with Colonel Orlov in Virginia, Sam McCready quietly entered the portals of the British Museum, which was located in the heart of Bloomsbury, and headed for the great circular reading room under its domed cupola.

There were two younger men with him, Denis Gaunt, on whom McCready was putting an increasing degree of trust and reliance, and another man called Patten. Neither of the backup team would see the face of Keepsake—they did not need to, and it might have been dangerous. Their job was simply to idle near the entrances while perusing the laid-out newspapers and ensure that their desk head would not be disturbed by interlopers.

McCready made for a reading table largely enclosed by bookshelves and courteously asked the man already seated there if he minded the intrusion. The man, his head bowed over a volume from which he took occasional notes, silently gestured to the chair opposite and went on reading. McCready waited quietly. He had selected a volume he wished to read, and in a few moments one of the reading room staff brought it to him and as quietly left. The man across the table kept his head bowed.

When they were alone McCready spoke. "How are you, Nikolai?"

"Well," murmured the man, making a note on his pad.

"There is news?"

"We are to receive a visit next week. At the *Rezidentsia*."

"From Moscow Center?"

"Yes. General Drozdov himself."

McCready made no sign. He kept reading his book, and his lips hardly moved. No one outside the enclave of book-lined shelves could have heard the low murmur, and no one would enter the enclave. Gaunt and Patten would see to that. But he was amazed by the name. Drozdov, a short chunky man who bore a startling resemblance to the late President Eisenhower, was the head of the Illegals Directorate and rarely ventured outside the USSR. To come into the lion's den of London was most unusual and could be very important.

"Is that good or bad?" he asked.

"I don't know," said Keepsake. "It's certainly odd. He is

not my direct superior, but he could not come unless he had
cleared it with Kryuchkov.''

(General Vladimir Kryuchkov, since 1988 Chairman of the
KGB, was then Head of the First Chief Directorate, the
foreign intelligence arm.)

''Will he discuss with you his illegals planted in Britain?''

''I doubt it. He likes to run his illegals direct. It may be
something to do with Orlov. There has been the most almighty
stink over that. The two other GRU officers in the delegation
are under interrogation already. The best they will get is a
court martial for negligence. Or maybe . . .''

''Is there another reason for his coming?''

Keepsake sighed and raised his eyes for the first time.
McCready stared back. He had become a friend of the Russian
over the years, trusted him, believed in him.

''It's just a feeling,'' said Keepsake. ''He may be checking
out the *Rezidentsia* over here. Nothing concrete, just an odor
on the wind. Maybe they suspect something.''

''Nikolai, it cannot go on forever. We know that. Sooner or
later, the pieces will add together. Too many leaks, too many
coincidences. Do you want to come out now? I can arrange
it. Say the word.''

''Not yet. Soon perhaps, but not yet. There is more I can
send. If they really start to pull the London operation apart, I
will know they have something. In time. In time to come out.
But not yet. By the way, please do not intercept Drozdov. If
there *are* suspicions, he would see it as another straw in the
wind.''

''Better tell me what he is coming as, in case of a genuine
accident at Heathrow,'' said McCready.

''A Swiss businessman,'' said the Russian. ''From Zurich.
British Airways, Tuesday.''

''I'll ensure he is left completely alone,'' said McCready.
''Anything on Orlov?''

''Not yet,'' said Keepsake. ''I know of him, never met him.
But I'm surprised at him defecting. He had the highest clearance.''

''So do you,'' said McCready. The Russian smiled.

''Of course. No accounting for taste. I will find out what I
can about him. Why does he interest you?''

''Nothing concrete,'' said McCready. ''As you said, an

odor on the wind. The manner of his coming, giving Joe Roth no time to check. For a sailor jumping ship, it's normal. For a colonel of the KGB, it's odd. He could have done a better deal."

"I agree," said the Russian. "I'll do what I can."

The Russian's position inside the embassy was so delicate that face-to-face meetings were hazardous, therefore infrequent. The next was set up at a small and seedy cafe in Shoreditch, London's East End. Early in the following month, May.

At the end of April, the Director of Central Intelligence had a meeting in the White House with the President. Nothing unusual in that; they met extremely regularly, either with others in the National Security Council or in private. But on this occasion the President was unusually flattering about the CIA. The gratitude that a number of agencies and departments had directed toward the Agency as a result of information stemming from the Ranch in southern Virginia had reached as high as the Oval Office.

The DCI was a hard man whose career went back to the days of the OSS in the Second World War, and he was a devoted colleague of Ronald Reagan. He was also a fair man and saw no reason to withold the general praise from the Head of Special Projects responsible for bringing in Colonel Orlov. When he returned to Langley, he summoned Calvin Bailey.

Bailey found the Director at the picture windows that occupy almost one side of the DCI's office on top of the CIA headquarters building. He was staring out toward the valley, where the wash of green trees in spring leaf had finally obscured the winter view of the Potomac River. When Bailey entered, he turned with an expansive smile.

"What can I say? Congratulations are in order, Cal. The Navy Department loves it, says keep it coming. The Mexicans are delighted; they just wrapped up a network of seventeen agents, cameras, communication radios, the works."

"Thank you," said Calvin Bailey carefully. He was known as a cautious man, not given to overt displays of human warmth.

"Fact is," said the DCI, "we all know Frank Wright is

retiring at the end of the year. I'm going to need a new DDO. Maybe, Calvin, just maybe I think I know who it ought to be."

Bailey's morose shrouded gaze flashed into a rare smile. In the CIA the Director himself is always a political appointment and has been for three decades. Under him come the two main divisions of the Agency: Operations, headed by the Deputy Director Ops (DDO), and Intelligence (analysis), headed by the Deputy Director Intel (DDI). These two posts are the highest to which a professional can reasonably aspire. The DDO is in charge of the entire information gathering side of the Agency, while the DDI is in charge of analyzing the raw information into presentable and usable intelligence.

Having delivered his bouquet, the DCI turned to more mundane matters. "Look, it's about the Brits. As you know, Margaret Thatcher was over."

Calvin Bailey nodded. The close friendship between the British Prime Minister and the U.S. President was known to all.

"She brought with her Sir Christopher. . . ." The DCI mentioned the name of the then chief of the British SIS. "We had several good sessions. He gave us some really good product. We owe them, Cal. Just a favor. I'd like to clean the slate. They have two beefs. They say they're very grateful for all the Minstrel product we've been sending over, but they point out that as regards Soviet agents being run in England, so far it's useful material but all code-names. Can Minstrel recall any actual names, or offices held—something to identify a hostile agent in their own pond?"

Bailey thought it over.

"He's been asked before," he said. "We've sent the Brits everything that remotely concerns them. I'll ask him again, have Joe Roth see if he can remember a real name. Okay."

"Fine, fine," said the DCI. "One last thing. They keep asking for access. Over there. This time around, I'm prepared to indulge them. I think we can go that far."

"I'd prefer to keep him over here. He's safe here."

"We can keep him safe over there. Look, we can put him on an American air base. Upper Heyford, Lakenheath, Alconbury. Whatever. They can see him, talk to him under supervision, then we bring him back."

"I don't like it," said Bailey.

"Cal—" there was a hint of steel in the DCI's voice—"I've agreed to it. Just see to it."

Calvin Bailey drove down to the Ranch for a personal talk with Joe Roth. They talked in Roth's suite of rooms above the central portico of the Ranch house. Bailey found his subordinate tired and drawn. Debriefing a defector is a tiring business, involving long hours with the defector followed by long nights spent working through the next day's line of questioning. Relaxing is not usually on the menu, and when, as often happens, the defector has established a personal relationship with his chief debriefing officer, it is not easy to give that officer time off and replace him with a substitute.

"Washington is pleased," Bailey told him. "More than pleased—delighted. Everything he says checks out. Soviet Army, Navy, and Air Force deployments, confirmed by other sources of satellite coverage. Weapons levels, readiness states, the Afghan mess—Pentagon loves it all. You've done well, Joe. Very well."

"There's still a long way to go," said Roth. "Lots more still to come. There must be. The man's an encyclopedia. Phenomenal memory. Sometimes stuck for a detail, but usually recalls it sooner or later. But . . ."

"But what? Look, Joe, he's pulling apart years of patient KGB work in Central and South America. Our friends down there are closing down network after network. It's okay. I know you're tired. Just keep at it."

He went on to tell Roth of the hint the DCI had given him about the forthcoming vacancy as Deputy Director Operations. He was not usually a confiding man, but he saw no reason not to give his subordinate the same kind of boost the DCI had given him.

"If it goes through, Joe, there'll be a second vacancy, head of Special Projects. My recommendation will count for a lot. It'll be for you, Joe. I wanted you to know that."

Roth was grateful but not ecstatic. He seemed more than tired. There was something else on his mind.

"Is he causing problems?" asked Bailey. "Has he got everything he wants? Does he need female company? Do you? It's isolated down here. It's been a month. These things can be arranged."

He knew Roth was divorced and single. The Agency has a legendary divorce rate. As they say at Langley, it comes with the territory.

"No, I've offered him that. He just shook his head. We work out together. It helps. Run through the woods until we can hardly stand. I've never been in such good shape. He's older, but he's fitter. That's one of the things that worries me, Calvin. He's got no flaws, no weaknesses. If he got drunk, screwed around, got maudlin for thinking about his homeland, lost his temper—"

"You've tried to provoke him?" asked Bailey. Provoking a defector into a rage, an outburst of pent-up emotions, can sometimes work as a release, a therapy. According to the in-house psychiatrists, anyway.

"Yes. I've taunted him with being a rat, a turncoat. Nothing. He just ran me into the ground and laughed at me. Then he got on with what he calls "the job." Blowing away KGB assets worldwide. He's a total pro."

"That's why he's the best we've ever had, Joe. Don't knock it. Be grateful."

"Calvin, that's not the main reason he bugs me. As a guy, I like him. I even respect him. I never thought I would respect a defector. But there's something else. He's holding something back."

Calvin Bailey went very quiet and very still. "The polygraph tests don't say so."

"No, they don't. That's why I can't be sure I'm right. I just feel it. There's something he's not saying."

Bailey leaned across and stared hard into Roth's face. An awful lot hung on the question he was about to ask.

"Joe, could there be any chance, in your considered view, that despite all the tests, he might still be a phony, a KGB plant?"

Roth sighed. What had been troubling him had finally come out.

"I don't know. I don't think so, but I don't *know*. For me, there's a ten-percent area of doubt. A gut feeling that he's holding something back. And I can't work out, if I'm right, why."

"Then find out, Joe. Find out," said Calvin Bailey. He did not need to point out that if there was anything phony about

Colonel Pyotr Orlov, two careers in the CIA were likely to go straight into the trash can. He rose.

"Personally I think it's nonsense, Joe. But do what you have to do."

Roth found Orlov in his living room, lying on a settee, listening to his favorite music. Despite the fact that he was virtually a prisoner, the Ranch was equipped like a well-appointed country club. Apart from his daily runs in the forest, always flanked by four of the young athletes from Quantico, he had acess to the gymnasium, the sauna and pool, an excellent chef, and a well-stocked bar that he used sparingly.

Soon after arriving, he had admitted to a taste for the ballad singers of the sixties and early seventies. Now, whenever he visited the Russian, Roth was accustomed to hearing Simon and Garfunkel, the Seekers, or the slow honeyed tones of Elvis Presley coming from the tape deck.

That evening when he walked in, the clear childlike voice of Mary Hopkin was filling the room. It was her one famous song. Orlov jackknifed himself off the settee with a grin of pleasure. He gestured at the tape deck.

"You like it? Listen."

Roth listened. " 'Those were the days, my friend, we thought they'd never end. . . .' "

"Yeah, it's nice," said Roth, who preferred traditional and mainstream jazz.

"You know what it is?"

"That British girl, isn't it?" said Roth.

"No, no—not the singer, the tune. You think it is British tune, yes? From the Beatles, perhaps."

"Guess so," said Roth, now also smiling.

"Wrong," said Orlov triumphantly. "It is old Russian song. *Dorogoy dlinnoyu da nochkoy lunayu.* 'By a long road on a moonlit night.' You didn't know that?"

"No, I certainly didn't."

The jaunty little tune ran to its end, and Orlov switched off the tape.

"You want we should talk some more?" asked Orlov.

"No," said Roth. "I just stopped by to see if you were okay. I'm going to turn in. It's been a long day. By the way, we are going back to England soon. Let the Limeys have a chance to talk to you for a little while. All right by you?''

Orlov frowned. ''My deal was to come here. Only here.''

''It's okay, Peter. We'll be staying for a short while on an American Air Force base. To all intents and purposes, still in America. I'll be there to protect you from the big bad Brits.''

Orlov did not smile at the joke.

Roth became serious. ''Peter, is there a reason you don't want to go back to England? Something I should know?''

Orlov shrugged. ''Nothing specific, Joe. Just gut feeling. The farther I am away from the USSR, the safer I feel.''

''Nothing will happen to you in England. I give you my word. You going to turn in now?''

''I stay up for a while. Read, play music,'' said the Russian.

In fact, the light burned in Orlov's room until half-past one in the morning. When the KGB assassination team struck, it was a few minutes before three.

Orlov was told later that they had silenced two guards on the perimeter with powerful crossbows, traversed the lawn at the rear of the house undetected, and entered the house via the kitchens.

On the upper floor, the first Roth or Orlov heard was a burst of submachine-gun fire from the lower hall, followed by the rapid pounding of feet up the stairs. Orlov awoke like a cat, came out of his bed, and was across the living room in no more than three seconds. He opened the door to the landing and caught a brief glimpse of the night duty guard from Quantico swerving off the landing and down the main stairs. A figure in a black cat–suit and ski mask, halfway up the stairs, loosed a brief burst. The American took the blast in the chest. He sagged against the banister, his front a wash of blood. Orlov slammed his door and turned back toward the bedroom.

He knew his windows would not open; there was no escape that way. Nor was he armed. He entered the bedroom as the man in black ran through the door from the corridor, followed by an American. The last thing Orlov saw before he slammed his bedroom door shut was the KGB assassin turn and blast the American behind him. The killing gave Orlov time to throw the lock.

But it was only a respite. Seconds later, the lock was blasted away and the door kicked open. By the dim light shining in from the corridor beyond the living room, Orlov saw the KGB man throw down his empty machine-pistol and pull a Makarov 9mm automatic from his belt. He could not see the face behind the mask, but he understood the Russian word and the contempt with which it was uttered.

The figure in black gripped the Makarov two-handed, pointed it straight at Orlov's face, and hissed, "*Predatel!*" Traitor.

There was a cut-glass ashtray on the bedside table. Orlov had never used it, since unlike most Russians, he did not smoke. But it was still there. In a last gesture of defiance, he swept it off the table and sent it spinning toward the Russian killer's face. As he did so he yelled back, "*Padla!*" Scum.

The man in black side-stepped the heavy glassware that was scything toward his face. It cost him a fraction of a second. In that time the Quantico security-team leader stepped into the living room and fired twice with his heavy Colt .44 Magnum at the black-suited back in the bedroom doorway. The Russian was thrown forward as the front of his chest exploded in a welter of blood that sprayed the sheets and the coverlet on the bed. Orlov stepped forward to kick the Makarov from the falling man's hand, but there was no need. No one stops two Magnum shells and keeps fighting.

Kroll, the man who had fired, crossed the sitting room to the bedroom door. He was white with rage and panting.

"You okay?" he snapped. Orlov nodded. "Someone fucked up," said the American. "There were two of them. Two of my men are down, maybe more outside."

A shaken Joe Roth came in, still in pajamas.

"Jesus, Peter, I'm sorry. We have to get out of here. Now. Fast."

"Where do we go?" asked Orlov. "I thought you said this was a safe house." He was pale but calm.

"Yeah, well, apparently not safe enough. Not anymore. We'll try and find out why later. Get dressed. Pack your things. Kroll, stay with him."

There was an army base only twenty miles from the Ranch. Langley fixed things with the army commander. Within two hours Roth, Orlov, and the remainder of the Quantico team had taken an entire floor of the bachelors' quarters building. Military police ringed the block. Roth would not even drive there by road; they went by helicopter, setting down right on the lawn by the Officers' Club and waking everyone up.

It was only temporary housing. Before nightfall, they had moved on to another CIA safe house, in Kentucky and much better protected.

While the Roth/Orlov group was in the army base, Calvin Bailey returned to the Ranch. He wanted a full report. He had already spoken to Roth by phone to hear his version of events. He listened to Kroll first, but the man whose evidence he really wanted was the Russian in the black ski mask who had confronted Orlov at point-blank range.

The young officer of the Green Berets was nursing a bruised wrist where Orlov had kicked the gun from his hand as he fell. The special-effects blood had long been wiped off him, and he had changed out of the black jumpsuit with the two holes in the front and removed the harness containing the tiny charges and sacs of realistic blood that had burst all over the bed.

"Verdict?" asked Bailey.

"He's for real," said the Russian-speaking officer. "Either that, or he doesn't care whether he lives or dies. That I doubt. Most men do."

"He didn't suspect you?" asked Bailey.

"No, sir. I saw it right in his eyes. He believed he was going to die. He just went right on fighting. Quite a guy."

"Any other choices?" asked Bailey.

The officer shrugged. "Only one. If he's a phony and thought he was being liquidated by his own side, he ought to have yelled something to that effect. Assuming he cares about living, that would make him about the bravest guy I ever met."

"I think," Bailey said to Roth by telephone later, "that we have our answer. He's okay, and that's official. Try and get him to recall a name—for the Brits. You're flying over next Tuesday, military executive jet, to Alconbury."

Roth spent two days with Orlov at their new home, going back over the sparse details the Russian had already provided from his days in the Illegals Directorate concerning Soviet agents planted in Britain. As he had specialized in Central and South America, Britain had not been his primary concern. But he racked his memory all the same. All he could recall were code-names. Then at the end of the second day, something came back to him.

A civil servant in the Ministry of Defense in Whitehall. But the money was always paid into the man's account at the Midland Bank in Croydon High Street.

"It's not a lot," said the man from the Security Service, MI-5, when he was given the news. He was sitting in the office of Timothy Edwards at the headquarters of his sister service, the SIS. "He might have moved long since. Might have banked under a false name. But we'll try."

He went back to Curzon Street in Mayfair and set the wheels in motion. British banks do not have the right of absolute confidentiality, but they decline to hand out details of private accounts to just anybody. One institution that always secures their cooperation, by law, is the Inland Revenue.

The Inland Revenue agreed to cooperate, and the manager of the Midland in Croydon High Street, an outer suburb of south London, was interviewed in confidence. He was new to the job, but his computer was not.

A Security Service man sitting with the real Inland Revenue inspector took over. He had a list of every civil servant employed by the Ministry of Defense and its many out-stations over the past decade. Surprisingly, the chase was very quick. Only one MOD civil servant banked at the Midland in Croydon High Street. The records of the accounts were sent for. The man had two, and still lived locally. He had a checking account and a higher-rate savings account.

Over the years a total of £20,000 had been paid into his deposit account, always by him and always in cash and fairly regularly. His name was Anthony Milton-Rice.

The Whitehall conference that evening involved the Director General and Deputy Director General of MI-5 and the Assistant Commissioner of the Metropolitan Police in charge of Special Branch. MI-5 in Britain cannot make arrests—only the police can do that. When the Security Service wants someone picked up, the Special Branch is called in to do the honors. The meeting was chaired by the Chairman of the Joint Intelligence Committee. He started the questioning.

"Who exactly is Mr. Milton-Rice?"

The Deputy Director of MI-5 consulted his notes. "Grade-two civil servant on the staff of the Procurement Office."

"Pretty low grade?"

"Sensitive work, though. Weapons systems, access to evaluations of new armaments."

"Mm," mused the Chairman. "So what do you want?"

"The point is, Tony," said the Director General, "we have very little to go on. Unexplained payments over a period of years into his account—not enough to hold him, let alone get a conviction. He could plead that he backs the horses, always on track, gets his cash that way. Of course, he might confess. Then again, he might not."

The policeman nodded his agreement. Without a confession, he would have a bad time trying to persuade the Crown Prosecution Office even to bring a case. He doubted the man who had denounced Milton-Rice, whoever he might be, would ever appear in court as a witness.

"We'd like to shadow him first," said the Director General. "Around the clock. If he makes one contact with the Russians, he's in the bag, with or without a confession."

It was agreed. The watchers, that elite team of MI-5 agents who—on their own turf, at least—are reckoned by all the Western services to be the best tailers in the world, were put on alert to envelop Anthony Milton-Rice the following morning as he approached the Defense Ministry with an invisible surveillance for twenty-four hours in every day.

Anthony Milton-Rice, like so many people with a regular job, had regular habits. He was a man of routine. On workdays he left his house in Addiscombe precisely at ten to eight and walked the half-mile to East Croydon Station—unless it was raining heavily, in which case the bachelor civil servant took a bus. He boarded the same commuter train every day, flashed his season ticket, and rode into London, descending at Victoria Station. From there, it was a short bus ride down Victoria Street to Parliament Square. There he got off and crossed Whitehall to the ministry building.

The morning after the conference about him, he did exactly

the same. He did not notice the group of youths who boarded at Norwood Junction. He noticed them when they entered his open-plan carriage, jammed with other commuters. There were screams from the women and shouts of alarm from the men as the teenagers, engaged in an orgy of casual robbery and assault called "steaming," swept through the carriage snatching women's handbags and jewelry, demanding men's wallets at knifepoint, and threatening anyone who seemed to oppose, let alone resist, them.

As the train hissed into the next station up the line, the crowd of two dozen young thugs, still screaming their rage at the world, quit the train and scattered, jumping the barrier and disappearing into the streets of Crystal Palace, leaving behind them hysterical women, badly shaken men, and frustrated Transport Police. No arrests were made—the outrage had been too fast and unforeseen.

The train was delayed, wreaking havoc on the commuter schedules as other trains backed up behind it, while Transport Police boarded to take statements. It was only when they tapped the commuter in the pale-gray raincoat dozing in the corner on his shoulder that the man toppled slowly forward onto the floor. There were further screams as the first blood from the thin stiletto wound to his heart began to seep from beneath the crumpled figure. Mr. Anthony Milton-Rice was very dead.

Ivan's Café, appropriately named for a meeting with a Russian, was situated in Crondall Street in Shoreditch, and Sam McCready, as always, arrived second, even though he had been the first in the street outside. The reason was that if anyone was being tailed, it would more likely be Keepsake than him. So he always sat for thirty minutes in his car, watched the Russian make the meet, then gave it another fifteen minutes to see if the asset from the Soviet Embassy had suddenly grown a tail.

When McCready entered Ivan's, he took a cup of tea from the counter and wandered over to the wall where two tables were side by side. Keepsake occupied the one in the corner and was engrossed in *Sporting Life*. McCready unfolded his *Evening Standard* and proceeded to study it.

"How was the good General Drozdov?" he asked quietly,

his voice lost in the babble of the café and the hissing of the tea urn.

"Amiable and enigmatic," said the Russian, studying the form of the horses in the three-thirty at Sandown. "I fear he may have been checking us out. I will know more if K-Line decide to visit, or if my own K-Line man gets hyperactive."

K-Line is the KGB's internal counterintelligence and security branch, charged not so much with espionage as with keeping a check on other KGB men and looking for internal leaks.

"Have you ever heard of a man called Anthony Milton-Rice?" asked McCready.

"No. Never. Why?"

"You didn't run him out of your *Rezidentsia*? A civil servant in the Ministry of Defense?"

"Never heard of him. Never handled his product."

"Well, he's dead now. Too late to ask him who did run him. If anyone did. Could he have been run directly from Moscow through the Illegals Directorate?"

"If he was working for us, that's the only explanation," muttered the Russian. "He never worked for us in PR-Line. Not out of the London Station. As I say, we never even handled such product. He must have communicated with Moscow via a case officer based here outside the embassy. Why did he die?"

McCready sighed. "I don't know."

But he did know that unless it was a remarkable coincidence, someone had to have set it up. Someone who knew the civil servant's routines, could brief the thugs on his regular train, his appearance—and pay them off. Possibly Milton-Rice had not even worked for the Russians at all. Then why the denunciation? Why the unaccounted-for money? Or perhaps Milton-Rice had indeed spied for Moscow but via a cut-out, unknown to Keepsake, who in turn reported directly back to the Illegals Directorate in Moscow. And General Drozdov had just been in town. And he *ran* the Illegals. . . .

"He was denounced," said McCready. "To us. And then he was dead."

"Who denounced him?" asked Keepsake. He stirred his tea, though he had no intention of drinking the sweet, milky mixture.

"Colonel Pyotr Orlov," said McCready quietly.

"Ah," said Keepsake in a low murmur. "I have something for you there. Pyotr Alexandrovitch Orlov is a loyal and dedicated KGB officer. His defection is as phony as a three-dollar bill. He is a plant, a disinformation agent. And he is well-prepared and very good."

Now that, thought McCready, is going to cause problems.

Chapter 3

Timothy Edwards listened carefully. McCready's narration and evaluation lasted thirty minutes. When he had finished, Edwards asked calmly, "And you are quite certain you believe Keepsake?"

McCready had expected this question. Keepsake had worked for the British for four years since he had first approached an SIS officer in Denmark and offered his services as an "agent-in-place," but this was a world of shadows and suspicions. There was always the possibility, however remote, that Keepsake might be a "double," his true loyalties still with Moscow. It was precisely the accusation he now made of Orlov.

"It's been four years," said McCready. "For four years Keepsake's product has been tested against every known criterion. It's pure."

"Yes, of course," said Edwards smoothly. "Unfortunately, if one word of this leaked to our Cousins, they would say exactly the opposite—that *our* man was lying and theirs was for real. The word is, Langley is deeply enamored of this Orlov."

"I don't think they should be told about Keepsake," retorted McCready. He was very protective of the Russian in the embassy in Kensington Palace Gardens. "Besides, Keepsake feels his time may be coming to an end. He has an instinct that suspicions are growing in Moscow that they have a leak somewhere. If they become convinced, it will only be a matter of time before they home in on their London Station. When Keepsake finally comes in from the cold, we can come clean with the Cousins. For the moment, it could be very dangerous to widen the circle who know."

Edwards made his decision.

"Sam, I agree. But I'm going to see the Chief on this one. He's up at the Cabinet Office this morning. I'll catch him later. Stay in touch."

During the lunch hour, which Edwards spent eating a sparse meal with the Chief in Sir Christopher's top-floor suite of offices, a military version of the Grumman Gulfstream III landed at the USAF base at Alconbury, situated just north of the market town of Huntingdon in the county of Cambridgeshire. It had taken off at midnight from the Air National Guard base in Trenton, New Jersey, its passengers having arrived from Kentucky and boarded under the cover of darkness and away from the air-base buildings.

In picking Alconbury, Calvin Bailey had chosen well. The base was the home of the 527 "Aggressor" Squadron of the USAF, whose pilots fly F-5 fighters with a very specific role. They are called the Aggressors because the F-5 has a configuration similar to the Russian MIG-29 and the Aggressors play the role of attacking Soviet fighters in midair combat practice with their fellow American and British jet-jockeys. They themselves study and are adept at all the Soviet air-battle tactics, and they so sink themselves into their role that they constantly talk Russian to each other when aloft. Their guns and rockets may be so adapted as to score only electronic hits and misses, but the rest—insignia, flight suits, maneuvers, and jargon—is all pure Russian.

When Roth, Orlov, Kroll, and the rest descended from the Grumman, they were outfitted in the flight suits of the Aggressor Squadron. They passed through unnoticed and were soon ensconced in a single-story building, set aside from the rest, and equipped with living quarters and kitchen, conference rooms, and one elctronically bugged room for the debriefing of Colonel Orlov. Roth had a talk with the base commander, and the British team was cleared to be allowed onto the base the following morning. Then somewhat jet-lagged, the American party turned in to get some sleep.

McCready's phone rang at three P.M. and Edwards asked to see him again.

"Proposals accepted and agreed," said Edwards. "We back our judgment that Keepsake is telling the truth and that the Americans have themselves a disinformation agent. That said, the problem is that whatever Orlov is here for, we don't know yet. It seems that for the moment he is producing good product, which makes it unlikely our Cousins would believe us—the more so as the Chief agrees that we cannot reveal the existence, let alone the identity, of Keepsake. So how do you suggest we handle it?"

"Let me have him," said McCready. "We have right of access. We can ask questions. Joe Roth is in charge, and I know Joe. He's no fool. Maybe I can push Orlov, push him hard, before Roth cries 'Enough.' Sow some seeds of doubt. Get the Cousins to begin to contemplate the notion that he may not be all he seems."

"All right," said Edwards. "You take it."

He made it sound like his own decision, his own act of magnanimity. The reality of his lunch with the Chief, who would be retiring at the end of the year, had been quite different. The ambitious Assistant Chief, who prided himself on his excellent personal relationship with the CIA, had in mind that one day Langley's approval of him could be a useful aid to his appointment as Chief.

During the lunch, Edwards had proposed a far less skilled but less abrasive debriefer than Sam McCready to handle the matter of Keepsake's embarrassing denunciation of the CIA's new treasure. He had been overruled. Sir Christopher, a former colleague in the field, had insisted that the Deceiver whom he had himself appointed be in charge of handling Orlov.

McCready set off for Alconbury by car early the following morning. Denis Gaunt drove. Edwards had cleared McCready's request that Gaunt sit in on the interrogation of the Russian. In the back of the car sat a woman from MI-5. The

Security Service had asked urgently that they too have someone at the meetings with the Russian, since a specific line of questioning would cover the area of Soviet agents working in and against Britain. Alice Daltry was in her early thirties, pretty, and very bright. She still seemed rather overawed by McCready. In their tight, closed world, despite the need-to-know principle, word had leaked of the previous year's Pankratin affair.

The car also contained a secure telephone. Looking like an ordinary car phone but larger, it could be switched to encrypted mode to communicate with London. There might well be points emerging from the talk with Orlov that would need to be checked with London.

For much of the journey McCready sat silently, staring through the windshield at the unfolding countryside in the early morning, marveling again at the beauty of England in the spring.

He ran his mind back over what Keepsake had told him. In London, according to the Russian, he had been marginally associated years earlier with the first preparatory stages for a deception operation of which Orlov could only be the final fruition. It had been code-named Project Potemkin.

An ironic title, thought McCready, a hint of KGB gallows humor. It almost certainly had been named not after the battleship *Potemkin*—nor even after Marshal Potemkin, whose name had been bestowed on the battleship—but after the Potemkin Villages.

Years ago, the Empress Catherine the Great, as ruthless a dictator as long-suffering Russia had ever endured, visited the newly conquered Crimea. Fearful of letting her see the shivering, huddled masses in their freezing shacks, her chief minister, Potemkin, had sent carpenters, plasterers, and painters ahead of her route to construct and paint handsome facades of clean, sturdy cottages with smiling, waving peasants in the windows. The shortsighted old queen was delighted by the picture of rural bliss and returned to her palace. Later, laborers dismantled the facades to reveal again the miserable shantytowns behind them. These deceptions were called Potemkin Villages.

"The target is the CIA," Keepsake had said. He did not know who the exact victim would be or how the sting would be accomplished. The project was not then being handled directly by his department, which had been asked only for peripheral assistance.

"But this has to be Potemkin coming into operation at last," he had said. "The proof will be in two parts. No information provided by Orlov will ever actually produce massive and irreversible damage to Soviet interests. Second, you will see an enormous loss of morale taking place inside the CIA."

At the moment, the latter was certainly not the case, mused McCready. Recovering from the undoubted embarrassment of the Urchenko affair, his American friends were riding high, largely due to their newfound asset. He determined to concentrate on the other area.

At the main gate of the air base, McCready offered an identification card (not in his real name) and asked for Joe Roth on a certain phone extension. Minutes later, Roth appeared in an Air Force jeep.

"Sam, good to see you again."

"Nice to see you back, Joe. That was quite a vacation you took."

"Hey, I'm sorry. I was given no choice, no chance to explain. It was a question of take the guy and run, or throw him back."

"That's okay," said McCready easily. "All has been explained. All is smoothed over. Let me present my two colleagues."

Roth reached into the car and shook hands with Gaunt and Daltry. He was relaxed and effusive. He foresaw no problems and was glad the Brits would be sharing in the goodies. He cleared the whole party with the Guard Commander, and they drove in line across the base to the isolated block where the CIA team was housed.

Like many service buildings, it was no architectural gem, but it was functional. A single corridor divided its entire length, from which doors led off to sleeping rooms, an eating room, kitchens, toilets, and conference rooms. A dozen Air Force police ringed the building, guns visible.

McCready glanced around before entering. He noted that while he and his two colleagues had excited no attention, many of the USAF personnel passing by stared curiously at the circle of armed guards.

"All they've managed to do," he muttered to Gaunt, "is identify the bloody place to any KGB team with a set of binoculars."

Roth led them to a room in the center of the block. Its windows were closed and shuttered; the only illumination was electric. Easy chairs formed a comfortable group around a coffee table in the center of the room; straight chairs and tables ringed the walls, for the note-takers.

Roth genially gestured to the British party to take the easy chairs and ordered some coffee.

"I'll go get Minstrel," he said, "unless you guys want to shoot the breeze first."

McCready shook his head. "Might as well get on with it, Joe."

When Roth was out, McCready nodded to Gaunt and Daltry to take chairs by the wall. The message was: Watch and listen, miss nothing. Joe Roth had left the door open. From down the corridor, McCready heard the haunting melody of "Bridge over Troubled Waters." The sound stopped as someone switched off the tape deck. Then Roth was back. He ushered into the room a chunky, tough-looking man in running shoes, slacks, and a polo sweater.

"Sam, let me present Colonel Pyotr Orlov. Peter, this is Sam McCready."

The Russian stared at McCready with expressionless eyes. He had heard of him. Most high-ranking officers of the KGB had by then heard of Sam McCready. But he gave no sign. McCready crossed the central carpet, his hand outstretched.

"My dear Colonel Orlov. I am delighted to meet you," he said with a warm smile.

Coffee was served, and they seated themselves, McCready facing Orlov, Roth to one side. On a side table a tape machine started to turn. There were no microphones on the coffee table. They would have been a distraction. As it was, the tape machine would miss nothing.

McCready began gently, flatteringly, and kept it up for the first hour. Orlov's answers came fluently and easily. But after the first hour McCready became more and more perplexed, or so it seemed.

"It's all very fine, wonderful stuff," he said. "I just have this tiny problem—well, I'm sure we all do. Everything you have given us is code-names. We have Agent Wildfowl somewhere in the Foreign Office; Agent Kestrel, who may be a serving officer in the Navy or a civilian working for the Navy. My problem, you see, Colonel, is that nothing could actually lead to a detection or an arrest."

"Mr. McCready, as I have explained many times, here and in America, my period in the Illegals Directorate was over four years ago, and I specialized in Central and South America. I did not have access to the files of agents in Western Europe, Britain, or America. These were heavily protected, as I am sure they are here."

"Yes, of course, silly of me," said McCready. "But I was thinking more of your time in Planning. As we understand it, that entails preparing cover stories, 'legends' for people about to be infiltrated or just recruited. Also, systems for making contact, passing information—paying off agents. It involves the banks they use, the sums paid, the periods payments are made, the running costs. All this you seem to have—forgotten."

"My time in Planning was even before my time in Illegals Directorate," retorted Orlov. "Eight years ago. Bank accounts are in eight-figure numbers, it is impossible to recall them all."

There was an edge to his voice. He was getting annoyed. Roth had begun to frown.

"Or even one number," mused McCready as if thinking aloud, "or even one bank."

"Sam." Roth leaned forward urgently. "What are you driving at?"

"I am simply trying to establish whether anything Colonel Orlov has given you or us over the past six weeks will really do massive and irreversible damage to Soviet interests."

"What are you talking about?" It was Orlov, on his feet, plainly angry. "I have given hour after hour of details of Soviet military planning, deployments, weapons levels, readiness states, personalities. Details of the Afghan afffair. Networks in Central and South America that have now been dismantled. Now you treat me like . . . like a criminal."

Roth was on his feet, too.

"Sam, could I have a word with you? Privately. Outside."

He made for the door. Orlov sat down again and stared disconsolately at the floor. McCready rose and followed Roth. Daltry and Gaunt remained at their tables, fixated. The young CIA man by the tape machine turned it off. Roth did not stop walking until he had reached the open grassland outside the building. Then he turned to McCready.

"Sam, what the hell do you think you're doing?"

McCready shrugged. "I'm trying to establish Orlov's bona fides," he said. "That's what I'm here for."

"Let's get this absolutely straight," said Roth tightly. "You are not, as in 'not,' here to establish Minstrel's bona fides. That has already been done. By us. Over and over again. We are satisfied that he is genuine, doing his best to recall what he can. You are here, as a concession from the DCI, to share in Minstrel's product. That's all."

McCready stared dreamily at the waving fields of young wheat beyond the perimeter fence.

"And what do you think that product is really worth, Joe?"

"A lot. Just what he said: Soviet military deployments, postings, weapons levels, plans—"

"Which can all be changed," murmured Sam, "quite quickly and easily. Provided they know what he's telling you."

"And Afghanistan," said Roth.

McCready was silent. He could not tell his CIA colleague what Keepsake had told him in the café twenty-four hours earlier, but he could hear in his mind's ear the murmuring voice from beside him.

"Sam, this new man in Moscow, Gorbachev. You know little about him, as yet. But I know him. When he was here to visit Mrs. Thatcher, before he became General Secretary, when he was just a Politburo member, I handled his security arrangements. We talked. He is unusual, very open, very frank. This perestroika *he talks about, this* glasnost. *You know what these will mean, my friend? In two years, by 1988, maybe 1989, all these military details won't matter anymore. He is not going to attack across the Central German Plain. He is really going to try and restructure the whole Soviet economy and society. He will fail, of course, but he will try. He will pull out of Afghanistan, pull back from Europe. All*

that this Orlov is telling the Americans will be for the archives in two years. But the Big Lie, when it comes—that will be important. For a decade, my friend. Wait for the Big Lie. The rest is calculated minor sacrifice by the KGB. They play good chess, my former colleagues."

"And the networks of agents in South America," said Roth. "Dammit—Mexico, Chile, and Peru are delighted. They've rolled up scores of Soviet agents."

"All locally recruited help," said McCready. "Not an ethnic Russian among them. Tired, clapped-out networks, greedy agents, low-level informants. Disposable."

Roth was staring at him hard.

"My God," he breathed, "you think he's phony, don't you? You think he's a double. Where did you get that, Sam? Do you have a source, an asset, that we don't know about?"

"Nope," said McCready flatly. He did not like to lie to Roth, but orders were orders. In fact, the CIA always received Keepsake's product, but disguised and attributed to seven different sources.

"I just want to push him hard. I think he's holding something back. You're no fool, Joe. I believe that in your deepest heart, you have the same impression."

That shaft went home. In his secret heart, that was exactly what Roth still thought. He nodded.

"All right. We'll ride him hard. He hasn't come here for a vacation, after all. And he's tough. Let's go back."

They resumed at a quarter to twelve. McCready returned to the question of Soviet agents in Britain.

"One I have already given you," said Orlov. "If you can detect him. The man they called Agent Juno. The one who banked in Croydon, at the Midland."

"We have traced him," said McCready evenly. "His name is, or rather was, Anthony Milton-Rice."

"So there you are," said Orlov.

"What do you mean, *was?*" queried Roth.

"He's dead."

"I didn't know," said Orlov. "It has been several years."

"That's another of my problems," said McCready sadly. "He didn't die several years ago. He died yesterday morning. Murdered, liquidated, just an hour before we could get the surveillance team around him."

There was a stunned silence. Then Roth was on his feet again, absolutely outraged. They were back outside the building again in two minutes.

"What the fuck do you think you're playing at, Sam?" he shouted. "You could have told me."

"I wanted to see Orlov's reaction," said Sam bluntly. "I thought if I told you, you might break the news yourself. Did you see his reaction?"

"No, I was watching you."

"There wasn't one," said McCready. "I would have thought he'd be pretty stunned. Worried, even. Bearing in mind the implications."

"He's got nerves of steel," said Roth. "He's a total pro. If he doesn't want to show anything, he doesn't. Is it true, by the way? Is the man dead? Or was it a ploy?"

"Oh, he's dead all right, Joe. Knifed by one of a gang of teenagers on his way to work. We call it 'steaming'; you call it 'wilding.' Which gives us a problem, doesn't it?"

"It could have leaked at the British end."

McCready shook his head. "No time. It took time to set up a killing like that. We only had the man's real identity the night before last, after twenty-four hours of detective work. They got him yesterday morning. No time. Tell me, what happens to Minstrel's product?"

"First to Calvin Bailey, direct, by hand. Then the analysts. Then the customers."

"When did Orlov produce the product about the spy in our Defense Ministry?"

Roth told him.

"Five days," mused McCready. "Before it reached us. Time enough. . . ."

"Now just hang in there a minute," protested Roth.

"Which gives us three choices," McCready continued. "Either it was a remarkable coincidence, and in our job we can't afford to believe too many of them. Or someone between you and the teletype operator leaked. Or it was set up in advance. I mean, the killing was prepared for a specific hour on a specific day. A certain number of hours before that time, Orlov had a rush of memory. Before the good guys could get their act together, the denounced agent was dead."

"I don't believe we have a leak in the Agency," said Roth tightly. "And I don't believe Orlov is a phony."

"Then why isn't he coming clean? Let's go back to him," suggested Sam gently.

When they returned, Orlov was subdued. The news that the British spy he had denounced had been so conveniently liquidated had evidently shaken him. In a change of tone, McCready spoke very gently.

"Colonel Orlov, you are a stranger in a strange land. You have anxieties about your future. So you wish to keep certain things back, for insurance. We understand that. I would do the same if I were in Moscow. We all need insurance. But Joe here informs me that your standing with the Agency is now so high, you need no more insurance. Now, are there any other real names you can offer us?"

There was utter silence in the room. Slowly, Orlov nodded. There was a general exhalation of breath.

"Peter," said Roth coaxingly, "this really is the time to bring them out."

"Remyants," said Pyotr Orlov, "Gennadi Remyants."

Roth's exasperation was almost visible. "We know about Remyants," he said. He looked up at McCready. "Washington-based representative of Aeroflot. That's his cover. The FBI picked him up and turned him two years ago. Been working for us ever since."

"No," said Orlov and raised his gaze. "You are wrong. Remyants is *not* a double. His exposure was arranged by Moscow. His pickup was deliberate. His turning was phony. Everything he provides has been carefully doctored by Moscow. It will cost America millions to repair the damage one day. Remyants is a KGB major of the Illegals Directorate. He runs four separate Soviet networks in mainland U.S.A. and knows all the identities."

Roth whistled. "If that is true, then it is real pay dirt. *If* it is true."

"Only one way to find out," suggested McCready. "Pick Remyants up, fill him full of Pentothal, and see what falls out. And I do believe it is the lunch hour."

"That's two good ideas in ten seconds," admitted Roth. "Guys, I have to go down to London to talk with Langley. Let's take a break for twenty-four hours."

*   *   *

Joe Roth got his link direct to Calvin Bailey at eight P.M. London time, three o'clock in Washington. Roth was buried deep in the cipher room below the U.S. Embassy in Grosvenor Square; Bailey was in his office in Langley. They were speaking in clear voices, their tones slightly tinny because of the encrypting cipher technology through which both voices had to pass to cross the Atlantic with security.

"I spent the morning with the Brits up at Alconbury," said Roth. "Their first meet with Minstrel."

"How did it go?"

"Badly."

"You're joking. Ungrateful bastards. What went wrong?"

"Calvin, the debriefer was Sam McCready. He's not anti-American, and he's no fool. He believes Minstrel is a phony, a plant."

"Well, bullshit to that. Did you tell him how many tests Minstrel has passed? That we are satisfied he's okay?"

"Yes, in detail. He sticks with his view."

"He produce any hard evidence for this fantasy?"

"No. Said it was the result of the British analysis of Minstrel's product."

"Jesus, that's crazy. Minstrel's product over a mere six weeks has been great. What's McCready's beef?"

"We covered three areas. On Minstrel's military product, he said Moscow could change it all, as long as they knew what Minstrel was telling us, which they would if they had sent him."

"Crap. Go on."

"On Afghanistan he was silent. But I know Sam. It was as if he knew something I didn't but wouldn't say what it was. All I could get out of him was a 'suppose.' He hinted the Brits thought Moscow might pull out of Afghanistan quite soon. That all Minstrel's stuff on Afghanistan would be for the archives if that happened. Do we have any such analysis?"

"Joe, we have no evidence the Russkies intend to pull out of Kabul, soon or ever. What else didn't satisfy Mr. McCready?"

"He said he thought the Soviet networks rolled up in Central and South America were tired networks—*clapped-out* was the word he used—and all locally recruited help with not an ethnic Russian among them.''

"Look, Joe, Minstrel has blown away a dozen networks run by Moscow in four countries down there. Sure the agents were locally recruited. They've been interrogated—not very pleasantly, I'll admit. Naturally, they were all run out of the Soviet embassies. A dozen Russian diplomats are being sent home in disgrace. He's smashed up years of KGB work down there. McCready's talking crap.''

"He did have one point. All Minstrel has given the Brits concerning Soviet agents over here are code-names. Nothing to identify a single Russian asset here. Except one, and he's dead. You heard about that?''

"Sure. Rotten luck. A miserable coincidence.''

"Sam thinks it's no coincidence. Thinks either Minstrel knew it was slated for a certain day and released his identification too late for the Brits to get their man, or we have a leak.''

"Bullshit to both.''

"He favors the first option. Thinks Minstrel works for Moscow Center.''

"Mr. Sam Smartass McCready offer you any hard evidence for this?''

"No. I asked him specifically if he had an asset inside Moscow who had denounced Minstrel. He denied it. Said it was just his people's analysis of the product.''

There was silence for a while, as if Bailey were deep in thought. Which he was. Then: "Did you believe his denial?''

"Frankly, no. I think he was lying. I suspect they're running someone we know nothing about.''

"Then why don't the Brits come clean?''

"I don't know, Calvin. If they have an asset who has denounced Minstrel, they're denying it.''

"Okay, listen, Joe. You tell Sam McCready from me, he has to put up or shut up. We have a major success in Minstrel, and I'm not about to let a sniping campaign out of Century House wreck it all. Not without hard evidence, and I mean really hard. Understood, Joe?''

"Loud and clear.''

"One other thing: Even if they have been tipped off that Orlov is phony, that would be standard Moscow Center practice. Moscow lost him, we got him, the Brits' noses were put out of joint. Of course Moscow would leak to the Brits that our triumph was hollow and useless. And the Brits would be susceptible to that scam because of their annoyance at not getting Minstrel to themselves. So far as I am concerned, the British tipoff is disinformation. If they have a man, it's their man who is lying. Ours is on the level.''

"Right, Calvin. If it arises again, can I tell Sam that?"

"Absolutely. That is Langley's official view, and we'll defend it.''

Neither man bothered to recall that by now the vindication of Orlov was linked to both their rising careers.

"Sam had one success," said Joe Roth. "He came at Minstrel hard and strong—I had to pull him out of there twice—but he got Minstrel to come up with a new name. Gennadi Remyants.''

"We run Remyants," retorted Bailey. "I've had his product coming across my desk for two years.''

Roth went on to reveal what Orlov had said about Remyants's true loyalties to Moscow and McCready's suggestion that the simple way to clear the whole thing up would be to pick up Remyants and break him.

Bailey was silent. Finally he said, "Maybe. We'll think it over. I'll talk to the DDO and the Bureau. If we decide to go with that one, I'll let you know. In the meantime, keep McCready away from Minstrel. Give them both a break.''

Joe Roth invited McCready to join him for breakfast the following morning at Roth's apartment, an invitation Mc-Cready accepted.

"Don't worry about it," said Roth. "I know there are some fine hotels nearby, and Uncle Sam can afford breakfast for two, but I make a pretty mean breakfast myself. Juice, eggs over easy, waffles, coffee suit you?''

McCready laughed down the phone. "Juice and coffee will do fine.''

When he arrived, Roth was in the kitchen, an apron over his shirt, proudly demonstrating his talent with ham and eggs. McCready weakened and took some.

"Sam, I wish you'd revise your opinion about Minstrel," said Roth over the coffee. "I spoke with Langley last night.''

"Calvin?"

"Yep."

"His reaction?"

"He was saddened by your attitude."

"Saddened, my butt," said McCready. "I'll bet he used some nice old-fashioned Anglo-Saxon language about me."

"Okay, he did. Not pleased. Figures we gave you a generous break on Minstrel. I have a message. Langley's view is this: We got Minstrel. Moscow is mad as hell. Moscow tries to discredit Minstrel by feeding London a skillful line on how Minstrel is really a Moscow plant. That's Langley's view. Sorry, Sam, but on this one you're wrong. Orlov is telling the truth."

"Joe, we're not complete fools over here. We are not going to fall for some Johnny-come-lately piece of disinformation like that. *If* we had some information, the source of which we could not divulge—which we do not—it would have to predate Orlov's defection."

Roth put down his coffee cup and stared at McCready open-mouthed. The distorted language had not fooled him for a minute.

"Jesus, Sam, you *do* have an asset somewhere in Moscow. For Christ's sake, come clean!"

"Can't," said Sam. "And we don't, anyway. Have someone in Moscow we haven't told you about."

Strictly speaking, he was not even lying.

"Then I'm sorry, Sam, but Orlov stays. He's good. Our view is that your man—the one who doesn't exist—is lying. It's you, not us, who's been taken for an awful ride. And that's official. Orlov has passed three polygraph tests, for God's sake. That's proof enough."

For answer, McCready produced a slip of paper from his breast pocket and laid it in front of Roth. It read:

We discovered that there were some East Europeans who could defeat the polygraph at any time. Americans are not very good at it because we are raised to tell the truth, and when we lie, it is easy to tell we are lying. But we find a lot of Europeans . . . can handle the polygraph without a blip. . . . There is an occasional individual who lives in that part of the world who has spent his life lying about one thing or another and therefore becomes so good at it that he can pass the polygraph test."

Roth snorted and tossed the paper back. "Some half-assed academic with no experience of Langley," he said.

"Actually," said McCready mildly, "it was said by Richard Helms two years ago."

Richard Helms had been a legendary Director of Central Intelligence. Roth looked shaken. McCready rose.

"Joe, one thing Moscow has always longed for is to have the Brits and the Yanks fighting like Kilkenny cats. That's exactly what we're heading for, and Orlov's only been in the country forty-eight hours. Think about it."

In Washington, the DCI and the FBI had agreed that to see if there was truth in Orlov's statement about Remyants, the only way to prove it was to pick him up. The planning took place through the day that Roth and McCready had their breakfast, and the arrest was fixed for the same evening, when Remyants left the Aeroflot office in downtown Washington, about five P.M. local time, long after dark in London.

The Russian emerged from the building a little after five and walked down the street, then cut across a pedestrian mall to where he had left his car.

The Aeroflot offices had been under surveillance, and Remyants was unaware of the six FBI agents, all armed, who moved in behind him as he crossed the mall. The agents intended to make the arrest as the Russian got into his car. It would be done quickly and discreetly. No one would notice.

The mall contained a series of paths between ragged and litter-strewn lawns, and various benches that had been intended for the good citizens of Washington to sit on while taking the sun or eating their brown-bag lunches. The city fathers could not have known that the small park would become a meeting place for drug pushers and their customers to score. On one of the benches, as Remyants crossed the mall toward the parking lot, a black man and a Cuban were negotiating a deal. Each dealer had backup men close by.

The fight was triggered by a scream of rage from the Cuban, who rose and pulled a knife. One of the black man's bodyguards drew a handgun and shot him down. At least eight others from the two gangs pulled weapons and fired at their opponents. The few noninvolved civilians nearby screamed and scattered. The FBI agents, stunned for a second by the suddenness of it all, reacted with their Quantico training, dropped, rolled, and drew their guns.

Remyants took a single soft-nosed bullet in the back of the head and toppled forward. His killer was shot at once by an FBI agent. The two gangs—the blacks and the Cubans—scattered in different directions. The whole firefight took seven seconds and left two men dead, one Cuban and the Russian killed in the crossfire.

The American way of doing things is very technology-dependent, and it is sometimes criticized for this; but no one can deny the results when the technology is working at peak.

The two dead men were removed to the nearest morgue, where the FBI took control. The handgun used by the Cuban went for forensic analysis but offered no clues. It was an untraceable Czech Star, probably imported from Central or South America. The Cuban's fingerprints gave better harvest. He was identified as Gonzalo Appio, and he was already on file with the FBI. Cross-checking by computer speedily revealed that he was also known to the Drug Enforcement Administration and the Metro–Dade Police Department covering Miami.

He was known as a drug dealer and contract hit man. Earlier in his miserable life he had been one of the *Marielitos*, those Cubans so generously "liberated" by Castro when he dispatched from the port of Mariel to Florida every criminal, psychopath, pederast, and low-life clogging up his prisons and asylums, and America was duped into taking them.

The only thing not proved about Appio, though suspected by the FBI, was that he was really a gunman for the DGI, Cuba's KGB-dominated secret police. The evidence was based on Appio's believed involvement in the slaying of two prominent and effective anti-Castro broadcasters who were working out of Miami.

The FBI passed the file to Langley, where it caused deep concern. It was the DDO, Frank Wright, who went over Bailey's head and spoke to Joe Roth in London.

"We need to know, Joe. Now, fast. If there is any substance to the British reservations about Minstrel, we need to know.

Gloves off, Joe. Lie-detector, the works. Get up there, Joe, and find out why things keep going wrong.''

Before he left for Alconbury, Roth saw Sam McCready again. It was not a happy meeting. He was bitter and angry.

"Sam, if you know something, really *know* something, you have got to come clean with me. I'm holding you responsible if we have made a bad mistake here, because you won't level with us. We've leveled with you. Now come clean—what have you got?''

McCready stared at his friend blank-faced. He had played too much poker to give away anything that he did not want to. He was in a dilemma. Privately, he would have liked to tell Joe Roth about Keepsake, given him the hard evidence he needed to lose his faith in Orlov. But Keepsake was walking a very tight wire indeed, and strand by strand that wire was soon going to be cut away by Soviet counterintelligence, as soon as they got the bit between their teeth, convinced they had a leak somewhere in Western Europe. He could not, dare not, blow away Keepsake's existence, let alone his rank and position.

"You have a problem, Joe," he said. "Don't blame me for it. I've gone as far as I can go. I think we both agree Milton-Rice might have been a coincidence, but not both.''

"There could have been a leak over here," said Roth, and regretted it.

"No way," said McCready calmly. "We'd have to have known time and place for the hit in Washington. We didn't. It's either Orlov setting them up by prearrangement, or it's on your side. You know what I think; it's Orlov. By the by, how many on your side have access to the Orlov product?''

"Sixteen," said Roth.

"Jesus. You could have taken an ad in the *New York Times*.''

"Me, two assistants, tape-deck operators, analysts—it mounts up. The FBI knew about the Remyants pickup, but not Milton-Rice. Sixteen would have known about both—in time. I'm afraid we have a loose nut—probably low level, a clerk, cryptographer, secretary.''

"And *I* think you have a phony defector.''

"Whatever, I'm going to find out.''

"Can I come?'' asked Sam.

"Sorry, buddy, not this time. This is CIA business now. In-house. See you, Sam."

Colonel Pyotr Orlov noticed the change in the people around him as soon as Roth arrived back at Alconbury. Within minutes, the jocular familiarity had vanished. The CIA staff within the building became withdrawn and formal. Orlov waited patiently.

When Roth took his place opposite him in the debriefing room, two aides wheeled in a machine on a trolley. Orlov glanced at it. He had seen it before. The polygraph. His eyes went back to Roth.

"Something wrong, Joe?" he asked quietly.

"Yes, Peter, something very wrong."

In a few brief sentences Roth informed the Russian of the fiasco in Washington. Something flickered in Orlov's eyes. Fear? Guilt? The machine would find out.

Orlov made no protest as the technicians fitted the disks to his chest, wrists, and forehead. Roth did not operate the machine—there was a technician for that—but he knew the questions he wanted to ask.

The polygraph looks and performs something like an electrocardiograph found in any hospital. It records heart rate, pulse, sweating—any symptom normally produced by someone telling lies while under pressure, and the mental pressure is exercised simply by the experience of being tested.

Roth began as always with simple questions designed to establish a response norm. The fine pen drifted lazily over the rolling paper in gentle rises and falls. Three times Orlov had been so tested, and three times he had produced no noticeable symptoms as of a man lying. Roth asked him about his background, his years in the KGB, his defection—the information he had given so far.

Then he went for the hard ones. "Are you a double agent working for the KGB?"

"No."

The pen kept drifting slowly up and down.

"Is the information you have given so far truthful?"

"Yes."

"Is there any last vital information you have not given us?"

Orlov was silent. Then he gripped the arms of his chair. "No."

The fine pen swerved violently up and down several times before settling. Roth glanced at the operator and got a nod of confirmation. He rose, crossed to the machine, glanced at the paper, and told the operator to switch it off.

"I'm sorry, Peter, but that was a lie."

There was silence in the room. Five people gazed at the Russian, who was looking at the floor. Finally, he raised his eyes.

"Joe, my friend, can I speak to you? Alone? Really alone? No microphones—just you and me?"

It was against the rules, and a risk. Roth thought it over. Why? What did this enigmatic man who had failed the lie-detector test for the first time want to say that even security-cleared staff were not to hear? He nodded abruptly.

When they were alone, all the technology disconnected, he said, "Well?"

The Russian gave a long, slow sigh.

"Joe, did you ever wonder at the manner of my defection? The speed? Not giving you a chance to check with Washington?"

"Yes, I did. I asked you about it. Frankly, I was never completely satisfied with the explanations. Why did you defect that way?"

"Because I didn't want to end like Volkov."

Roth sat as if he had been punched in the belly. Everyone in the "business" knew of the disastrous Volkov case. In early September 1945, Konstantin Volkov, apparently Soviet Vice-Consul in Istanbul, Turkey, turned up at the British Consulate-General and told an astonished official that he was really the deputy head of the KGB in Turkey and wanted to defect. He offered to blow away 314 Soviet agents in Turkey and 250 in Britain. Most vital of all, he said, there were two British diplomats in the Foreign Office working for Russia and another man high in the British Secret Intelligence Service.

The news was sent to London while Volkov returned to his consulate. In London the matter was given to the head of the Russian Section. This agent took the necessary steps and flew out to Istanbul. The last that was seen of Volkov was a heavily bandaged figure being hustled aboard a Soviet transport plane bound for Moscow, where he died after hideous torture in the Lubyanka. The British Head of the Russian Section had arrived too late—not surprisingly, for he had informed Moscow from his London base. His name was Kim Philby, the very Soviet spy whom Volkov's evidence would have exposed.

"What exactly are you saying to me, Peter?"

"I had to come over the way I came because I knew I could trust you. You were not high enough."

"Not high enough for what?"

"Not high enough to be him."

"I'm not following you, Peter," said Roth, though he was.

The Russian spoke slowly and clearly, as if liberating himself from a long-held burden.

"For seventeen years the KGB has had a man inside the CIA. I believe that by now he has risen very high."

Chapter 4

Joe Roth lay on his cot in his bedroom in the isolated building on Alconbury field and wondered what to do. A task that six weeks earlier had appeared fascinating and likely to advance his career by leaps and bounds had just turned into a nightmare.

For forty years, since its creation in 1948, the CIA had had one obsessive concern: to keep itself pure from the infiltration of a Soviet "mole." To this end billions of dollars had been spent in counterintelligence precautions. All staff had been checked and checked again, given lie-detector tests, questioned, vetted, and vetted again.

And it had worked. While the British had been rocked in the early fifties by the treachery of Philby, Burgess, and Maclean, the Agency had remained pure. The Philby affair had rumbled on as the ousted British SIS man had eked out a living in Beirut until his final departure to Moscow in 1963, but the Agency had remained clean.

When France was shaken by the Georges Paques affair and Britain again by George Blake in the early sixties, the CIA stayed unpenetrated. Through all of that time, the counterintelligence arm of the Agency, the Office of Security, had been headed by a remarkable man, James Jesus Angleton, a lonely, secretive, and obsessive man who lived and breathed for one thing: to keep the Agency free from Soviet infiltration.

Finally, Angleton had fallen victim to his own innate suspicions. He began to believe that despite his efforts, there really *was* a mole loyal to Moscow inside the CIA. Despite all the tests and all the vetting, he became convinced that a traitor had somehow gotten in. His reasoning seemed to be, "If there isn't a mole, there ought to be. So there must be; so there is." The hunt for the suspected "Sasha" took up more and more time and effort.

The paranoid Russian defector Golytsin, who held the KGB responsible for everything bad on the planet, agreed.

This was music to Angleton's ears. The hunt for Sasha was stepped up. Rumor began that his name started with K. Officers whose name started with K found their lives being pulled apart. One resigned in disgust; others were dismissed because they could not prove their innocence—a prudent move, perhaps, but not very good for morale, which slumped. For ten more years, from 1964 to 1974, the hunt went on. Finally, Director William Colby had had enough. He eased Angleton into retirement.

The Office of Security passed into other hands. Its duties to keep the Agency free of Soviet penetration continued, but at a lower and less aggressive tenor.

Ironically, the British, having gotten rid of their older-generation ideological traitors, suffered no more spy scandals from within their intelligence community. Then the pendulum seemed to swing. America, so free of traitors since the late forties, suddenly produced a rash of them—not ideologues, but wretches prepared to betray their country for money. Boyce, Lee, Harper, Walker, and finally Howard had been inside the CIA and betrayed American agents working in their native Russia. Denounced by Urchenko before his bizarre redefection, Howard had managed to slip away to Moscow before he could be arrested. The affairs of Howard's treachery and Urchenko's redefection, both the previous year, had left the Agency with a very red face.

But all this was as nothing compared with the potential effect of Orlov's claim. If it was true, the manhunt alone could tear the Agency apart. If it was true, the damage assessment would take years—the realignment of thousands of agents, codes, foreign networks, and alliances would last for a decade and cost millions. The reputation of the Agency would be badly damaged for years to come.

The question that raged through Roth's mind as he tossed the night away was, "Who the hell can I go to?"

Just before dawn, he made up his mind, rose, dressed, and packed a suitcase. Before leaving he looked in on Orlov, who was sound asleep, and said to Kroll, "Look after him for me. No one enters, no one leaves. That man has just become incredibly valuable."

Kroll did not understand why, but he nodded. He was a man who followed orders and never questioned why.

Roth drove to London, avoided the embassy, went to his apartment, and took a passport in a name other than his own. He secured one of the last seats on a private British carrier to Boston and connected at Logan Airport into Washington National. Even with the five-hour time saving, it was dusk when he drove a rented car into Georgetown, parked, and walked down K Street to the far end, close to the campus of Georgetown University.

The house he sought was a fine building of red brick, distinguished from others near it only by extensive security systems that scanned the street and all approaches to it. He was intercepted as he crossed the road toward the portico, and he flashed his CIA pass. At the door he asked to see the man he had come for, was told he was at dinner, and asked that a message be passed. Minutes later, he was admitted and shown into a paneled library redolent of leatherbound books and a hint of cigar. He sat and waited. Then the door opened, and the Director of Central Intelligence entered.

Though he was not accustomed to receiving youthful and relatively junior CIA staffers at his home, except on a summons, he seated himself in a leather club chair, gestured Roth to sit opposite him, and quietly asked for the meaning of the visit. Carefully, Roth told him.

The DCI was over seventy, an unusual age for the post, but he was an unusual man. He had served with the OSS in World War II, running agents into Nazi-occupied France and the Low Countries. After the war, with the OSS disbanded, he had returned to private life, taking over a small factory from his father and building it to a huge conglomerate. When the CIA had been formed to succeed the OSS, he had been offered a chance to join by the first Director, Allen Dulles, but had declined.

Years later, a wealthy man and a major contributor to the Republican party, he had noticed and attached himself to a rising ex-actor who was running for the governorship of California. When Ronald Reagan won the White House, he had asked his trusted friend to take over the CIA.

The DCI was a Catholic, long widowed, and a strict moral puritan, and he was known in the corridors of Langley as a tough old bastard. He rewarded talent and intelligence, but his passion was loyalty. He had known good friends go to the torture chambers of the Gestapo because they had been betrayed, and betrayal was the one thing he would not tolerate under any circumstances. For traitors, he had only a visceral loathing. For them, in the mind of the DCI, there could be no mercy.

He listened carefully to Roth's narration, staring at the gas log fire where no flame burned on such a warm night. He gave no sign of what he felt, save a tightening of the muscles around the dewlapped jaw.

"You came straight here?" he asked when Roth finished. "You spoke to no one else?"

Roth explained how he had come, like a thief in the night into his own country, on a false passport, by a circuitous route. The old man nodded; he had once slipped into Hitler's Europe like that. He rose and went to fill a tumbler from the brandy decanter on the antique side-table, pausing to tap Roth reassuringly on the shoulder.

"You did well, my boy," he said. He offered brandy to Roth, who shook his head. "Seventeen years, you say?"

"According to Orlov. All my own superior officers, right up to Frank Wright, have been with the Agency that long. I didn't know who else to come to."

"No, of course not."

The DCI returned to his chair and sat lost in thought. Roth did not interrupt.

Finally the old man said, "It has to be the Office of Security. But not the Chief. No doubt he's totally loyal, but he's a twenty-five-year man. I'll send him on vacation. There's a very bright young man who works as his deputy. Ex-lawyer. I doubt if he's been with us more than fifteen.''

The DCI summoned an aide and caused several phone calls to be made. It was confirmed the deputy Head of the Office of Security was forty-one and had joined the Agency from law school fifteen years earlier. He was summoned from his home in Alexandria. His name was Max Kellogg.

"Just as well he never worked under Angleton," said the DCI. "His name begins with K."

Max Kellogg, flustered and apprehensive, arrived just after midnight. He had been about to go to bed when the call came, and he was stunned to hear the DCI himself on the line.

"Tell him," said the DCI. Roth repeated his story.

The lawyer took it all in without blinking, missed nothing, asked two supplementary questions, took no notes. Finally he asked the DCI: "Why me, sir? Harry's in town?"

"You've only been with us fifteen years," said the DCI.

"Ah."

"I have decided to keep Orlov—Minstrel, whatever we call him—at Alconbury," said the DCI. "He's probably as safe there, even safer, than back over here. Stall the British, Joe. Tell them Minstrel has just come up with more information of only U.S. interest. Tell them their access will be resumed as soon as we've checked it out.

"You'll fly in the morning"—he checked his watch—"this morning by designated flight straight to Alconbury. No holds barred now. Too late for that. The stakes are too high. Orlov will understand. Take him apart. I want it all. I want to know two things, fast. Is it true, and if so, who?

"As of now, you two work for me—only for me. Report direct. No cut-outs. No questions. Refer them to me. I'll handle things at this end."

The light of combat was in the old man's eyes again.

Roth and Kellogg tried to get some sleep on the Grumman from Andrews back to Alconbury. They were still ragged and tired when they arrived. The west-east crossing is always the worst. Fortunately, both men avoided alcohol and drank only water. They hardly paused to wash and brush up before going to Colonel Orlov's room.

As they entered Roth heard the familiar tones of Art Garfunkel coming from the tape deck.

Appropriate, thought Roth grimly. We *have* come to talk with you again. But this time there will be no sounds of silence.

But Orlov was cooperation itself. He seemed resigned to the fact that he had now divulged the last piece of his precious "insurance." The price of the bride had been offered in full. The only question was whether it would be acceptable to the suitors.

"I never knew his name," he said in the debriefing room. Kellogg had elected to have the microphones and tape recorders switched off. He had his own portable recorder and backed it up with his own handwritten notes. He wanted no other tape to be copied, no other CIA staff present. The technicians had been sent away; Kroll and two others guarded the passage beyond the now-soundproofed door. The technicians' last job had been to sweep the room for bugs and declare it clean. They were plainly puzzled by the new regimen.

"I swear to that. He was known only as Agent Sparrowhawk, and he was run personally by General Drozdov."

"Where and when was he recruited?"

"I believe in Vietnam in '68 or '69."

"Believe?"

"No, I know it was Vietnam. I was with Planning, and we had a big operation down there, mainly in and around Saigon. Locally recruited help was Vietnamese, of course, Viet Cong; but we had our own people. One of them reported that the Viet Cong had brought him an American who was dissatisfied. Our local *Rezident* cultivated the man and turned him. In late 1969 General Drozdov personally went to Tokyo to talk with the American. That was when he was code-named Sparrowhawk."

"How do you know this?"

"There were arrangements to be made, communication links set up, funds to be transferred. I was in charge."

They talked for a full week. Orlov recalled banks into which sums had been paid over the years, and the months (if not the actual days) on which these transfers were made. The sums increased as the years passed, probably to account for promotion and better product.

"When I moved to the Illegals Directorate and came directly under Drozdov, my association with Case Sparrowhawk continued. But I was not now concerned with bank transfers. It was more operational. If Sparrowhawk gave us an agent working against us, I would inform the appropriate department, usually Executive Action—known as 'wet affairs'—and they would liquidate the hostile agent if he was out of our territory or pick him up if he was inside. We got four anti-Castro Cubans that way."

Max Kellogg noted everything and reran his tapes through the night. Finally he said to Roth, "There is only one career that fits all these allegations. I don't know whose it is, but the records will prove it. It's a question of cross-checking now. Hours and hours of cross-checking. I can only do that in Washington, in the Central Registry. I have to go back."

He flew the following day, spent five hours with the DCI in his Georgetown mansion, then closeted himself with the records. He had carte blanche, on the personal orders of the DCI. No one dared deny Kellogg anything. Despite the secrecy, word began to spread through Langley. Something was up. There was a flap going on, and it had to do with internal security. Morale began to flag. These things can never be kept truly quiet.

At Golders Hill in North London there is a small park, an adjunct to the much larger Hampstead Heath, that contains a menagerie of deer, goats, ducks, and other wildfowl. McCready met Keepsake there on the day Max Kellogg flew back to Washington.

"Things are not so good at the embassy," said Keepsake. "The K-Line man, on orders from Moscow, has started asking for files that go back years. I think a security investigation, probably of all our embassies in Western Europe, has been started. Sooner or later, it will narrow to the London embassy."

"Is there anything we can do to help?"

"Possibly."

"Suggest it," said McCready.

"It would help if I could give them something really useful—some good news about Orlov, for example."

When a defector-in-place like Keepsake changes sides, it
would be suspicious if he produced no information for the
Russians year after year. So it is customary for his new
masters to give him some genuine intelligence to send home
to prove what a fine fellow he is.

Keepsake had already given McCready the name of every
real Soviet agent in Britain that he knew about, which was
most of them. The British had clearly not picked them all
up—that would have given the game away. Some had been
shifted away from classified material, not in an obvious manner but slowly, in the course of "administrative" changes.
Some had been promoted in rank but been moved out of the
handling of secret matters. Some had had the material crossing their desks doctored so that it would do more harm than
good.

Keepsake had even been allowed to recruit a few new agents
to prove his worth to Moscow. One of these was a clerk in the
Central Registry of the SIS itself, a man utterly loyal to Britain
but who would pass on what he was told. Moscow had been
quite delighted by the recruitment of Agent Wolverine. It was
agreed that two days later, Wolverine would pass to Keepsake
a copy of a draft memorandum in Denis Gaunt's hand to the
effect that Orlov was now ensconced at Alconbury, where the
Americans had fallen for him hook, line, and sinker—and so
had the British.

"How are things with Orlov?" inquired Keepsake.

"Everything has gone quiet," said McCready. "I had one
half-day with him, got nowhere. I think I sowed some seeds
of doubt in Joe Roth's mind, there and in London. He went
back to Alconbury, talked again with Orlov, then shot off
back to the States on a different passport. He thought we
hadn't spotted him. Seemed in a hell of a hurry. Hasn't
reappeared—at least, not through a regular airport. May have
flown direct into Alconbury on a military flight."

Keepsake stopped tossing crumbs to the ducks and turned
to McCready. "They have talked to you since, invited you
back to resume?"

"No. It's been a week. Total silence."

"Then he has produced the Big Lie, the one he came to produce. That is why the CIA is involved within themselves."

"Any idea what it could be?"

Keepsake sighed. "If I were General Drozdov, I would think like a KGB man. There are two things the KGB has always lusted after. One is to start a major war between the CIA and the SIS. Have they started fighting you?"

"No, they are being very polite. Just noncommunicative."

"Then it is the other. The other dream is to tear the CIA apart from the inside. Destroy its morale. Set colleague against colleague. Orlov will denounce someone as a KGB agent inside the CIA. It will be an effective accusation. I warned you; Potemkin is a long-planned affair."

"How will we spot him if they don't tell us?"

Keepsake began to stroll back to his car. He turned and called over his shoulder, "Look for the man to whom the CIA suddenly grows cold. That will be the man, and he will be innocent."

Edwards was aghast.

"Let Moscow know that Orlov is now based at Alconbury? If Langley ever finds out, there'll be a war. Why in heaven's name do that?"

"A test. I believe in Keepsake. I'm convinced he's genuine. I trust him. So I think Orlov is phony. If Moscow does not react, makes no attempt to harm Orlov, that will be the proof. Even the Americans will believe that. They'll be angry, of course, but they'll see the logic."

"And if by any chance they attack and kill Orlov? You're going to be the one to tell Calvin Bailey?"

"They won't," said McCready. "As night follows day, they won't."

"By the way, he's coming here. On vacation."

"Who?"

"Calvin. With wife and daughter. There's a file on your desk. I'd like the Firm to offer him some hospitality. A couple of dinners with people he'd like to meet. He's been a good friend of Britain over the years. Least we can do."

Glumly, McCready stumped downstairs and looked at the file. Denis Gaunt sat opposite him.

"He's an opera buff," said McCready, reading from the

file. "I suppose we can get him tickets for Covent Garden, Glyndebourne, that sort of thing."

"Jesus, I can't get into Glyndebourne," said Gaunt enviously. "There's a seven-year waiting list."

The magnificent country mansion in the heart of Sussex, set amid rolling lawns and containing one of the country's finest opera houses, was and remains a most sought-after treat for any opera lover on a summer's evening.

"You like opera?" asked McCready.

"Sure."

"Fine. You can mother-hen Calvin and Mrs. Bailey while they're here. Get tickets for the Garden and Glyndebourne. Use Timothy's name. Pull rank, swing it. This miserable job must have some perks, though I'm damned if I ever get any."

He headed for lunch. Gaunt grabbed the file.

"When's he due?" he asked.

"In a week," called McCready from the door. "Call him up. Tell him what you're fixing. Ask what his favorites are. If we're going to do it, let's do it right."

Max Kellogg shut himself inside the archives and lived there for ten days. His wife in Alexandria was told he was out of town and believed it. Kellogg had his food sent in, but he mainly survived on a diet of coffee and too many filter kings.

Two archive clerks were at his personal disposal. They knew nothing of his investigation but simply brought him the files he wanted, one after the other. Photographs were dug out of files long buried as being of little further use or relevance. Like all covert agencies, the CIA never threw anything away, however obscure or outdated; one never knew whether someday that tiny detail, that fragment of newsprint or photograph, might be needed. Many were needed now.

Halfway through his investigation, two agents were dispatched to Europe. One visited Vienna and Frankfurt; the other, Stockholm and Helsinki. Each carried identification as an agent of the Drug Enforcement Administration and a personal letter from the Secretary of the Treasury asking for the cooperation of a major bank in each city. Aghast at the thought that it was being used to launder drug money, each bank conferred among its directors and opened its files.

Tellers were summoned from their desks and shown a

photograph. Dates and bank accounts were quoted. One teller could not remember; the other three nodded. The agents took receipt of photocopies of accounts, sums deposited, transfers made. They took away samples of signatures in a variety of names for graphology analysis back at Langley. When they had what they came for, they returned to Washington and put their trophies on the desk of Max Kellogg.

From an original group of more than twenty CIA officers who had served in Vietnam in the relevant period—and Kellogg had expanded the time frame to include a period of two years on either side of the dates quoted by Orlov—the first dozen were quickly eliminated. One by one, the others went out of the frame.

Either they were not in the right city at the right time, or they could not have divulged a certain piece of information because they never knew it, or they could not have made a certain rendezvous because they were on the other side of the world. Except one.

Before the agents arrived back from Europe, Kellogg knew he had his man. The evidence from the banks merely confirmed it. When he was ready, when he had it all, he went back to the house of the DCI in Georgetown.

Three days before he went, Calvin and Mrs. Bailey with their daughter, Clara, flew from Washington to London. Bailey loved London; in fact, he was a staunch anglophile. It was the history of the place that enthused him.

He loved to visit the old castles and stately mansions built in a bygone era, to wander the cool cloisters of ancient abbeys and seats of learning. He installed himself in a Mayfair apartment that the CIA retained for the housing of visiting VIPs, rented a car, and went to Oxford, avoiding the motorway and meandering instead through the byways, taking lunch in the sun at The Bull at Bisham, whose oak beams were set before Queen Elizabeth I was born.

On his second evening, Joe Roth stopped by for a drink. For the first time he met the remarkably plain Mrs. Bailey and Clara, a gawky child of eight with straight plaits of ginger hair, eyeglasses, and buck teeth. He had never met the Bailey family before; his superior was not the sort of man one associated with bedtime stories and barbecues on the lawn.

But the frostiness of Calvin Bailey seemed to have mellowed, though whether it was the fact of enjoying an extended vacation among the operas, concerts, and art galleries that he so admired, or the prospect of promotion, Roth could not tell.

He wanted to tell Bailey of the strain caused by Orlov's bombshell, but the DCI's orders had been adamant. No one, not even Calvin Bailey, the Head of Special Projects, was to be allowed to know—yet. When the Orlov accusation had been either shown to be false, or had been justified with hard evidence, the top echelon of the officers who ran the CIA would be personally briefed by the DCI himself. Until then, silence. Questions were asked, but none answered, and certainly nothing was volunteered. So Joe Roth lied.

He told Bailey the debriefing of Orlov was progressing well but at a slower pace. Naturally, the product Orlov remembered most clearly had already been divulged. Now it was a question of dragging smaller and smaller details from his memory. He was cooperating well, and the British were happy with him. Areas already covered were now being gone over again and again. It took time, but each recovering of an area of product brought a few more tiny details—tiny but valuable.

As Roth sipped his drink, Sam McCready turned up at the door. He had Denis Gaunt with him, and introductions were made again. Roth had to admire his British colleague's performance. McCready was flawless, congratulating Bailey on a remarkable success with Orlov, and producing a menu of proposals the SIS had come up with to enhance Bailey's visit to Britain.

Bailey was delighted with the tickets to the operas at Covent Garden and Glyndebourne. They would form the high point of the family's twelve-day visit to London.

"And then back to the States?" asked McCready.

"No. A quick visit to Paris, Salzburg, and Vienna, then home," said Bailey. McCready nodded. Salzburg and Vienna both had operas that were among the pinnacles of that art form anywhere in the world.

It turned into quite a jolly evening. The overweight Mrs. Bailey lumbered around dispensing drinks; Clara came to be presented before bed. She was introduced to Roth, Gaunt, and McCready, who gave her his lopsided grin. She smiled shyly. Within ten minutes he was delighting her with conjuring tricks. He took a coin from his pocket, flicked it in the air, and caught it, but when Clara forced open his clenched fist, it was gone. Then he produced the coin from her left ear. The child shrieked with delight. Mrs. Bailey beamed.

"Where did you learn that sort of thing?" asked Bailey.

"Just one of my more presentable talents," said McCready.

Roth had watched in silence. Privately the troubled CIA agent wondered if McCready could make the allegations made by Orlov disappear with the same ease as the coin. He doubted it.

McCready caught his eye, reading his thoughts. Gently, he shook his head. Not now, Joe. Not yet. He turned his attention back to the now-devoted little girl.

The three visitors left after nine o'clock. On the pavement McCready murmured to Roth, "How goes the investigation, Joe?"

"You're full of crap," said Roth.

"Do be careful," said McCready. "You're being led up the garden path. By the nose."

"That's what we believe of you, Sam."

"Who's he nailed, Joe?"

"Back off," snapped Roth. "As of now, Minstrel is Company business. Nothing to do with you."

He turned and walked quickly away toward Grosvenor Square.

Max Kellogg sat with the DCI in the latter's library two nights later with his files and his notes, copies of bank drafts, and photographs, and he talked.

He was tired unto death, exhausted by a workload that would and should normally have taken a team of men double the time. Dark smudges ringed his eyes.

The DCI sat on the other side of the old oak refectory table he had caused to be placed between them to carry the paperwork. The old man seemed hunched into his velvet smoking jacket. The lights shone on his bald and wrinkled head, and beneath his brows his eyes watched Kellogg and flicked over the proffered documents like those of an aged lizard.

When Kellogg had finally finished, he asked, "There can be no doubt?"

Kellogg shook his head. "Minstrel provided twenty-seven points of evidence. Twenty-six check out."

"All circumstantial?"

"Inevitably. Except the testimony of the three bank tellers. They have made positive ID—from photographs, of course."

"Can a man be convicted on circumstantial evidence alone?"

"Yes, sir. It is well precedented and amply documented. You do not always need a body to convict of murder."

"No confession needed?"

"Not necessary. And almost certainly not forthcoming. This is one shrewd, skilled, tough, and very experienced operator."

The DCI sighed. "Go home, Max. Go home to your wife. Stay silent. I'll send for you when I need you again. Do not return to the office until I give the word. Take a break. Rest."

He waved a hand toward the door. Max Kellogg rose and left. The old man summoned an aide and ordered a coded telegram on an "eyes only" basis to be sent to Joe Roth in London. It said simply: "Return at once. Same route. Report to me. Same place." It was signed with the code word that would tell Roth it came directly from the DCI.

The shadows over Georgetown deepened that summer night, as did the shadows in an old man's mind. The DCI sat alone and thought of the old days, of friends and colleagues, bright young men and women whom he had sent beyond the Atlantic wall and who had died under interrogation because of an informer, a traitor. There had been no excuses in those days, no Max Kelloggs to sift the evidence and produce an overwhelming case. And there had been no mercy in those days—not for an informer. He stared at the photo before him.

"You bastard," he said softly, "you double-dyed traitorous bastard."

The following day a messenger entered Sam McCready's office at Century House and deposited a chit from the cipher room. McCready was busy; he gestured to Denis Gaunt to open it. Gaunt read it, whistled, and passed it over. It was a request from the CIA in Langley: During his vacation in Europe, Calvin Bailey was to be provided with access to no classified information.

"Orlov?" asked Gaunt.

"Gets my vote," said McCready. "What the hell can I do to convince them?"

He made his own decision on that. He used a dead-letter drop to get a message to Keepsake, asking for a meeting without delay.

In the lunch hour McCready was informed in a routine note from Airport Watch, a division of MI-5, that Joe Roth had left London again for Boston, still using the same phony passport.

That same evening, having gained five hours crossing the Atlantic, Joe Roth sat at the refectory table at the DCI's mansion. The Director sat opposite him, Max Kellogg to his right. The old man looked grim, Kellogg merely nervous. At his home in Alexandria he had slept for most of the twenty-four hours between his arrival there the previous evening and the telephoned summons to return to Georgetown. He had left all his documents with the Director, but they were again in front of him now.

"Begin again, Max. At the beginning. Just the way you told it to me."

Kellogg glanced at Roth, adjusted his eyeglasses, and took a sheet from the top of the pile.

"In May 1967, Calvin Bailey was sent as a Provincial Officer, a G-12, to Vietnam. Here is the posting. He was assigned, as you see, to the Phoenix Program. You've heard of that, Joe."

Roth nodded. At the height of the Vietnam war, the Americans had mounted an operation to attempt to counter the drastic effects being secured by the Viet Cong on the local population through selective, public, and sadistic assassinations. The notion was to use counterterror against the terrorists, to identify and eliminate Viet Cong activists. It was the Phoenix Program. Just how many Viet Cong suspects were sent to their maker without benefit of evidence or trial has never been established. Some have put the figure at twenty thousand; the CIA put it at eight thousand.

How many of the suspects were really Viet Cong remains even more problematic, for it soon became the practice for Vietnamese to denounce any person against whom they had a grudge. People were denounced on the basis of family feuds, clan wars, land squabbles, even debts owed and never to be collected if the creditor was dead.

Usually the denounced person was handed over to the Vietnamese secret police or the army, the ARVN. The interrogations they underwent and the ways they died tested even oriental ingenuity.

"There were young Americans, fresh out of the States, who saw things down there that no man should be asked to watch. Some quit, some needed professional help. One turned, in his mind, to the very philosophy of the men he had been sent to fight. Calvin Bailey was that man, as George Blake had turned in Korea. We have no proof of that because it happened inside a human head, but the evidence that follows makes the supposition totally reasonable.

"In March 1968 came what we believe to be the climactic experience. Bailey was present at the village of My Lai just four hours after the massacre. You recall My Lai?"

Roth nodded again. It was all part of his youth. He recalled it all too well. On March 16, 1968, an American infantry company came across a small village called My Lai, where they suspected there might be Viet Cong or sympathizers hiding. Exactly why they lost control and went berserk was only inadequately established later. They started firing when they could get no response to their questions, and once it started, it did not stop until at least 450 unarmed civilians— men, women, and children—lay dead in mangled heaps. It took eighteen months for the news to leak out in America, and three years almost to the day for Lieutenant William Calley to be convicted by court-martial. But Calvin Bailey had reached the spot after four hours and seen it all.

"Here is his report at the time," said Kellogg, passing over several sheets, "written in his own hand. As you can see, it was written by a badly shaken man. Unfortunately, it seems this experience turned Bailey into a Communist sympathizer.

"Six months later, Bailey reported he had recruited two Vietnamese cousins, Nguyen Van Troc and Vo Nguyen Can, and infiltrated them into the Viet Cong's own intelligence setup. It was a major coup, the first of many. According to Bailey, he ran these men for two years. According to Orlov, it was the other way around. They ran him. Look at this."

He passed Roth two photographs. One photograph showed

two young Vietnamese males, taken against a background of the jungle. One man had a cross over his face, indicating he was now dead. The other photograph, taken much later and in a setting of verandah with rattan chairs, showed a group of Vietnamese officers at ease, being served tea. The steward was looking up at the camera and smiling.

"The tea-server ended up as a boat-person, a refugee, at a camp in Hong Kong. The photo was his prize possession, but the British were interested in the group of officers and took it from him. Look at the man to the steward's left."

Roth looked. It was Nguyen Van Troc, ten years older but the same man. He wore a senior officer's shoulder boards.

"He's now deputy head of Vietnamese counterintelligence," said Kellogg. "Point made.

"Next, we have Minstrel's assertion that Bailey was passed on to the KGB right there in Saigon. Minstrel named a now-dead Swedish businessman as the KGB *Rezident* for Saigon in 1970. We have known since 1980 that the businessman was not who he said he was, and Swedish counterintelligence long broke his cover story. He never came from Sweden, so he probably came from Moscow. Bailey could have seen him whenever he wanted.

"Next, Tokyo. Minstrel says Drozdov himself went there in the same year, 1970, and took over Bailey, giving him the name Sparrowhawk. We cannot prove Drozdov was there, but Minstrel is dead accurate on the dates. And Bailey was there on those dates. Here is his movement order by Air America, our own airline. It all fits. He returned to America in 1971 a dedicated KGB agent."

After that, Calvin Bailey had served in two posts in Central and South America and three in Europe, a continent he had also visited many times as he rose in the hierarchy and undertook flying visits to inspect out-stations.

"Help yourself to a drink, Joe," growled the DCI. "It gets worse."

"Minstrel named four banks into which his department in Moscow had made transfers of cash to the traitor. He even got the dates of the transfers right. Here are the four accounts, one in each of the banks he named: in Frankfurt, Helsinki, Stockholm, and Vienna. Here are the deposit slips, large sums and in cash. Payments all made within a month of the accounts being opened. Four tellers were shown a photograph; three identified it as the man who opened the accounts. This photograph.''

Kellogg slipped a photograph of Calvin Bailey across to Roth. He stared at the face as if at the face of a stranger. He could not believe it. He had eaten with the man, drunk with him, met his family. The face in the photo stared back blankly.

''Minstrel gave us five pieces of information that were in the possession of the KGB that should never have entered its possession. And he gave the times those pieces entered their possession. Each piece was known to Calvin Bailey and only a few others.

''Even Bailey's triumphs, the coups that secured him his promotions, were fed to him by Moscow—genuine sacrifices made by the KGB to enhance their man's standing with us. Minstrel names four successful operations conducted by Bailey. And he's right—except that he claims they were all permitted by Moscow, and I'm afraid he's right, Joe.

''That makes in all twenty-four precise items extracted from Orlov, and twenty-one check out. That leaves three, much more recent. Joe, when Orlov called you that day in London, what name did he use?''

''Hayes,'' said Roth.

''Your professional name. How did he know it?''

Roth shrugged.

''Finally we come to the two recent killings of the agents named by Orlov. Bailey told you to get the Orlov product to him first, by hand, right?''

''Yes. But that would be normal. It was a Special Operations project, bound to be serious material. He would want to check it over first.''

''When Orlov fingered the Brit, Milton-Rice, Bailey got that first?''

Roth nodded.

''The Brits three days later?''

''Yes.''

''And Milton-Rice was dead before the Brits could get to him. Same with Remyants. I'm sorry, Joe. It's watertight. There's just too much evidence.''

Kellogg closed his last file and left Roth staring at the

material in front of him: the photos, the bank statements, the airline tickets, the movement orders. It was like a jigsaw puzzle assembled, not a piece missing. Even the motive, those awful experiences in Vietnam, was logical.

Kellogg was thanked and dismissed. The DCI stared across the table.

"What do you think, Joe?"

"You know the British think Minstrel's a phony," said Roth. "I told you the first time I came what London's view was."

The DCI made an irritable gesture of dismissal. "Proof, Joe. You asked them for hard proof. Did they give you any?"

Roth shook his head.

"Did they say they had a high-placed asset in Moscow who had denounced Minstrel?"

"No, sir. Sam McCready denied that."

"So they're full of shit," said the DCI. "They have no proof, Joe—just the loser's resentment at not having gotten Minstrel to themselves. This is proof, Joe. Pages and pages of it."

Roth stared dumbly at the papers. To know that he had worked closely with a man who was steadily and with deliberate malice betraying his country over many years was like having a chunk blown out of his midriff. He felt sick. Quietly he said, "What do you want me to do, sir?"

The DCI rose and paced his elegant library. "I am the Director of the Central Intelligence Agency. Appointed by the President himself. As such, I am asked to protect this country as best I can and may, from all her enemies. Some within, some without. I cannot and will not go to the President and tell him we have yet another massive scandal that makes all previous treacheries right back to Benedict Arnold look like nickel-and-dime affairs. Not after the recent series of breaches of security.

"I will not expose him to the savaging of the media and the ridicule of foreign nations. There can be no arrest and trial, Joe. The trial has been here, the verdict has been reached, and the sentence must be from me, God help me."

"What do you want me to do?" repeated Roth.

"In the last analysis, Joe, I could steel myself not to worry about the broken trusts, the traduced secrets, the loss of confidence, the wrecked morale, the scavenging media, the snickering foreign nations. But I *cannot* expel from my mind the images of the agents blown away, the widows and the orphans. For a traitor, there can be only one verdict, Joe.

"He does not return here, ever. He does not soil this land with his feet ever again. He is consigned to outer darkness. You will return to England, and before he can skip to Vienna and thence across the border into Hungary—which is assuredly what he has been preparing to do ever since Minstrel came over—you will do what has to be done."

"I'm not certain I can do that, sir."

The DCI leaned over the table, and with his hand he raised Roth's chin so that he stared into the younger man's eyes. His own were as hard as obsidian.

"You will do it, Joe. Because it is my order as Director, because through our President I speak for this land, and because you will do it for your country. Go back to London and do what has to be done."

"Yes, sir," said Joe Roth.

Chapter 5

The steamer pulled away from Westminster Pier precisely at three and began its leisurely journey downriver toward Greenwich. A crowd of Japanese tourists lined the rail, cameras clicking like subdued machine-gun fire to record the images of the Houses of Parliament slipping away.

As the boat neared midriver, a man in a light gray suit quietly rose and walked to the stern, where he stood at the rail gazing down into the churning wake. Minutes later another man, in a light summer raincoat, rose from a different bench and went to join him.

"How are things at the embassy?" asked McCready quietly.

"Not so good," said Keepsake. "The fact of a major counterintelligence operation is confirmed. So far, only the behavior of my junior staff is being gone over. But intensively. When they have been cleared, the focus of search will move higher—toward me. I am covering tracks as best I can, but there are some things, losing entire files, that would do more harm than good."

"How long do you think you've got?"

"A few weeks at most."

"Be careful, my friend. Err on the side of caution. We absolutely do not want another Penkovsky."

In the early 1960s, Colonel Oleg Penkovsky of the GRU worked for the British for two and a half brilliant years. Until then and for many years afterward, he had been by far the most valuable Soviet agent ever recruited, and the most damaging to the USSR. In his brief span he passed over more than five thousand top-secret documents, culminating in vital intelligence on the Soviet missiles in Cuba in 1962, information that enabled President Kennedy to play a masterly hand against Nikita Khrushchev. But he overstayed his time. When urged to come out, he insisted on staying for a few more weeks, was unmasked, interrogated, tried, and shot.

Keepsake smiled. "Don't worry, no Penkovsky affair. Not again. And how are things with you?"

"Not good. We believe Orlov has denounced Calvin Bailey."

Keepsake whistled. "That high. Well, well. Calvin Bailey himself. So *he* was the target of Project Potemkin. Sam, you must persuade them they are wrong, that Orlov is lying."

"I can't," said McCready. "I've tried. They've got the bit between their teeth."

"You must try again. There is a life at stake here."

"You don't really think—"

"Oh yes, old friend, I do," said the Russian. "The DCI is a passionate man. I don't think he can allow another major scandal, bigger than all the rest put together, at this stage in his President's career. He will take the option of ensuring silence. Forever. But of course, it won't work. He will think, if the act is done, that it will never get out. We know better, don't we? The rumors will start quite soon because the KGB will ensure that they start. They are very good at that.

"Ironically, Orlov has already won. If Bailey is arrested and goes on trial, with hugely damaging publicity, he has won. If Bailey is silenced and the news gets out, CIA morale will hit an all-time low and he has won. If Bailey is expelled without pension, he will claim his innocence, and the controversy will roll for years. Again, Orlov will have won. You must dissuade them."

"I have tried. They still think Orlov's product is immensely valuable and pure. They believe him."

The Russian stared at the foaming water beneath the stern as the Dockland Redevelopment Area, then still a mass of cranes and part-demolished derelict warehouses, slid past.

"Did I ever tell you of my ashtray theory?"

"No," said McCready, "I don't think you did."

"When I taught at the KGB training school, I told my pupils that you take a cut-glass ashtray and smash it into three pieces. If you recover one piece, you know only that you have a piece of glass. If you recover two, you know you have two-thirds of an ashtray, but you cannot stub out your cigarette. To have the whole and usable article, you need all three pieces of the ashtray."

"So?"

"So everything Orlov has provided only makes up one or two pieces of a whole range of ashtrays. He has never actually given the Americans a whole ashtray. Something really secret that the USSR has treasured for years and does not want to give away. Ask them to give Orlov an acid test. He will fail it. But when I come out, I will bring the whole ashtray. Then they will believe."

McCready pondered. Finally he asked, "Would Orlov know the name of the Fifth Man?"

Keepsake thought it over. "Almost certainly, though I do not," he said. "Orlov spent years in the Illegals Directorate. I never did. I was always PR-Line, operating out of embassies. We have both been in the Memory Room—it is a standard part of the training. But only he would have seen the Black Book. Yes, he will know the name."

Deep in the heart of Number 2, Dzerzhinsky Square, headquarters of the KGB, lies the Memory Room, a kind of shrine in a godless building to commemorate the great precursors of the present generation of KGB officers. Among the revered portraits hanging there are those of Arnold Deutsch, Teodor Maly, Anatoli Gorsky, and Yuri Modin, successive recruiters and controllers of the most damaging spy ring ever recruited by the KGB among the British.

The recruitings took place mainly among a group of young students at Cambridge University in the mid- and late thirties. All had flirted with Communism, as had many others who later abandoned it. But five did not, and they went on to serve

Moscow so brilliantly that to this day they are known there as
the Magnificent Five, or the Five Stars.

One was Donald Maclean, who left Cambridge to join the
Foreign Office. In the late forties he was in the British Embassy in Washington and was instrumental in passing to
Moscow hundreds of the secrets of the new atomic bomb,
which America was sharing with Britain.

Another in the Foreign Office was Guy Burgess, a chain-
smoking drunk and rabid homosexual who somehow managed
to avoid being dismissed for far too long. He acted as runner
and go-between for Maclean and their Moscow masters. Both
were finally blown in 1951, avoided arrest after a tipoff, and
fled to Moscow.

A third was Anthony Blunt, also gay, a superb intellect and
talent-spotter for Moscow. He moved on to exploit his other
talent, for the history of art, and rose to become curator of
the Queen's personal art collection and a knight of the realm.
It was he who tipped off Burgess and Maclean of their pending
arrest in 1951. Having successfully brazened out a series of
investigations, he was finally exposed, stripped of his title,
and disgraced only in the 1980s.

The most successful of all was Kim Philby, who joined the
SIS and rose to control the Soviet desk. The flight of Burgess
and Maclean in 1951 pointed the finger at him, too; he was
interrogated, admitted nothing, and was ousted from the
Service, finally quitting for Moscow, from Beirut, only in
1963.

The portraits of all four hang in the Memory Room. But
there was a fifth, and the fifth portrait is a black square. The
real identity of the Fifth Man was to be found only in the
Black Book. The reason was simple.

Confusing and demoralizing the opposition is one of the
principal aims of covert war and was the reason behind the
belated formation of the Deception, Disinformation, and Psychological Operations desk, which McCready now headed.
Since the early fifties, the British had known that there was a
Fifth Man in that ring recruited so long ago, but they could
never prove just who it was. This was all grist for Moscow's
mill.

Over the years—thirty-five in all—and to Moscow's delight,

the enigma wracked British Intelligence, aided by a hungry press and a series of books.

Over a dozen loyal and long-serving officers came under suspicion and had their careers curbed and their lives torn apart. The principal suspect was the late Sir Roger Hollis, who rose to become Director General of MI-5. He became the target of another obsessive like James Angleton, Peter Wright, who went on to make a fortune from a book in which he trotted out his conviction that Roger Hollis was the Fifth Man.

Others were also suspected, including two of Hollis's deputies and even the deeply patriotic Lord Victor Rothschild. It was all bunk, but the puzzle went on. Was the Fifth Man still alive—perhaps still in office, highly placed in the government, the civil service, or the intelligence community? If so, it would be disastrous. The matter could rest only when the Fifth Man, recruited all those years ago, was finally identified. The KGB, of course, had jealously guarded that secret for thirty-five years.

"Tell the Americans to ask Orlov for the name," said Keepsake. "He will not give it to you. But I will find it out and bring it with me when I come over."

"There is the question of time," said McCready. "How long can you hang on?"

"Not more than a few more weeks—maybe less."

"They may not wait, if you are right about the DCI's reaction."

"Is there no other way you can persuade them to stay their hand?" asked the Russian.

"There is. But I must have your permission."

Keepsake listened for several minutes. Then he nodded.

"If this Roth will give his solemn, sworn word. And if you trust him to keep it. Then yes."

When Joe Roth stepped out of the airport terminal the next morning, having flown through the night from Washington, he was jet-lagged and not in the best of moods.

This time he had drunk heavily on the plane, and as he reached the door, he was not amused that a caricature of an Irish voice spoke in his ear.

"Top of the morning to you, Mr. Casey, and welcome back again."

He turned. It was Sam McCready at his elbow. The bastard had evidently known about his "Casey" passport all along and had checked passenger lists at the Washington end to be sure to meet the right plane.

"Jump in," said McCready when they reached the pavement. "I'll give you a lift to Mayfair."

Roth shrugged. Why not? He wondered what else Mc-Cready knew, or had guessed. The British agent kept the conversation to small talk until they entered London's outskirts. When the serious stuff came, it was without warning.

"What was the DCI's reaction?" he asked.

"Don't know what you're talking about."

"Come on, Joe. Orlov has denounced Calvin Bailey. It's horseshit. You're not taking it seriously, are you?"

"You're way off line, Sam."

"We've had a note at Century: "Keep Bailey away from all classified material." So we know he's under suspicion. You're saying it's not because Orlov has accused him of being a Soviet agent?"

"It's just routine, for Christ's sake. Something about his having too many girlfriends."

"My arse," said McCready. "Calvin may be many things, but a philanderer he ain't. Try another one."

"Don't push me, Sam. Don't push our friendship too far. I told you before—this is Company business now. Back off."

"Joe, for God's sake. It's already gone too far. It's got out of hand. Orlov's lying to you, and I fear you are going to do something terrible."

Joe Roth lost his temper. "Stop the car," he shouted. "Stop the goddamned car!"

McCready swerved the Jaguar into the curb. Roth reached into the back for his suitcase and unlatched his door. Mc-Cready grabbed his arm.

"Joe, tomorrow, two-thirty. I have something to show you. Pick you up outside your apartment block at two-thirty."

"Get lost," said the American.

"A few minutes of your time. Is that too much to ask? For the old times, Joe—for all the old times."

Roth stepped out of the car and swung away down the pavement looking for a cab.

But he was there, on the pavement outside his apartment block, at half-past two the next day. McCready waited in the Jaguar until Roth climbed in and drove without saying a word. His friend was still angry and suspicious. The journey was less than half a mile. Roth thought he was being driven to his own embassy, so close did they come to Grosvenor Square, but McCready stopped in Mount Street, a block away.

Halfway down Mount Street is one of London's finest fish restaurants, Scott's. At three precisely, a trim man in a pale gray suit stepped out of the doors and paused just clear of the portico. A black limousine from the Soviet Embassy eased down the street to pick him up.

"You asked me twice if we had an asset in the KGB in Moscow," said McCready quietly. "I denied it. I was not entirely lying. He's not in Moscow—he's here in London. You're looking at him."

"I don't believe what I'm seeing," whispered Roth. "That's Nikolai Gorodov. He's the head of the whole goddam KGB *Rezidentura* in Britain."

"In the flesh. And he works for us, has done for four years. You've had all his product, source disguised, but pure. And he says Orlov is lying."

"Prove it," said Roth. "You're always telling Orlov to prove it. Now *you* prove it. Prove he's really yours."

"If Gorodov scratches his left ear with his right hand before he gets into the car, he's our man," said McCready.

The black limousine was abreast of the portico. Gorodov never glanced toward the Jaguar. He just raised his right hand, reached across his chest, tugged at his left earlobe, and climbed in. The embassy car purred away.

Roth leaned forward and buried his face in his hands. He breathed deeply several times, then raised his face.

"I have to tell the DCI," he said. "Personally. I can fly back."

"No deal," said McCready. "I have given Gorodov my word, and ten minutes ago you gave me yours."

"I have to tell the DCI. Otherwise, the die is cast. There's no going back now."

"Then delay. You can get other proof, or at least grounds for delay. I want to tell you about the ashtray theory."

He told Roth what Keepsake had told him on the river steamer two days earlier.

"Ask Orlov for the name of the Fifth Man. He knows, but he will not tell you. But Keepsake will get it and bring it with him when he comes over."

"When is that to be?"

"Soon now. A few weeks at most. Moscow is suspicious. The net is closing."

"One week," said Roth. "Bailey leaves for Salzburg and Vienna in one week. He must not reach Vienna. The DCI thinks he's going to slip into Hungary."

"Have him recalled as a matter of urgency. Have him recalled to Washington. If he obeys, that merits a further delay. If he refuses, I'll throw in the towel."

Roth considered the proposition. "I'll try it," he said. "First I'm going to Alconbury. Tomorrow, when I get back, if Orlov has refused to name the Fifth Man, I'll send a cable to the DCI saying the Brits have produced fresh evidence that Orlov may be lying and asking for Bailey's instant recall to Langley. As a test. I think the DCI will grant that, at least. It will cause a delay of several weeks."

"Enough, old friend," said McCready. "More than enough. Keepsake will have come across by then, and we can all level with the DCI. Trust me."

Roth was at Alconbury just after sundown. He found Orlov in his room, lying on his bed, reading and listening to music. He had exhausted Simon and Garfunkel—Kroll said the body-guard team had memorized nearly every word of the twenty top hits—and had passed on to the Seekers. He switched off "Morningtown" as Roth entered and jackknifed off the bed with a grin.

"We go back to the States?" he asked. "I am bored here. The Ranch was better, despite the risks."

He had put on weight from the lying around without a chance of exercise. His reference to the Ranch was a joke. For a while, after the dummy assassination attempt, Roth had kept up the pretense that it was a KGB project, and that Moscow must have learned details of the Ranch from Ur-

chenko, who had been debriefed there before he foolishly
went back to the KGB. Then he had admitted to Orlov that it
had all been a CIA ploy to test the Russian's reactions. Orlov
had been angry at first—"You bastards, I thought I was going
to die," he had yelled—but later he had begun to laugh at the
incident.

"Soon," said Roth. "Soon we will be finished here."

He dined with Orlov that night and put to him the notion of
the Memory Room in Moscow.

Orlov nodded. "Sure, I have seen it. All inducted officers
are taken there. To see the heroes and admire them."

Both steered the conversation to the portraits of the Magnificent Five.

Chewing on a mouthful of steak, Orlov shook his head.
"Four," he said. "Only four pictures. Burgess, Philby, Maclean, and Blunt. Four Stars."

"But there's a fifth frame, with just black paper in it?"
suggested Roth.

Orlov was chewing much more slowly. "Yes," he admitted
as he swallowed. "A frame, but no picture."

"So there *was* a Fifth Man?"

"Apparently."

Roth's conversational tone did not vary, but he watched
Orlov over the top of his fork.

"But you were a full major in the Illegals Directorate. You
must have seen the name in the Black Book."

Something flickered in Orlov's eyes. "They never showed
me any Black Book," he said evenly.

"Peter, who *was* the Fifth Man? His name, please."

"I do not know, my friend. I swear that to you." He smiled
again, his wide and attractive grin. "You want me to take the
lie detector on it?"

Roth smiled back, but he thought, No, Peter, I rather think
you can beat the lie detector—when you want to. He resolved
to return to London in the morning and send his cable asking
for a delay and a recall of Bailey to Washington—as a test. If
there was one tiny element of doubt—and despite Kellogg's
pulverizing case, he now entertained an element of doubt—
Roth would not carry out the order, not even for the DCI and
his own flowering career. Some prices were just too high.

*   *   *

The following morning, the cleaners came in to the Alconbury quarters. These were local Huntingdon ladies, the same as those used by the rest of the base. Each had been security-cleared and given a pass to enter the cordoned area. Roth was eating breakfast opposite Orlov in the mess hall, trying to talk above the noise of a rotary floor-buffer polishing the corridor outside. The insistent hum of the machine went up and down as the buffing head swirled around and around.

Orlov wiped the coffee from his lips, mentioned that he needed to go to the men's room, and left. In later life, Roth would never again mock the notion of a sixth sense. Seconds after Orlov had left, Roth noticed a change in the tone of the buffing machine. He walked out into the corridor to look at it. The buffer stood alone, its brushes turning, its motor emitting a single, high whine.

He had seen the cleaner when he went in for breakfast—a thin lady in print overalls, curlers in her hair, and a scarf wrapped over them. She had stepped aside to let him pass, then continued with her drudgery without raising her eyes. Now she was gone. At the end of the corridor, the men's room door was still swinging gently.

Roth yelled, "Kroll!" at the top of his voice and raced down the corridor. She was on her knees in the middle of the men's room floor, her plastic bucket of cleaning fluids and dusters spilled around her. In her hand she had the silenced Sig Sauer that the dusters had hidden. From the far end of the room, a cubicle door opened, and Orlov stepped out. The kneeling assassin raised the gun.

Roth did not speak Russian, but he knew a few words. He yelled *"Stoi!"* at the top of his voice.

She turned on her knees, Roth threw himself to the floor, there was a low *phut*, and Roth felt the shock waves near his head. He was still on the tiles when there was a crashing boom from behind him, and he felt more waves of reverberation beating around him. An enclosed toilet is no place to loose off a .44 Magnum.

Behind him, Kroll stood in the doorway, his Colt gripped two-handed. There was no need for a second shot. The woman lay on her back on the tiles, a blooming red stain vying with the roses on her overalls. Later, they would discover the real charlady bound and gagged at her home in Huntingdon.

Orlov still stood by the door of the cubicle, white-faced.

"More games!" he shouted. "It is enough of CIA games!"

"No games," said Roth as he eased himself up. "This was no game. This was the KGB."

Orlov looked again and saw that the dark red pool spreading across the tiles was not Hollywood makeup. Not this time.

It took Roth two hours to secure Orlov and the rest of the team a fast passage back to America and to secure their immediate transfer to the Ranch. Orlov left gladly, taking his precious collection of ballads with him. When the Air Force transport lifted off for the States, Roth took his car and headed back to London. He was deeply and bitterly angry.

In part, he blamed himself. He should have realized that after the exposure of Bailey, Alconbury could no longer be considered a safe haven for Orlov. But he had been so busy with McCready's intervention, it had slipped his mind. Everyone is fallible. Had it been anyone but McCready, Roth would have been a hundred-percent convinced that the Brits were wrong and that Orlov was telling the truth, but because it was McCready, Roth was still prepared to concede to his friend a five-percent chance that he was right and that Bailey was straight.

But the ball now lay firmly in McCready's court. He wondered why Bailey had not tipped off Moscow to arrange the assassination of Orlov sooner, before the KGB colonel had had a chance to name him. Perhaps he had hoped Orlov would not name him, did not have that information. It was Bailey's mistake. Everyone is fallible.

Roth drove to the American Embassy. There was only one thing to do to back the claim that Gorodov was a real defector and Orlov a phony, and therefore Bailey was in the clear, an innocent man wrongly but cunningly set up. McCready would have to pull Gorodov out *now* so that Langley could talk to the man directly and sort it out once and for all. He went to his desk to make the call to McCready in Century House.

His head of station passed him in the corridor before he reached his desk.

"Oh, by the way," said Bill Carver. "Something just came

in, courtesy of Century. Seems our friends in Kensington
Palace Gardens are moving things around. Their *Rezident*,
Gorodov, flew back to Moscow this morning. It's on your
desk."

Roth did not make the call to McCready. He sat at his desk.
He was stunned. He was also vindicated—he and his DCI and
his Agency. He even found it in his heart to be sorry for
McCready. To have been so wrong, to have been so thoroughly duped for four years, must be a devastating blow. As
for himself, he was relieved in a strange sort of way, despite
what must now lie ahead. He had no more doubts now, not a
shred. The two events of a single morning had swept his last
doubts away. The DCI was right. What had to be done had to
be done.

He was still sorry for McCready. Down at Century they
must be pulling him apart, he thought.

They were—or rather, Timothy Edwards was.

"I'm sorry to have to say this, Sam, but it's an utter bloody
fiasco. I've just had a word with the Chief, and the received
wisdom is that we may now seriously have to contemplate the
notion that Keepsake was a Soviet plant all along."

"He wasn't," said McCready flatly.

"So you say, but the present evidence points to the clear
possibility that our American Cousins have got it right and
we've been duped. Do you know what the perspectives of
that are?"

"I can guess."

"We'll have to rethink, reevaluate every damned thing
Keepsake gave us over four years. It's a massive task. Worse,
the Cousins shared it all, so we'll have to tell them to rethink
as well. The damage assessment will take years. Apart from
that, it's a major embarrassment. The Chief is not pleased."

Sam sighed. It was ever thus. When Keepsake's product
was flavor-of-the-month, running him was a Service operation. Now it was entirely the Deceiver's fault.

"Did he give you any indication that he intended to return
to Moscow?"

"No."

"When was he due to quit and come across to us?"

"Two, three weeks," said McCready. "He was going to let

me know when his situation had become hopeless, then jump the fence.''

"Well, he hasn't. He's gone home. Presumably voluntarily. Port Watch report that he passed through Heathrow without any coercion. We have to assume now that Moscow *is* his real home.

"And then there's this damned Alconbury business. What on earth could have possessed you? You said it was a test. Well, Orlov has passed it with flying colors. The bastards tried to kill him. We're extremely lucky no one's dead but the assassin. That's one thing we cannot tell the Cousins, ever. Bury it.''

"I still don't believe Keepsake was 'bent.' ''

"Why ever not? He's gone back to Moscow.''

"Possibly to get one last suitcase of documents for us.''

"Damned dangerous. He must be crazy. In his position—''

"True. A mistake, perhaps. But he's like that. He promised years ago to bring back one last big consignment before he came over. I think he's gone back for it.''

"Any evidence for this remarkable leap of faith?''

"Gut feeling.''

"Gut feeling!'' expostulated Edwards. "We can't achieve anything on gut feeling.''

"Columbus did. Mind if I see the Chief?''

"Appeal to Caesar, eh? You're welcome. I don't think you'll get any change.''

But McCready did. Sir Christopher listened to his proposal carefully, then asked, "And supposing he's loyal to Moscow after all?''

"Then I'll know within seconds.''

"They could pick you up,'' said the Chief.

"I don't think so. Mr. Gorbachev doesn't seem to want a diplomatic war at the moment.''

"He won't get one,'' said the Chief flatly. "Sam, you and I go back a long way. Back to the Balkans, the Cuban missile crisis, the first days of the Berlin Wall. You were damned good then, and you still are. But Sam, I may have made a mistake in bringing you into the Head Office. This is a job for a field team.''

"Keepsake won't trust anyone else. You know that.''

The Chief sighed. "True. If anyone goes, you go. Is that it?"

" 'Fraid so."

The Chief thought it over for a moment. To lose Keepsake would be a devastating blow. If there was a tenth of a chance that McCready was right and Gorodov was not a plant after all, the Service should try to pull him out of there. But the political fallout of a major scandal—the Deceiver caught red-handed in Moscow—would ruin him. He sighed and turned from the window.

"All right. Sam. You can go. But you go alone. As of now, I have never heard of you. You are on your own."

McCready prepared to go on those terms. He just hoped Mr. Gorbachev did not know them. It took him three days to make his plans.

On the second day, Joe Roth rang Calvin Bailey.

"Calvin, I've just come back from Alconbury. I think we should talk."

"Sure, Joe, come on over."

"Actually, there's no great hurry. Why don't you let me offer you dinner tomorrow night?"

"Ah, well now, that's a nice thought, Joe. But Gwen and I have a pretty full schedule. I had lunch at the House of Lords today."

"Really?"

"Yep. With the Chief of Defense Staff."

Roth was amazed. At Langley, Bailey was chilly, distant, and skeptical. Let him loose in London, and he was like a child in a candy store. Why not? In six days, he'd be safely across the border in Budapest.

"Calvin, I know this marvelous old inn up the Thames at Eton. Serves wonderful seafood. They say Henry VIII used to have Anne Boleyn rowed up the river for secret meetings with her there."

"Really? That old? Okay, look, Joe, tomorrow night we're at Covent Garden. Thursday is clear."

"Right. Thursday, Calvin. You've got it. I'll be outside your apartment at eight. Thursday it is."

The following day, Sam McCready completed his arrangements and slept what might turn out to be his last night in London.

On Thursday, three men entered Moscow on different flights. The first in was Rabbi Birnbaum. He arrived from Zurich by Swissair. The passport control officer at Scheremetyevo was from the KGB's Border Guards Directorate, a young man with corn-blond hair and chill blue eyes. He gazed at the rabbi at length, then turned his attention to the passport. It was American, denoting the holder to be one Norman Birnbaum, age fifty-six.

Had the passport officer been older, he would have recalled the days when Moscow and indeed all Russia had many Orthodox Jews who looked like Rabbi Birnbaum. The rabbi was a stout man in a black suit with a white shirt and black tie. He wore a full gray beard and moustache. On his face, topped by a black homburg, his eyes were masked by lenses so thick, the pupils blurred as the man peered to see. Twisted gray ringlets hung from beneath his hatband down each side of his face. The face in the passport was exactly the same, but without the hat.

The visa was in order, issued by the Soviet Consulate General in New York.

The officer looked up again. "The purpose of your visit to Moscow?"

"I want to visit my son for a short stay. He works at the American Embassy here."

"Moment, please," said the officer. He rose and retired. Behind a glass door he could be seen consulting with a senior officer who studied the passport. Orthodox rabbis were rare in a country where the last rabbinical school had been abolished decades earlier. The junior officer returned.

"Wait, please." He gestured for the next in line to approach.

Phone calls were made. Someone in Moscow consulted a diplomatic list. The senior officer returned with the passport and whispered to the junior. Apparently there was a Roger Birnbaum listed at the Economic Section of the U.S. Embassy. The diplomatic list did not record, however, that Roger Birnbaum's real father had retired to Florida and had last been to synagogue for his son's bar mitzvah twenty years earlier. The rabbi was waved through.

They still checked his suitcase at customs. It contained the usual changes of shirt, socks, and shorts, another black suit, a washkit, and a copy of the Talmud in Hebrew. The customs officer flicked through it uncomprehendingly. Then he let the rabbi go.

Rabbi Birnbaum took the Aeroflot coach into central Moscow, drawing several curious or amused glances all the way. From the terminus building, he walked to the National Hotel on Manezh Square, entered the men's room, used the urinal until the only other occupant left, and slipped into a cubicle.

The spirit gum solvent was located in his cologne flask. When he emerged, he was still in a dark jacket, but the reversible trousers were now medium gray. The hat was inside the suitcase, along with the bushy eyebrows, the beard and moustache, and the shirt and tie. His hair, instead of gray, was chestnut brown, and his torso was covered by a canary yellow polo-neck sweater that had been under his shirt. He left the hotel unnoticed, took a cab, and was dropped at the gates of the British Embassy, on the embankment opposite the Kremlin.

Two militia from the MVD stood guard duty outside the gates, on Soviet territory, and asked for his identification. He showed them his British passport and simpered at the young guard as it was examined. The young militiaman was embarrassed and handed it quickly back. Irritably, he gestured the gay Englishman into the grounds of his own embassy and raised his eyebrows expressively to his colleague as he did so. Seconds later, the Englishman disappeared through the doors.

In fact, Rabbi Birnbaum was neither a rabbi nor an American nor gay. His real name was David Thornton, and he was one of the best makeup artists in British films. The difference between makeup for the stage and that needed for films is that on stage the lights are fierce and the distance from the audience considerable. In films there are also lights, but the camera may have to work in tight closeup, a few inches from the face. Film makeup therefore has to be more subtle, more realistic.

David Thornton had worked for years at Pinewood Studios, where he was always in demand. He was also one of that corps of experts that the British Secret Intelligence Service seems amazingly able to draw upon when it needs one.

The second man to arrive in Moscow came direct from London by British Airways. He was Denis Gaunt, looking exactly like himself, save that his hair was gray and he looked fifteen years older than his real age. He had a slim attaché case chained discreetly to his left wrist, and he wore the blue tie bearing the motif of the greyhound, the sign of one of the Corps of Queen's Messengers.

All countries have diplomatic couriers who spend their lives ferrying documents from embassy to embassy and back home. They are covered by the usages of the Treaty of Vienna as diplomatic personnel, and their luggage is not searched. Gaunt's passport was in another name, but it was British and completely valid. He presented it and was waved through the formalities.

A Jaguar from the embassy met him, and he was taken at once to the embassy building, arriving there an hour after Thornton. He was then able to give Thornton all the tools of the makeup artist's trade, which he had brought in his own suitcase.

The third to arrive was Sam McCready, on a Finnair flight from Helsinki. He, too, had a valid British passport in a false name, and he, too, was disguised. But in the heat of the aircraft, something had gone wrong.

His ginger wig had come slightly askew, and a wisp of darker hair showed from beneath it. The spirit gum that retained one corner of his equally ginger moustache seemed to have melted so that a fragment of the moustache had detached itself from his upper lip.

The passport officer stared at the picture in the passport and back at the man in front of him. The faces were the same—hair, moustache and all. There is nothing illegal about wearing a wig, even in Russia; many bald men do. But a moustache that comes unstuck? The passport officer, not the same one who had seen Rabbi Birnbaum—for Scheremetyevo is a big airport—also consulted a senior officer, who peered through a one-way mirror.

From behind the same mirror, a camera clicked several times, orders were given, and a number of men went from standby to full operation status. When McCready emerged

from the concourse, two unmarked Moskvitch cars were
waiting. He too was collected by a British Embassy car, of
lower standing than a Jaguar, and was driven to the embassy,
followed all the way by the two KGB vehicles, who reported
back to their superiors in the Second Chief Directoráte.

In the late afternoon the photos of the strange visitor
arrived at Yazenevo, the headquarters of the KGB's foreign
intelligence arm, the First Chief Directorate. They ended up
on the desk of the Deputy Head, General Vadim V. Kirpichenko. He stared at them, read the attached report about the
wig and the corner of the moustache, and took them down to
the photographic lab.

"See if you can remove the wig and moustache," he
ordered. The technicians went to work with the airbrush.

When General Kirpichenko saw the finished result, he
almost laughed out loud. "Well, I'll be damned," he murmured. "It's Sam McCready."

He informed the Second Chief Directorate that his own
people would take over the tail forthwith. Then gave his
orders: "Twenty-four hours in twenty-four. If he makes a
contact, pick them both up. If he makes a collection from a
drop, pick him up. If he farts in the direction of Lenin's
mausoleum, pick him up."

He put down the phone and read again the details from
McCready's passport. He was supposed to be an electronics
expert from London via Helsinki, come to sweep the embassy
for listening devices, a regular chore.

"But what the hell are you really doing here?" he asked
the picture staring up from his desk.

In the embassy on the embankment, McCready, Gaunt, and
Thornton dined alone. The ambassador was not much pleased
to have three such guests, but the request had come from the
Cabinet Office, and he was assured that the disruption would
last for only twenty-four hours. So far as His Excellency was
concerned, the sooner these dreadful spooks were gone, the
better.

"I hope it works," said Gaunt over the coffee. "The
Russians are extremely good at playing chess."

"True," said McCready soberly. "Tomorrow we'll find out
how good they are at the three-card trick."

Chapter 6

At precisely five minutes to eight on a warm July morning, an unmarked Austin Montego sedan eased out of the gates of Britain's Moscow embassy and drove across the bridge over the Moskva toward the center of the city.''

According to the KGB report, Sam McCready was at the wheel, driving alone. Although his ginger wig and moustache were now impeccably in place, they were clearly visible to the watchers behind the windshields of their several cars. Telephoto-lens pictures were taken at the time, and several more were secured during the course of the day.

The British agent drove carefully through Moscow and out to the Park of Technological Achievement to the north of the city. On the way he made several attempts to shake any tail he may have had, but he failed. Nor did he even spot the tail. The KGB was using six cars, each intercutting with the other so that no single car was ever behind the Montego for more than a few hundred yards.

After entering the enormous park, the SIS man left his car and proceeded on foot. Two of the KGB vehicles remained on station close to the parked Montego. The crews of the other four descended and fanned out between the scientific exhibits until the Englishman was enveloped on all sides by an invisible screen.

He bought an ice cream and sat for much of the morning on a bench pretending to read a newspaper, frequently glancing at his watch as if waiting for someone to show up. No one did, except an old lady who asked him for the time. He showed her his watch without a word, she read the time, thanked him, and walked on.

She was promptly taken into custody, searched, and questioned. By the following morning, the KGB had satisfied themselves that she was an old lady who wanted to know the time. The ice cream seller was also detained.

Shortly after twelve, the agent from London took a packet of sandwiches from his pocket and slowly ate them. When he had finished he rose, dropped the wrapping paper into a waste basket, bought another ice cream, and sat down again.

The trash basket was kept under observation, but no one retrieved the wrappers until the park's hygiene team arrived with their cart to empty the basket. The wrappers were taken by the KGB and subjected to intensive forensic analysis. Tests included those for invisible writing, microdots, and microfilm secreted between two layers of paper. Nothing was found. Traces were in evidence, however, of bread, butter, cucumber, and egg.

Long before this, just after one P.M., the London agent had risen and left the park in his car. His first rendezvous had clearly aborted. He went, apparently to keep a second or backup rendezvous, to a hard-currency *beriozka* shop. Two KGB agents entered the shop and loitered among the shelves to see if the Englishman would deposit a message among the exclusive goods on offer there or pick one up. Had he made a purchase, he would have been arrested, as per orders, on the grounds that his purchase probably contained a message and that the shop was being used as a dead-letter box. But he made no purchases and was left alone.

On leaving the shop, he drove back to the British Embassy. Ten minutes later, he left again, now seated in the back of a Jaguar being driven by an embassy chauffeur. As the Jaguar left the city heading for the airport, the leader of the watcher team was patched straight through to General Kirpichenko.

"He is approaching the concourse now, Comrade General."

"He has made no contact of any kind? Any kind at all?"

"No, Comrade General. Apart from the old lady and the ice cream seller—now both in custody—he has spoken to no one, nor has anyone spoken to him. His discarded newspaper and sandwich wrappers are in our possession. Otherwise, he has touched nothing."

"It's a mission-abort," thought Kirpichenko. "He'll be back. And we'll be waiting."

He knew that McCready, under the guise of a British Foreign Office technician, was carrying a diplomatic passport.

"Let him go," he said. "Watch for a brush-pass inside the airport concourse. If there is none, see him through the departure lounge and into the aircraft."

Later, the general would examine his team's telephoto pictures of McCready in the Montego and at the park, call for a large microscope, look again, straighten up with a face pink with anger, and shout: "You stupid pricks, that's not McCready."

At ten past eight on the morning of the same day, a Jaguar driven by Barry Martins, the SIS Station Head in Moscow, left the embassy and drove sedately toward the old district of the Arbat where the streets are narrow and flanked by the elegant houses of long-gone prosperous merchants. A single Moskvitch took up the tail, but this was purely routine. The British referred to these KGB agents who followed them all over Moscow in one of life's more boring chores as "the second eleven." The Jaguar drove aimlessly around the Arbat. The man at the wheel occasionally pulled into the curb to consult a city map.

At twenty past eight a Mercedes sedan left the embassy. At the wheel, in a blue jacket and peaked cap, was an embassy chauffeur. No one looked in the rear, so no one saw another figure crouched low down near the floor and covered with a blanket. Another Moskvitch fell in behind.

Entering the Arbat district, the Mercedes passed the parked Jaguar. At this point Martins, still consulting his city map, made up his mind and swerved out from the curb, taking space between the Mercedes and the following Moskvitch.

The convoy now constituted a Mercedes, a Jaguar, and two Moskvitches, all in line astern.

The Mercedes entered a narrow one-way street, followed by the Jaguar, which then developed engine trouble, coughed, spluttered, lurched, and came to a halt. The two Moskvitches piled up behind it, spilling out KGB agents. Martins flicked the hood release, climbed out, and raised the hood. He was at once surrounded by protesting men in leather jackets.

The Mercedes disappeared down the street and turned the corner. Amused Muscovites gathered on the narrow pavements to hear the Jaguar driver saying to the KGB team leader, "Now, look here, my good man. If you think you can make the bugger work, you go right ahead."

Nothing entertains a Muscovite as much as the sight of the *chekisti* making a mess of things. One of the KGB men reentered his car and got on the radio.

Clearing the Arbat, David Thornton, at the wheel of the Mercedes, took his guidance from Sam McCready, who emerged from his blanket and gave directions, without any disguise at all and looking precisely like himself.

Twenty minutes later, on a lonely road screened by trees in the middle of Gorki Park, the Mercedes halted. At the rear, McCready ripped off the CD plate, which was secured by a quick-release snaplock, and stuck a new license plate, prepared with strong adhesive on one side, over the British plate. Thornton did the same at the front. McCready retrieved Thornton's makeup box from the trunk and climbed into the rear seat. Thornton swapped his hard blue peaked cap for a more Russian black leather cap and got back behind the wheel.

At eighteen minutes past nine, Colonel Nikolai Gorodov left his apartment in Shabolovsky Street on foot and began to walk toward Dzerdzinsky Square and the headquarters of the KGB. He looked haggard and pale; the reason soon appeared behind him. Two men emerged from a doorway and without a pretense of subtlety took station behind him.

He had gone two hundred yards when a black Mercedes drew to the curb beside him and kept pace. He heard the hiss of an electric window coming down, and a voice said in English, "Good morning, Colonel. Going my way?"

Gorodov stopped and stared. Framed in the window,

shielded by the rear curtains from the two KGB men up the street, was Sam McCready. Gorodov was stunned, but not triumphant.

"That," thought McCready, "is the look I wanted to see."

Gorodov recovered and said loudly enough for the KGB ferrets to hear, "Thank you, Comrade. How kind."

Then he entered the car, which sped away. The two KGB men paused for three seconds—and lost. The reason they paused was because the license plates of the Mercedes bore the letters *MOC* and then two figures.

The extremely exclusive MOC plates belong only to the members of the Central Committee, and it is a bold KGB footsoldier who dares stop or harass a Central Committee man. But they took the number and frantically used their hand communicators to tell the head office.

Martins had chosen well. The particular registration plates on that Mercedes belonged to a Politburo candidate member who happened to be in the Far East, somewhere near Khabarovsk. It took four hours to find him and learn that he had a Chaika, not a Mercedes, and that it was safely garaged in Moscow. By then it was too late; the Mercedes was back in its British Embassy livery, the Union Jack jauntily fluttering from its pennant-staff.

Gorodov leaned back in the seat, his bridges now completely burned behind him.

"If you are a long-term Soviet mole, I am dead," remarked McCready.

Gorodov considered this. "And if *you* are a long-term Soviet mole," he replied, "then *I* am dead."

"Why did you return?" asked McCready.

"As it turned out, a mistake," said Gorodov. "I had promised you something, and I found I could not discover it in London. When I give my word, I like to keep it. Then Moscow summoned me back for urgent consultations. To disobey would have meant coming over to the West immediately. No excuse would have been accepted for my not returning. I thought I could come for one week, find out what I needed, and be allowed to return to London. Only when I got here did I learn that it was too late. I was under deep suspicion, my apartment and office bugged, followed everywhere, forbidden to go out to Yazenevo, confined to meaningless work in Moscow Center. By the way, I have something for you."

He opened his attaché case and passed McCready a slim file. There were five sheets in the file, each with a photograph and a name. The first picture had beneath it *Donald Maclean*, and the second *Guy Burgess*. Both moles were by then dead and buried in their adopted Moscow. The third sheet showed the familiar face and name of Kim Philby, who was then still alive in Moscow. The fourth had the thin, ascetic features and the name of Anthony Blunt, who was then disgraced in England. McCready turned to the fifth page.

The photo was very old. It showed a thin young man with wild wavy hair and large, owlish glasses. Beneath the photo were two words. *John Cairncross*. McCready leaned back and sighed.

"Bloody hell, him all along."

He knew the name. Cairncross had been a senior civil servant during and after the war, senior despite his youth. He had served in a variety of capacities—private secretary to War Cabinet Minister Lord Hankey; in signals intelligence at Bletchly Park, in the Treasury and the War Office. He had had access to nuclear secrets in the late forties. In the early fifties he had come under suspicion, conceded nothing, and been eased out. Nothing could be proved, so he was allowed to move on to the Food and Agriculture Organization in Rome. By 1986, he was in retirement in France.

The Fifth Man. Keepsake had made good on his promise. The thirty-five-year hunt was over, and no more innocent men need be accused.

"Sam," asked Gorodov mildly, "where exactly are we going?"

"My horoscope," replied McCready, "says I am to travel west today. Yours, too."

Thornton parked again in the trees of Gorki Park, changed places with one of the men in the rear, and went to work. The other man sat in the front pretending to be the chauffeur. No one would care to interfere with a Central Committee member's limousine, even if they saw it. Senior Party members always shrouded the rear of their cars with inner curtains, and these were now drawn. Thornton worked on his client—he always referred to those he made up as his clients—by the sunlight that filtered through the curtains.

On went the thin, inflatable undervest to give the slimmer man the sturdy bulk of Rabbi Birnbaum. Then the white shirt, black trousers, tie, and jacket. Thornton affixed the rich gray beard and moustache, dyed the client's hair to the same color, and appended the curling gray ringlets of the orthodox rabbi to his temples. With the addition of the black homburg and single handgrip, Rabbi Birnbaum had been recreated exactly as he had arrived the previous day—except that he was a different man. Finally, the car was changed back to a British Embassy vehicle.

The rabbi was dropped off at the entrance to the National Hotel, where he had a sustaining lunch, paid in U.S. dollars, and took a cab to the airport after lunch. He was booked on the afternoon flight to London, his ticket showing that he was connecting to New York.

Thornton drove the car back into the British Embassy compound with his other client crouched under the rug in the back. He went to work again almost at once, with an identical ginger wig and moustache, foundation creams, colorants, tinted contact lenses, and tooth stain. Ten minutes after Denis Gaunt, hot and itchy under the ginger wig he had worn all day for the benefit of the KGB, drove back in his Montego, the other man left for the airport in the Jaguar, driven by a real chauffeur. Within an hour Thornton, transformed into the Queen's Messenger, was himself driven to Scheremetyevo by Barry Martins.

The rabbi drew the usual curious glances, but his papers were in order, and he was passed through the formalities in fifteen minutes and into the departure lounge. He sat and read his Talmud, occasionally murmuring prayers in an unintelligible mutter.

The man in the ginger wig and moustache was almost escorted to the door of the departure lounge, so numerous were the KGB team trying to ensure he neither passed nor received a message or package.

Last to arrive was the Queen's Messenger, his attaché case chained to his left wrist. This time, Thornton's precious workbox was in his own suitcase; he did not need anyone to carry it for him, as his case could not be searched.

Denis Gaunt remained inside the embassy. Three days later, he would be exfiltrated when another SIS man posing as a messenger would enter Moscow and pass Gaunt a passport in the same name as his own—Mason. At precisely the identical moment, two Masons would pass out through the controls at different points in the concourse, and British Airways would be briefed to board two Masons for the price of one.

But that afternoon the passengers for London were boarded on time, and the British Airways flight cleared Soviet air space at five-fifteen. Shortly after that, the rabbi lumbered to his feet and walked down to the smoking section, and said to the man in the ginger wig and moustache: "Nikolai, my friend, you are now in the West."

Then Sam McCready bought champagne for them both, and for the Queen's Messenger. The scam had worked because McCready had noticed that he, Gaunt, and Gorodov were all of the same height and build.

With the gain in time caused by flying west, they landed at Heathrow just after seven. A team from Century House, alerted by Martins from Moscow, was there to meet them. They were enveloped as they left the aircraft and spirited away.

As a concession, Timothy Edwards allowed McCready to take Nikolai Gorodov to his own apartment in Abingdon Villas for the evening.

"I'm afraid, Colonel, the real debriefing must start in the morning. A very agreeable country house has been prepared. You will want for nothing, I assure you."

"Thank you. I understand," said Gorodov.

It was just after ten that evening when Joe Roth arrived, summoned by a phone call from McCready. He found two SIS heavies in the hallway and two more in the corridor outside McCready's modest flat, which surprised him.

McCready answered his ring on the doorbell, appearing in slacks and sweater, a glass of whiskey in his hand.

"Thanks for coming, Joe. Come on in. There's someone I have wanted you to meet for a long time. You'll never know how much."

He led the way into the sitting room. The man at the window turned and smiled.

"Good evening, Mr. Roth," said Gorodov. "Good to meet you at last."

Roth stood as if paralyzed. Then he slumped into a chair and took McCready's proffered whiskey. Gorodov seated himself opposite Roth.

"You'd better tell it," said McCready to the Russian. "You know it better than I."

The Russian sipped his drink as he pondered where to begin.

"Project Potemkin started eight years ago," he said. "The original idea came from a junior officer, but General Drozdov took it up personally. It became his personal baby. The aim was to denounce a senior CIA officer as a Soviet plant, but in a manner so convincing and with such a wealth of apparently fireproof evidence that no one could reasonably not be taken in.

"The long-term aim was to sow years of feuding inside the Agency and thus destroy morale among the staff for a decade and wreck the relationship with the SIS in Britain.

"At first, no particular officer was the target, but after half a dozen were considered, the choice fell on Calvin Bailey. There were two reasons for this. One was that we knew he was not a much-liked man inside the Agency because of his personal manner. The second was that he had served in Vietnam, a suitable place for a possible recruitment.

"Calvin Bailey was spotted as a CIA agent in Vietnam purely as routine. You know we all try to identify each other's staffers, and when we do, their movements and progress up the promotions ladder are carefully noted. Sometimes a lack of promotion may sow resentment, which can be exploited by a cunning recruiter. Well, this you know—we all do it.

"Also like the CIA, the KGB throws nothing away. Every tiny scrap of information, every fragment, is carefully kept and stored. Drozdov's breakthrough came when he was once again examining the material that came to us from the Vietnamese after the final fall of Saigon in 1975. Most of your papers were burned, but in the confusion some survived. One mentioned a certain Nguyen Van Troc, who had worked for the Americans.

"That paper was the end for Van Troc. He and his cousin were picked up—they had not managed to escape. The cousin was executed, but Van Troc, although brutally interrogated for many months, was finally sent to a North Vietnamese slave labor camp. That was where Drozdov found him, still alive in 1980. Under torture, he confessed he had worked for Calvin Bailey inside the Viet Cong.

"The Hanoi government agreed to cooperate, and the photo session was set up. Van Troc was taken from the camp, fattened on good food, and dressed in the uniform of a colonel of Hanoi's intelligence arm. The photos were taken of him enjoying tea with other officers just after the invasion of Cambodia. Three separate tea-servers were used, all Hanoi agents, and then sent to the West with their photos. After that, Van Troc was liquidated.

"One of the stewards posed as a boat-person and showed his proud possession to any British officer in Hong Kong who would look at it. Finally, it was confiscated and sent to London—as planned."

"We sent a copy to Langley," said McCready, "just as a courtesy. It seemed to have no value."

"Drozdov already knew Bailey had been involved in the Phoenix Program," Gorodov resumed. "He had been spotted by our *Rezident* in Saigon, a man posing as a Swedish importer of liquor for the foreign community. And Drozdov learned that Bailey had been at My Lai when Bailey gave evidence at the court-martial of that young officer. You are very open with your public records in America. The KGB scours them avidly.

"Anyway, it seemed that a likely scenario for a change of allegiance in Bailey had been established. His 1970 visit to Tokyo had been noticed and noted—purely routine. Drozdov only had to brief Orlov to say that he, Drozdov himself, had been in Tokyo on a certain date to take over the running of an America CIA renegade, and when you checked—presto—the same dates. Of course, Drozdov was not there at all in 1970. That was added later.

"From that point on, the case against Bailey was built up, brick by brick. Pyotr Orlov was chosen as the disinformation agent about 1981; he has been in training and rehearsal ever since. Urchenko, when he foolishly came back and before he died, provided valuable information on exactly how you Americans treat defectors. Orlov could prepare himself to avoid the traps, beat the polygraph, and always tell you what you wanted to hear. Not too much, but enough that when you checked it out, it fit.

"After Drozdov picked Bailey as the victim, Bailey went under intensive scrutiny. Wherever he went, it was noted. After he rose in rank and began to travel to Europe and elsewhere to visit the out-stations, the bank accounts began. Bailey would be spotted in a European city, and immediately a bank account would be opened, always in a name he might choose, like that of his wife's married sister or his maternal grandmother.

"Drozdov prepared an actor, a dead ringer for Bailey, to fly at a moment's notice to open these accounts so that the bank teller would later recognize Bailey as the client. Later, large sums were deposited in these accounts, always in cash and always by a man with a strong Central European accent.

"Information learned from a variety of sources—loose talk, radio intercepts, phone taps, technical publications (and some of your American technical publications are incredibly open)—was attributed to Bailey. Even conversations in your own embassy in Moscow are tapped—did you know that? No? Well, more of that later.

"What Drozdov did was change the dates. Pieces of secret intelligence that we did not learn until the early eighties were, according to Orlov, acquired in the midseventies and attributed to Calvin Bailey. All lies, but cunning. And of course, Orlov memorized it all.

"Triumphs secured by the KGB against the CIA were attributed to Bailey. CIA operations that went sour were attributed to Bailey. And always the dates were changed so that it looked as if we had found out earlier than we possibly could have—without a CIA traitor, that is.

"But two years ago, Drozdov still lacked something. He needed inside-Langley gossip, nicknames known only inside the building—your own professional name of Hayes, Mr. Roth. Then Edward Howard defected to Russia, and Drozdov had it all. He could even name hitherto unknown successes secured by Bailey and rehearse Orlov to say they had been permitted by the KGB to secure the promotion of their agent, Sparrowhawk. Of course, these successes were not permitted by Moscow—they were hard won by Bailey.

"Finally, Orlov was allowed to come over, in a manner so bizarre that he could later claim he feared he would be stopped and betrayed by Sparrowhawk if he did it any other way. For the same reason, he had to go to the Americans, not the British. The British would have questioned him about other things.

"Then he came and denounced two KGB agents just before they were liquidated. It was all pretimed. But it looked as if there were a leak in Washington, feeding his debriefing details back to Moscow. When the customer was ready for the bait, he finally came clean with news of a Soviet mole high in the CIA. No?"

Roth nodded. He looked haggard. "That assassination attempt against Orlov at Alconbury. Why?" he asked.

"That was Drozdov overinsuring. He did not know about me, of course. He just wanted to pile on a bit more evidence. The killer was one of the best—a very dangerous lady. She was briefed to wound, not kill, then make her escape."

There was silence in the room. Joe Roth stared at his drink. Then he rose. "I must go," he said shortly.

McCready accompanied him out into the passage and down the stairs. In the hall he clapped the American on the back.

"Cheer up, Joe. Hell, everyone in this game makes mistakes. My Firm has made some real beauties in the past. Look on the bright side. You can go back to the embassy and cable the DCI that everything's worked out. Bailey's in the clear."

"I'll think I'll fly back and tell him myself," muttered Roth, and left.

McCready escorted him to the door of the building, puzzled by his friend's silence. When he returned to the door of his apartment, the two bodyguards parted to let him through and closed it after him. In the sitting room, he found Gorodov sitting staring at a copy of the *Evening Standard* that he had been glancing through while he waited. Without a word, he flicked it across the table and pointed to a series of paragraphs on page five.

Police divers today recovered the body of an American tourist from the Thames at Teddington Lock. According to an official spokesman, the body is believed to have entered the water somewhere near Eton yesterday eve-

ning. The dead man has been identified as one Calvin
Bailey, an American civil servant on holiday in London.

According to the U.S. Embassy, Mr. Bailey had been
to dinner at Eton with a friend, a Second Secretary at
the embassy. After dinner, Mr. Bailey felt faint and left
to take a turn in the fresh air. His friend stayed to settle
the bill. When he went out to rejoin Mr. Bailey, he could
not find him. After waiting for an hour he assumed Mr.
Bailey had decided to return to London alone. When a
phone call proved this was not so, the friend consulted
Eton police. A search was made of the town in the
darkness, but without result.

This morning a police spokesman at Eton said it
appeared Mr. Bailey had taken a stroll along the tow-
path and, in the darkness, had slipped and fallen in.
Mr. Bailey was a nonswimmer. Mrs. Gwen Bailey was
unavailable for comment. She remains under sedation
at the couple's rented apartment.

McCready put down the paper and stared toward the door.

"Oh, you bastard," he whispered, "you poor bloody bastard."

Joe Roth took the first morning flight to Washington and
went to the Georgetown mansion. He handed in his resigna-
tion, effective twenty-four hours later. He left the DCI a wiser
and chastened man. Before he left, he had made one request.
The DCI granted it.

Roth reached the Ranch very late that night.

Colonel Orlov was still awake, alone in his room, playing
chess against a minicomputer. He was good, but the computer
was better. The computer was playing the white pieces; Orlov
had the others, which, instead of being black, were a dark
red. The tape deck was playing a Seekers album from 1965.

Kroll came in first, stepped to one side, and took up
position by the wall. Roth followed him and closed the door
behind him. Orlov looked up, puzzled.

Kroll stared at him, eyes blank, face expressionless. There
was a bulge under his left armpit. Orlov took it in and looked
inquiringly at Roth. Neither spoke. Roth just stared at him
with very cold eyes. Orlov's puzzlement ebbed, and a resigned awareness took its place. No one spoke.

The pure, clear voice of Judith Durham filled the room.

> *Fare thee well, my own true lover,*
> *This will be our last good-bye. . . .*

Kroll's hand moved sideways toward the tape deck.

For the carnival is over. . . .

Kroll's finger hit the "off" button, and silence returned. Orlov spoke one word, almost his first in Russian since he had arrived in America. He said: *"Kto?"* It means "Who?"

Roth said, "Gorodov."

It was like a punch in the stomach. Orlov closed his eyes and shook his head as if in disbelief.

He looked at the board in front of him and placed the tip of one forefinger on top of the crown of his king. He pushed. The red king toppled sideways and fell, the chessplayer's admission of capitulation. The price of the bride had been paid and accepted, but there would be no wedding. The red king rolled once and lay still.

Kroll pulled out his gun.

"Let's go," he said.

Then Colonel Pyotr Alexandrovich Orlov, a very brave man and a patriot, rose and went into the darkness to meet the mighty God who made him.

Interlude

"Well, now, that's all very fine, Denis, and most impressive," said Timothy Edwards when the board reconvened on Wednesday morning. "But we have to ask ourselves: Will these remarkable talents ever be needed in the future?"

"I don't think I quite follow you, Timothy," said Denis Gaunt.

Sam McCready sat back in his chair, as far as the upright chair would permit him, and allowed them to drone on. They were talking about him as if he had already become a piece of furniture, something from the past, a discussion point to muse upon during the serving of the port at the club.

He looked out at the bright blue sky of the summer day beyond the windows. There was a whole world out there, another world, one that he would soon have to join and in which he would have to make his way without the membership of his own small peer group, the intelligence officers among whom he had lived for most of his adult life.

He thought of his wife. If she had still been alive, he would have wanted to retire with her, find a small cottage by the sea in Devon or Cornwall. He had sometimes dreamed of his own small fishing boat, bobbing in a stone-walled harbor, safe from the winter gales, waiting to be taken out on a summer's sea to bring home a supper of cod or plaice or slick, gleaming mackerel.

In his dream he would have been just Mr. McCready from the house above the harbor, or Sam, when taking his beer in the snug of the local inn with the fishermen and crabbers of the town. It was just a dream, of course, that had come to him sometimes in the dark, rain-swept alleys of Czechoslovakia or Poland as he waited for a "meet" or watched a dead-letter box to see if it had been staked out, before he moved close to reach for the message inside.

But May was gone, and he was alone in the world, cocooned only by the camaraderie of that smallest of small worlds, the other men who had chosen to serve their countries and spend their lives in the shadowed places where destruction came not in a blaze of glory but in the flash of a torch in the face and the rasp of soldiers' boots on cobbles. He had survived them all, but he knew he would not survive the mandarins.

Besides, he would be lonely living all alone down in the southwest, far away from the other old war horses who drank their gins in the Special Forces Club at the end of Herbert Crescent. Like most men who had spent their lives in the Service, he was a loner at heart and made new friends uneasily, like an old dog fox preferring the coverts he knew to the open plain.

"I mean simply," Timothy Edwards was saying, "that the days of slipping into and out of East Germany are a thing of the past. This October, East Germany will actually cease to exist—even today it exists only in name. Relations with the USSR have changed out of all recognition; there will be no more defectors, just honored guests—"

"Bloody hell," thought McCready, "he really has fallen for that one. And what happens, dickbrain, when the famine strikes Moscow and the hard men close in on the embattled Mikhail Gorbachev? Never mind, you'll see."

He let his attention drift and thought of his son. He was a good boy, a fine lad, just out of college and wanting to be an architect. Good for him. He had a pretty blond girlfriend living with him—they all seemed to do that nowadays—no need for the pretty girl to have security clearance. And Dan came around to see him now and again. That was nice. But the boy had a life of his own, a career to head for, friendships to make, places to go and see, and he hoped they would be brighter, safer places than the ones he had seen.

He wished he had spent more time with his son when he was small, wished he had had the time to roll on the sitting-room carpet and read him bedtime stories. Too often, he had left that to May because he had been away on some godfor-saken border, staring at the barbed wire, waiting for his agent to come crawling through, or listening for the klaxons that would mean the man would never be seen again.

There was so much he had missed, and so many things he had done, and seen, and places he had been that he could not really discuss with the young man who still called him Dad.

"I am most grateful, Timothy, for your suggestion, which, in a way, preempted my own."

Denis Gaunt was doing a good job, making the bastards listen, growing in confidence as he spoke. He was a good man, a Head Office man really, but good.

"Because," Gaunt went on, "Sam here realizes just as well as any of us that we cannot dwell in the past, chewing over the Cold War all over again. The point is, there are other menaces that threaten our country and that are on the in-crease. Proliferation of high-tech weaponry to highly unstable tyrants in the Third World—we all know exactly what France has been selling Iraq—and of course terrorism.

"In that regard"—he took a buff folder from the Records clerk and opened it—"let me remind you of the affair that began in April 1986 and ended, if indeed the Irish question will ever end, in the late spring of 1987. Such affairs will probably happen again, and it will be the Firm's task to head them off—again. Get rid of Sam McCready? Frankly, gentle-men, that could be very foolish."

The Controllers for Western Hemisphere and Domestic Operations nodded, while Edwards glowered at them. This was the sort of agreement he did not need. But Gaunt was bland as he read out the events on April 1986 that had triggered the case that took up most of the spring of 1987.

" 'On April 16, 1986, fighters from American carriers in the Gulf of Sirte and fighter-bombers flying from British bases blasted the private living quarters of Colonel Qaddafi outside

Tripoli. The good Colonel's sleeping area was hit by a fighter flying from the USS *Exeter*, call-sign Iceman Four.

" 'Qaddafi survived, but he had a nervous breakdown. When he recovered he vowed vengeance, just as much on Britain as upon America, because we had allowed the F-111 strike bombers to fly out of our bases at Upper Heyford and Lakenheath.

" 'In the early spring of 1987 we learned how Qaddafi intended to extract that revenge upon Britain, and the case was given to Sam McCready. . . .' "

A CASUALTY
OF WAR

Chapter 1

Father Dermot O'Brien received the message from Libya by the normal route for such first communications—by mail.

It was a perfectly ordinary letter, and had anyone opened it—which they had not, because the Republic of Ireland does not intercept mail—they would have found nothing of interest in it. The postmark said that it came from Geneva, as indeed it had, and the return address indicated the writer worked for the World Council of Churches, which he did not.

Father O'Brien found it in his pigeonhole in the main hall beside the refectory one morning in the early spring of 1987 as he emerged from taking his breakfast. He glanced through the other four letters addressed to him, but his gaze returned to the one from Geneva. It bore the slight pencil mark on the rear flap that told him it should not be opened in public or left lying around.

The priest nodded amiably to two colleagues about to enter the refectory and went back to his bedroom on the first floor.

The letter had been typed on the usual onionskin airmail paper. The text was warm and friendly, beginning "My dear Dermot . . . ," and was written in the tone of one old friend involved in pastoral work to another. Even though the World

Council of Churches is a Protestant organization, no casual
observer would have seen anything strange in a Lutheran
clergyman writing to a friend who happened to be a Catholic
priest. These were the days of cautious ecumenism, especially
in the international field.

The friend in Geneva wished him well, trusted he was in
good health and chatted about the work of the WCC in the
Third World. The meat was in the third paragraph of the
script. The writer said that his bishop recalled with pleasure a
previous meeting with Father O'Brien and would be delighted
to meet him again. The signoff was simply, "Your good friend
Harry."

Father O'Brien laid the letter down thoughtfully and gazed
from his window across the green fields of County Wicklow
toward Bray and, beyond it, the gray waters of the Irish Sea.
The waters were hidden by the roll of the hills, and even the
spires of Bray were dim and distant from the old manor house
at Sandymount that contained the headquarters of his Order.
But the sun shone brightly on the green meadows that he
loved so dearly, as dearly indeed as he hated the great enemy
that lay beyond the sea.

The letter intrigued him. It had been so long, almost two
years, since he had visited Tripoli for a personal audience
with Colonel Muammar Qaddafi, the Great Leader of the
Libyan Jamahariya, Keeper of Allah's Word, the man referred
to as "the bishop" in the letter.

It had been a rare and privileged occasion, but despite the
flowery language, the soft voice, and the extravant promises,
nothing had finally been forthcoming. No money, no arms for
the Irish Cause. Finally, it had been a disappointment and the
man who had arranged the meeting, Hakim al-Mansour, head
of the foreign arm of the Libyan Secret Service, the Moukha-
barat, who now signed himself "Harry," had been apologetic.

And now this, a summons, for that was what it was. Though
no time had been suggested for the meeting with the bishop,
Father O'Brien knew none was necessary. Harry meant
"without delay." Although the Arabs can delay for years
when they are so minded, when Qaddafi summoned in this
manner, one went—if one wanted his largesse.

Father O'Brien knew that his trusted friends in the Cause
did indeed want that largesse. Funds from America were

down; the constant appeals from the Dublin government—
men Father O'Brien regarded as traitors—not to send arms
and money to Ireland had had their effect. It would not be
wise to ignore the summons from Tripoli. The snag would be
to find a good excuse to travel again so soon.

In a perfect world, Father O'Brien could have done with a
few weeks' break. He had but three days earlier returned
from Amsterdam, ostensibly from a seminar of the War on
Want.

During his time in Europe he had been able to slip away
from Amsterdam and, using funds he had earlier salted away
in Utrecht, take two long-term leases in false names for one
apartment in Roermond, Holland, and another in Münster,
West Germany. These would later become safe houses for the
young heroes who would go over there to carry the war to the
enemy where they least expected it.

Traveling was, for Dermot O'Brien, a constant part of his
life. His Order busied itself with missionary and ecumenical
work, and he was its International Secretary. It was the
perfect cover for the war. Not the War on Want, but the war
against the English, which had been his calling and his life
since he had held the broken head of the dying young man in
Derry all those years ago and seen the British paratroopers
running down the street, and spoken the last rites, and made
his other, personal vow, of which his Order and his bishop
knew nothing.

Since then, he had nurtured and honed his visceral loathing
of the people across the water and had offered his services to
the Cause. They had been welcomed, and for ten years he
had been the principal international "fixer" for the Provisional IRA. He had raised the funds, moved the money from
one deep-cover bank account to another, secured false passports, and arranged for the safe arrival and storage of the
Semtex and the detonators.

With his help, the bombs in Regent's Park and Hyde Park
had torn apart the young bandsmen and the horses; through
his assistance, the sharpened coach bolts had scythed through
the street outside Harrods, ripping out entrails and severing
limbs. He regretted that it was necessary, but he knew it was
just. He read the reports in the newspapers and watched
beside his horrified colleagues in the television room at the

manor; and he would go, when invited by a colleague in parish work, and take the Mass with a calm soul.

His problem that spring morning was fortuitously solved by a small announcement in the *Dublin Press*, a copy of which was still lying across his bed where he had read it while drinking his morning tea.

His room also served as his office, and he had his own telephone. He made two calls, and during the second he received a warm welcome to join the group whose forthcoming pilgrimage had been announced in the paper. Then he went to see his Superior.

"I need the experience, Frank," he said. "If I stay in the office the phone never stops ringing. I need the peace, and the time to pray. If you can spare me, I would like to go."

The Superior glanced at the itinerary and nodded.

"Go with my blessing, Dermot. Pray for us all while you are there."

The pilgrimage was one week away. Father O'Brien knew he did not need to contact the Army Council to ask them also for permission. If he had news when he returned, so much the better. If not, no need to trouble the Army Council. He sent a letter to London, paying the extra to guarantee twenty-four-hour delivery, knowing it would reach the Libyan People's Bureau—the Libyan government's term for its embassies—within three days. That would give Tripoli time to make their arrangements.

A week later, the pilgrimage began with Mass and prayers at the Irish shrine of Knock. Thence it moved to Shannon Airport and a chartered jet to Lourdes, in the foothills of the French Pyrenees. There Father O'Brien slipped away from the crowd of lay men and women, nuns and priests, who made up the pilgrims, and boarded the small charter plane waiting for him at the Lourdes airport. It deposited him four hours later at Valletta, Malta, where the Libyans took him over. Their unmarked executive jet landed at a small military base outside Sirte just twenty-four hours after the Irish priest had departed from Shannon. Hakim al-Mansour, urbane and gracious as ever, was there to meet him.

Because of the urgency of getting back to Lourdes and rejoining the group of pilgrims, there was no meeting with

Colonel Qaddafi. In fact, it had never even been envisaged. This was an operation al-Mansour had been charged to handle alone. The two men talked in a room at the base set aside for them and ringed by al-Mansour's personal guards. When they had finished and the Irishman had snatched a few hours' sleep, he left again for Malta and Lourdes. He was excited. What he had learned, if it came to fruition, would constitute a huge breakthrough for his Cause.

Hakim al-Mansour secured his personal interview with the Great Leader three days later. He was summoned, as always, at a moment's notice to present himself at the place where Qaddafi was staying that day. Since the bombing of the previous year, the Libyan leader had taken more than ever to shifting his quarters from place to place, spending more and more time out in the desert, an hour's drive from Tripoli.

He was in what al-Mansour privately called "the Bedouin mood" that day, lounging at ease on a pile of cushions in a large and ornate tent at his desert encampment, dressed in a white kaftan. He appeared as languid as ever as he listened to the reports of the two nervous ministers who sat cross-legged before him. The ministers, townsmen by birth, would clearly have preferred to be seated behind their desks. But if the Great Leader's whim was that they squat on cushions on the carpet, they would squat on cushions.

Qaddafi acknowledged al-Mansour's entry with a gesture of the hand to be seated to one side and await his turn. When the ministers had been dismissed, Qaddafi took a sip of water and asked for a report on progress.

The younger officer gave his report without frills or exaggerations. Like all those around the Libyan leader, he was somewhat in awe of Muammar Qaddafi. The man was an enigma, and men are always in awe of an enigma, especially one who, with a wave of his hand, could require your immediate execution.

Al-Mansour knew that many foreigners, particularly the Americans, including those at the highest level, believed Qaddafi to be mad. He, al-Mansour, knew there was nothing mad about Muammar Qaddafi. The man would not have survived eighteen years of supreme and unquestioned mastery of this turbulent, fragmented, and violent land if he had been deranged.

He was in fact a subtle and skilled political operator. He had made his mistakes, and he entertained his illusions—notably about the world outside his own country and his status in that world. He genuinely believed he was a lonely superstar, occupying the center of the world stage. He really believed that his long, rambling speeches were received with reverence by millions of "the masses" beyond his own borders as he encouraged them to overthrow their own leaders and accept his inevitable supremacy in the cause of the purification of Islam according to the message he had personally received to accomplish this task. No one in his personal entourage dared to contradict this.

But within Libya he was unchallenged and virtually unchallengeable. He relied for advice upon a small circle of trusted intimates. Ministers would come and go, but his personal inner circle, unless he suspected one of them of treachery, had his ear and wielded the real power. Few of them knew anything about that strange place "abroad." On this, Hakim al-Mansour, raised in a British public school, was the expert. Al-Mansour knew Qaddafi had a soft spot for him. It was justified—the head of the foreign arm of the Mukhabarat had, in younger days, proved his loyalty by personally executing three of Qaddafi's political opponents in their European boltholes.

Still, the Bedouin dictator needed careful handling. Some did this with flowery flattery. Al-Mansour suspected Qaddafi accepted the flattery but took it with a pinch of salt. Al-Mansour's own approach was respectful, but he did not varnish the truth. Rather, he phrased the truth carefully and certainly did not offer all of it—that would have been suicidal. But he suspected that behind the dreamy smile and the almost effeminate gestures, Muammar Qaddafi wanted to be told the truth.

That day, in April 1987, Hakim al-Mansour told his leader of the visit of the Irish priest and of their discussions. As he talked, one of Qaddafi's personal team of doctors, who had been mixing a potion at a table in the corner, approached and offered the small cup to Qaddafi. The Libyan leader swallowed the draught and waved the doctor away. The man

packed up his medicaments and a few minutes later left the
tent.

Although a year had passed since the American bombers
had devastated his personal living quarters, Muammar Qaddafi had not completely recovered. He still suffered occasional nightmares and the effects of hypertension. The doctor
had given him a mild sedative.

"The fifty-fifty split of the material—it is accepted?" he
asked now.

"The priest will report that condition," said al-Mansour.
"I am confident the Army Council will agree."

"And the matter of the American ambassador?"

"That, too."

Qaddafi sighed, in the manner of one on whose shoulders
too many of the world's burdens are placed. "Not enough,"
he said dreamily. "There must be more. On mainland America."

"The search goes on, Excellency. The problem remains the
same. In Britain, the Provisional IRA will exact your just
revenge for you. The infidels will destroy the infidels at your
behest. It was a brilliant idea."

The idea of using the Provisional IRA as the conduit and
tool of Qaddafi's revenge on Britain had actually come from
the brain of al-Mansour, but Qaddafi now believed the notion
had been his, inspired by Allah.

Al-Mansour went on: "In America there is, alas, no in-
place partisan network that can be used in the same way. The
search goes on. The tools of your vengeance will be found."

Qaddafi nodded several times, then gestured that the interview was over. "See to it," he murmured softly.

The gathering of intelligence is a strange business. Rarely
does one single coup provide all the answers, let alone solve
all the problems. The search for the single, wonderful solution
is a particularly American trait. Mostly, the picture appears
as if a jigsaw puzzle is being carefully asesembled, piece by
piece. Usually, the last dozen pieces never appear at all; a
good intelligence analyst will discern the picture from a collection of fragments.

Sometimes the pieces themselves do not come from the
jigsaw picture under study at all, but from another one.

Sometimes the pieces are themselves untrue. And they never lock together quite as neatly as in a real jigsaw puzzle, with the fretted edges of each and every piece matched.

There are men at Century House, home of the British Secret Intelligence Service, who are experts at jigsaw puzzles. They seldom leave their desks; the gatherers—the field agents—are the ones who bring in the pieces. The analysts try to assemble them. Before the end of April, two pieces of a new puzzle had arrived at Century House.

One came from the Libyan doctor who had given Qaddafi his medicine in the tent. The man had once had a son whom he dearly loved. The student had been in England trying to become an engineer when the Mukhabarat had approached him and suggested that if he loved his father, he should carry out a task for the Great Leader. The bomb they had given him to plant had gone off prematurely. The father had hidden his grief well and had accepted the condolences, but his heart had turned to hatred, and he passed what information he could glean from his position at the court of Muammar Qaddafi to the British.

His report of half a conversation, which he had heard in the tent before he was dismissed, was not sent via the British Embassy in Tripoli, for this was watched night and day. Instead, it went to Cairo, arriving a week later. From Cairo it was flashed to London, where it was considered important enough to go straight to the top.

"He's going to do *what*?" asked the Chief, when he was told.

"It seems he has offered a gift of explosives and weaponry to the IRA," said Timothy Edwards, who had that month been promoted from Assistant Chief to Deputy Chief. "That, at least, seems to be the only interpretation of the overheard conversation."

"How was the offer made?"

"Apparently via an Irish priest flown in to Libya."

"Do we know which one?"

"No, sir. Might not be a real priest at all. Could be a cover for an Army Council man. But the offer seems to have originated with Qaddafi."

"Right. Well, we must find out who this mysterious cleric is. I'll tell the Box and see if they have anything. If he's in the

North, he's theirs. If he's in the South or elsewhere, we take him.''

"Box Five Hundred" is the in-house slang term for MI-5, the British Security Service, the internal counterintelligence arm that has the task of counterterrorism in Northern Ireland, as British territory. The SIS had the mandate for intelligence and offensive counterintelligence operations outside Britain, including the Republic of Ireland, the "South."

The Chief lunched with his colleague, the Director General of MI-5 that same day. The third man at the table was the Chairman of the Joint Intelligence Committee; it would be his job to alert the Cabinet Office.

Two days later, an MI-5 operation came up with the second piece of the jigsaw puzzle.

There was nothing foreseen about it; it was just one of those flukes that occasionally make life easier. A young IRA man, driving a car with an Armalite in the trunk, came up against an unexpected roadblock manned by the Royal Ulster Constabulary. The teenager hesitated, thought of the rifle in his car—which would guarantee him several years imprisonment in the Maze jail—and tried to crash the roadblock.

He almost made it. Had he been more experienced, he might have. The sergeant and two constables at the roadblock had to throw themselves to one side as the stolen car suddenly surged ahead. But a third officer, standing well back, brought up his rifle and fired four shots into the accelerating car. One of them took off the top of the teenager's head.

He was only a messenger boy, but the IRA decided he merited a full funeral with military honors. It took place in Bollycrane, the dead youth's native village, a small place in South Armagh. The grieving family was comforted by Sinn Fein president Gerry Adams and asked for a favor. Would they allow a visiting priest, presented as a longtime friend of the family, to conduct the funeral service in place of the parish priest? The family, hardline Republicans all, with another son serving life for murder, agreed without hesitation. The service was duly conducted by Father Dermot O'Brien.

A little-known fact about the funerals of IRA men buried in Northern Ireland is that they provide a constant and useful venue for IRA leaders to get together and confer. The ceremonies are extremely tightly controlled by IRA "hard men."

*   *   *

Usually, every single person among the mourners—men, women, and children—is a staunch supporter of the IRA. In some of the small villages of South Armagh and Fermanagh and South Tyrone, entire villages down to the last inhabitant are fanatic supporters.

The TV cameras are often fixed upon the ceremony, and the IRA chiefs, shielded by the crowd even from lip-reading, can hold muttered conferences, plan, decide, relay information, or set up future operations—not always an easy task for men under constant surveillance. For a British soldier or a Royal Ulster Constabulary man even to approach a funeral party would be a signal for a riot or even the murder of the soldier, as has been proved.

So a watch is kept with Long Tom cameras, but these usually cannot detect a muttered conversation from the side of the mouth. Thus, the IRA uses the supposed sanctity of death to plan further slaughter.

When the British first learned of this, they were not slow to catch up. It was once said that the most important thing an English gentleman ever learns is precisely when to stop being one.

So the British bug the coffins.

On the night before the funeral at Ballycrane, two Special Air Service soldiers, acting under cover in civilian clothes, broke into the funeral parlor where the empty coffin stood waiting for the morrow. The body, in Irish tradition, was still laid out in the family's front parlor down the street. One of the soldiers was an electronics expert, the other a skilled French polisher and carpenter. Within an hour they implanted the bug in the woodwork of the coffin. It would have a short life, since before noon the next day it would be under six feet of earth.

From their deep cover on a hillside above the village the next day, the SAS soldiers kept watch on the funeral, photographing every face present with a camera whose lens resembled a bazooka tube. Another man monitored the sounds emanating from the device in the wood of the coffin as it came through the village street and into the church. The device recorded the entire funeral service, and the soldiers watched the coffin re-emerge and move toward the open grave.

The priest, his cassock billowing in the morning breeze,

intoned the last words and scattered a little earth on the coffin as it went down. The sound of the earth hitting the woodwork caused the listening soldier to wince, it was so loud. Above the open grave, Father Dermot O'Brien stood beside a man known by the British to be the deputy Chief of Staff of the IRA Army Council. Heads down, lips hidden, they began to mutter.

What they said went onto the tape on the hillside. From there it went to Lurgan, thence to Aldergrove airport, and thence to London. It had been only a routine operation, but it had come up with pure gold. Father O'Brien had reported to the Army Council the full details of Colonel Qaddafi's offer.

"*How* much?" asked Sir Anthony, the Chairman of the Joint Intelligence Committee, two days later in London.

"Twenty tons, Tony. That's the offer."

The Director General of MI-5 closed the file that his colleagues had just finished reading and returned it to his briefcase. The actual tape was not present. Sir Anthony was a busy man; a written synopsis was all he needed.

The tape had been with MI-5 in London for over a day, and they had been working fast. The sound quality, inevitably, had not been good. For one thing, the bugging device had been straining to hear the words through half a centimeter of wood, and it was being lowered downward into the grave as the conversation began. For another, there were extraneous sounds: the wailing of the young terrorist's mother nearby, the rustle of the brisk wind across the open grave and through the priest's flowing robes, the crack of the IRA honor guard in black balaclava woolen masks firing three rounds of blanks into the air.

A radio producer would have thought the tape a mess. But this tape was never intended for broadcast. Moreover, the technology of electronic sound-enhancement is very advanced. Carefully, sound engineers had phased out the background noises, "lifting" the spoken words into a different frequency mode and separating them from everything else. The voices of the officiating priest and the Army Council man beside him would never win prizes for elocution, but what they had said was clear enough.

"And the conditions?" asked Sir Anthony. "No doubt about them?"

"None," said the DG. "Within the twenty tons will be the usual machine guns, rifles, grenades, launchers, mortars, pistols, timers, and bazookas—probably the Czech RPG-7. Plus two metric tons of Semtex-H. Of this, half must be used for a bombing campaign on mainland Britain, to include selective assassinations, including that of the American ambassador. Apparently the Libyans were very insistent on that."

"Bobby, I want you to take it all to the SIS," said Sir Anthony at last. "No interservice rivalry, if you please. Total cooperation, all the way. It looks as if this will be an overseas operation—their pigeon. From Libya right up to some godforsaken bay on the coast of Ireland, it'll be a foreign operation. I want you to give them your absolute cooperation, from you downward."

"No question," said the DG. "They'll have it."

Before nightfall, the Chief of the SIS and his Deputy Timothy Edwards attended a full and lengthy briefing at the Curzon Street headquarters of their sister service. Exceptionally, the Chief was prepared to admit that he could, in part, corroborate the Ulster information from the report of the Libyan doctor. Normally, wild horses would not drag from him the slightest admission concerning SIS assets abroad, but this was not a normal situation.

He asked for, and was given, the cooperation he wanted. MI-5 would increase surveillance, both physical and electronic, on the IRA Army Council man. So long as Father O'Brien remained in the North, the same would apply to him. When he returned to the Irish Republic, the SIS would take over. Surveillance would also be doubled on the one other man mentioned in the graveside conversation, a man well known to British security forces but who had never yet been charged or imprisoned.

The Chief ordered his own networks in the Irish Republic to keep watch for the return of Father O'Brien, to tail him, and above all else, to alert London if he left by air or sea for foreign parts. A pickup would be much easier on the continent of Europe.

When he returned to Century House, the Chief summoned Sam McCready.

"Stop it, Sam," he said finally. "Stop it at its source in Libya or in transit. Those twenty tons must not get through."

Sam McCready sat for hours in a darkened viewing room watching the film of the funeral. As the tape played through the entire service inside the church, the camera roamed over the graveyard outside, picking up the handful of IRA guards placed there to ensure no one came near. They were all unrecognizable in black balaclava woolen masks.

When the cortège reemerged from the portico of the church to proceed to the open grave, with six masked pall-bearers carrying the coffin, McCready asked the technicians to synchronize sound and vision. Nothing remotely suspicious was said until the priest stood, his head bowed, by the grave with the IRA Army Council man beside him. The priest raised his head once to offer words of comfort to the teenager's weeping mother.

"Freeze frame. Closeup. Enhance."

When the face of Father O'Brien filled the screen, McCready stared at it for twenty minutes, memorizing every feature until he would know the face anywhere.

He read the transcript of the section of the tape in which the priest reported on his Libyan visit, over and over again. Later he sat alone and stared at photographs in his office.

One of the photographs was of Muammar Qaddafi, his bouffant black hair bulging from beneath his army cap, mouth half open as he spoke. Another was of Hakim al-Mansour, stepping out of a car in Paris, exquisitely tailored by Savile Row, smooth, urbane, bilingual in English, fluent in French, educated, charming, cosmopolitan, and utterly lethal. A third was the Chief of Staff, IRA Army Council, addressing a public meeting in Belfast in his other role as a law-abiding and responsible local government councilor of the Sinn Fein political party. There was a fourth picture: that of the man mentioned by the graveside as the one the Army Council would probably choose to take over and run the operation, the one Father O'Brien would have to introduce and recommend by letter to Hakim al-Mansour. The British knew he was a former commander of the IRA's South Armagh Brigade, now removed from local tasks to head up Special Projects, a very intelligent, highly experienced, and ruthless killer. His name was Kevin Mahoney.

McCready stared at the photographs for hours, trying to glean some knowledge of the brains behind the faces. If he was to win, he would have to match his mind with theirs. So far, they had the edge. They knew, presumably, not only what they were going to do, but how they were going to do it. And when. He knew the first, but not the second or the third.

He had two advantages. One, he knew what they had in mind, but they did not know he knew. And two, he could recognize them, but they did not know him. Or did al-Mansour know his face? The Libyan had worked with the KGB; the Russians knew McCready. Had they briefed the Libyan on the face of the Deceiver?

The Chief was not prepared to take the risk.

"I'm sorry, Sam. You are absolutely not going in yourself. I don't care if there's only a one-percent chance they have your face on file, the answer is no. Nothing personal. But you are not, under any circumstances, being taken alive. I will not contemplate another Buckley affair."

Richard Buckley, the CIA chief of station in Beirut, had been taken alive by the Hezbollah. He had died slowly and hideously. The zealots had finally sent the CIA a videotape, complete with soundtrack, as they skinned him alive. And of course he had talked, told it all.

"You'll have to find someone else," said the Chief. "And may the Lord look after him."

So McCready went through the files, day after day, backward and forward, sifting and sorting, considering and rejecting. Eventually he came up with a name, a "possible." And he took it to Timothy Edwards.

"You're crazy, Sam," said Edwards. "You know he's absolutely unacceptable. MI-5 hate his guts. We're trying to cooperate with them, and you produce this—turncoat. Dammit, he's a literary renegade, a biter of the hand that fed him. We'd never employ him."

"That's the point," said Sam quietly. Edwards shifted his ground.

"Anyway, he'd never work for us."

"He might."

"Give me one good reason why."

McCready gave it.

"Well," said Edwards, "as far as the record goes, the man's an outsider. Use of him is forbidden. Absolutely forbidden. Is that clear?"

"Completely," said McCready.

"On the other hand," added Edwards, "you'll probably follow your own instincts anyway."

As McCready left the office, Edwards reached under the desk to flick off the hidden tape deck. Without the last sentence, he was covered. Thus are long and glittering careers created.

McCready, who had been tipped off about the tape machine by an old friend, the engineer who had installed it, muttered as he walked down the corridor, "All right, arsehole, you can start editing now."

McCready had no illusions about the Provisional IRA. The journalists in the tabloid press who designated the Irish terrorist group as a bunch of dense idiots who occasionally got it right simply did not know what they were talking about.

It might have been like that in the old days, the late 1960s and early 1970s, when the IRA leadership was composed of a bunch of middle-aged ideologues in trenchcoats, carrying small-caliber handguns and making bombs in back-street garages from garden fertilizer. Those were the days when they could have been "taken out" and stopped in their tracks. But as usual, the politicians had got it wrong, underestimated the danger, accepted that the bombers were just an extension of the civil rights movement. Now, those days were long gone. By the mid-1980s, the IRA had graduated, becoming arguably the most efficient terrorist group in the world.

They had four qualities without which no terrorist group can survive for twenty years, as they had. First, they had a pool of tribal support, from whose youth a constant stream of new recruits could step in to fill the shoes of the dead and the "gone away"—those in prison. Although they had never had more than 150 active terrorists deployed at once and probably no more than twice that number of "active" supporters ready to offer safe houses, locations for arms caches, and technical backup, and although they had lost well over one hundred dead and several hundred gone away, the new young recruits constantly came forward from the die-hard Republican community in the North and the South to take their places. The recruit pool would never dry up.

Second, they had the safe refuge of the South, the Irish Republic, from which to mount operations into the British-ruled North. Though many lived permanently in the North, the South was always available, and into it a wanted terrorist could slip away and disappear. Had the six counties of Northern Ireland been an island, the IRA would have been coped with years ago.

Third, they had dedication and ruthlessness; there was no threshold of atrocity beyond which they would not go. Over the years, the old men of the late 1960s had been eased out, still nursing their idealistic fervor for the reunification of their island into a single United Ireland under democratic rule. In their place had come hard-nosed zealots of skill and cunning, whose education and good brains masked their cruelty. The new breed were dedicated to a United Ireland all right—but under their rule, and according to the principles of Marx, a dedication that still had to be kept hidden from their American cash-donors.

Last, they had established a constant supply of money, the real lifeblood of a terrorist or revolutionary campaign. In the early days, it had been a question of donations from the bars of Boston or the occasional local bank raid. By the mid-1980s, the Provisionals controlled a nationwide network of drinking clubs, protection rackets, and "normal" criminal enterprises that yielded a huge annual income with which to underpin the terror campaign. As they had learned about money, they had learned too about internal security, the need-to-know rule, and strict compartmentalization. The old days when they talked too much and drank too much had long gone.

Their Achilles' heel was in the area of arms. Having the money to buy weapons was one thing. Parlaying money into M-60 machine guns, mortars, bazookas, or ground-to-air missiles was another. They had had their successes—and their failures. They had tried many operations to bring the arms from America, but usually the FBI got them first. They had had weapons from the Communist bloc, via Czechoslovakia, with a nod from the KGB. But since the arrival of Mr.

Gorbachev, the Soviet preparedness to sanction terror in the West had waned and was finally disappearing.

The IRA needed arms, McCready knew; and if these were an offer, they would send in the best and the brightest to get them. Such were his thoughts as he steered his car out of the small town of Cricklade and across the unmarked county line into Gloucestershire.

The converted barn was where he had been told it would be, tucked down a side road, an old Cotswold stone affair that had once housed cattle and hay. Whoever had done the conversion to a quiet country house had worked hard and well. It was surrounded by a stone wall set with wagon wheels, and the garden was bright with late spring flowers. McCready drove through the gate and drew up outside the timber door. A pretty young woman, weeding a flowered border, put down her trowel and stood up.

"Hello," she said. "Have you come about a rug?"

So, he thought, he's selling rugs as a sideline. Perhaps the information about the books not selling too well was true.

"No, 'fraid not," he said. "Actually, I've come to see Tom."

Her smile faded, and an element of suspicion entered her eyes, as if she had seen men like him enter her husband's life before and knew they meant trouble.

"He's writing. In his shed at the bottom of the garden. He finishes in about an hour. Can you wait?"

"Certainly."

She gave him coffee in the bright, chintz-curtained sitting room, and they waited. Conversation wilted. At last they heard the tramp of feet coming through the kitchen. She jumped up.

"Nikki—"

Tom Rowse appeared in the door and stopped. His smile did not flicker, but his eyes took in McCready and became very watchful.

"Darling, this gentleman has come to see you. We've been waiting. Would you like a coffee?"

He did not look at her, just kept his eyes on his visitor. "Sure, love a coffee."

She left. McCready introduced himself. Rowse sat down.

The records had said he was thirty-three. They did not say that he looked extremely fit. They did not need to.

Tom Rowse had been a captain in the Special Air Service regiment. Three years earlier, he had left the army, married Nikki, and bought a decrepit barn west of Cricklade. He had done the conversion himself, working out his rage through the long days of bricks and mortar, beams and rafters, windows and waterpipes. He had hacked the rough meadow into smooth lawn, laid the flower beds, built the wall. That was by day; by night, he had written.

It had to be a novel, of course; a nonfiction work would have been banned under the Official Secrets Act. But even as a novel, his first book had caused outrage in the Curzon Street headquarters of MI-5. The book was about Northern Ireland, seen from the point of view of an undercover soldier, and it had mocked the counterintelligence efforts of MI-5.

The British Establishment can be very vindictive toward those it sees to have turned against it. Tom Rowse's novel eventually found a publisher and came out to a modest success for a first novel by an unknown writer. The publishers had since commissioned a second book, on which he was now working. But the word had gone out from Curzon Street that Tom Rowse, former captain in the SAS, was an outsider, beyond the pale—not to be touched, approached, or helped in any way. He knew it, and he did not give a damn. He had built himself a new world with his new house and his new wife.

Nikki served coffee, absorbed the atmosphere, and left. She was Rowse's first wife, but Rowse was not her first husband.

Four years earlier, Rowse, crouched behind a van in a mean street in West Belfast, had watched his friend Nigel Quaid move slowly forward like a giant armored crab toward a red Ford Sierra a hundred yards down the road.

Rowse and Quaid suspected there was a bomb in the trunk of the car. A controlled explosion would have disposed of it. The senior brass wanted the bomb defused if possible. The British know the identity of just about every IRA bomb-maker in Ireland. Each one of them leaves a personal signature in the way the bomb is assembled. That signature is blown apart if the bomb goes off, but if the bomb can be defused and retrieved, it provides a harvest of information: where the explosive came from, the source of the primer, the detonator, maybe even fingerprints. And even without fingerprints, usually the identity of the hands that put it together.

So Quaid, his friend since school days, had gone forward, swathed in body armor till he could hardly walk, to open the trunk and try to dismantle the antihandling devices. He had failed. The trunk lid had come open, but the device was taped on the underside of the lid. Quaid was looking downward, half a second too long. When daylight hit the photosensitive cell, the bomb went off. Despite Quaid's armor, it removed his head.

Rowse had comforted the young widow, Nikki Quaid. The comfort had turned to affection, and affection to love. When he asked her to marry him, she had one condition: Leave Ireland, leave the Army. When she saw McCready today, she had suspected something, for she had seen men like him before. They were the quiet ones, always the quiet ones. It had been a quiet one who had come to Nigel that day and asked him to go to the mean street in West Belfast. Outside in the garden she dug angrily into the weeds while her man talked with the quiet one.

McCready spoke for ten minutes. Rowse listened. When the older man had finished, the ex-soldier said, "Look outside."

McCready did so. The rich farming land stretched away to the horizon. A bird sang.

"I have made a new life here. Far away from that filth, from those scum. I'm out, McCready. Right out. Didn't Curzon Street tell you that? I've made myself untouchable. A new life, a wife, a home that isn't a soaking scrape in an Irish bog, even a modest living from the books. Why the hell should I go back?"

"I need a man, Tom. A man in on the ground. Inside. Able to move through the Middle East with a good cover. A face they don't know."

"Find another."

"If that metric ton of Semtex-H goes off here in England, divided into five hundred two-kilo packages, there'll be another hundred Nigel Quaids. Another thousand Mary Feeneys. I'm trying to stop it arriving, Tom."

"No, McCready. Not me. Why the hell should I?"

"They're putting a man in charge, from their side. Someone I think you know. Kevin Mahoney."

Rowse stiffened as if he had been hit.

"He will be there?" he asked.

"We believe he will be in charge. If he fails, it will destroy him."

Rowse stared out at the landscape for a long time. But now he saw a different countryside, one that was a deeper green but less well tended; and a garage forecourt; and a small body by the roadside that had once been a little girl called Mary Feeney.

He rose and went outside. McCready heard low voices and the sound of Nikki crying. Rowse came back and went to pack a suitcase.

Chapter 2

Rowse's briefing took a week, and McCready handled it personally. There was no question of bringing Rowse to the environs of Century House, let alone to Curzon Street. Mc-Cready borrowed one of the three quiet country houses not an hour's drive from London that the SIS keeps for such purposes, and he had the briefing materials sent from Century House.

There was written material and movie film, much of the latter rather indistinct, having been shot from great distance or through a hole in the side of a van, or from between the branches of a bush at long range. But the faces were clear enough.

Rowse saw the film and heard the tape from the graveyeard scene at Ballycrane a week earlier. He studied the face of the Irish priest who had acted as messenger, and that of the Army Council man beside him. But when the still photographs were laid side by side, his gaze always came back to the cold, handsome features of Kevin Mahoney.

Four years earlier, Rowse had almost killed the IRA gunman. Mahoney was on the run, and the operation to track him down had taken weeks of patient undercover work. Finally, he had been suckered by a deception operation into venturing into Northern Ireland from his hideout near Dundalk in the South. He was being driven by another IRA man, and they stopped for petrol at a filling station near Moira. Rowse had been driving behind him, well back, receiving radio briefings from the watchers along the route and in the sky. When he heard that Mahoney had stopped for fuel, he decided to close in.

By the time he reached the forecourt of the filling station, the IRA driver had filled his tank and was back in the car. No one was with him yet. For a moment Rowse thought he had lost the quarry. He told his partner to cover the IRA driver and got out. It was while he was busying himself with the petrol pump that the door of the men's room opened and Mahoney came out.

Rowse was carrying his SAS-issue Browning 13-shot in his waistband at the back, under his blue duffle jacket. A scruffy woolen cap covered most of his head, and several days of stubble obscured his face. He looked like an Irish workman, which was his cover.

As Mahoney emerged, Rowse dropped into a crouch beside the petrol pump, pulled his gun, took up the double-handed aim position, and yelled, "Mahoney—freeze!"

Mahoney was fast. Even as Rowse was drawing, he was reaching for his own gun. By law, Rowse could have finished him there and then. Later, he wished he had. But he shouted again, "Drop it, or you're dead!"

Mahoney had his gun out, but it was still by his side. He looked at the man half-hidden by the pump, saw the Browning, and knew he could not win. He dropped his Colt.

At that moment, two old ladies in a Volkswagen pulled onto the concrete apron of the filling station. They had no idea what was going on, but they drove straight between Rowse by the petrol pump and Mahoney by the wall. That was enough for the IRA man. He dropped like a stone and retrieved his gun. His partner tried to drive to his rescue, but Rowse's backup man was beside him, a gun stuck straight through the car window into the man's temple.

Rowse could not fire because of the two women, who had now stalled their engine and were sitting in their Volkswagen screaming. Mahoney came out from behind the Volkswagen, dodged around the back of a parked lorry, and ran out into the road. By the time Rowse cleared the lorry, Mahoney was in the middle of the highway.

At that moment, a Morris Minor drove by. The elderly driver of the Morris jammed on his brakes to avoid hitting the running man. Mahoney kept the Morris between himself and Rowse, hauled the old man out by the jacket, clubbed him to the ground with the Colt, jumped into the driving seat, and was off.

There was a passenger in the car. The old man had been taking his granddaughter to the circus in the Morris. Rowse, in the road, watched as the passenger door flew open and the child was thrown out. He heard her thin scream from down the road, saw her small body hit the road, then saw her body struck by an oncoming van.

"Yes," said McCready softly, "we know it was him. Despite the eighteen witnesses who said he was at a bar in Dundalk at that hour."

"I still write to her mother," said Rowse.

"The Army Council wrote, too," said McCready. "They expressed regret. Said she fell accidentally."

"She was thrown," said Rowse. "I saw his arm. He's really going to be in charge of this?"

"We think so. We don't know whether the transshipment will be by land, sea, or air, or where he'll show up. But we think he'll command the operation. You heard the tape."

McCready briefed Rowse on his cover stories. He would have two, not one. The first would be reasonably transparent. With luck, those investigating it would penetrate the lie and discover the second story. With luck (again), they would be satisfied with the second cover.

"Where do I start?" asked Rowse as the week neared its end.

"Where would you like to start?" asked McCready.

"Anyone researching international arms traffic for his next novel would soon find out that the two European bases for that traffic are Antwerp and Hamburg," said Rowse.

"True," said McCready. "Do you have any contacts in either city?"

"There's a man I know in Hamburg," said Rowse. "He's

dangerous, crazy, but he may have contacts in the international underworld.''

"His name?''

"Kleist. Ulrich Kleist.''

"Jesus, you know some strange bastards, Tom.''

"I saved his butt once,'' said Rowse. "At Mogadishu. He wasn't crazy then. That came later, when someone turned his son into a druggie. The boy died.''

"Ah, yes,'' said McCready, "that can have an effect. Right, Hamburg it is. I'll be with you all the time. You won't see me, and neither will the bad guys. But I'll be there, somewhere nearby. If things turn sour, I'll be close, with two of your former colleagues from the SAS Regiment. You'll be okay— we'll come for you if things get rough. I'll need to contact you now and again for regular updates on progress.''

Rowse nodded. He knew it was a lie, but it was a nice one. McCready would need his regular updates so that if Rowse abruptly departed this planet, the SIS would know how far he had got. For Rowse possessed that quality so beloved of spymasters: He was quite dispensable.

Rowse arrived in Hamburg in the middle of May. He was unannounced, and he came alone. He knew McCready and the two "minders'' had gone ahead of him. He did not see them, and he did not look. He realized he would probably know the two SAS men with McCready, but he did not have their names. It did not matter; they knew him, and their job was to stay close but invisible. It was their specialty. Both would be fluent German speakers. They would be at Hamburg Airport, in the streets, near his hotel, just watching and reporting to McCready, who would be farther back.

Rowse avoided the luxury hotels like the Vier Jahrzeiten and the Atlantik, choosing a more unpretentious hotel near the railway station. He had hired a small car from Avis and stuck to his modest budget, in keeping with the limitations of a moderately successful novelist trying to research his next book. After two days he found Ulrich Kleist, who was working as a forklift driver on the docks.

The big German had switched off his machine and was climbing down from the cab when Rowse called to him. For a second Kleist spun around, prepared to defend himself, then recognized Rowse. His craggy face broke into a grin.

"Tom. Tom, my old friend."

Rowse was embraced in a crushing bear hug. When he was released, he stood back and looked at the former Special Forces soldier whom he had first met in a baking Somali airport in 1977 and had last seen four years ago. Rowse had been twenty-four then, and Kleist was six years his senior. But he looked as if he were older than forty now, much older.

On October 13, 1977, four Palestinian terrorists had hijacked a Lufthansa flight from Mallorca to Frankfurt, with eighty-six passengers and a crew of five. Tracked by the authorities, the captive jet had landed in succession at Rome, Larnaca, Bahrain, Dubai, and Aden before finally coming to rest, out of fuel, at Mogadishu, the bleak capital of Somalia.

Here, a few minutes after midnight on the night of October 17, the jet had been stormed by the West German special force, the GSG 9, which modeled itself on, and had been largely trained by, the British SAS. It had been the first foreign "outing" for Colonel Ulrich Wegener's crack troops. They were good, very good, but two SAS sergeants had come along anyway. One was Tom Rowse—that was before he was commissioned.

The reason for the presence of the British was twofold. One, they were very experienced at taking off sealed airliner doors in a fraction of a second; two, they knew how to handle the British-developed stun grenades. These grenades produced three things designed to paralyze a terrorist for two vital seconds. One was the flash, which blinded the naked eye; one was the shock wave, which caused disorientation; the third was the bang, which rattled the brain through the eardrums and paralyzed reaction.

After the successful liberation of the Lufthansa airline, Chancellor Helmut Schmidt lined up the warriors and gave them all medals on behalf of a grateful nation. The two Britishers had vaporized before the politicians and the press could appear.

Although the two SAS sergeants had been there only as technical advisers—the British Labour government had been adamant on that—what had really happened was this: The British had gone up the ladder first in order to take off the rear passenger door. They had approached the airliner from behind and beneath to avoid detection by the terrorists.

Because it was impossible to change position at the top of an aluminium ladder in pitch darkness, the SAS men had gone through the gaping hole before the Germans and had thrown their stun grenades. Then they stepped aside to let the GSG 9 team pass them and finish the job. The first two Germans were Uli Kleist and another trooper. They entered the center aisle and dropped flat as ordered, their guns trained forward toward where they had been told the terrorists would be.

And they *were* there, up by the forward bulkhead, recovering from the blast. Zohair Yussef Akache, alias Captain Mahmoud, who had already murdered the Lufthansa captain, Jürgen Schumann, was rising with a submachine gun in his hands. Beside him, one of the two women, Nadia Hind Alameh, was climbing to her feet with a grenade in one hand, her other hand reaching for the pin. Uli Kleist had never done it at point-blank range before, so Rowse stepped into the aisle from the lavatory bay and did it for him. Then the GSG 9 team finished the job, blowing away the second male terrorist, Nabi Ibrahim Harb, and wounding the other female, Suheila Saleh. In all, it had taken eight seconds.

Ten years later, Uli Kleist now stood in the sun on a Hamburg quayside and grinned at the slim young man who had fired those two shots over his head in the cramped airliner cabin so long ago.

"What brings you to Hamburg, Tom?"

"Let me buy you dinner, and I'll tell you."

They ate spicy Hungarian food at a *csarda* in one of the back streets of Sankt Pauli, well away from the bright lights and high prices of the Reeperbahn, and washed it down with Bull's Blood. Rowse talked, Kleist listened.

"*Ja,* sounds like a good plot," he said eventually. "I didn't read your books yet. They are translated into German?"

"Not yet," said Rowse. "My agent's hoping to get a German contract. It would help—Germany's a big market."

"So, there is a living to be made from writing this thriller fiction?"

Rowse shrugged. "It pays the rent."

"And this new one, the one about terrorists and arms dealers and the White House—you have a title for it?"

"Not yet."

The German considered. "I will try and get you some information—research purposes only, yes?" He laughed and tapped his nose, as if to say, Of course, there's more to it than that, but we all have to make a living.

"Give me twenty-four hours. I'll talk with some friends, see if they know where you could get this sort of stuff. So, you have done well since leaving the Army. I—not so well."

"I heard about your troubles," said Rowse.

"Ach, two years in Hamburg jail. A piece of cake. Another two, and I could have been running the place. Anyway, it was worth it."

Kleist, although divorced, had had a son. He had been only sixteen when someone turned him on to cocaine, then crack. The boy overdosed and died. Rage had made Uli Kleist rather unsubtle. He had found out the names of the Colombian wholesaler and the German distributor of the consignment that had killed his son, walked into a restaurant where they were dining, and blown both their heads off. When the police came, Kleist did not even resist. An old-school judge who shared his personal views about drug traffickers listened to the defense plea of provocation and gave Kleist four years. He served two, and had come out six months before. Word was, there was a contract on him. Kleist did not give a damn. Some said he was crazy.

They parted at midnight, and Rowse took a cab back to his hotel. A single man on a motorcycle followed all the way. The motorcyclist spoke twice into a hand-communicator. When Rowse paid off the taxi, McCready emerged from the shadows.

"You haven't got a tail," he said. "Not yet, anyway. Feel like a nightcap?"

They drank beer in an all-night bar near the station, and Rowse filled him in.

"He believes your tale of researching a novel is poppycock?" McCready asked.

"He suspects it."

"Good—let's hope he puts it about. I doubt if you'll get to

the real bad guys in this scenario. I'm rather hoping they'll come to you."

Rowse made a remark about feeling like the cheese in a mousetrap and climbed off his bar stool.

"In a successful mousetrap," remarked McCready as he followed Rowse out of the bar, "the cheese does not get touched."

"I know it, and you know it, but tell that to the cheese," said Rowse, and retired to bed.

Rowse met Kleist the following evening. The German shook his head.

"I have asked around," he said, "but what you mentioned is too sophisticated for Hamburg. That kind of material is made in government-owned laboratories and arms factories. It is not on the black market. But there is a man, or so is the whisper."

"Here in Hamburg?"

"No, Vienna. The Russian military attaché there is a certain Major Vitali Kariagin. As you no doubt know, Vienna is the main outlet for the Czech manufacturer Omnipol. The broad mass of their exports they are allowed to make on their own account, but some stuff and some buyers have to be cleared out of Moscow. The channeling agent for these permissions is Kariagin."

"Why should he help?"

"Word is, he has a taste for the good things of life. He's GRU, of course, but even Soviet military intelligence officers have private tastes. It appears he likes girls—expensive girls, the sort to whom you have to give expensive presents. So he himself takes presents, cash presents, in envelopes."

Rowse thought it over. He knew that corruption was more the rule than the exception in Soviet society, but a GRU major on the take? The arms world is very bizarre; anything is possible.

"By the way," said Kleist, "in this . . . novel of yours. Would there be any IRA in it?"

"Why do you ask?" said Rowse. He had not mentioned the IRA.

Kleist shrugged. "They have a unit here. Based in a bar run by Palestinians. They do liaison with other terror groups in the international community, and arms-buying. You want to see them?''

"In God's name, why?''

Kleist laughed, a mite too loud. "Might be fun," he said.

"These Palestinians—they know you once blew away four of their number?'' asked Rowse.

"Probably. In our world everyone knows everyone. Especially their enemies. But I still go to drink in their bar.''

"Why?''

"Fun. Pulling the tiger's tail.''

"You really *are* crazy," thought Rowse.

"I think you should go," said McCready later that night. "You might learn something, see something. Or they might see you and wonder why you are here. If they inquire, they'll come up with the novel-researching story. They won't believe it, and they'll deduce you really *are* out buying weapons for use in America. Word gets around. We want it to get around. Just have a few beers, and stay cool. Then distance yourself from that mad German.''

McCready did not feel it necessary to mention that he knew of the bar in question. It was called the Mausehöhle, or Mousehole, and the rumor persisted that a German undercover agent, working for the British, had been unmasked and shot in an upstairs room there a year earlier. Certainly the man had disappeared without a trace. But there was not enough for the German police to raid the place, and German counterintelligence preferred to leave the Palestinians and the Irish where they were. Smashing up their headquarters would simply mean they would reestablish somewhere else. Still, the rumors persisted.

The following evening Uli Kleist paid off their cab on the Reeperbahn. He led Rowse up the Davidstrasse, past the steel-gated entrance to Herbertstrasse, where the whores sat night and day in their windows; past the brewery gates; and down to the far end where the Elbe glittered under the moon. He turned right into Bernhard Nochtstrasse and after two hundred yards stopped at a studded timber door.

He rang the discreet bell by its side, and a small grill slid back. An eye looked at him, there was a whispered conference inside, and the door opened. The doorman and the dinner-jacketed man beside him were both Arabs.

"Evening, Mr. Abdallah," Kleist said cheerfully in German. "I'm thirsty, and I'd like a drink."

Abdallah glanced at Rowse.

"Oh, he's all right, he's a friend," said Kleist. The Arab nodded at the doorman, who opened the door wide to let them in. Kleist was big, but the doorman was massive, shaven-headed, and not to be trifled with. Years earlier, back in the camps in Lebanon, he had been an enforcer for the PLO. In a way, he still was.

Abdallah led them both to a table, summoned a waiter with a flick of the hand, and ordered in Arabic that his guests be looked after. Two busty bar-girls, both German, left the bar and sat at their table.

Kleist grinned. "I told you. No problem."

They sat and drank. Now and then, Kleist danced with one of the girls. Rowse toyed with his drink and surveyed the room. Despite the sleazy street in which it was situated, the Mousehole was lushly decorated, the music was live, and the drink was unwatered. Even the girls were pretty and well dressed.

Some of the clientèle were Arabs from abroad, others Germans. They seemed prosperous and concerned only with having a good time. Rowse had put on a suit; only Kleist remained in his brown leather bomber jacket over an open-neck shirt. Had he not been who he was, with the reputation he had, Mr. Abdallah might well have excluded him on grounds of dress.

Apart from the redoubtable doorman, Rowse could see no sign that this was a hangout for anything other than businessmen who were prepared to be parted from a lot of money in the hope, almost certainly to be dashed, of taking one of the bar-girls home. Most drank champagne; Kleist had ordered beer.

Above the bar, a large mirror dominated the seating area. It was a one-way mirror; behind it was the manager's office. Two men stood and looked down.

"Who's your man?" one asked softly in the harsh burr of Belfast.

"German called Kleist. Comes in occasionally. Once GSG 9.

Not anymore—he's on the outside. Did two years for murder."

"Not him," said the first man, "the other, the one with him. The Brit."

"No idea, Seamus. Just came in."

"Find out," said the first man. "I think I've seen him somewhere before."

They came in when Rowse was visiting the men's room. He had used the urinal and was washing his hands when the two men entered. One approached the urinal, stood in front of it, and jiggled with his fly. He was the big one. The slimmer, good-looking Irishman stayed by the door. He slipped a small wooden wedge out of his jacket pocket, dropped it to the floor, and with the side of one foot eased it under the restroom's entrance door. There would be no distractions.

Rowse caught sight of the gesture in the mirror but pretended not to notice. When the big man turned away from the urinal, he was ready. He turned, ducked the first hammer blow from the big fist that came at his head, and lashed a toe-kick into the sensitive tendon beneath the man's left knee-cap.

The big man was taken by surprise and grunted in pain. His left leg buckled, bringing his head down to waist-level. Rowse's knee came up hard, finding the point of the jaw. There was a crunch of breaking teeth and a spray of fine blood from the broken mouth in front of him. He felt pain running up his thigh from his bruised knee. The fight was stopped by his third blow—four rigid knuckles into the base of the big man's throat. Then he turned to the man by the door.

"Easy now, friend," said the man called Seamus. "He only wanted to talk to you."

He had a wide, broth-of-a-boy smile that must have worked wonders with the girls. The eyes stayed cold and watchful.

"Qu'est-ce que se passe?" asked Rowse. On entering the club, he had passed himself as a visiting Swiss.

"Drop it, Mr. Rowse," said Seamus. "For one thing, you have Brit written all over you. For another, your picture was on the back of your book, which I read with great interest. For a third, you were an SAS man in Belfast years ago. Now I remember where I've seen you before."

"So what?" said Rowse. "I'm out, well out. I write novels for a living now. That's all."

Seamus O'Keefe thought it over. "Could be," he admitted. "If the Brits were sending undercover men into my pub, they'd hardly use a man with his face plastered all over so many books. Or would they?"

"They might," said Rowse, "but not me. 'Cause I wouldn't work for them anymore. We had quite a parting of the ways."

"So I heard, to be sure. Well then, SAS man, come and have a drink. A real drink. For old times' sake."

He kicked the wedge away from the door and held it open. On the tiles, the big man hauled himself to his hands and knees. Rowse passed through the door. O'Keefe paused to whisper in the big man's ear.

In the bar Uli Kleist was still at his table. The girls had gone. The manager and the enormous doorman stood by his table. As Rowse passed, he raised an eyebrow. If Rowse had said so, he would have fought, even though the odds were impossible.

Rowse shook his head. "It's all right, Uli," he said. "Stay cool. Go home. I'll see you."

O'Keefe took Rowse to his own apartment. They drank Jamesons with water.

"Tell me about this 'research,' SAS man," said O'Keefe quietly.

Rowse knew there were two others in the passage within call. No need for any more violence. He told O'Keefe the outline of the plot of his intended next novel.

"Not about the lads in Belfast, then?" said O'Keefe.

"Can't use the same plot twice," said Rowse. "The publishers wouldn't have it. This one's about America."

They talked through the night. And drank. Rowse had a rock-hard head for whiskey, which was just as well. O'Keefe let him go at dawn. He walked back to his hotel to blow away the whiskey fumes.

The others worked on Kleist in the abandoned warehouse to which they had taken him after Rowse left the club. The big doorman held him down, and another Palestinian used the instruments.

Uli Kleist was very tough, but the Palestinians had learned

about pain in South Beirut. Kleist took all he could, but he talked before dawn. They let him die as the sun rose. It was a welcome release.

The big Irishman from the men's room watched and listened, occasionally dabbing his bleeding mouth. His orders from O'Keefe were to find out what the German knew about Rowse's presence in Hamburg. When it was over, he reported what he had learned. The IRA station head nodded.

"I thought there was more to it than a novel," he said. Later, he sent a cable to a man in Vienna. It was carefully worded.

When Rowse left O'Keefe's flat and walked back through the waking city to the railway station hotel, one of his minders moved quietly in behind him. The other kept watch on the abandoned warehouse but did not interfere.

In the lunch hour, Rowse ate a large bratwürst, heavily laced with sweet German mustard. He bought it from a *Schnellimbiss*, one of those stands on streetcorners that prepare the delicious sausages as snacks for those in a hurry. As he ate, he talked out of the side of his mouth to the man beside him.

"Do you think O'Keefe believed you?" asked McCready.

"He may have done. It's a plausible enough explanation. Thriller writers, after all, have to research some odd things in some strange places. But he may have had doubts. He's no fool."

"Do you think Kleist believed you?"

Rowse laughed. "No, not Uli. He's convinced I'm some sort of renegade turned mercenary, looking for arms on behalf of a client. He was too polite to say so, but the novel-research story didn't fool *him*."

"Ah," said McCready. "Well, perhaps last night was an added bonus. You're certainly getting yourself noticed. Let's see if Vienna gets you farther down the trail. By the way, you booked yourself on a flight tomorrow morning. Pay cash at the airport."

The Vienna flight was via Frankfurt and took off on time. Rowse was in business class. After takeoff, the stewardess distributed newspapers. As it was an internal flight, there were no English ones. Rowse could speak halting German and decipher headlines. The one covering much of the lower half of the front page of the *Morgenpost* did not need deciphering.

The face in the picture had its eyes closed and was surrounded by garbage. The headline read, SLAYER OF DRUG BARONS FOUND DEAD. The text below said two garbage collectors had found the body near a rubbish bin close to the docks. The police were treating the case as a gangland revenge killing.

Rowse, however, knew better. He suspected that an intervention by his SAS minders could have saved his German friend. He rose and walked through the curtains down the aisle to the economy-class toilets. Near the rear of the plane, he dropped the newspaper into the lap of a rumpled-looking man reading the in-flight magazine.

"You bastard," he hissed.

Somewhat to Rowse's surprise, Major Kariagin took his call at the Soviet Embassy at his first attempt. Rowse spoke in Russian.

SAS soldiers—most especially the officers—have to be multitalented creatures. As the basic SAS fighting unit has only four men, a wide spectrum of proficiencies is necessary. Within the four-man group, all will have advanced medical training, and all will be able to handle a radio. They will have several languages among them, apart from their varied fighting skills. As the SAS has operated in Malaya, Indonesia, Oman, and Central and South America, apart from its NATO role, the favored languages have always been Malay, Arabic, and Spanish. For the NATO role, the preferred proficiencies have been Russian (of course) and one or two Allied languages. Rowse spoke French, Russian, and Irish Gaelic.

For a complete stranger to telephone Major Kariagin at the embassy was not so odd, bearing in mind the major's secondary task of keeping an eye on the stream of applications made to the Czech arms outlet, Omnipol.

Intergovernmental applications were made to the Husak government in Prague. They did not concern him. Others, from more dubious sources, came to the external office of Omnipol, based in neutral Vienna. Kariagin saw them all.

Some he approved, some he referred to Moscow for a decision, others he vetoed out of hand. What he did not tell Moscow was that his judgment could be influenced by a generous tip. He agreed to meet Rowse that evening at Sacher's.

Kariagin did not look like a caricature Russian. He was smooth, groomed, barbered, and well tailored. He was known at the famous restaurant. The headwaiter showed him to a corner table away from the orchestra and the babble of the voices of the other diners. The two men sat and ordered *Schnitzel* with a dry, light Austrian red wine.

Rowse explained his need for information for his next novel.

Kariagin listened politely. "These American terrorists . . ." he said when Rowse had finished.

"Fictional terrorists," said Rowse.

"Of course. These fictional American terrorists—what would they be looking for?"

Rowse passed over a typed sheet that he took from his breast pocket. The Russian read the list, raised an eyebrow, and passed it back.

"Impossible," he said. "You are talking to the wrong man. Why did you come to see me?"

"A friend in Hamburg said you were extremely well informed."

"Let me change the question: Why come to see anyone? Why not make it up? It is for a novel, after all."

"Authenticity," said Rowse. "The modern novelist cannot get things hopelessly wrong. Too many readers today are not fooled by schoolboy howlers in the text."

"I'm afraid you are still in the wrong place, Mr. Rowse. That list contains some items that simply do not come under the heading of conventional weaponry. Booby-trapped briefcases, Claymore mines—these are simply not provided by the Socialist bloc. Why not use simpler weaponry in your . . . novel?"

"Because the terrorists—"

"Fictional terrorists," murmured Kariagin.

"Of course. The fictional terrorists apparently—that is, as I intend them in the book . . . wish to carry out an outrage involving the White House. Mere rifles obtainable in a Texan gunshop will not do."

"I cannot help you," said the Russian, wiping his lips. "These are the days of *glasnost*. Weaponry of the type of the Claymore mine, which in any case is American and unobtainable—"

"There is an East Bloc copy," said Rowse.

"—are simply not provided, except between government and government, and only then for legitimate defense purposes. My country would never dream of supplying such materiel or sanctioning its supply by a friendly state."

"Like Czechoslovakia."

"As you say, like Czechoslovakia."

"And yet these weapons do appear in the hands of certain terrorist groups," said Rowse. "The Palestinians, for example."

"Possibly, but I have not the faintest idea how," said the Russian. He made to rise. "And now, if you will excuse me—"

"I know it's a lot to ask," said Rowse, "but in the pursuit of authenticity, I do have a modest research fund."

He lifted the corner of his folded newspaper, which lay on the third chair at the table. A slim white envelope rested between the pages. Kariagin sat down again, extracted the envelope, and glanced at the Deutschmark bills inside. He looked thoughtful, then slipped the envelope into his breast pocket.

"If I were you, and wished to acquire certain kinds of materiel to sell on to a group of American terrorists—all fictional, of course—I think I might go to Tripoli and try to seek an interview with a certain Colonel Hakim al-Mansour. And now, I really must rush. Good night, Mr. Rowse."

"So far, so good," McCready said as they stood side by side in the men's room of a sleazy bar near the river. The two SAS sergeants had confirmed that neither man was being tailed, or the meeting could not have taken place. "I think you should go there."

"What about a visa?"

"The Libyan People's Bureau at Valletta would be your

best chance. If they grant a visa without delay, it will mean you have been preannounced."

"You think Kariagin will tip off Tripoli?" asked Rowse.

"Oh, I think so. Otherwise, why advise you to go there? Yes, Kariagin was offering his friend al-Mansour the chance to have a look at you and check out your ridiculous story a bit more deeply. At least no one believes the novel-research story anymore. You have crossed the first hurdle. The bad guys really are beginning to think you're a renegade trying to make a fast buck by working for some shadowy group of American madmen. Al-Mansour will want a lot more than that, of course."

Rowse flew from Vienna to Rome and thence to the capital of Malta. Two days later—no need to rush them off their feet, said McCready—he made his application to the People's Bureau for a visa to visit Tripoli. The reason he gave was a desire to do research for a book on the amazing progress of the People's Jamahariya. The visa came through in twenty-four hours.

The following morning, Rowse took the Libyan Airways flight from Valletta to Tripoli. As the ochre-brown coast of Tripolitania came into view across the glittering blue Mediterranean, he thought of Colonel David Stirling and the others, Paddy Mayne, Jock Lewis, Reilly, Almonds, Cooper, and the rest, the first of the SAS men, just after the group's formation, who had raided and blasted German bases along this coast more than a decade before he was born.

And he thought of McCready's words in the Valletta airport as the two minders waited in the car: "I'm afraid Tripoli is one place I cannot follow you. This is where you lose your backup. When you go in there, you will be alone."

Like his predecessors in 1941, some of whom were still buried down there in the desert, he would find that in Libya, he was completely alone.

The airliner tipped one wing and began to drop toward the Tripoli airport.

Chapter 3

At first, there seemed to be no problem. Rowse had been sitting in economy class and was one of the last out of the airliner. He followed the other passengers down the steps into the blazing sun of a Libyan morning.

From the observation terrace of the modern white airport building, a pair of impassive eyes picked him out, and binoculars trained briefly on him as he crossed the tarmac toward the Arrivals door. After several seconds the binoculars were laid aside, and a few calm words were muttered in Arabic.

Rowse entered the air-conditioned cool of the terminal and took his place at the end of the queue waiting for passport clearance. The sloe-eyed immigration officers took their time, scanning every page of each passport, gazing at each passenger's face, comparing it lengthily with the passport photo, and consulting a manual that was kept out of sight beneath their desks. Libyan passport holders were in a separate queue.

Two American oil engineers who had been in the smoking section and were behind Rowse made up the rear of the queue. It took twenty minutes for Rowse to reach the passport desk.

The green-uniformed officer took his passport, opened it, and glanced down at a note beneath the grill. Without expression, he raised his gaze and nodded to someone behind Rowse. There was a tug at Rowse's elbow. He turned. Another green uniform—younger, courteous but firm. Two armed soldiers stood farther back.

"Would you please come with me?" the young officer said in passable English.

"Is there something wrong?" asked Rowse. The two Americans had gone silent. In a dictatorship the removal of a passenger from the passport queue is a great conversation-stopper.

The young officer at his elbow reached under the grill and retrieved Rowse's passport.

"This way, if you please," he said. The two soldiers closed up from behind, one at each elbow. The officer walked, Rowse followed, the soldiers came behind. They turned out of the main concourse and down a long white passage. At the far end, on the left, the officer opened a door and gestured to Rowse to enter. The soldiers took up position at either side of the door.

The officer followed Rowse inside and closed the door. It was a bare white room with barred windows. A table and two facing chairs stood in the center, nothing else. A portrait of Muammar Qaddafi hung on one wall. Rowse took one of the chairs; the officer sat down facing him and began to study the passport.

"I don't understand what is wrong," said Rowse. "My visa was issued yesterday by your People's Bureau in Valletta. Surely it is in order?"

The officer simply made a gesture with one languid hand to suggest that Rowse should be quiet. He was. A fly buzzed. Five minutes elapsed.

From behind him, Rowse heard the door open. The young officer glanced up, shot to his feet, and saluted. Then without a word, he left the room.

"So, Mr. Rowse, here you are at last."

The voice was deep and modulated, the English of a kind that can only be learned in one of Britain's better public schools. Rowse turned. He allowed no trace of recognition to cross his face, but he had studied pictures of this man for hours in McCready's briefing sessions.

"He's slick and highly educated—by us," McCready had

said. "He's also utterly ruthless and quite deadly. Be careful of Hakim al-Mansour."

The Libyan head of external intelligence was more youthful than his pictures had suggested, barely older than Rowse himself. Thirty-three, the dossier had said.

In 1969, Hakim al-Mansour had been a fifteen-year-old schoolboy attending Harrow public school outside London, the son and heir of an extremely wealthy courtier and close confidant of Libyan King Idris.

It was in that year that a group of radical young officers headed by an unknown colonel of Bedouin origin called Qaddafi had carried out a coup d'état while the King was abroad, and had toppled him. They immediately announced the formation of the People's Jamahariyah, the socialist republic. The King and his court took refuge with their considerable wealth in Geneva and appealed to the West for help in their own restoration. None came.

Unknown to his father, the young Hakim was entranced by the turn of events in his own country. He had already repudiated his father and all his politics, for only a year earlier his young imagination had been fired by the riots and near-revolution of the radical students and workers in Paris. It is not unknown for the impassioned young to turn to radical politics, and the Harrow schoolboy had converted in body and soul. Rashly, he bombarded the Libyan Embassy in London with requests to be allowed to leave Harrow and return to his homeland to join the socialist revolution.

His letters were noted and rejected. But one diplomat, a supporter of the old regime, tipped off al-Mansour Senior in Geneva. There was a blazing row between father and son. The boy refused to recant. At seventeen, his funds cut off, Hakim al-Mansour left Harrow prematurely. For a year he moved around Europe, trying to persuade Tripoli of his loyalty and always rejected. In 1972 he pretended to reform his views, made peace with his father, and joined the court-in-exile in Geneva.

While he was there, he learned details of a plot by a number of former British Special Forces officers, funded by King Idris's financial chancellor, to create a countercoup against Qaddafi. They intended to mount a commando raid against the Libyan coastline in a ship called the *Leonardo da Vinci*, out of Genoa. The aim was to break open Tripoli's main jail, the so-called Tripoli Hilton, and release all the desert clan chiefs who supported King Idris and detested Muammar Qaddafi. They would then scatter, raise the tribes, and topple the usurper. Hakim al-Mansour immediately revealed the entire plan to the Libyan Embassy in Paris.

In fact, the plan had already been "blown away" by the CIA, who later regretted it, and it was dismantled by the Italian security forces at America's request. But al-Mansour's gesture earned him a long interview at the Paris embassy.

He had already memorized most of Qaddafi's rambling speeches and zany ideas, and his enthusiasm impressed the interviewing officer enough to earn the young firebrand a journey home. Two years after he was seconded to the Intelligence Corps, the Mukhabarat.

Qaddafi himself met and took to the younger man, promoting him beyond his years. Between 1974 and 1984, al-Mansour carried out a series of "wet affairs" for Qaddafi abroad, passing effortlessly through Britain, America, and France, where his fluency and urbanity were much appreciated, and through the terrorist nests of the Middle East, where he could become totally Arab. He carried out three personal assassinations of Qaddafi's political opponents abroad, and he liaised extensively with the PLO, becoming a close friend and admirer of the Black September planner and mastermind Abu Hassan Salameh, whom he much resembled.

Only a head cold had prevented him from joining Salameh for his dawn game of squash that day in 1979, when the Israeli Mossad finally closed on the man who had planned the butchery of their athletes at the Munich Olympics and blown him to bits. Tel Aviv's *kidon* team never knew how close they had come to taking two similar birds with one bomb.

In 1984, Qaddafi had promoted him to direct all foreign terror operations. Two years later, Qaddafi was reduced to a nervous wreck by American bombs and rockets. He wanted revenge, and it was al-Mansour's job to deliver it—quickly. The British angle was not a problem—the men of the IRA, whom al-Mansour privately regarded as animals, would leave a trail of blood and death across Britain if they were given the wherewithal. The problem was finding a group that would do the same thing inside America. And here was this young Britisher, who might or might not be a renegade. . . .

"My visa, I repeat, is in perfect order," Rowse said indignantly. "So may I ask what is going on?"

"Certainly, Mr. Rowse. The answer is simple. You are being denied entry into Libya."

Al-Mansour strolled across the room to stare out of the windows at the airline-maintenance hangars beyond.

"But why?" asked Rowse. "My visa was issued in Valletta yesterday. It is in order. All I want to do is try to research some passages for my next novel."

"Please, Mr. Rowse, spare me the bewildered innocence. You are a former soldier of the British Special Forces, apparently turned novelist. Now you turn up here saying you want to describe our country in your next book. Frankly, I doubt that your description of my country would be particularly flattering, and the Libyan people, alas, do not share your British taste for self-mockery. No, Mr. Rowse, you cannot stay. Come, I will escort you back to the plane to Malta."

He called an order in Arabic, and the door opened. The two soldiers entered. One took Rowse's grip. Al-Mansour picked up the passport from the table. The other soldier stood aside to let the two civilians pass.

Al-Mansour led Rowse down a different passage and out into the sunlight. The Libyan airliner stood ready for takeoff.

"My suitcase," said Rowse.

"Already back onboard, Mr. Rowse."

"May I know who I have been speaking to?" asked Rowse.

"Not for the moment, my dear fellow. Just call me . . . Mr. Aziz. Now, where will you go from here for your research?"

"I don't know," said Rowse. "I seem to have reached the end of the line."

"Then take a break," said al-Mansour. "Have a brief holiday. Why not fly on to Cyprus? A lovely island. Personally, I always favor the cool air of the Troodos Mountains at this time of year. Just outside Pedhoulas in the Marathassa Valley is a charming old hostelry called the Apollonia. I recommend it. Such interesting people tend to stay there. Safe journey, Mr. Rowse."

*   *   *

It was a lucky coincidence that one of the SAS sergeants spotted Rowse coming through the Valletta airport. They had not expected him back so soon. Both men were sharing a room at the airport hotel, spelling each other in the Arrivals hall on a four-hours-on, four-hours-off basis. The duty man was reading a sports magazine when he spotted Rowse emerging from customs, his suitcase in one hand and his grip in the other. Without raising his head, he let Rowse pass and watched him approach the desk beneath the logo for Cyprus Airways. Then he used a wall phone to rouse his colleague in the hotel. The colleague raised McCready in central Valletta.

"Damn," swore McCready. "What the hell's he doing back so fast?"

"Dunno, boss," said the sergeant, "but according to Danny, he's inquiring at the Cyprus Airways desk."

McCready thought furiously. He had hoped Rowse would stay in Tripoli for several days and that his cover story of seeking sophisticated weaponry for a bunch of fictional American terrorists would eventually lead to his arrest and interrogation by al-Mansour himself. Now it looked as if he had been thrown out. But why Cyprus? Had Rowse gone out of control?

McCready needed to get to him and find out what had happened in Tripoli. But Rowse was not checking into a hotel, where he could be covertly approached for a situation report. He was moving on. Perhaps he thought he was now under surveillance by the bad guys.

"Bill," he said down the line, "tell Danny to stay with him. When the coast is clear, get to the Cyprus Airways desk and try to find where they went. Then book us two on the same flight, and two more on the next flight, in case I can't get there on time. I'll be out there as soon as I can."

The traffic in downtown Valletta is fierce at sundown, and by the time McCready reached the airport, the evening flight for Nicosia had gone—with Rowse and Danny onboard. The next flight was not till the following day.

McCready checked into the airport hotel. At midnight, a call came in from Danny.

"Hallo, Uncle. I'm at the Nicosia airport hotel. Auntie's gone to bed."

"She must be tired," said McCready. "Is it a nice hotel?"

"Yes, it's lovely. We've got a super room. Six ten."

"I'm so glad. I'll probably stay there myself when I arrive. How's the holiday so far?"

"Great. Auntie's rented a car for tomorrow. I think we're going up into the mountains."

"That'll be lovely," McCready said jovially to his "nephew" across the eastern Mediterranean. "Why don't you reserve that room for me? I'll join you and Auntie as soon as I can. Good night, dear boy."

He put the phone down. "Bugger's going up into the mountains tomorrow," he said gloomily. "What the hell did he learn in that stopover in Tripoli?"

"We'll know tomorrow, boss," said Bill. "Danny'll leave a message in the usual place."

Never seeing the point of wasting good sleeping time, Bill rolled over, and in thirty seconds he was fast asleep. In his profession, one never knew when one would sleep next.

McCready's plane from Valletta touched down at the airport of the Cypriot capital just after eleven, having lost an hour because of the change of time zone. He was well separated from Bill, although they emerged from the same plane and took the same courtesy shuttle to the airport hotel. McCready settled into the lobby bar while Bill went up to room 610.

There was a maid cleaning it. Bill nodded and smiled, explained he had forgotten his razor, and went into the bathroom. Danny had left his situation report taped to the underside of the lavatory cistern lid. He emerged from the bathroom, nodded again to the maid, held up the razor he had produced from his pocket, was rewarded with an answering smile, and went back downstairs.

They made the exchange in the men's toilet off the lobby. McCready retired to a cubicle and read the sitrep.

It was just as well that Rowse had not tried to make contact. According to Danny, shortly after Rowse had appeared from the customs hall at Valletta, his tail had followed, a sallow young man in a fawn suit. The Libyan agent had shadowed Rowse until the Cyprus Airways plane took off for Nicosia, but he had not joined the flight. Another tail, presumably called up from the Libyan People's Bureau in Nicosia, had been waiting at the Nicosia airport and had shadowed Rowse to the hotel, where he had spent the night in the lobby. Rowse might have spotted either man, but he had given no sign. Danny had spotted both and stayed well back.

Rowse had asked the reception desk to order him a hired car for seven the following morning. Much later, Danny had done the same. Rowse had also asked for a map of the island and had consulted the reception manager on the best route to the Troodos Mountains.

In the last passage of the sitrep, Danny had said he would leave the hotel at five, park at a place where he could see the only route out of the car park, and wait for Rowse to emerge. He could not know whether the resident Libyan would follow Rowse all the way into the mountains or just see him off. He, Danny, would stay as close as he could and would call the hotel lobby when he had run Rowse to earth and could find a public phone. He would ask for Mr. Meldrum.

McCready returned to the lobby and made a brief call from one of the public phones to the British Embassy. Minutes later, he was speaking to the SIS Head of Station, an important post, bearing in mind Britain's bases on Cyprus and its proximity to Lebanon, Syria, Israel, and the Palestinian strongholds across the sea. McCready knew his colleague from their days in London, and he soon got what he wanted— an unmarked car with a driver who spoke fluent Greek. It would arrive within the hour.

The call for Mr. Meldrum came at ten past two. McCready took the phone from the hand of the reception manager. Once again it was the uncle-and-nephew routine.

"Hallo, dear boy. How are you? How nice to hear from you."

"Hallo, Uncle. Auntie and I have stopped for lunch at a lovely hotel high in the mountains outside the village of Pedhoulas. It's called the Apollonia. I think she may stay here, it's so lovely. The car gave a bit of problem at the end, so I've brought it to a garage in Pedhoulas run by a Mr. Demetriou."

"Never mind. How are the olives?"

"There are no olives up here, Uncle. Just apple and cherry orchards. Olives only grow down in the plain."

McCready put the phone down and headed for the men's room. Bill followed him. They waited till the only other occupant had left, checked the cubicles, and talked.

"Is Danny all right, boss?"

"Sure. He tailed Rowse to a hotel high in the Troodos Mountains. Seems Rowse has checked in. Danny's in the village at a garage called Demetriou's. He'll wait for us there. The Libyan tail, the olive-skinned one, remained down here, apparently satisfied that Rowse would go where he was supposed to go.

"The car will be here shortly. I want you to take your grip and leave. Wait for us half a mile down the road."

Thirty minutes later, Mr. Meldrum's car indeed appeared— a Ford Orion with several dents, the only true sign of an "unmarked" car in Cyprus. The driver was an alert young staffer from the Nicosia Station. His name was Bertie Marks, and he spoke fluent Greek. They picked up Bill from under the shade of a tree by the wayside and headed for the mountains to the southwest. It was a long drive. It was dusk before they entered the picturesque village of Pedhoulas, heart of the Troodos Mountains cherry industry.

Danny was waiting for them in a café opposite the garage. Poor Mr. Demetriou had still not mended the rented car— Danny had ensured when he sabotaged it that it would take at least half the day to fix.

He pointed out the Hotel Apollonia, and he and Bill surveyed the surrounding countryside in the darkening light with professional eyes. They fixed on the mountain slope across the valley from the hotel's splendid dining terrace, hefted their grips, and disappeared silently into the cherry orchards. One of them carried the hand-held communicator that Marks had brought from Nicosia. The other communicator stayed with McCready. The two SIS men found a smaller and less pretentious *taverna* in the village and checked in.

Rowse had arrived during the lunch hour, after a pleasant and leisurely drive from the airport hotel. He assumed he was being tailed by his SAS minders—and he certainly hoped he was.

The previous evening at Malta, he had deliberately dawdled through the passport and customs formalities. All the other passengers but one had cleared the formalities before him. Only the sallow young man from the Libyan Mukhabarat had hung back. That was when he knew "Mr. Aziz"—Hakim al-

Mansour—had given him a tail. He did not look around for
the SAS sergeants in the Malta concourse, hoping they would
not try to approach him.

The Tripoli tail had not joined the flight to Nicosia, so he
assumed another would be waiting for him there. And he was.
Rowse had behaved perfectly naturally and had slept well. He
had seen the Libyan leave him on the road out of the Nicosia
airport complex, and he hoped there was an SAS man somewhere behind him. He took his time, but he never looked
around or tried to make contact. There might be another
Libyan posted in the hills.

There was a room available at the Apollonia, so he took it.
Perhaps al-Mansour had arranged for it to be available—
perhaps not. It was a pleasant room with stunning views over
the valley to a hillside covered with cherry trees, which were
now just beyond their bloom.

He lunched lightly but well off a local lamb casserole,
washed down by a light Omhodos red wine, followed by fresh
fruit. The hotel was an old *taverna*, well refurbished and
modernized with added features such as a dining terrace built
on piles out over the valley; the tables were set well apart
under striped awnings. Whoever else was staying there, few
had turned up for lunch. There was an elderly man with jet-
black hair at a corner table on his own, who addressed the
waiter in mumbled English, and several couples who were
clearly Cypriots and might have simply come for lunch. When
he entered the terrace, a very pretty younger woman had
been leaving. Rowse had turned to look at her; she was quite
a head-turner, and with her mane of corn-gold hair, she was
almost certainly not Cypriot. All three admiring waiters had
bowed her out of the restaurant before one of them showed
him to his table.

After lunch he went to his room and took a nap. If al-
Mansour's laborious hint meant that he was now "in play,"
there was nothing further he could do but watch and wait. He
had done what he had been advised to do. The next move, if
any, was in the Libyan's court. He only hoped, if the going
got rough, that he still had some backup out there somewhere.

The backup was indeed in place, by the time Rowse awoke
from his nap. The two sergeants had found a small stone hut

among the cherry trees on the mountainside opposite the
hotel terrace. They had carefully removed one of the stones
of the wall facing across the valley, which gave them a nice
aperture from which to observe the hotel at a range of seven
hundred yards. Their high-powered field glasses brought the
dining terrace to a range that appeared to be twenty feet.

Dusk was deepening when they called up McCready and
gave him directions to approach their hideout from the other
side of the mountain. Bertie Marks drove according to the
instructions, out of Pedhoulas and down two tracks, until they
saw Danny standing in their way.

Abandoning the car, McCready followed Danny around the
curve of the mountain. They disappeared into the cherry
orchard and made the hut without being perceived from
across the valley. There, Bill handed McCready his image-
intensifying night glasses.

On the dining terrace the lights were coming on, a ring of
colored bulbs strung around the perimeter of the dining area,
with candles in sconces on each table.

"We'll need Cypriot peasant clothes tomorrow, boss,"
murmured Danny. "Can't move around this hillside dressed
as we are for long."

McCready made a mental note to have Marks go to a village
some miles away in the morning and buy the sort of canvas
smocks and trousers they had seen farm workers by the
wayside wearing. With luck, the hut would remain undis-
turbed; in May it was too late for the spraying of the blossom
and too early for the harvest. The hut was clearly abandoned,
its roof half-collapsed. Dust was everywhere; a few broken-
hafted hoes and mattocks stood against one wall. For the SAS
sergeants, who had lain for weeks among soaking scrapes on
the hillsides of Ulster, it was like a four-star hotel.

"Hallo," muttered Bill, who had taken back the night
glasses. "Tasty." He passed the glasses to McCready.

A young woman had entered the terrace from the recesses
of the hotel. A beaming waiter was showing her to a table.
She wore a simple but elegant white dress over a golden
suntan. Blonde hair hung about her shoulders. She sat down
and apparently ordered a drink.

"Keep your minds on your work," grumbled McCready.
"Where's Rowse?"

The sergeants grinned. "Oh yeah, him. One line of windows above the terrace. Third window to the right."

McCready swiveled his glasses. None of the windows had their curtains drawn. Several had lights on. McCready saw a figure, naked but for a towel around his waist, emerge from the shower room and cross the floor of the bedroom. It was Rowse. So far, so good.

But none of the bad guys had shown up. Two other guests took their places on the terrace: a plump Levantine business-man with flashing rings on both hands, and an elderly man who sat alone at one corner of the terrace and studied the menu. He sighed. His life had involved a hell of a lot of waiting, and he still hated it. He handed back the glasses and checked his watch. Seven-fifteen. He would give it two hours before he took Marks back to the village for supper. The sergeants would keep the vigil through the night. It was what they were best at—apart from violent physical action.

Rowse dressed and checked his watch: seven-twenty. He locked his room and went down to the terrace for a drink before dinner. Beyond the terrace the sun had dropped below the mountains, bathing the far side of the valley in thick gloom while the silhouette of the hills was brilliantly back-lit. On the western coast, Paphos would still be enjoying a warm late-spring evening with another hour of sunshine to go.

There were three people on the dining terrace: a fat man of Mediterranean look, an old fellow with unlikely black hair, and the woman. She had her back to him, staring at the view across the valley. A waiter approached. Rowse nodded to the table next to the woman's, up against the terrace balustrade. The waiter grinned and hastened to show him to it. Rowse ordered ouzo and a carafe of local spring water.

As he took his seat, she glanced sideways. He nodded and murmured, "Evening." She nodded back and continued to gaze at the view of the darkening valley. His ouzo arrived. He too looked at the valley.

After a while he said, "May I propose a toast?"

She was startled. "A toast?"

He gestured with his glass to the shadow-shrouded sentinels of the mountains all around them and the wash of blazing orange sunset behind them.

"To tranquility. And spectacular beauty."

She gave a half-smile. "To tranquility," she said, and drank a sip of her dry white wine. The waiter brought two menus. At separate tables they studied their cards. She ordered mountain trout.

"I can't better that. The same for me, please," Rowse told the waiter, who left.

"Are you dining alone?" asked Rowse quietly.

"Yes, I am," she said carefully.

"So am I," he said. "And it worries me, for I'm a God-fearing man."

She frowned in puzzlement. "What's God got to do with it?"

He realized her accent was not British. There was a husky twang; American? He gestured beyond the terrace. "The view, the peace, the hills, the dying sun, the evening. He created all of this, but surely not for dining alone."

She laughed, a flash of clear white teeth in a sun-golden face. Try to make them laugh, his dad had told him. They like to be made to laugh.

"May I join you? Just for dinner?"

"Why not? Just for dinner."

He took his glass and crossed to sit opposite her. "Tom Rowse," he said.

"Monica Browne," she replied.

They talked, the usual small talk. He explained that he was the writer of a moderately successful novel and had been doing some research in the area for his next book, which would involve Levantine and Middle East politics. He had decided to end his tour of the eastern Mediterranean with a brief break at this hotel, recommended by a friend for its good food and restfulness.

"And you?" he asked.

"Nothing so exciting. I breed horses. I've been in the area buying three thoroughbred stallions. It takes time for the shipment papers to come through. So"—she shrugged—"time to kill. I thought it would be nicer here than stewing on the dockside."

"Stallions? In Cyprus?" he asked.

"No, Syria. The yearling sales at Hama. Pure Arabs, the finest. Did you know that every race horse in Britain is ultimately descended from three Arabian horses?"

"Just three? No, I didn't."

She was enthused by her horses. He learned that she was married to the much older Major Eric Browne and that together they owned and ran a breeding stud at Ashford. Originally she was from Kentucky, which was where she had gained her knowledge of bloodstock and horse-racing. He knew Ashford vaguely—it was a small town in Kent, on the road from London to Dover.

The trout arrived, deliciously grilled over a charcoal brazier. It was served with a local dry white wine from up the Marathassa Valley.

Inside the hotel, beyond the patio doors open to the terrace, a group of three men had moved into the bar.

"How long will you have to wait?" asked Rowse. "For the stallions?"

"Any day now, I hope. I worry about them. Maybe I should have stayed with them in Syria. They're terribly mettlesome. Get nervous in transit. But my shipping agent here is very good. He'll call me when they arrive, and I'll ship them out personally."

The men in the bar finished their whiskey and were shown out onto the terrace to a table. Rowse caught a hint of their accents. He raised a steady hand to his mouth with a forkful of trout.

"Ask yer man to bring another round of the same," said one of the men.

Across the valley, Danny said quietly, "Boss."

McCready jackknifed to his feet and came to the small aperture in the stone wall. Danny handed him the glasses and stood back. McCready adjusted focus and let out a long sigh.

"Bingo," he said. He handed the glasses back. "Keep it up. I'm going back with Marks to watch the front of the hotel. Bill, come with me."

By then, it was so dark on the mountainside that they could walk around to where the car was still waiting without fear of being seen from across the valley.

On the terrace, Rowse kept his attention fixed entirely on Monica Browne. One glance had told him all he needed to know. Two of the Irishmen he had never seen before. The third—clearly leader of the group—was Kevin Mahoney.

Rowse and Monica Browne declined desserts and took coffee. Small sticky sweetmeats came with it. Monica shook her head.

"No good for the figure—no good at all," she said.

"And yours should in no way be harmed, for it is quite stunning," said Rowse. She laughed away the compliment, but not with displeasure. She leaned forward. By the candlelight Rowse caught a brief but dizzying glance of the channel between her full breasts.

"Do you know those men?" she asked earnestly.

"No, never seen 'em before," said Rowse.

"One of them seems to be staring at you a lot."

Rowse did not want to turn and look at them, but after that remark it would have been suspicious not to. The dark handsome features of Kevin Mahoney were fixed on him. As he turned, Mahoney did not bother to glance away. Their eyes met. Rowse knew the glance: puzzlement. Unease. As of someone who thinks he has seen a person somewhere before but cannot place him.

Rowse turned back. "Nope. Total strangers."

"Then they are very rude strangers."

"Can you recognize their accent?" asked Rowse.

"Irish," she said. "Northern Irish."

"Where did you learn to detect Irish accents?" he asked.

"Horse racing, of course. The sport is full of them. And now, it's been lovely, Tom, but if you'll excuse me, I'm going to turn in."

She rose. Rowse followed, his fleeting suspicion allayed.

"I agree," he said. "It was a wonderful dinner. I hope we can eat together again."

He looked for a hint that she might want him to accompany her, but there was none. She was in her early thirties, her own woman, and not stupid. If she wanted that, she would indicate it in some small way. If not, it would be foolish to spoil things. She gave him a radiant smile and swept off the terrace. Rowse took another coffee and turned away from the Irish trio to look out across the dark mountains. Soon he heard them retire back to the bar and their whiskey.

"I told you it was a charming place," said a deep, cultured voice behind him.

Hakim al-Mansour, as beautifully tailored as ever, slipped into the vacant chair and gestured for coffee.

Across the valley, Danny laid down his glasses and muttered urgently into his communicator. In the Ford Orion, parked up the road from the Apollonia's main entrance, McCready listened. He had not seen the Libyan enter the hotel, but he might have been there for hours.

"Keep me posted," he told Danny.

"You did indeed, Mr. Aziz," said Rowse calmly. "And it is. But if you wanted to talk to me, why did you expel me from Libya?"

"Oh, please—not expel," drawled al-Mansour. "Just decline to admit. And well, the reason was that I wished to talk to you in complete privacy. Even in my homeland there are formalities, records to be kept, the curiosity of superiors to satisfy. Here—nothing but peace and quiet."

"And the facility," thought Rowse, "to carry out a quiet liquidation and leave the Cypriot authorities with a British body to explain."

"So," he said aloud, "I must thank you for your courtesy in agreeing to help me with my research."

Hakim al-Mansour laughed softly. "I think the time for that particular foolishness is over, Mr. Rowse. You see, before certain—animals—put him out of his misery, your late friend Herr Kleist was quite communicative."

Rowse spun around on him, bitterly angry. "The papers said he was killed by the drug people, in revenge for what he did to them."

"Alas, no. The people who did to him what was done do indeed deal in drugs. But their principal enthusiasm is for planting bombs in public places, principally in Britain."

"But why? Why should those bloody Paddies have been interested in Ulrich?"

"They weren't, my dear Rowse. They were interested in finding out what you were really up to in Hamburg, and they thought your friend might know. Or suspect. And he did. He seemed to believe your tarradiddle about "fictional" Ameri-

can terrorists masked a quite different purpose. That information, coupled with further messages received from Vienna,
brought me to the view that you might be an interesting man
to talk to. I hope you are, Mr. Rowse; for your sake, I
sincerely hope you are. And the time has come to talk. But
not here.''

Two men had appeared behind Rowse. They were big and
olive-skinned.

"I think we should go for a little ride," said al-Mansour.

"Is this the sort of ride from which one returns?" asked
Rowse.

Hakim al-Mansour rose. "That depends very much on
whether you are able to answer a few simple questions to my
satisfaction," he said.

McCready was waiting for the car when it emerged from
the portico of the Apollonia onto the road, having been tipped
off by Danny across the valley. He saw the Libyans' car—
with Rowse in the back seat between the two heavies—turn
away from the hotel.

"Do we follow, boss?" asked Bill from the rear seat of the
Orion.

"No," said McCready. To try and follow without lights
would have been suicide on those hairpin curves. To put on
headlights would give the game away. Al-Mansour had chosen
his terrain well. "If he comes back, he'll tell us what went on.
If not . . . well, at least he's in play at last. The bait is being
examined. We'll know by morning whether it has been taken
or rejected. By the way, Bill, can you enter that hotel unseen?"

Bill looked as if he had been grievously insulted.

"Slip that under Rowse's door," said McCready, and he
passed the sergeant a tourist brochure.

The drive took an hour. Rowse forced himself not to look
around. But twice, after the Libyan driver had negotiated
hairpin bends, Rowse could look back the way they had come.
There was no moving wash of another car's headlights behind
them. Twice the driver pulled to the side of the road, doused
his lights, and waited for five minutes. No one came past
them. Just before midnight, they arrived at a substantial villa
and drove through wrought-iron gates. Rowse was decanted

and pushed through the door, which was opened by another heavyweight Libyan. With al-Mansour himself, that made five. Too heavy odds.

And there was another man waiting for them in the large drawing room into which he was pushed, a heavy-set, jowly, big-bellied man in his late forties with a brutal, coarsened face and big red hands. He was clearly not a Libyan. In fact, Rowse easily recognized him though he gave no sign. The face had been in McCready's rogue's gallery, shown to him as a face he might one day see if he agreed to plunge into the world of terrorism and the Middle East.

Frank Terpil was a CIA renegade, fired by the Agency in 1971. Soon after, he had gravitated to his true and very lucrative vocation in life—supplying torture equipment, terrorist tricks, and expertise to Uganda's Idi Amin. Before the Ugandan monster was toppled and his hideous State Research Bureau broken up, he had introduced the American to Muammar Qaddafi. Since then Terpil, sometimes in association with another renegade, Edwin Wilson, had specialized in providing a vast range of terrorist equipment and technology to the most extreme groups around the Middle East, always remaining the servitor of the Libyan dictator.

Even by then, Terpil had been well out of the Western intelligence community for fifteen years, but he was still regarded in Libya as the "American" expert. It suited him well to hide the fact that by the late 1980s, he was completely out of touch.

Rowse was told to take a chair in the middle of the room. The furniture was almost entirely shrouded in dust sheets. Clearly, the villa was a holiday home for a wealthy family who had shut it up for the winter. The Libyans had simply taken it over for the night, which was why Rowse had not been blindfolded.

Al-Mansour removed a dust sheet and fastidiously seated himself in a brocade high-back chair. A single bulb hung over Rowse. Terpil took a nod from al-Mansour and lumbered over.

"Okay, boy, let's talk. You've been going around Europe looking for arms. Very special weapons. What the hell are you really up to?"

"Researching a new novel. I've tried to explain that a dozen times. It's a novel. That's my job, that's what I do. I write thriller novels. About soldiers, spies, terrorists—fictional terrorists.''

Terpil hit him once on the side of the face—not hard, but enough to indicate there was more where that came from and plenty of it.

"Cut the shit," he said without animosity. "I'm going to get the truth anyway, one way or the other. Might as well keep it painless—all the same to me. Who are you really working for?"

Rowse let the story come out slowly, as he had been briefed, sometimes recalling things exactly, sometimes having to search his memory.

"Which magazine?"

"Soldier of Fortune."

"Which edition?"

"April . . . May, last year. No, May, not April."

"What did the ad say?"

" 'Weapons expert needed, European area, for interesting assignment' . . . something like that. A box number."

"Bullshit. I take that magazine every month. There was no such ad."

"There was. You can check."

"Oh, we will," murmured al-Mansour from the corner of the room. He was making notes with a slim gold pen on a Gucci pad.

Rowse knew Terpil was bluffing. There had been such an ad in the columns of *Soldier of Fortune*. McCready had found it, and a few calls to his friends in the CIA and the FBI had ensured—or so Rowse fervently hoped—that the placer of the ad would not be available to deny he had ever received a reply from Mr. Thomas Rowse of England.

"So you wrote back."

"Yep. Plain paper. Accommodation address. Giving my background, areas of expertise. Instructions for a reply, if any."

"Which were?"

"Small ad in the London *Daily Telegraph*." He recited the wording. He had memorized it.

"The ad appeared? They made contact?"

"Yep."

"What date?"

Rowse gave it. Previous October. McCready had found that ad as well. It had been chosen at random, a perfectly genuine small advertisement from an innocent British citizen, but with wording that would suit. The *Telegraph* staff had agreed to alter the records to show it had been placed by someone in America and paid for in cash.

The interrogation went on. The phone call he had taken from America after placing a further ad in The *New York Times*. (That too had been found after hours of searching—a real ad listing a British phone number. Rowse's own unlisted number had been changed to tally with it.)

"Why the roundabout way of getting in touch?"

"I figured I needed discretion in case the placer of the original ad was crazy. Also that my secretiveness might impress whoever it was."

"And did it?"

"Apparently. The speaker said he liked it. Set up a meet."

When? Last November. Where? The Georges Cinq in Paris. What was he like?

"Youngish, well dressed, well spoken. Not registered at the hotel. I checked. Called himself Galvin Pollard. Certainly phony. A yuppie type."

"A what?"

"Young, upwardly mobile professional," drawled al-Mansour. "You're out of touch."

Terpil went red. Of course. He had seen the term but forgotten it.

What did he say? He said he represented a group of ultra-radical people, Rowse replied, who were sick and tired of the Reagan Administration, of its hostility to the Soviet and Third Worlds, and particularly of the use of American planes and taxpayer money to bomb women and children in Tripoli the previous April.

"And he produced a list of what he wanted?"

"Yes."

"This list?"

Rowse glanced at it. It was a copy of the list he had shown Kariagin in Vienna. The Russian must have a superb memory.

"Yes."

"Claymore mines, for God's sake. Semtex-H. Booby-

trapped briefcases. This is high-tech stuff. What the hell did
they want all that for?''

"He said his people wanted to strike a blow. A real blow.
He mentioned the White House, and the Senate. He seemed
particularly keen on the Senate.''

He allowed the money side of it to be dragged out of him.
The account at the *Kreditanstalt* in Aachen with half a million
dollars in it. (Thanks to McCready, there really was such an
account, backdated to the appropriate period. And bank
secrecy is not really all that good. The Libyans could confirm
it if they wanted to.)

"So what did you get involved for?''

"There was a twenty percent commission. A hundred thousand dollars.''

"Peanuts.''

"Not to me.''

"You write thriller novels, remember.''

"Which don't sell all that well. Despite the publisher's
blurb. I wanted to make a few bob.''

"Bob?''

"Shillings,'' murmured al-Mansour. "British equivalent for
"greenbacks'' or "dough.''

At four in the morning, Terpil and al-Mansour went into a
huddle. They talked quietly in an adjacent room.

"Could there really be a radical group in the States prepared to carry out a major outrage at the White House and
the Senate?'' asked al-Mansour.

"Sure,'' said the burly American who hated his homeland.
"In a country that size, you get all kinds of weirdos. Jesus,
one Claymore mine in a briefcase on the lawn of the White
House. Can you imagine it?''

Al-Mansour could. The Claymore is one of the most devastating antipersonnel weapons ever invented. Shaped like a
disk, it leaps into the air when detonated, then sends thou-
sands of ball-bearings outward from the perimeter of the disk
at waist-height. A moving sheet of these missiles will slice
through hundreds of human beings. Loosed in an average
railway concourse, a Claymore will leave few of the thousands
of commuters in the area alive. For this reason, the sale of the

Claymore is fiercely vetted by America. But there are always replicas. . . .

At half-past four, the two men returned to the sitting room. Although Rowse did not know it, the gods were smiling on him that night. Al-Mansour needed to bring something to his Leader without further delay to satisfy the insistent pressure for revenge against America; Terpil needed to prove to his hosts that he was still the man they needed to advise them about America and the West. Finally, both men believed Rowse for the reason that most men believe: because they wanted to.

"You may go, Mr. Rowse," said al-Mansour mildly. "We will check, of course, and I will be in touch. Stay at the Apollonia until I or someone sent by me gets in touch."

The two heavies who had brought him drove him back and dropped him at the hotel doorway before driving off. When he entered his room, he switched on the light, for the dawn was not yet bright enough to fill his west-facing room. Across the valley, Bill, who was on the shift, activated his communicator and awoke McCready in his hotel room in Pedhoulas.

Rowse stooped to pick something from the carpet inside his room. It was a brochure inviting visitors to visit the historic Kykko Monastery and admire the Golden Icon of the Virgin. A single script in pencil beside the paragraph said "Ten A.M."

Rowse set his alarm for three hours' sleep. "Screw Mc-Cready," he said as he drifted off.

Chapter 4

Kykko, the largest monastery in Cyprus, was founded in the twelfth century by the Byzantine emperors. They chose their spot well, bearing in mind that the lives of monks are supposed to be spent in isolation, meditation, and solitude.

The vast edifice stands high on a peak west of the Marathassa Valley in a situation so remote that only two roads lead to it, one from each side. Finally, below the monastery, the two roads blend into one, and a single lane leads upward to the monastery gate.

Like the emperors of Byzantium, McCready, too, chose his spot well. Danny had stayed behind in the stone hut across the valley from the hotel, watching the curtained windows of the room where Rowse slept, while Bill, on a motorcycle acquired for him locally by the Greek-speaking Marks, had ridden ahead to Kykko. At dawn, the SAS sergeant was well hidden in the pines above the single track to the monastery.

He saw McCready himself arrive, driven by Marks, and he watched to see who else came. Had any of the Irish trio appeared, or the Libyan car (they had noted its number), McCready would have been alerted by three warning blips on the communicator and would have vaporized. But only the

usual stream of tourists—most of them Greek and Cypriot—
trundled up the track on that May morning.

During the night the head of station in Nicosia had sent one
of his young staffers up to Pedhoulas with several messages
from London and a third communicator. Each sergeant now
had one, aside from McCready.

At half-past eight Danny reported that Rowse had appeared
on the terrace and taken a light breakfast of rolls and coffee.
There was no sign of Mahoney and his two friends, or Rowse's
girl from the evening before, or any of the other guests at the
hotel.

"He's looking tired," said Danny.

"No one said this would be a holiday for any of us,"
snapped McCready from his seat in the courtyard of the
monastery twenty miles away.

At twenty-past nine Rowse left. Danny reported it. Rowse
drove out of Pedhoulas, past the great painted church of the
Archangel Michael that dominated the mountain village, and
turned northwest on the road to Kykko. Danny continued his
watch on the hotel. At half-past nine the maid entered
Rowse's room and drew the curtains back. That made life
easier for Danny. Other curtains were withdrawn on the
facade of the hotel facing the valley. Despite the rising sun in
his eyes, the sergeant was rewarded by the sight of Monica
Browne doing ten minutes of deep-breathing exercises quite
naked in front of her window.

"Beats South Armagh," murmured the appreciative veteran.

At ten to ten, Bill reported that Rowse had come into sight,
climbing the steep and winding track to Kykko. McCready
rose and went inside, wondering at the labor that had brought
these massive stones so high into the mountain peaks, and at
the skill of the masters who had painted the frescoes in the
gold leaf, scarlet, and blue that decorated the incense-sweet
interior.

Rowse found McCready in front of the famous Golden Icon
of the Virgin. Outside, Bill insured that Rowse had not grown
a tail, and he gave McCready two double-blips on the communicator in the senior agent's breast pocket.

"It seems you're clean," murmured McCready as Rowse
appeared beside him. There was no strangeness in talking in

a low voice; all around them, the other tourists conversed in whispers, too, as if afraid to disturb the calm of the shrine.

"So shall we start at the beginning?" said McCready. "I remember seeing you off at the Valletta airport on your very brief visit to Tripoli. Since then, if you please, every detail."

Rowse started at the beginning.

"Ah, so you met the notorious Hakim al-Mansour," said McCready after a few minutes. "I hardly dared hope he'd turn up at the airport himself. Kariagin's message from Vienna must have tickled his fancy. Go on."

Part of Rowse's narrative McCready could confirm from his own and the sergeants' observations—the sallow-faced young agent who had followed Rowse back to Valletta and seen him on the Cyprus flight, the second agent at Nicosia who had tailed him until he left for the mountains.

"Did you see my two sergeants? Your two former colleagues?"

"No, never. I remain to be convinced they're even there," said Rowse. Together they stared up at the Madonna who, with calm and pitying eyes, stared back down at them.

"Oh, they're here, all right," said McCready. "One's outside at the moment, just to see that neither you nor I was followed. Actually, they're taking quite a lot of pleasure in your adventures. When this is all over, you can have a drink together. Not yet. So . . . after you arrived at the hotel?"

Rowse skipped through to the moment he first saw Mahoney and his two cronies.

"Wait a minute, the girl. Who is she?"

"Just a vacation pickup. An American race-horse breeder waiting for the arrival of three Arab stallions she bought last week at the Hama yearling sales in Syria. Monica Browne. With an "e." No problem, just a dining companion."

"Are you sure?"

"Yes, Sam. Quite sure. Just a civilian. And a very pretty one, as it happens."

"So we noticed," muttered McCready. "Go on."

Rowse narrated the arrival of Mahoney and the suspicious glances his companion had intercepted across the terrace.

"You think he recognized you? From that filling station forecourt?"

"He couldn't have done," said Rowse. "I had a wool cap

down to my eyes and stubble all over my face, and I was half-hidden by the petrol pumps. No, he'd stare like that at any Englishman as soon as he heard the accent. You know how much he hates us all."

"Maybe. Go on."

It was the sudden appearance of Hakim al-Mansour and the nightlong interrogation by Frank Terpil that really interested McCready. He made Rowse stop a dozen times to clarify tiny points. The Deceiver was carrying a hard-cover book on Cypriot Byzantine churches and monasteries. As Rowse talked, he made copious notes in the book, writing over the Greek text. No mark appeared from the point of his pencil—that would only come later when the chemicals were applied. To any bystander, he was just a tourist making notes on what he saw around him.

"So far, so good," mused McCready. "Their arms shipment operation seems to be on hold, ready for some ''go'' order. Mahoney and al-Mansour turning up at the same hotel in Cyprus is too much to mean anything else. What we have to know is when, where, and how. Land, sea, or air? From where and to where? And the carrier—truck, air freight, or cargo ship?"

"You're still sure they'll go ahead? Not call the whole thing off?"

"I'm sure."

There was no need to tell Rowse why he was sure. Rowse had no need to know. But there had been another message from the Libyan doctor who attended Muammar Qaddafi. It would be a multipackage shipment, when it came. Some of the weapons would be for the Basque separatists, the ETA. More would be for the French ultra-Left group, the Action Directe. Another consignment for the small but lethal Belgian terrorists, the CCC. A large present for the German Red Army Faction—at least half, no doubt, to be used on bars frequented by U.S. servicemen. More than half the shipment was for the IRA.

It was reported that one of the IRA's tasks would be the assassination of the American ambassador to London. McCready suspected that the IRA, mindful of its fund-raising operations in America, would farm that job out—probably to the Germans of the Faction, successors to the Baader-Meinhof gang, who were diminished in numbers but still deadly and prepared to take contract work in exchange for arms.

"Did they ask where you would want the shipment for the American terror group, if they agree to sell?" McCready asked Rowse.

"Yes."

"And you told them?"

"Anywhere in Western Europe."

"Plans for getting it to the States?"

"Told them what you said. I'd remove the consignment, which is quite small in bulk, from wherever they delivered it to a rented garage known only to me. I'd return with a camper van or mobile home, with hidden compartments behind the walls. Drive the van north through Denmark, on the ferry to Sweden, up to Norway and take it on one of the many freighters crossing to Canada. Just another tourist on a wild-life-watching vacation."

"They like that?"

"Terpil did. Said it was neat and clean. Al-Mansour objected that it would mean crossing several national frontiers. I pointed out that in the holiday season, camper vans pour across Europe, and that at each stage I would say I was picking up my wife and kids at the next capital's airport after they flew in. He nodded several times."

"All right. We've made our pitch. Now we have to wait and see if you've convinced them. Or if their greed for revenge against the White House will outweigh natural caution. It has been known."

"What happens next?" asked Rowse.

"You go back to the hotel. If they swallow the American scheme and include your package in the shipment, al-Mansour will contact you, either personally or by courier. Follow his instructions to the letter. I'll only close in on you for a situation report when the coast is clear."

"And if they don't swallow it?"

"Then they'll try to silence you. Probably ask Mahoney and his boys to do the job as a sign of good faith. That'll give you your chance at Mahoney. And the sergeants will be close by. They'll move in to pull you out alive."

"The hell they will," thought Rowse. That would blow away London's awareness of the plot. The Irish would scatter, and the whole shipment would reach them by another route at another time and place. If al-Mansour came for him directly or indirectly, he would be on his own.

"Do you want a warning bleeper?" asked McCready. "Something to bring us running?"

"No," said Rowse shortly. There was no point in having one. No one would come.

"Then go back to the hotel and wait," said McCready. "And try not to tire yourself to exhaustion with the pretty Mrs. Browne. With an 'e.' You might need your strength later."

McCready then drifted away into the throng. He too knew he could not intervene if the Libyans or the Irish came for Rowse. What he had decided to do, in case the Libyan fox had not believed Rowse, was to bring in a far larger team of watchers and to keep an eye on Mahoney. When he moved, the Irish arms consignment would be moving. Now that he had found Mahoney, the IRA man was the better bet as a trace to the shipment.

Rowse completed his tour of the monastery and emerged into the brilliant sunshine to find his car. Bill, from his cover under the pines up on the hill below the tomb of the late President Makarios, watched him go and alerted Danny that their man was on his way back. Ten minutes later, McCready left, driven by Marks. On the way down the hill they gave a lift to a Cypriot peasant standing by the roadside and thus brought Bill back to Pedhoulas.

Fifteen minutes into the forty-minute drive, McCready's communicator crackled into life. It was Danny.

"Mahoney and his men have just entered our man's room. They're ransacking it. Giving it a right going over. Shall I get out on the road and warn him?"

"No," said McCready. "Stay put and keep in touch."

"If I speed up, we might be able to overtake him," suggested Marks.

McCready glanced at his watch. An empty gesture. He was not even calculating the miles and the speed to Pedhoulas.

"Too late," he said. "We'd never catch him."

"Poor old Tom," said Bill from the back.

Unusually with subordinates, Sam McCready lost his temper. "If we fail, if that load of shit gets through, poor old shoppers at Harrods, poor old tourists in Hyde Park, poor old women and children all over our bloody country,'' he snapped.

There was silence all the way to Pedhoulas.

Rowse's key was still hanging on its hook in the reception lobby. He took it himself—there was no one behind the desk—and walked upstairs. The lock to his room was undamaged; Mahoney had used the key and replaced it in the lobby. But the door was unlocked. Rowse thought the maid might still be bed-making, so he walked right in.

As he entered, a powerful shove from the man behind the door sent him staggering forward. The door slammed shut, access to it barred by the stocky one. Danny's long-range photographs had been sent down to Nicosia with the courier before dawn, faxed to London, and identified. The stocky one was Tim O'Herlihy, a killer from the Derry Brigade; the beefy ginger-haired one by the fireplace Eamonn Kane, an enforcer from West Belfast. Mahoney sat in the room's only armchair, his back to the window, whose curtains had been drawn to filter the brilliant daylight.

Without a word Kane grabbed the staggering Englishman, spun him around, and flattened him against the wall. Skilled hands ran quickly over Rowse's short-sleeved shirt and down each leg of his trousers. If he had been carrying McCready's offered bleeper, it would have been discovered and ended the game there and then.

The room was a mess, every drawer opened and emptied, the contents of the wardrobe scattered all over. Rowse's only consolation was that he carried nothing that an author on a research trip would not have had—notebooks, story outline, tourist maps, brochures, portable typewriter, clothes, and washkit. His passport was in his back trouser pocket. Kane fished it out and tossed it to Mahoney. Mahoney flicked through it, but it told him nothing he did not already know.

"So, Sass-man, now perhaps you'll tell me just what the feck you're doing here."

There was the usual charming smile on his face, but it did not reach the eyes.

"I don't know what the hell you're talking about," said Rowse indignantly.

Kane swung a fist that caught Rowse in the solar plexus.

He could have avoided it, but O'Herlihy was behind him and
Kane was to one side. The odds were loaded, even without
Mahoney. These men were not Sunday-school teachers.
Rowse grunted and doubled, leaning against the wall and
breathing heavily.

"Don't you now? Don't you now?" said Mahoney without
rising. "Well, normally I have other ways than words of
explaining myself, but for you, Sass-man, I'll make an exception. A friend of mine in Hamburg identified you there a
couple of weeks back. Tom Rowse, former captain in the
Special Air Service Regiment, well-known fan club of the
Irish people, asking some very funny questions. Two tours in
the Emerald Isle behind him, and now he turns up in the
middle of Cyprus just when my friends and I are trying to
have a nice quiet holiday. So once again, what are you doing
here?"

"Look," said Rowse. "Okay, I was in the regiment. But I
quit. Couldn't take any more of it. Denounced them all, the
bastards, three years ago. I'm out, well out. The British
Establishment wouldn't piss on me if I was on fire. Now I
write novels for a living. Thriller novels. That's it."

Mahoney nodded to O'Herlihy. The punch from behind
caught him in the kidneys. He cried out and dropped to his
knees. Despite the odds, he could have fought back and
finished at least one of them, maybe two, before going down
himself for the last time. But he took the pain and slumped to
his knees.

Despite Mahoney's arrogance, Rowse suspected the terrorist chief was puzzled. He must have noticed Rowse and Hakim
al-Mansour in conversation on the terrace last night, before
driving off. Rowse had returned from that all-night session,
and Mahoney was on the point of receiving a very big favor
from al-Mansour. No, the IRA man had not turned lethal—
yet. He was just having fun.

"You're lying to me, Sass-man, and I don't like it. I've
heard this just-doing-my-research story before. You see, we
Irish are a very literary people. And some of the questions
you have been asking are not literary at all. So what are you
doing here?"

"Thrillers," wheezed Rowse. "Thrillers nowadays have to
be accurate. Can't get away with vague generalizations. Look

at le Carré, Clancy—you think they don't research every last detail? It's the only way nowadays.''

"Is it now? And a certain gentleman from across the water that you were talking with last night—he one of your co-writers?"

"That's between us. You'd better ask him."

"Oh, I did, Sass-man. This morning, by phone. And he asked me to keep an eye on you. If it were left to me, I'd have the lads drop you off a very tall mountain. But my friend asked me to keep an eye on you. Which I will do, day and night, until you leave. But that was all he asked me. So just between us, here's a little something for the old times."

Kane and O'Herlihy waded in. Mahoney watched. When Rowse's legs gave way, he went down to the floor, doubling up, protecting the lower stomach and genitals. He was too low for a good punch, so they used the feet. He rolled his head away to avoid brain damage, feeling the toecaps thud into his back, shoulders, chest, and ribs, choking on the wave of pain until the merciful blackness came after a kick on the back of the head.

He came to in the manner of people who have been in a road accident: first gingerly aware that he was not dead, and then conscious of the pain. Beneath his shirt and trousers, his body was one large ache.

He was lying on his face, and for a while he studied the pattern of the carpet. Then he rolled over: a mistake. He ran a hand to his face. There was one lump on the cheek below the left eye; otherwise it was more or less the same face he had been shaving for years. He tried to sit up and winced. An arm went behind his shoulders and eased him into a sitting position.

"What the hell happened here?" she asked.

Monica Browne was on her knees beside him, one arm around his shoulders. The cool fingers of her right hand touched the lump below his left eye.

"I was passing, saw the door ajar. . . ."

Quite a coincidence, he thought, then dismissed the idea.

"I must have fainted and thumped myself as I went down," he said.

"Was that before or after you wrecked the room?"

He glanced around. He had forgotten about the tumbled drawers and the scattered clothes.

She unbuttoned his shirt front. "Jesus, that was some fall," was all she said. Then she helped him up and led him to the bed. He sat on it. She pushed him backward, lifted his legs, and rolled him onto the mattress.

"Don't go away," she said unnecessarily. "I have some liniment in my room."

She was back in minutes, closing the door behind her and giving the key a swift turn. She unbuttoned his Sea Island cotton shirt and slipped it from his shoulders, tut-tutting at the sight of the four bruises, now turning a fetching blue, that adorned his torso and ribs.

He felt helpless, but she seemed to know what she was doing. A small bottle was uncorked, and gentle fingers rubbed liniment into the bruised areas. It stung. He said, "Ow."

"It'll do you good, take the swelling down, help the discoloration. Roll over."

She eased more liniment into the bruises on his shoulders and back.

"How come you carry liniment around?" he mumbled. "Do all your dining partners end up like this?"

"It's for horses," she said.

"Thanks a lot."

"Stop fussing—it has the same effect on stupid men. Roll back."

He did so.

She stood over him, her golden hair falling about her shoulders. "They hit you in the legs as well?"

"All over."

She unbuttoned the waistband of his trousers, unzipped them, and eased them down and off without a fuss. It was no strange task for a young wife with a husband who drank too much. Apart from one lump on the right shin, there were another half-dozen bluish areas on the thighs. She massaged the liniment into them. After the sting, the sensation was of pure pleasure. The odor reminded him of the days when he played Rugby at school. She paused and set the bottle down.

"Is that a bruise?" she asked.

He glanced down toward his jockey shorts. No, it was not a bruise.

"Thank God," she murmured. She turned away and reached for the zipper at the back of her cream shantung dress. The filtered light from the curtains gave the room a low, cool glow.

"Where did you learn about bruises?" he asked.

After the beating and the massage, he was feeling drowsy. His head was drowsy, anyway.

"Back in Kentucky, my kid brother was an amateur jockey," she said. "I patched him up a few times."

Her cream dress slid to the floor in a pool. She wore tiny Janet Reger panties. No bra strap crossed her back. Despite the fullness of her breasts, she needed none. She turned around. Rowse swallowed.

"But this," she said, "I did not learn from any brother."

He thought fleetingly about Nikki back in Gloucestershire. He had not done this before, not since marrying Nikki. But, he reasoned, a warrior occasionally needs solace, and if it is offered, he would be less than human to refuse.

He reached up for her as she straddled him, but she took his wrists and pressed them back on the pillow.

"Lie still," she whispered. "You're far too ill to participate."

But for the next hour or so she seemed quite content to be proved wrong.

Just before four she rose and crossed the room to open the curtains. The sun had passed its azimuth and was moving toward the mountains.

Across the valley Danny the sergeant adjusted his focus and said, "Cor, you dirty bastard, Tom."

The affair lasted for three days. The horses did not arrive from Syria, nor any message for Rowse from Hakim al-Mansour. She checked with her agent on the coast regularly, but always the answer was "Tomorrow." So they walked through the mountains, took picnics high above the cherry orchards where the conifers grow, and made love among the pine needles.

They breakfasted and dined on the terrace, while Danny and Bill watched in silence from across the valley and Mahoney and his colleagues glowered from the bar.

McCready and Marks stayed at their pension in Pedhoulas

village while McCready organized more men from Nicosia Station and a few from Malta. As long as Hakim al-Mansour made no contact with Rowse to indicate that their prepared story had, or had not, been accepted, the key was the Irishman Mahoney and his two colleagues. They were running the IRA enterprise; so long as they stayed, the operation would not move into the shipment phase.

The two SAS sergeants were to give backup to Rowse; the rest would keep the IRA men under surveillance at all times.

On the second day after Rowse and Monica first made love, McCready's team was in place, scattered through the hills covering every road in and out of the area from observation posts in the hills.

The telephone line to the hotel had been intercepted and tapped. The monitoring listeners were ensconced in another nearby hotel. Few of the newcomers could speak Greek, but fortunately tourists were common enough for another dozen not to arouse suspicions.

Mahoney and his men never left the hotel. They, too, were waiting for something: a visit, or a phone call, or a hand-delivered message.

On the third day Rowse was up as usual just after dawn broke. Monica slept on, and it was Rowse who took the tray of morning coffee from the waiter at the door. When he lifted the coffee pot to pour his first cup, he saw a folded wafer of paper beneath it. He put the wafer between the cup and the saucer, poured the coffee, and walked with it into the bathroom.

The message said simply, "Club Rosalina, Paphos, 11 P.M. Aziz."

That posed a problem, Rowse mused as he flushed the fragments of the message down the toilet. Easing Monica out of the picture for the few hours it would take to get to Paphos and back in the middle of the night would not be easy.

The problem was solved at midday, when fate intervened in the form of Monica's shipping agent, who called to say that the three stallions would be arriving from Latakia in the port of Limassol that evening, and could she please be present to see them signed for and settled in their stables outside the port?

She left at four o'clock, and Rowse made life easier for his backup team by walking up to Pedhoulas village and ringing the manager of the Apollonia to say that he had to go to Paphos that evening for dinner and what, please, was the best route? The message was picked up by the listeners and passed to McCready.

The Rosalina Club turned out to be a casino in the heart of the Old Town. Rowse entered it just before eleven and soon saw the slim, elegant figure of Hakim al-Mansour seated at one of the roulette tables. There was a chair vacant next to him. Rowse slid into it.

"Good evening, Mr. Aziz. What a pleasant surprise."

Al-Mansour inclined his head gravely. *"Faites vos jeux,"* called the croupier.

The Libyan placed several high-denomination chips on a combination of the higher numbers. The wheel spun, and the dancing white ball elected to fall into the slot number four. The Libyan showed no annoyance as his chips were swept away. That single throw would have kept a Libyan farmer and his family for a month.

"Nice of you to come," said al-Mansour as gravely. "I have news for you. Good news, you will be pleased to hear. It is always so agreeable to impart good news."

Rowse felt relieved. That morning, the fact that the Libyan had sent the message to him instead of an order to Mahoney to lose the Englishman forever among the mountains had been hopeful. Now, it looked even better.

Rowse watched as the Libyan lost another pile of chips. He was inured to the temptation of gambling, regarding the roulette wheel as the most stupid and boring artifact ever invented. But the Arabs compare only with the Chinese as gamblers, and even the cool al-Mansour was entranced by the spinning wheel.

"I am happy to tell you," said al-Mansour as he placed more chips, "that our glorious Leader has acceded to your request. The equipment you seek will be provided—in full. There. What is your reaction?

"I'm delighted," said Rowse. "I'm sure my principals will put it to . . . good use."

"We must all fervently hope so. That is, as you British soldiers say, the object of the exercise."

"How would you like payment?" asked Rowse.

The Libyan waved a deprecatory hand. "Accept it as a gift from the People's Jamahariya, Mr. Rowse."

"I am very grateful. I am sure my principals will be, too."

"I doubt it, for you would be a fool ever to tell them. And you are not a fool. A mercenary, perhaps, but not a fool. So as you will now be making a commission of not one hundred thousand dollars but half a million, perhaps you will split that with me? Shall we say, fifty-fifty?"

"For the fighting funds, of course."

"Of course."

Retirement fund, more like, Rowse thought, then said aloud, "Mr. Aziz, sir, you have a deal. When I can pry the money out of the clients, half will come to you."

"I do hope so," murmured al-Mansour. This time he won, and a pile of chips was pushed toward him. Despite his urbanity, he was delighted. "My arm is very long."

"Trust me," said Rowse.

"Now that, my dear chap, would be insulting . . . in our world."

"I need to know about shipment. Where to collect, when."

"And so you shall. Soon. You asked for a port in Europe. I think that can be arranged. Return to the Apollonia, and I will be in touch very soon."

He rose and handed Rowse his remaining pile of chips. "Do not leave the casino for another fifteen minutes," he said. "Here—enjoy yourself."

Rowse waited for fifteen minutes, then cashed in the chips. He preferred to buy Nikki something nice.

He left the casino and strolled toward his car. Because of the narrow streets of the Old Town, parking was at a premium even late at night. His car was two streets away. He never saw Danny or Bill, who were in doorways up and down the road.

As he approached his car, an old man in blue denim and a forage cap was brushing the garbage from the gutters with a yard-broom.

"*Kali spera,*" croaked the old road-sweeper.

"*Kali spera,*" replied Rowse. He paused. The old man was one of those, finally beaten by life, who do the menial jobs all over the world. He remembered the wad of money from al-Mansour's winnings, pulled out a large-denomination note, and tucked it into the old man's top pocket.

"My dear Tom," said the road-sweeper, "I always knew you had a good heart."

"What the hell are you doing here, McCready?"

"Just keep jiggling with your car keys and tell me what happened," said McCready as he pushed his broom.

Rowse told him.

"Good," said McCready. "It looks like a ship. That probably means they're tacking your small cargo onto the much larger one for the IRA. We must hope so. If yours is simply sent as a one-shot by a different route in a different container, we're back to where we started. Left with Mahoney. But as your load is only a van-full, they may pack them all together. Any idea which port?"

"No, just Europe."

"Go back to the hotel, and do what the man says," ordered McCready.

Rowse drove off. Danny, on a motorcycle, went after him to ensure that Rowse had no follower other than himself. Ten minutes later, Marks arrived with the car and Bill to pick up McCready.

On the drive back, McCready sat in the rear and thought. The ship, if ship it was, would not be Libyan registered. That would be too obvious. Probably a chartered freighter, with a no-questions-asked captain and crew. There were scores of such to be found all over the eastern Mediterranean, and Cyprus was a favored country of registry.

If it was chartered locally, it would have to go to a Libyan port to take on the arms, probably to be buried beneath a perfectly normal cargo like crated olives or dates. The IRA team would probably go with it. When they left the hotel, it was vital that they be followed to the loading dock so the name of the ship could be noted for later interception.

Once noted, the plan was for the vessel to be tracked by a submarine at periscope depth. The submarine was on standby under the waters off Malta. A Royal Air Force Nimrod from the British air base at Akrotiri on Cyprus would guide the sub toward the steaming freighter, then make itself scarce. The sub would do the rest until Royal Navy surface vessels could make the intercept in the English Channel.

McCready needed the ship's name, or at least the port of destination. With the name of the port, he could have his friends at Lloyds Shipping Intelligence find out what vessels had reserved berthings in that port and for which days. That would narrow the choice down. It could be he no longer needed Mahoney, if only the Libyans would tell Rowse.

The message to Rowse came twenty-four hours later by telephone. It was not al-Mansour's voice but another. Later, McCready's engineers traced it to the Libyan People's Bureau in Nicosia.

"Go home, Mr. Rowse. You will be contacted there shortly. Your olives will arrive by ship at a European port. You will be contacted personally with arrival and collection details."

McCready studied the intercept in his hotel room. Did al-Mansour suspect something? Had he seen through Rowse but decided on a double-bluff? If he suspected Rowse's real employers, he would know that Mahoney and his group were also under surveillance. So was he ordering Rowse to England in order to take the watchers off Mahoney? Possibly.

In case it was not only possible but true, McCready decided to play both ends. He would leave with Rowse for London, but the watchers would stay with Mahoney.

Rowse decided to tell Monica the next morning. He had got back to the hotel from Paphos before her. She arrived from Limassol at three A.M., flushed and excited. Her stallions were in beautiful condition, now stabled outside Limassol, she told him as she undressed. She only needed the transit formalities to be completed to bring them to England.

Rowse awoke early, but she was ahead of him. He glanced at the empty space in the bed, then went down the corridor to check her room. They gave him a message at the reception desk, a brief note in one of the hotel's envelopes.

Dear Tom,
   It was beautiful but it's over. I'm gone, back to my husband and my life and my horses. Think kindly of me, as I will of you.
                                             Monica.

He sighed. Twice he had briefly thought she might be something other than she seemed. Reading her note, he real-

ized he had been right at the beginning—she was just a
civilian. He also had his life—with his country home and his
writing career and his Nikki. Suddenly he wanted to see Nikki
very badly.

As he drove back to the Nicosia Airport, Rowse guessed his
two sergeants were somewhere behind him. They were. But
McCready was not. Using the Head of Station in Nicosia, he
had found a Royal Air Force communications flight heading
for Lyneham, Wiltshire, that would get in ahead of the scheduled British Airways flight. McCready was already on it.

Just before midday, Rowse glanced out of the porthole of
the plane and saw the green mass of the Troodos Mountains
slipping away beneath the wing. He thought of Monica, and
Mahoney still propping up the bar, and al-Mansour, and he
was glad to be going home. For one thing, the green fields of
Gloucestershire were a good deal safer than the caldron of the
Levant.

Chapter 5

Rowse's flight touched down just after lunch, with the time gained from flying west from Cyprus. McCready had preceded him by an hour, though Rowse did not know it. As he emerged from the airplane cabin into the jetway connecting to the terminal, a trim young woman in a British Airways uniform was holding up a sign saying, MR. ROWSE.

He identified himself.

"Ah, there's a message for you at the Airport Information desk, just outside the customs hall," she said.

He thanked her, puzzled, and walked on toward passport control. He had not told Nikki he was coming, wishing to surprise her. When he got to the information desk, the message said, "Scott's. Eight P.M. Lobsters on me!"

He cursed. That meant he would not get home to Gloucestershire and Nikki until morning.

His car was in the long-term car park—no doubt, if he had not returned, the ever-efficient Firm would have had it removed and returned to his widow. He took the courtesy shuttle, retrieved his car, and checked into one of the airport hotels. It gave him time for a bath, a shave, sleep, and to change into a suit. Since he intended to drink a lot of fine wine if the Firm was paying, he decided to take a taxi to and from the West End of London.

First he rang Nikki. She was ecstatic, her voice shrill with a mixture of relief and delight. "Are you all right, darling?"

"Yes, I'm fine."

"And is it over?"

"Yes, the research is finished, all bar a couple of extra details that I can sort out here in England. How have you been?"

"Oh, great. Everything's great. Guess what happened?"

"Surprise me."

"Two days after you left, a man came. Said he was furnishing a large company flat in London, looking for carpets and rugs. He bought the lot, all our stock. Paid cash. Sixteen thousand pounds. Darling, we're flush!"

Rowse held the receiver and stared at the Degas print on the wall.

"This buyer, where was he from?"

"Mr. Da Costa? Portugal. Why?"

"Dark-haired, olive-skinned?"

"Yes, I suppose so."

Arab, Rowse thought. Libyan. That meant that while Nikki was out in the barn where they kept the stock of carpets and rugs that they sold as a sideline, someone had been in the house and probably bugged the phone. Al-Mansour certainly liked to cover all the angles. Had he made a single ill-judged phone call to Nikki from Vienna or Malta or Cyprus, as he had been tempted to do, he would have blown away himself and the mission.

"Well," he said cheerfully, "I don't care where he was from. If he paid cash, he's wonderful."

"When are you coming home?" she asked excitedly.

"Tomorrow morning. Be there about nine."

He presented himself at the superb fish restaurant in Mount Street at ten past eight and was shown to where Sam Mc-Cready already sat at a corner table. McCready liked corner tables. That way, each diner could sit with his back to a wall, at right angles to each other. It was easier to converse that way than sitting side by side, yet each was able to see the restaurant. "Never take it in the back," one of his training

officers had told him years ago. The same man was later
betrayed by George Blake and "took it" in a KGB interrogation cell. McCready had spent much of his life with his back
to the wall.

Rowse ordered lobster and asked for it Newberg. McCready
had his cold, with mayonnaise. Rowse waited until a glass of
Meursault had been poured for each and the sommelier had
departed before he mentioned the mysterious buyer of the
rugs. McCready chewed on a mouthful of Benbecula lobster,
swallowed, and said, "Damn. Did you phone Nikki from
Cyprus anytime before I tapped the hotel phone?"

"Not at all," said Rowse. "My first call was from the Post
House Hotel, a few hours ago."

"Good. Good and bad. Good that there were no inadvertent
slipups. Bad that al-Mansour is going to such lengths."

"He's going a bloody sight farther than that," said Rowse.
"I can't be sure, but I think there was a motorcycle, a Honda,
both at the long-term car park when I got my car back, and at
the Post House. Never saw it from the taxi into London, but
the traffic was very thick."

"Damn and blast!" said McCready with feeling. "I think
you're right. There's a couple at the end of the bar who keep
peering through the gap. And they're looking at us. Don't
turn around—keep eating."

"Man and woman, youngish?"

"Yes."

"Recognize either?"

"I think so. The man, anyway. Turn your head and call the
wine waiter. See if you can spot him. Lank hair, downturned
moustache."

Rowse turned to beckon the waiter. The couple were at the
end of the bar, separated from the main dining area by a
screen.

Rowse had once done intensive antiterrorist training. It had
meant scouring hundreds of photographs, not only of the
IRA. He turned back to McCready.

"Got him. A German lawyer. Ultraradical. Used to defend
the Baader-Meinhof crowd, later became one of them."

"Of course. Wolfgang Ruetter. And the woman?"

"No. But the Red Army Faction uses a lot of groupies. A
new face. More watchers from al-Mansour?"

"Not this time. He'd use his own people, not German radicals. Sorry, Tom, I could kick myself. Since al-Mansour didn't have a tail on you in Cyprus, and since I was so busy ensuring that you passed all of the Libyan's tests, I momentarily took my eye off that bloody paranoid psycho Mahoney. If those two at the bar are Red Army Faction, they'll be on an errand from him. I thought there'd be no heat on you once you got back here. I'm afraid I was wrong."

"So what do we do?" asked Rowse.

"They've already seen us together. If that gets out, the operation's finished, and so are you."

"Couldn't you be my agent, my publisher?"

McCready shook his head. "Won't work," he said. "If I leave by the back door, it'll be all they need. If I go by the front like a normal diner, it's short odds I'll be photographed. Somewhere in Eastern Europe that photo will be identified. Keep talking naturally, but listen. Here's what I want you to do."

During the coffee, Rowse summoned the waiter and asked for directions to the men's room. It was staffed, as McCready knew it would be. The tip he gave the attendant was more than generous—it was outrageous.

"Just for a phone call? You got it, guv'nor."

The call to the Special Branch of the Metropolitan Police, a personal call to a friend of McCready's, was placed while McCready was signing the slip for his credit card. The woman had left the restaurant as soon as he called for the bill.

When Rowse and McCready emerged under the illuminated portico, the woman was half-hidden in the alley beside the poultry shop just down the street. Her camera lens picked up McCready's face, and she ran off two quick shots. There was no flash; the portico lights were enough. McCready caught the movement, but he gave no sign.

The pair walked slowly to McCready's parked Jaguar. Ruetter emerged from the restaurant and crossed to his motorcycle. He took his helmet from the pannier and put it on, visor down. The woman left the alley and straddled the machine behind him.

"They've got what they want," said McCready. "They may peel off anytime. Let's just hope their curiosity keeps them there for a short while."

McCready's car phone trilled. On the other end was his friend in the Special Branch.

McCready filled him in. "Terrorists, probably armed. Battersea Park, near the Pagoda." He replaced the receiver and glanced in his mirror. "Two hundred yards—still with us."

Apart from the tension, it was an uneventful drive to the sprawl of Battersea Park, which was normally closed and locked at sundown. As they approached the Pagoda, McCready glanced up and down the road. Nothing. Not surprising—the park had been reopened by Rowse's telephone call.

"Diplomatic protection drill—remember it?"

"Yep," said Rowse, and reached for the handbrake.

"Go."

Rowse yanked hard on the brake as McCready pulled the Jaguar into a savage turn. The rear end of the car slid around, tires screaming in protest. In two seconds, the sedan turned around and was heading the other way. McCready drove straight at the oncoming single headlight of the motorcycle. Two unmarked parked cars nearby put on their headlights, and their engines came to life.

Ruetter swerved to avoid the Jaguar and succeeded. The powerful Honda veered off the road, over the curb, and onto the parkland. It almost missed the bench, but not quite. Rowse, in the passenger seat, caught a glimpse of the motorcycle somersaulting over, its passengers spilling onto the grass. The other cars drew up and decanted three men.

Ruetter was winded but unharmed. He sat up and reached under his jacket.

"Armed police. Freeze," said a voice beside him. Ruetter turned and looked into the barrel of a service-issue Webley .38. The face above it was smiling. Ruetter had seen the film *Dirty Harry* and decided not to make anyone's day. He withdrew his hand. The Special Branch sergeant stood back, the Webley pointed double-handed at the German's forehead. A colleague removed the Walther P38 Parabellum from inside the motorcycle jacket.

The woman was unconscious. A large man in a light gray coat walked from one of the cars toward McCready. Commander Benson, Special Branch.

"What have you got, Sam?" he asked.

"Red Army Faction. Armed, dangerous."

"The woman is not armed," said Ruetter clearly, in English. "This is an outrage."

The Special Branch Commander took a small handgun from his pocket, walked over to the woman, pressed the automatic into her right hand, then dropped it in a plastic bag.

"She is now," he said mildly.

"I protest!" said Ruetter. "This is in flagrant breach of our civil rights."

"How true," said the Commander sadly. "What do you want, Sam?"

"They have my picture, they know my name. And they saw me with him." He jerked his head at Rowse. "If that gets out, there'll be an awful lot of grief on the streets of London. I need them held incommunicado. No trace, no appearances. They must be badly hurt after that crash—a secure hospital, perhaps?"

"Isolation ward, I shouldn't wonder. What with the poor darlings being in a coma and no papers on them, it'll take me weeks even to identify them."

"My name is Wolfgang Ruetter," said the German. "I am a lawyer from Frankfurt and I demand to see my ambassador."

"Funny how deaf you can get in middle age," complained the Commander. "Into the car with them, lads. As soon as I can identify them, of course, I'll bring them to court. But it could take a long time. Keep in touch, Sam."

In Britain, as a rule, even when an armed and identified member of a terrorist group is arrested, he or she cannot be held without a court appearance for longer than seven days, under the Prevention of Terrorism Act. But all rules occasionally have their exceptions, even in a democracy.

The two unmarked police cars drove away. McCready and Rowse climbed into the Jaguar. They had to get out of the park so it could be locked up again.

"When this is over," asked Rowse, "will they come for me or Nikki?"

"They've never done that yet," said McCready. "Hakim al-Mansour is a pro. Like me, he accepts that in our game, you win some and you lose some. He'll shrug and get on with his next operation. Mahoney is trickier, I know, but for twenty years the IRA has targeted only their own informers

and holders of high office. I'm convinced he'll go back to
Ireland to make his peace with the IRA Army Council. They,
at least, will warn him off personal vengeance missions. So
hang on in there for just a few more days. It'll be okay after
that."

Rowse drove back to Gloucestershire the following morning
to take up the reins of his life again and await the promised
contact from Hakim al-Mansour. As he saw it, when he
received the information concerning the docking of the arms
ship, he would pass the tip to McCready. The SIS would trace
the ship backward from that, identify it in the Mediterranean,
and pick it up in the Eastern Atlantic or in the English
Channel, with Mahoney and his team on board. It was as
simple as that.

The contact came seven days later. A black Porsche crept
into the courtyard of Rowse's home, and a young man
climbed out. He looked around at the green grass and beds of
flowers in the late May sunshine. He was dark-haired and
saturnine, and he came from a drier, harsher land.

"Tom," called Nikki. "Someone to see you."

Rowse came around from the rear garden. He let no trace
of expression mask the polite inquiry on his face, but he
recognized the man: It was the tail who had followed him
from Tripoli to Valletta, then seen him off on the flight to
Cyprus two weeks earlier.

"Yes?" he said.

"Mr. Rowse?"

"Yes."

"I have a message from Mr. Aziz." His English was reasonable but careful, too careful to be fluent. He recited his
message as he had learned it.

"Your cargo will arrive at Bremerhaven. Three crates, all
marked as office machinery. Your normal signature will secure release. Bay Zero Nine, Warehouse Neuberg. Ross-
mannstrasse. You must remove them within twenty-four
hours of their arrival date, otherwise they will disappear. Is
that clear?"

Rowse repeated the exact address, fixing it in his mind. The
young man climbed back into his car.

"One thing. When? Which day?"

"Ah, yes. The twenty-fourth. They arrive at noon of the twenty-fourth."

He drove away, leaving Rowse with his mouth open. Minutes later he was racing to the village to use the public phone, having ensured he was still clean of a tail. His own phone was still tapped, the experts had confirmed, and it would have to stay that way for a while longer.

"What the hell can they mean, the twenty-fourth?" raged McCready for the tenth time. "That's in three days! Three bloody days!"

"Mahoney's still in place?" asked Rowse. He had just driven up to London at McCready's insistence, and they were meeting at one of the Firm's safe houses, an apartment in Chelsea. It was still not safe to bring Rowse to Century House—officially, he was persona non grata there.

"Yes, still propping up the bar at the Apollonia, still surrounded by his team, still waiting for a word from al-Mansour, still surrounded by my watchers."

McCready had already worked out that there were only two choices. Either the Libyans were lying about the twenty-fourth—another test for Rowse, to see if the police would raid the Neuberg warehouse. In which case al-Mansour would have time to divert his ship somewhere else. Or else he, McCready, had been duped—Mahoney and his team were decoys and probably did not know it themselves.

Of one thing he was certain: No ship could get from Cyprus to Bremerhaven via Tripoli or Sirte in three days. While Rowse was motoring to London, McCready had consulted his friend at Dibben Place, Colchester, home of Lloyds Shipping Intelligence. The man was adamant. First, it would take one day to sail from, say, Paphos to Tripoli or Sirte. Allow another day for loading, more likely a night. Two days to Gibraltar, and four or five more to northern Germany. Seven days minimum, more likely eight.

So either it was a test for Rowse, or the arms ship was already at sea. According to the man from Lloyds, to dock at Bremerhaven on the twenty-fourth, it would now be somewhere west of Lisbon, heading north to clear Finisterre.

Checks were being made by Lloyds as to the names of ships expected in Bremerhaven on the twenty-fourth with a Mediterranean port of departure. The phone rang. It was the Lloyds expert on a patch-through to the Chelsea safe house.

"There aren't any," he said. "Nothing from the Mediterranean is expected on the twenty-fourth. You must have been misinformed."

With a vengeance, thought McCready. In Hakim al-Mansour, he had come up against a master of the game.

He turned to Rowse.

"Apart from Mahoney and his crew, was there *anyone* in that hotel who even smelled of IRA?"

Rowse shook his head.

"I'm afraid it's back to the photograph albums," said McCready. "Go through them over and over again. If there's any face—anything at all—that you spotted in your time in Tripoli, Malta, or Cyprus, let me know. I'll leave you with them. I have some errands to run."

McCready did not even consult Century House about asking for American help. Time was too short to go through channels. He went to see the CIA Station Head in Grosvenor Square, Bill Carver.

"Well, Sam, I don't know. Diverting a satellite isn't that easy. Can't you use a Nimrod?"

Royal Air Force Nimrods can take high-definition pictures of ships at sea, but they tend to fly so low that they are seen themselves. Without added altitude, they have to make many passes to cover a large area of ocean.

McCready considered long and hard. If he knew the consignment had gotten through and was firmly in the hands of the IRA, he would have wasted no time alerting the CIA to the threat to their ambassador in London, as reported by the Libyan doctor in Qaddafi's tent.

But for weeks his concern had been just to stop the arms shipment from getting through to the final destination. Now, needing CIA help, he produced his bombshell—he told Carver of the threat.

Carver came out of his chair as if jet-propelled. "Jesus H. Christ, Sam!" he exploded. Both men knew that apart from the catastrophe of a U.S. ambassador being slaughtered on British soil, Charles and Carol Price had proved the most popular American emissaries in decades. Mrs. Thatcher would not easily forgive an organization that allowed anything to happen to Charlie Price.

"You'll get your fucking satellite," said Carver. "But next time you damned well better tell me earlier than this."

It was almost midnight before Rowse went wearily back to Album One, the old days. He was sitting with a photo expert brought over from Century House. A projector and screen had been installed so that photographs could be thrown onto the screen and alterations made to the faces.

Just before one o'clock, Rowse paused.

"This one," he said. "Can you put it on the screen?"

The face filled almost one wall.

"Don't be daft," said McCready. "He's been out of it for years. A has-been, over the hill."

The face stared back, tired eyes behind thick-rimmed glasses, iron-gray hair over the creased brow.

"Lose the glasses," Rowse said to the photo expert. "Give him brown contact lenses."

The technician made adjustments. The glasses vanished, and the eyes went from blue to brown.

"How old is this photo?"

"About ten years," said the technician.

"Age him ten years. Thin the hair, more lines, dewlaps under the chin."

The technician did as he was told. The man looked about seventy now.

"Turn the hair jet black. Hair dye."

The thin gray hair turned deep black. Rowse whistled.

"Sitting alone in the corner of the terrace," he said, "at the Apollonia. Talking to no one, keeping himself to himself."

"Stephen Johnson was Chief of Staff of the IRA—the *old* IRA—twenty years ago," said McCready. "Quit the whole organization ten years ago, after a blazing row with the new generation over policy. He's now sixty-five. Sells agricultural machinery in County Clare, for heaven's sake."

Rowse grinned. "Used to be an ace, had a row, quit in disgust, known to be out in the cold, untouchable by those inside the Establishment—remind you of anyone you know?"

"Sometimes, young Master Rowse, you can even be half-way smart," admitted McCready.

He called up a friend in the Irish police, the Garda Sio-
chana. Officially, contacts between the Irish Garda and their
British counterparts in the fight against terrorism are supposed to be formal but at arm's length. In fact, between
professionals, those contacts are often warmer and closer
than some of the more hardline politicians would wish.

This time it was a man in the Irish Special Branch, awakened at his home in Ranelagh, who came up trumps around
the breakfast hour.

"He's on holiday," said McCready. "According to the local
Garda, he's taken up golf and departs occasionally for a
golfing holiday, usually in Spain."

"Southern Spain?"

"Possibly. Why?"

"Remember the Gibraltar affair?"

They both remembered it all too well. Three IRA killers,
planning to plant a huge bomb in Gibraltar, had been "taken
out" by an SAS team—prematurely but permanently. The
terrorists had arrived on the Rock as tourists from the Costa
del Sol and the Spanish police and counterintelligence force
had been extremely helpful.

"There was always rumored to be a fourth in the party, one
who stayed in Spain," recalled Rowse. "And the Marbella
area is stiff with golf courses."

"The bugger," breathed McCready. "The old bugger. He's
gone active again."

In the middle of the morning, McCready took a call from Bill
Carver, and they went over to the American Embassy. Carver
received them in the main hall, signed them in, and took them
to his office in the basement, where he too had a room all set
up for viewing photographs.

The satellite had done its job well, rolling gently high in
space over the eastern Atlantic, pointing its Long Tom cameras downward to cover a strip of water from the Portuguese,
Spanish, and French coasts to more than one hundred miles
out into the ocean in a single pass.

Acting on a suggestion from his Lloyds contact, McCready
had asked for a study of a rectangle of water from Lisbon
north to the Bay of Biscay. The continuous welter of photographs that had poured back to the receiving station of the

National Reconnaissance Office outside Washington had been broken down into individual snaps of every ship afloat in that rectangle.

"The bird photographed everything bigger than a floating Coke can," remarked Carver proudly. "You want to start?"

There were more than a hundred and twenty ships in that rectangle of water. Nearly half were fishing vessels. McCready discounted them, though he might wish to return to them later. Bremerhaven had a port for fishing vessels, too, but they would be of German registry, and a stranger showing up to unload not fish but general cargo would look odd. He concentrated on the freighters and a few large and luxurious private yachts, also ignoring the four passenger liners. His reduced list numbered fifty-three.

One by one, he asked that the small slivers of metal on the great expanse of water be blown up until each filled the screen. Detail by detail, the men in the room examined them. Some were heading the wrong way. Those heading north for the English Channel numbered thirty-one.

At half-past two, McCready called a halt.

"That man," he said to Bill Carver's technician, "the one standing on the wing of the bridge. Can you come in closer?"

"You got it," said the American.

The freighter had been photographed off Finisterre just before sundown on the previous day. A crewman was busying himself with a routine task on the foredeck, while another man stood on the wing of the bridge looking at him. As McCready and Rowse watched, the ship grew bigger and bigger on the screen, and still the definition held. The forepeak and stern of the vessel disappeared offscreen and the figure of the man standing alone grew larger.

"How high is that bird?" asked Rowse.

"Hundred and ten miles," said the technician.

"Boy, that's some technology," said Rowse.

"Pick up a license plate, clearly readable," said the American proudly.

There were more than twenty frames of that particular freighter. When the man on the bridge-wing filled most of the wall, Rowse asked for all of them to be screened with the same magnification. As the images flashed, the man seemed

to move, like one of those stick figures in a Victorian bio-
graph.

The figure turned from looking at the seaman and stared
out to sea. Then he removed his peaked cap to run a hand
through his thin hair. Perhaps a seabird called above him.
Whatever, he raised his face.

"Freeze," called Rowse. "Closer."

The technician magnified the face until finally it began to
blur.

"Bingo," McCready whispered over Rowse's shoulder.
"That's him. Johnson."

The tired old eyes beneath the thin jet-black hair stared out
at them from the screen. The old man from the corner of the
Apollonia dining terrace. The has-been.

"The name of the ship," said McCready. "We need the
name of the ship."

It was on her bow, and the satellite, as she dropped over
the horizon to the north, had still been filming. A single, low-
angle shot caught the words beside the anchor: *Regina IV.*
McCready reached for the phone and called his man at Lloyds
Shipping Intelligence.

"Can't be," said the man when he called back thirty
minutes later. "*Regina IV* is over ten thousand tons, and
she's off the coast of Venezuela. You must have got it wrong."

"No mistake," said McCready. "She's about two thousand
tons, and she's steaming north, by now off Bordeaux."

"Hang about," said the cheerful voice from Colchester.
"Is she up to something naughty?"

"Almost certainly," said McCready.

"I'll call you back," said the Lloyds man. He did, almost
an hour later. McCready had spent most of that time on the
telephone to some people based at Poole, in Dorset.

"*Regina,*" said the man from Lloyds, "is a very common
name. Like *Stella Maris.* That's why they have letters or
Roman numerals after the name. To distinguish one from
another. It happens there's a *Regina VI* registered at Limassol, now believed to be berthed at Paphos. About two thousand tons. German skipper, Greek Cypriot crew. New owners—a shell company registered in Luxembourg."

"The Libyan government," thought McCready. It would
be a simple ruse. Leave the Mediterranean as the *Regina VI*;

out in the Atlantic, paint out the single numeral after the *V* and paint another in before it. Skilled hands could alter the ship's papers to match. The agents would book the thoroughly reputable *Regina IV* into Bremerhaven with a cargo of office machinery and general cargo from Canada, and who would know that the real *Regina IV* was off Venezuela?

At dawn of the third day, Captain Holst stared out of the forward windows of his bridge at the slowly lightening sea. There was no mistaking the flare that had burst into the sky straight ahead of him, hung for a moment, then fluttered back to the water. Maroon. A distress flare. Peering through the half-light, he could make out something else a mile or two ahead of him: the yellow fluttering of a flame. He ordered his engine room to make half-speed, lifted a handset, and called one of his passengers in his bunk below. The man joined him less than a minute later.

Captain Holst pointed silently through the windshield. On the calm water ahead of them, a forty-foot motor fishing vessel rolled drunkenly. She had clearly suffered an explosion in her engine area; a black smudge of smoke drifted up from below her deck, mingling with a flicker of orange flame. Her topsides were scorched and blackened.

"Where are we?" asked Stephen Johnson.

"In the North Sea, between Yorkshire and the Dutch coast," said Holst.

Johnson took the Captain's binoculars and focused on the small fishing boat ahead. *Fair Maid, Whitby,* could be made out on her bow.

"We have to stop and give them help," Holst said in English. "It is the law of the sea."

He did not know what his own vessel was carrying, and he did not want to know. His employers had given him their orders and an extremely extravagant bonus. His crew had also been taken care of financially. The crated olives from Cyprus had come onboard at Paphos and were totally legitimate. During the two-day stopover in Sirte, on the coast of Libya, part of the cargo had been removed and then returned. It looked the same. He knew there must be illicit cargo in there somewhere, but he could not spot it and did not want to try.

The proof that his cargo was extremely dangerous lay in the six passengers—two were from Cyprus, and four more were from Sirte. And the changing of the numerals as soon as he had passed the Pillars of Hercules. In twelve hours, he expected to be rid of them all. He would sail back through the North Sea, convert again to the *Regina VI* at sea, and return calmly to his home port of Limassol, a much richer man.

Then he would retire. The years of running strange cargoes of men and crates into West Africa, the bizarre orders now coming to him from his new Luxembourg-based owners—all would be a thing of the past. He would retire at fifty with his savings enough for him and his Greek wife, Maria, to open their little restaurant in the Greek islands and live out their days in peace.

Johnson looked dubious. "We can't stop," he said.

"We have to."

The light was getting better. They saw a figure, scorched and blackened, emerge from the wheelhouse of the fishing vessel, stagger to the forward deck, make a pain-wracked attempt to wave, then fall forward onto his face.

Another IRA officer came up behind Holst. He felt the muzzle of a gun in his ribs.

"Sail on by," said a flat voice.

Holst did not ignore the gun, but he looked at Johnson. "If we do, and they are rescued by another ship, as they will be sooner or later, they will report us. We will be stopped and asked why we did that."

Johnson nodded.

"Then ram them," said the one with the gun. "We don't stop."

"We can give first aid and call up the Dutch coast guard," said Holst. "No one comes aboard. When the Dutch cutter appears, we continue. They will wave their thanks and think no more of it. It will cost us thirty minutes."

Johnson was persuaded. He nodded. "Put up your gun," he said.

Holst moved his speed control to "full astern," and the *Regina* slowed rapidly. Giving an order in Greek to his helmsman, he left the bridge and went down to the waist before moving up to the foredeck. He looked down at the approaching fishing vessel, then waved a hand to the helmsman. The engines went to "midships," and the momentum of the *Regina* carried her slowly up to the stricken fisherman.

"Ahoy, *Fair Maid!*" called Holst, peering down as the fishing boat came under the bow. They saw the fallen man on the foredeck try to stir, then faint again. The *Fair Maid* bobbed along the side of the larger *Regina* until she came to the *Regina*'s waist, where the deck rail was lower. Holst walked down his ship and shouted an order in Greek for one of his crew to throw a line aboard the *Fair Maid*.

There was no need. As the fisherman slid past the waist of the *Regina*, the man on the foredeck came to, jumped up with remarkable agility for one so badly burned, seized a grappling hook beside him, and hurled it over the rail of the *Regina*, securing it fast to a cleat on the *Fair Maid*'s bow. A second man ran out of the fishing boat's cabin and did the same at the stern. The *Fair Maid* stopped drifting.

Four more men ran from the cabin, vaulted to the roof, and jumped straight over the rail of the *Regina*. It happened so fast and with such coordination that Captain Holst had only time to shout, "*Was zum Teufel ist denn das?*"

The men were all dressed alike: black one-piece overalls, cleated rubber boots, and black woollen caps. Their faces were blackened, too, but not by soot. A very hard hand took Captain Holst in the solar plexus, and he went down on his knees. He would later say that he had never seen the men of the SBS, the Special Boat Squadron, the seaborne equivalent of the Special Air Service, in action before, and he never wished to again.

By now, there were four Cypriot crewmen on the main deck. One of the men in black shouted a single order to them, in Greek, and they obeyed. They went flat onto the deck, face down, and stayed there. Not so the four IRA members, who came pouring out of the side door of the superstructure. They all had handguns.

Two had the sense to see quickly that a handgun is a poor bargain when faced with a Heckler and Koch MP5 submachine carbine. They threw their hands up and tossed their pistols to the deck. Two tried to use their guns. One was lucky: He took the brief burst in the legs and survived to spend his life in a wheelchair. The fourth was not so lucky and collected four bullets in the chest.

There were now six black-clad men swarming over the deck area of the *Regina*. The third to come aboard had been Tom Rowse. He ran for the companionway that led upward to the bridge. As he reached the wing, Stephen Johnson emerged from the interior. Seeing Rowse, he threw his hands in the air.

"Don't shoot, Sass-man. It's over!" he shouted.

Rowse stood aside and jerked the barrel of his machine pistol toward the staircase.

"Down," he said.

The old IRA man began to descend to the main deck. There was a movement behind Rowse, someone in the door of the wheelhouse. He sensed the movement, half turned, and caught the crash of the handgun. The bullet plucked at the shoulder of his cloth overall. There was no time to pause or shout. He fired as they had taught him, the quick double-burst, then another, loosing two pairs of nine-millimeter slugs in less than half a second.

He had an image of the figure in the doorway that had taken four bullets in the chest, being thrown back into the doorjamb, cannoning forward again—the wild swing of the corn-blond hair. Then she had been on the steel deck, quite dead, a thin trickle of blood seeping from the mouth he had kissed.

"Well, well," said a voice at his elbow. "Monica Browne. With an 'e.' "

Rowse turned. "You bastard," he said slowly. "You knew, didn't you?"

"Not knew. Suspected," McCready said gently. In civilian clothes, he had come at a more sedate pace out of the fishing vessel when the shooting was over.

"We had to check her out, you see, Tom, after she made contact with you. She is—was—indeed Monica Browne, but Dublin-born and bred. Her first marriage, at twenty, took her to Kentucky for eight years. After the divorce, she married Major Eric Browne, much older but rich. Through his alcoholic haze, he no doubt had not a whit of suspicion of his young wife's fanatical devotion to the IRA. And yes, she did run a stud farm, but not at Ashford, Kent, England. It was at Ashford, County Wicklow, Ireland."

The team spent two hours tidying up. Captain Holst proved keen to cooperate. He admitted there had been an open-sea transfer of crates, to a fishing boat off Finisterre. He gave the name, and McCready passed it to London for the Spanish authorities. With speed, they would intercept the arms for the ETA while still on board the trawler—a way for the SIS to say thank you for the Spanish help over the Gibraltar affair.

Captain Holst also agreed that he had been just within British territorial waters when the boarding took place. After that, it would be a matter for the lawyers, so long as Britain had jurisdiction. McCready did not want the IRA men removed to Belgium and promptly liberated, like Father Ryan.

The two bodies were brought to the main deck and laid side by side, covered in sheets from the cabins below. With the aid of the Greek-Cypriot crewmen, the covers were taken from the holds, and the cargo searched. The commandos of the SBS team did that. After two hours, the lieutenant who commanded them reported to McCready.

"Nothing, sir."

"What do you mean, nothing?"

"A lot of olives, sir."

"Nothing but olives?"

"Some crates marked office machinery."

"Containing?"

"Office machinery, sir. And the three stallions. They're pretty upset, sir."

"Bugger the horses—so am I," said McCready grimly. "Show me."

He and Rowse followed the officer below. The lieutenant gave them a tour of the ship's four holds. In one, copying machines and typewriters from Japan were visible through the sides of their smashed crates. In the second and third holds, tins of Cypriot olives spilled from broken boxes. No crate or carton had been left untouched. The fourth hold contained three substantial horse boxes. In each of them a stallion whinnied and shied in fear.

There was a feeling in McCready's stomach, that awful feeling that comes with knowing you have been duped, have taken the wrong course of action, and that there will be the devil to pay. If all he could come up with was a cargo of olives and typewriters, London would nail his hide to a barn door.

A young SBS man was standing with the horses in their

hold. He seemed to know about animals; he was talking to them quietly, calming them down.

"Sir?" he asked.

"Yes?"

"Why are they being shipped?"

"Oh. They're Arabs. Thoroughbreds, destined for a stud farm," said Rowse.

"No, they're not," said the young commando. "They're riding-school hacks. Stallions, but hacks."

Between the inner and outer walls of the specially constructed transport boxes, there was a good foot of space. With crowbars they hacked at the planks of the first loose box. As the shattered timber fell away, the search was over. The watching men saw piled blocks of Semtex-H, serried ranks of RPG-7 rocket launchers, and rows of shoulder-borne surface-to-air missiles. The other horse boxes yielded heavy machine guns, ammunition, grenades, mines, and mortars.

"I think," said McCready, "we can call in the Navy now."

They left the hold and went back to the warm morning sunshine of the main deck. The Navy would take over the *Regina* and bring her to Harwich. There she would be formally seized and her crew and passengers arrested.

The *Fair Maid* had been pumped out to repair her wallowing list. The special-effects smoke grenades that had given her the appearance of being on fire had long been thrown into the sea.

For the IRA man with the shattered knee, the bleeding had been stopped by a rough but skillful tourniquet applied by the commandos. He now sat ashen-faced with his back against a bulkhead and waited for the naval surgeon-commander, who would come with the frigate, now only half a mile off the beam. The other two had been handcuffed to a stanchion farther down the deck, and McCready had the key to the cuffs.

Captain Holst and his crew had descended without demur into one of the holds—not the one containing the weaponry—and sat among the olives until the Navy men could drop them a ladder.

Stephen Johnson had been locked in his cabin belowdecks.

When they were ready, the five SBS men vaulted onto the cabin roof of the *Fair Maid,* then disappeared below. Her engine started. Two of the commandos reappeared and cast her loose. The lieutenant waved a last farewell to McCready, still on the *Regina*, and the fishing boat chugged away. These were the secret warriors; they had done their job, and there was no need for them to wait around.

Tom Rowse sat down, shoulders hunched, on the coaming of one of the holds, next to the supine body of Monica Browne. On the other side of the *Regina*'s deck, the frigate eased alongside, threw graplines, and sent the first of the boarding party across. They conferred with McCready.

A puff of wind blew a corner of the sheet away from the face beneath it. Rowse stared down at the beautiful face, so calm in death. The breeze blew a frond of corn-blond hair across the forehead. He reached down to push it back. Someone sat down beside him, and an arm came round his shoulders.

"It's over, Tom. You weren't to know. You weren't to blame. She knew what she was doing."

"If I'd known she was here, I wouldn't have killed her," said Rowse, dully.

"Then she'd have killed you. She was that kind of person."

Two seamen unlocked the IRA men and led them toward the frigate. Two orderlies under the supervision of a surgeon lifted the wounded one onto a stretcher and carried him away.

"What happens now?" asked Rowse.

McCready stared at the sea and the sky and sighed. "Now, Tom, the lawyers take over. The lawyers always take over, reducing all of life and death, passion, greed, courage, lust, and glory to the dessicated vernacular of their trade."

"And you?"

"Oh, I will go back to Century House and start again. And go back each night to my small flat and listen to my music and eat my baked beans. And you will go back to Nikki, my friend, and hold her very tight, and write your books and forget all this. Hamburg, Vienna, Malta, Tripoli, Cyprus— forget it. It's all over."

Stephen Johnson was led past. He paused to look down at the two Englishmen. His accent was as thick as the heather of the west coast.

"Our day will come," he said. It was the slogan of the Provisional IRA.

McCready looked up and shook his head. "No, Mr. Johnson, your day has long gone."

Two orderlies loaded the body of the dead IRA man onto a stretcher and removed it.

"Why did she do it, Sam? Why the hell did she do it?" asked Rowse.

McCready leaned forward and drew the sheet back over the face of Monica Browne. The orderlies returned to take her away.

"Because she believed, Tom. In the wrong thing, of course. But she believed."

He rose, pulling Rowse up with him.

"Come on, lad, we're going home. Let it be, Tom. Let it be. She's gone the way she wanted, by her own wish. Now she's just another casualty of war. Like you, Tom. Like all of us."

Interlude

Thursday, when the hearing began for its fourth day, was the day that Timothy Edwards had determined would be its last. Before Denis Gaunt could begin, Edwards decided to preempt him.

Edwards had become aware that his two colleagues behind the table, the Controllers for Domestic Operations and Western Hemisphere, had indicated a softening of their attitudes and were prepared to make an exception in the case of Sam McCready and retain him by some ruse or other. After the close of the Wednesday hearing, his two colleagues had taken Edwards to a quiet corner of the Century House bar and made their feelings more than plain, proposing that somehow the old Deceiver be retained within the Service.

That was emphatically not in Edwards's scenario. Unlike the others, he knew that the decision to make a class action out of the case for the early retirement of the Deceiver stemmed from the Permanent Under-Secretary of the Foreign Office, a man who one day would sit in conclave with four others and decide the identity of the next Chief of the SIS. It would be foolish to antagonize such a man.

"Denis, we have all listened with the greatest interest to

THE DECEIVER

your recall of Sam's many services, and we are all mightily impressed. The fact is, however, that we now have to face the challenge of the nineties, a period when certain—how shall I put it?—active measures, riding roughshod over agreed procedures, will have no place. Must I remind you of the brouhaha occasioned by Sam's chosen course of action in the Caribbean last winter?"

"Not in the slightest, Timothy," said Gaunt. "I had in mind to recall the episode myself, as my last instance of Sam's continuing value to the Service."

"Then please do so," invited Edwards, relieved that this was the last plea he would have to listen to before proceeding to his unavoidable judgment. Besides, he reasoned, this episode would surely sway his two colleagues to the view that McCready's actions had been more those of a cowboy than of a local representative of her Gracious Majesty. It was all very well for the juniors to give Sam a round of applause when he walked into the Hole in the Wall bar on his return, just before the New Year, but it was he, Edwards, who had had to interrupt his festivities to smooth the ruffled feathers of Scotland Yard, the Home Office, and the outraged Foreign Office, an interlude he still recalled with intense exasperation.

Denis Gaunt reluctantly crossed the room to the desk of the Records clerk and took the proffered folder. Despite what he had said, the Caribbean affair was the one he would most have liked to avoid. Deep though his admiration for his desk chief ran, he knew that Sam had really taken the bit between his teeth on that one.

He recalled only too well the memoranda that had rained on Century House early in the New Year, and the lengthy one-on-one meeting with the Chief to which McCready had been summoned in mid-January.

The new Chief had taken over the Service only a fortnight earlier, and his New Year present had been to have details of Sam's Caribbean exploits land on his desk. Fortunately, Sir Mark and the Deceiver went back a long way, and after the official fireworks the Chief had, apparently, produced a six-pack of McCready's favorite ale for a New Year toast and a promise—no more rule-bending.

Six months later, for reasons McCready could only guess at, the Chief had been much less accessible to him.

Gaunt assumed, wrongly, that Sir Mark had bided his time and waited until the summer to ease McCready out. He had no idea from how high a level the order had really come.

McCready knew. He did not need to be told, had no requirement of proof. But he knew the Chief. Like a good commanding officer, Sir Mark would tell you to your face if you were out of line, chew you off if he felt you deserved it, even fire you if things were that bad. But he would do it personally. Otherwise, he would fight like a tiger for his own people against the outsiders. So this business had come from higher up, and the Chief himself had been overruled.

As Denis Gaunt returned to his own side of the room with the file, Timothy Edwards caught McCready's eye and smiled.

You really are a bloody menace, Sam, he thought. Brilliantly talented, but you just don't fit anymore. Such a pity, really. If only you'd smarten yourself up and abide by the rules, there could be a place for you. But not now. Not now that you have really upset people like Robert Inglis. It will be a different world in the nineties—my world, a world for people like me. In three years, maybe four, I shall have the Chief's desk, and there will be no place for people like you anyway. Might as well go now, Sam, old boy. We'll have a whole new officer group by then—bright young staffers who do what they're told, abide by the rules, and do not upset people.

Sam McCready smiled back.

You really are a prize asshole, Timothy, he thought. You really think the gathering of intelligence is about committee meetings and computer print-outs and kissing Langley's butt. All right, it's good, the American signals-intelligence, and their electronic intelligence. The best in the world—they have the technology with their satellites and listening devices. But it can be fooled, Timothy, old boy.

There's a thing called *maskirovka,* which you have hardly heard of. It's Russian, Timothy, and it means the art of building phony airfields, hangars, bridges—entire tank divisions—out of tinplate and plywood, and it can fool the American Big Birds. So sometimes you simply have to go in on the ground, put an agent deep inside the citadel, recruit a malcontent, employ a defector-in-place. Timothy, you'd never have made a field man, with all your club ties and your aristocratic wife. The KGB would have had your balls for cocktail olives in two weeks flat.

Gaunt was beginning his last defense, trying to justify what had happened in the Caribbean, trying not to lose the sympathy of the two Controllers who last night had appeared willing to change their minds and recommend a reprieve. McCready stared out of the window.

Things were changing, all right, but not the way Timothy Edwards thought. The world, in the aftermath of the Cold War, was going quietly crazy—the noise would come later.

In Russia, the bumper harvest was still ungathered for lack of equipment, and by the autumn it would be rotting in the sidings for lack of rolling stock. Famine would come in December, maybe January, driving Gorbachev back into the arms of the KGB and the High Command, and they would exact their price for his heresy of this summer of 1990. The year 1991 would be no fun at all.

The Middle East was a powder keg, and the best-informed agency in the region, the Israeli Mossad, was being treated like a pariah by Washington, and Timothy Edwards was taking his cue from there. McCready sighed. The hell with them all. Perhaps a fishing boat in Devon was the answer after all.

"It all really began," said Gaunt, opening the file in front of him, "in early December, on a small island in the northern Caribbean."

McCready was jerked back to the realities of Century House. Ah yes, the Caribbean, he thought—the bloody Caribbean.

A LITTLE BIT
OF SUNSHINE

Chapter 1

The *Gulf Lady* came home across a bright and glittering sea
an hour before the sun went down. Julio Gomez sat forward,
his ample rear end supported by the cabin roof, his mocca-
sined feet upon the foredeck. He drew contentedly on one of
his Puerto Rican cheroots, whose foul odors were blown away
across the uncomplaining Caribbean waters.

He was, in that moment, a truly happy man. Ten miles
behind him lay the underwater dropoff, where the Great
Bahama Bank falls into the Santaren Channel; where the
kingfish run with the wahoo, and the tuna hunt the bonito,
who in turn hunt the ballyhoo and all on occasions are
pursued by the sailfish and the big marlin.

In the scarred old box astern of the open fishing deck lay
two fine dorado, one for him and one for the skipper, who
now held the tiller and steered his game fisherman home to
Port Plaisance.

Not that two fish had been his entire day's take; there had
been a fine sailfish that had been tagged and returned to the
ocean; a mess of smaller bonito that had been used for
baitfish; a yellowfin tuna that he had estimated at seventy
pounds before it dived so hard and so deep he had had to cut

line or see his reel stripped before his eyes; and two big
amberjack that he had fought for thirty minutes each. He had
returned the big fish to the sea, taking only the dorado
because they are among the finest eating fish in the tropics.

Julio Gomez did not like to kill. What brought him on his
annual pilgrimage to these waters was the thrill of the hissing
reel and the running line, the tension of the bowed rod, and
the sheer excitement of the contest between air-breathing
man and monstrously strong fighting fish. It had been a
wonderful day.

Far away to his left, way out beyond the Dry Tortugas,
invisible well below the western horizon, the big red ball of
the sun was dropping to meet the sea, giving up its skin-
flaying heat, conceding finally to the cool of the evening
breeze and the oncoming night.

Three miles ahead of the *Gulf Lady,* the island straddled
the water. They would berth in twenty minutes. Gomez
flicked the stub of his cheroot to a sputtering grave in the
water and rubbed his forearms. Despite his naturally saturnine
complexion and olive skin, he would need to apply a good
layer of after-sun cream when he got back to his boarding
house. Jimmy Dobbs on the tiller had no such problem: He
was an islander born and bred, and he owned his boat and
chartered it for the visiting tourists who wanted to fish. On
his deep ebony skin, the sun had no effect.

Julio Gomez swung his feet off the foredeck and dropped
from the cabin roof into the stern.

"I'll take over, Jimmy. Give you a chance to swab down."

Jimmy Dobbs gave his ear-to-ear grin, handed over the
tiller, took bucket and broom, and began to swab the fish
scales and fragments of gut out through the scuppers. Half a
dozen terns appeared from nowhere and took the floating
scraps from the wake. Nothing goes to waste in the ocean—
nothing organic, that is.

There were, of course, more modern charter fishing boats
plying the Caribbean—boats with engine-linked power hoses
for cleaning down, with cocktail bars, with television and
even video shows; with banks of electronic technology for
finding fish, and enough navigational aids to go around the
world. *Gulf Lady* had none of these things. She was an old
and chipped clinker-built timber vessel powered by a smoky

Perkins diesel, but she had seen more white water than the smart boys from the Florida Keys could shake a radar scanner at. She had a small forward cabin, a tangle of rods and lines, redolent of fish and oil, and an open afterdeck with ten rod-holders and a single fighting chair homemade in oak, cushions extra.

Jimmy Dobbs had no silicon chips to find the fish for him; he found them himself, the way his father had taught him, with eyes for the slightest hint of change in the water color, the ripple on the surface that should not be there, the diving of a frigate bird far, far away; he had the gut instinct to know where they were running this week and what they were feeding on. But find them he did, every day. That was why Julio Gomez came every vacation to fish with him.

The sheer lack of sophistication of the islands pleased Julio, the lack of technology of the *Gulf Lady*. He spent much of his professional life handling America's modern technology, tapping queries into a computer, steering a car through the tangled traffic of central Miami. For his vacation, he wanted the sea, the sun, and the wind—those and the fish, for Julio Gomez only had two passions in life, his job, and his fishing. He had had five days of the latter, and just two more to go, Friday and Saturday. On Sunday he would have to fly home to Florida and on Monday morning report for work with Eddie. He sighed at the prospect.

Jimmy Dobbs was also a happy man. He had had a good day with his client and friend, he had a few dollars in his pocket to buy a dress for his old lady and a fine fish to make supper for them both and their brood of kids. What more, he reasoned, had life to offer?

They berthed just after five at the rickety old wooden fishing quay that ought to have fallen down years ago but never had. The previous Governor had said he would ask London for a grant to build a new one, but then he had been replaced by the present man, and Sir Marston Moberley had no interest in fishing. Nor in the islanders, if the bar talk in Shantytown was to be believed—and it always was.

There was the usual scuttling of children to see what the catch had been and to help carry the fish ashore, and the usual banter in the lilting, singsong accents of the islanders as the *Gulf Lady* was made fast for the night.

"You free tomorrow, Jimmy?" asked Gomez.

"Sure am. You wanna go again?"

"That's what I'm here for. See you at eight."

Julio Gomez paid a small boy a dollar to carry his fish for him, and together the pair walked off the dock and into the dusky streets of Port Plaisance. They had not far to go, for no distance was far in Port Plaisance. It was not a large town—more a village really.

It was the sort of town found in most of the smaller Caribbean islands, a jumble of mainly wooden houses painted in bright colors with shingle roofs and lanes of crushed shells between them. Along the seashore, around the small harbor bounded by a curving mole of coral blocks against which the weekly trading steamer berthed, stood the more resplendent structures—the custom house, the court house, and the war memorial. All were built of blocks of coral, cut and mortared long ago.

Farther into the town were the town hall, the small Anglican church, the police station, and the principal hotel, the Quarter Deck. Apart from these and an unsightly corrugated-iron warehouse at one end of the port, the buildings were mainly of wood. Along the shore, just out of town, stood the Governor's residence, Government House, all white and walled in white, with two old Napoleonic cannon by the front gate and the flagpole in the middle of the carefully cultured green-grass lawn. During the day the British Union Jack fluttered from the mast, and even as Julio Gomez made his way through the small town to the boarding house where he lodged, the flag was being ceremoniously hauled down by a police constable in the presence of the Governor's adjutant.

Gomez could have stayed at the Quarter Deck, but he preferred the homey atmosphere of Mrs. Macdonald's boarding house. She was a widow, with a cap of snow-white frizzy hair, as amply proportioned as he was himself, and she made a conch chowder that was to die for.

He turned into the street where she lived, ignoring the garish election posters clipped to most of the walls and fences, and saw that in the dusk she was sweeping down the front steps of her neat, detached residence—a ritual she carried out several times a day. She greeted him and his fish with her usual beaming smile.

"Why, Mistah Gomez, that is one very fine fish."

"For our supper, Mrs. Macdonald, and enough, I think, for all of us."

Gomez paid off the boy, who scampered away with his new-found wealth, and went up to his room. Mrs. Macdonald retired to her kitchen to prepare the dorado for the grill. Gomez washed, shaved, and changed into cream slacks and a bright short-sleeved beach shirt. He decided he could use a very large, very cold beer and walked back through the town to the bar of the Quarter Deck.

It was only seven o'clock, but night had come and the town was quite dark, save where it was lit by the glimmer from the windows. Emerging from the back streets, Gomez entered Parliament Square with its neat, enclosed patch of palm trees at the center and three of its sides garnished respectively by the Anglican church, the police station, and the Quarter Deck Hotel.

He passed the police station, where electric lights, powered by the municipal generator that hummed away down on the docks, still burned. From this small, coral-block building Chief Inspector Brian Jones and an impeccably turned-out force of two sergeants and eight constables represented law and order in the community with the lowest crime rate in the Western Hemisphere. Coming from Miami, Gomez could not but wonder at a society that seemed to have no drugs, no gangs, no muggings, no prostitution, no rapes, one bank (no robberies therefrom), and only half a dozen reportable thefts a year. He sighed, passed in front of the darkened church, and entered the portico of the Quarter Deck.

The bar lay to the left. He took a corner stool at the far end and ordered his large, cold beer. It would be an hour before his fish was ready—time for a second beer to keep company with the first. The bar was already half full, for it was the town's favorite watering hole with tourists and expatriates. Sam, the cheerful white-jacketed barman, administered his nightly array of rum punches, beers, juices, Cokes, daiquiris, and soda-mixers to help down the fiery shots of Mount Gay rum.

At five to eight, Julio Gomez reached into his pocket for a handful of dollars with which to settle his bill. When he looked up, he stopped, fixed rigid, and stared at the man who had entered the bar and was ordering a drink at the far end. After two seconds, he eased back on his stool so that the bulk of the drinker sitting next to him blocked him from view. He could hardly believe his eyes, but he knew he was not wrong. You do not spend four days and four nights of your life sitting across a table from a man, staring into his eyes, and seeing hatred and contempt coming back at you—and later forget that face, even eight years on. You do not spend four days and nights trying to get a single word out of a man and get absolutely nothing, not even a name, so that you have to give him a nickname just to have something to put on the file—and later forget that face.

Gomez gestured to Sam to refill his glass, paid for all three beers, and retired to a corner seat in the shadows. If the man was here, he was here for a reason. If he had checked into a hotel, he would have a name. Gomez wanted that name. He sat in the corner, waited, and watched. At nine the man, who had drunk alone, always Mount Gay rums, rose and left. Emerging from his corner, Gomez went after him.

In Parliament Square, the man climbed into an open Japanese-made jeep, started the ignition, and drove away. Gomez looked desperately around. He had no transportation of his own. Parked near the hotel entrance was a small motor scooter, its key still in the ignition. Wobbling precariously, Gomez set off after the jeep.

The jeep left the town and drove steadily out along the coast road—the only road—which went right round the entire island. Properties situated in the hilly interior were all reached by individual service roads, dusty tracks, that ran down to the one coastal highway. The jeep passed the island's other residential community, the native village known as Shantytown, then went on past the grass strip airport.

It kept going until it reached the other side of the island. Here the road flanked the expanse of Teach Bay—named after Edward Teach, Blackbeard the Pirate, who had once anchored and victualed here. The jeep pulled off the coast road and up a short track to a pair of wrought-iron gates that protected a large walled estate. If the driver had seen the single wobbling headlamp that had been behind him all the way from the Quarter Deck Hotel, he gave no sign of it. But seen it he surely had.

At the gates a man stepped out of the shadows to open them for the jeep driver, but the driver slowed and stopped. He reached above his head to the rollbar and detached a powerful hand-held spotlamp. As Gomez rode past the entrance to the track, the beam of the spotlamp swept over him, came back, and held him in its glare until he passed out of sight down the road.

Gomez returned the scooter to its place outside the hotel thirty minutes later and walked home. He was deep in thought and deeply worried. He had seen whom he had seen, and he knew he had not been wrong. He now also knew where the man was living. But he himself had been seen. He could only pray that after eight years, in the darkness of a Caribbean night, sputtering past for a few seconds on a motor scooter, he had not been recognized.

Mrs. Macdonald was perturbed at his failure to arrive for supper until almost two hours late, and said so. She served the dorado anyway and watched her guest eat it with no pleasure. He was lost in thought and only made one remark.

"Nonsense, man," she chided. "We don't even have them things in these islands."

Julio Gomez spent the night lying awake and considering his choices. How long the man would remain in the islands, he did not know. But his presence here was something the British ought to hear about, he thought, especially his actual location. Surely that was significant. He could go to the Governor, but what could that official do? The man probably had no cause to be arrested. He was not on U.S. territory now. Nor did Gomez believe that Chief Inspector Jones, with his toytown force, would have any more weight than the Governor. This would need an order from London, following an extradition request from Uncle Sam personally. He could telephone in the morning—then he discarded that thought. The island's communication, for public use, was an old-style open phone line running to Nassau, the Bahamas, and thence to Miami. He had no choice; he would have to return to Florida in the morning.

That same evening, a Delta Airlines flight from Washington touched down at Miami Airport. Among its passengers was a tired British civil servant whose passport said he was Mr.

Frank Dillon. He had other papers—which he had no need to show on arrival from an internal American flight—that specified he was on the staff of the British Foreign Office and asked all whom it might concern to be as helpful to him as possible.

Neither his passport, which he had no need to show, nor his papers revealed that his real name was Sam McCready. This was known only to the group of senior staff members of the CIA at Langley, Virginia, in whose company he had spent an intensive week attending a seminar on the role of the intelligence community of the Free World in the forthcoming decade of the nineties. It had meant listening to a raft of professors and other assorted academics, none of whom favored using one simple word where ten complicated ones would do.

McCready hailed a cab outside the airport terminal and asked to be taken to the Sonesta Beach Hotel on Key Biscayne. Here he checked in and treated himself to a lobster supper before retiring for a deep and untroubled sleep. He faced, or so he thought, the prospect of seven days of toasting himself by the pool, working his way through several light-hearted spy novels, and occasionally raising his gaze from a chilled daiquiri to watch a Florida girl sway by. Century House was a long way away, and the business of Disinformation, Deception, and Psychological Operations could remain in the capable hands of his newly appointed deputy, Denis Gaunt. It was time, he thought as he fell asleep, for the Deceiver to get a suntan.

On Friday morning, Julio Gomez checked out of Mrs. Macdonald's boarding house without asking for a rebate for his unused two days and with profuse apologies. He hefted his suitcase and walked to Parliament Square, where he took one of the town's two taxis and asked to be driven to the airstrip.

His ticket was for the Sunday-morning scheduled flight by BWIA to Nassau, with a connection to Miami. Although it was actually a shorter distance direct to Miami, there were no scheduled flights on the direct run, only via Nassau. There was no travel agent in town—bookings were always made right at the airstrip—so he could only hope that there was a Friday-morning BWIA flight. He did not notice that he was being watched as he took the taxi out of the square.

At the airstrip he was disappointed. The airport building, a single long shed containing a customs area and little else, was not closed, but it was almost deserted. A single passport officer sat in the morning sun reading a week-old *Miami Herald* that someone, probably Gomez himself, had left behind.

"Not today, man," he replied cheerfully. "Never on a Friday."

Gomez surveyed the grass field. Outside the single metal hangar stood a Piper Navajo Chief. A man in ducks and shirt was checking it over.

Gomez moved across. "You flying today?" he asked.

"Yep," said the pilot, a fellow American.

"Available for charter?"

"No way," said the pilot. "This is a private plane. Belongs to my employer."

"Where you heading? Nassau?" asked Gomez.

"Nope. Key West."

Gomez's heart rose. From Key West, he could take one of the frequent scheduled flights up to Miami.

"Any chance I can have a talk with your employer?"

"Mr. Klinger. He'll be here in about an hour."

"I'll wait," said Gomez.

He found a shady spot near the hangar wall and settled down. Someone in the bushes withdrew, took a motorcycle from the undergrowth, and motored away down the coast road.

Sir Marston Moberley checked his watch, rose from his breakfast table in the walled garden behind Government House, and sauntered toward the steps that led up to his verandah and his office. That tiresome delegation was due anytime.

Britain retains very few of her former colonies in the Caribbean. The colonial days are long gone. And yet five still remain, charming mementoes of a bygone era. No longer called colonies—an unacceptable word—they are today classed as Dependent Territories. One is the Cayman Islands, well known for its numerous and very discreet offshore banking facilities. In a referendum, when London offered the people of the three Cayman Islands independence, they voted

overwhelmingly to stay British. Since then, they have prospered like the green bay tree, in contrast to some of their
neighbors.

Another group is the British Virgin Islands, now a haven
for yachtsmen and anglers. A third, even more obscure, is the
small island of Anguilla, whose inhabitants conducted the
only known revolution in colonial history in order to stay
British rather than be forcibly amalgamated with two neighboring islands, of whose prime minister they had the most
lively and well-founded suspicions.

Even more obscure are the Turks and Caicos, where life
proceeds on its somnolent way beneath the palm trees and
the Union Jack, untroubled by drug peddlers, secret police
forces, coups d'état, and election thuggery. In all four, London rules with a fairly light hand, its principal role in the last
three being to pick up the annual budget deficit. In exchange,
the local populations appear content to have the Union Jack
run up and down the flagpole twice a day and the insignia of
Queen Elizabeth on their currency notes and policemen's
helmets.

In the winter of 1989, the fifth and last Dependent Territory
group was the Barclays, a collection of eight small islands
situated at the western edge of the Great Bahama Bank, west
of the Bahamas's Andros Island, northeast of Cuba, and due
south of the Florida Keys.

Why the Barclays were not amalgamated into the Bahamas
when that archipelago secured its independence, few can
recall. A wag in the Foreign Office suggested later they might
simply have been overlooked, and he could have been right.
The tiny group had no more than twenty thousand inhabitants,
and only two of the eight islands were inhabited at all. The
chief island and home of the Government rejoiced in the name
of Sunshine, and the fishing was superb.

They were not rich islands. Industry was nil, and income
not much more. Most of that came from the wages of the
young people who left to become waiters, chambermaids, and
bellhops in the smart hotels elsewhere and who became
favorites with visiting European and American tourists for
their sunny good nature and beaming smiles.

Other income came from a smattering of tourism, the
occasional game fisherman who would make the pilgrimage

via Nassau, aircraft-landing rights, the sale of their very obscure stamps, and the sale of lobster and conch to passing yachtsmen. This modest income permitted the importation by weekly steamer of some basic commodities not available from the sea.

The generous ocean provided most of the food, along with fruit from the forests and gardens tended along the slopes of Sunshine's two hills, Spyglass and Sawbones.

Then in early 1989, someone in the Foreign Office decided that the Barclays were ripe for independence. The first "position paper" became a "submission" and went on to become policy. The British Cabinet that year was wrestling with a huge trade deficit, slumping popularity polls, and restiveness over a divided mood on European policy. The bagatelle of an obscure island group in the Caribbean going independent passed without debate.

The then Governor objected, however, and was duly recalled and replaced by Sir Marston Moberley. A tall, vain man who prided himself on his resemblance to the late actor George Sanders, he had been sent to Sunshine with a single brief, carefully spelled out to him by an Assistant Principal Secretary in the Caribbean Department. The Barclays were to accept their independence. Candidates for Prime Minister would be invited, and a general election day was set. After the democratic election of the Barclays' first Prime Minister, a decent interval (say, three months) would be agreed to by him and his Cabinet, after which full independence would be granted—nay, insisted upon.

Sir Marston was to ensure that the program went through and another burden removed from Britain's exchecquer. He and Lady Moberley had arrived on Sunshine in late July. Sir Marston had set about his duties with a will.

Two potential candidates had soon presented themselves for the office of Prime-Minister-to-be. Mr. Marcus Johnson, a wealthy local businessman and philanthropist, had returned to the islands of his birth after making a fortune in Central America. He now resided on a fine estate the other side of Sawbones Hill and had formed the Barclays Prosperity Alliance, pledged to develop the islands and bring wealth to the people. The more rough-hewn but populist Mr. Horatio Livingstone, who lived down in Shantytown, of which he owned a substantial part, had formed the Barclays Independence Front. The elections were but three weeks away, scheduled for January 5. Sir Marston was pleased to see that vigorous electioneering campaigns were under way, with both candidates earnestly canvassing the islanders for support with speeches, pamphlets, and posters on every wall and tree.

There was but one fly in Sir Marston's ointment: the CCC, or Committee for Concerned Citizens, which was opposed to independence. It was led by that tiresome man Reverend Walter Drake, the local Baptist minister. Sir Marston had agreed to receive a delegation from the CCC at nine that morning.

There were eight of them. The Anglican vicar—a pale, washed-out, and ineffectual Englishman—he knew he could deal with. Six were local worthies—the doctor, two shopkeepers, a farmer, a bar owner, and a boarding-house keeper called Mr. Macdonald. They were all elderly and of rudimentary education. They could not match Sir Marston for fluency in English or persuasiveness in argument. For each one of them, he could find a dozen who were in favor of independence.

Marcus Johnson, the "prosperity" candidate, was supported by the airport manager, the owners of dockside property (Johnson had promised to build a thriving international marina in its place), and most of the business community, who would become richer with development. Livingstone was securing backing from the proletariat, the have-nots, to whom he had promised a miraculous rise in living standards based on the nationalization of property and assets.

The problem was the CCC delegation leader, Reverend Drake, a big black bull of a man in a black suit who now wiped perspiration from his face. He was a compulsive preacher, lucid and loud, who had secured an education on the American mainland. He wore the small sign of a fish in his lapel, a born-again Christian. Sir Marston wondered idly from what previous state he had been born again, but it never occurred to him to ask. Reverend Drake thumped a pile of paper on the Governor's desk.

Sir Marston had ensured there were not enough seats for all, so they had to stand. He stood himself—it would make the meeting shorter. He glanced at the pile of paper.

"That, Governor," boomed Reverend Drake, "is a petition. Yes, sir, a petition. Signed by more than one thousand of our citizens. We want this petition conveyed to London and put before Mrs. Thatcher herself. Or even the Queen. We believe these ladies will listen to us, even if you will not."

Sir Marston sighed. It was all going to be—he searched for his favorite adjective—more tiresome than he had expected.

"I see," he said. "And what does your petition require?"

"We want a referendum, just like the British people had over the Common Market. We *demand* a referendum. We do not want to be forced into independence. We want to go on as we are, as we have always been. We do not want to be ruled by Mr. Johnson or Mr. Livingstone. We appeal to London."

Down at the airstrip, a taxi arrived, and Mr. Barney Klinger stepped out. He was a short, rotund man who lived in a substantial Spanish-style property in Coral Gables, next to Miami. The chorus girl who accompanied him was neither short nor rotund; she was stunning, and young enough to be his daughter. Mr. Klinger kept a cottage on the slopes of Spyglass Hill, which he used occasionally for discreet vacations away from Mrs. Klinger.

He intended to fly to Key West, put his girlfriend on a scheduled flight to Miami, then proceed home in his own plane, clearly alone, a tired businessman returning from a commercial visit to discuss a boring old contract. Mrs. Klinger would meet him at Miami Airport and note that he was alone. One could not be too careful. Mrs. Klinger knew some very fine lawyers.

Julio Gomez heaved himself to his feet and approached.

"Mr. Klinger, sir?"

Klinger's heart jumped. A private detective? "Who wants to know?"

"Look, I have a problem, sir. I was vacationing down here, and I just got a call from my wife. Our kid's had an accident back home. I have to get back, I really do. There are no flights today. None. Not even for charter. I was wondering, could you give me a lift to Key West? I'd be forever in your debt."

Klinger hesitated. The man could still be a private eye hired by Mrs. Klinger. He handed his grip to a baggage porter, who

began to load it and the rest of his valises into the hold of the
Navajo.

"Well," said Klinger, "I don't know."

There were six people grouped around: the passport officer,
the baggage porter, Gomez, Klinger, his girlfriend, and another man who was helping with the luggage. The porter
assumed this man was from the Klinger party, and the Klinger
party assumed he belonged to the airstrip. The pilot was out
of earshot inside his cabin, and the taxi driver was relieving
himself in the vegetation twenty yards away.

"Gee, honey, that's dreadful. We've got to help him," said
the chorus girl.

"Okay," said Klinger. "So long as we take off on time."

The passport officer quickly stamped the three passports,
the baggage locker was closed, the three passengers boarded,
the pilot revved up both engines, and three minutes later the
Navajo lifted off Sunshine with a filed flight plan for Key
West, seventy minutes' cruising time away.

"My dear friends, and I do hope I may call you friends," said
Sir Marston Moberley. "Please try to understand the position
of Her Majesty's government. At this juncture a referendum
would be quite inappropriate. It would be administratively
complex to an impossible degree."

He had not become a senior diplomat with a series of
Commonwealth postings behind him without learning to pa-
tronize.

"Please explain," rumbled Reverend Drake, "why a referendum is more complex than a general election. We want the
right to decide whether to have an election at all."

The explanation was simple enough, but it was not to be
mentioned here. The British government would have to pay
for a referendum; but in the election, the candidates were
paying for their own campaigns though exactly how, Sir
Marston had not inquired. He changed the subject.

"Tell me, if you feel this way, why not stand for the post of
Prime Minister yourself? According to your view, you would
have to win."

Seven of the delegation looked baffled. But the Reverend
Drake stabbed a sausagelike finger in his direction. "You
know why, Governor. These candidates are using printing

presses, public address systems, even campaign managers brought in from outside. And they're offering a lot of cash around among the people."

"I have no evidence of that—none at all," interrupted the Governor, now a shade of pink.

"Because you won't go outside and see what's going on!" roared the Baptist minister. "But *we* know. It happens on every streetcorner. And intimidation of those who oppose them."

"When I receive a report from Chief Inspector Jones to that effect, I will take action," snapped Sir Marston.

"Surely we need not quarrel," pleaded the Anglican vicar. "The point is, will you send our petition to London, Sir Marston?"

"Certainly I will," said the Governor. "It is the least I can do for you. But it is also, I fear, the *only* thing I can do. My hands, alas, are tied. And now, if you will excuse me."

They trooped out, having done what they came for. As they left the building, the doctor, who happened to be the uncle of the police chief, asked, "Do you think he really will?"

"Oh, certainly," said the vicar. "He has said he will."

"Yes, by surface mail," growled the Reverend Drake. "It should arrive in London around mid-January. We have to get rid of that Governor and get ourselves a new one."

"No chance, I'm afraid," said the vicar. "Sir Marston will not resign."

In its continuing war against the narcotics invasion of its own southern coast, the American government has resorted to using some expensive and ingenious surveillance techniques. Among these is a series of covert balloons, tethered in out-of-the-way places, owned, bought, or leased by Washington.

Suspended in the gondolas beneath these balloons are an array of extra-high-technology radar scanners and radio monitors. They cover the entire Caribbean basin, from Yucatan in the west to Anegada in the east, from Florida in the north to the Venezuelan coast. Every airplane, however big or small, that takes off within this bowl is spotted at once. Its course, height, and speed are monitored and reported back. Every yacht, cruiser, freighter, or liner that leaves port is picked up and tailed by unseen eyes and ears high in the sky and far away. The technology in these gondolas is mainly made by Westinghouse.

When it lifted from Sunshine Island, the Piper Navajo Chief was picked up by Westinghouse 404. It was routinely tracked across the ocean toward Key West on its course of 310 degrees, which, with the wind drift from the south, would have brought it right over Key West's approach beacon. Fifty miles short of Key West, it disintegrated in midair and disappeared from the screens. A U.S. Coast Guard vessel was sent to the spot, but it found no wreckage.

On Monday, Julio Gomez, a detective on the force of the Metro-Dade Police Department, did not show up for work. His partner, Detective Eddie Favaro, was extremely annoyed. They were due in court together that morning, and now Favaro had to go alone. The judge was scathing, and it was Favaro who had to bear her sarcasm. In the late morning he got back to the MDPD headquarters building at 1320 Northwest Fourteenth Street (the force was then on the threshold of moving to its new complex in the Doral District) and checked with his superior officer, Lieutenant Broderick.

"What's with Julio?" asked Favaro. "He never showed up at court."

"You're asking me? He's your partner," replied Broderick.

"He didn't check in?"

"Not to me," said Broderick. "Can't you get by without him?"

"No way. We're handling two cases, and neither defendant speaks anything but Spanish."

Mirroring its own local population, the Metro-Dade Police Department, which covers most of what people know as Greater Miami, employs a wide racial mix. Half the population of Metro-Dade is of Hispanic origin, some with a very halting command of English. Julio Gomez had been of Puerto Rican parentage and raised in New York, where he had joined the police. A decade ago, he had re-migrated south to join Metro-Dade. Here nobody referred to him as a "spick." In this area, that was not wise. His fluent Spanish was invaluable.

His partner of nine years, Eddie Favaro, was an Italian-American, his grandparents having emigrated from Catania as young newlyweds seeking a better life. Lieutenant Clay Broderick was black. Now he shrugged. He was overworked and understaffed, with a backlog of cases he could have done without.

"Find him," he said. "You know the rules."

Favaro did indeed. In Metro-Dade, if you are three days late back from a vacation without adequate good reason and without checking in, you are deemed to have dismissed yourself.

Favaro checked his partner's apartment, but there was no sign that anyone had returned from vacation. He knew where Gomez had gone—he always went to Sunshine—so he checked the passenger lists on the previous evening's flights from Nassau. The airline computer revealed the flight reservation and prepaid ticket, but it also showed the ticket had not been taken up. Favaro went back to Broderick.

"He could have had an accident," he urged. "Game fishing can be dangerous."

"There are phones," said Broderick. "He has our number."

"He could be in a coma. Maybe in a hospital. Maybe he asked someone else to phone in, and they didn't bother. They're pretty laid back in those islands. We could at least check it out."

Broderick sighed. Missing detectives he could also do without.

"Okay," he said. "Get me the number of the police department for this island—what do you call it? Sunshine? Jeez, what a name. Get me the local police chief, and I'll make the call."

Favaro had it for him in half an hour. It was so obscure, it was not even listed in International Directory Inquiries. He got it from the British Consulate, who rang Government House on Sunshine, and they passed it on. It took another thirty minutes for Lieutenant Broderick to get his connection.

He was lucky—he found Chief Inspector Jones in his office. It was midday.

"Chief Inspector Jones, this is Lieutenant of Detectives Clay Broderick, speaking from Miami. Hallo? Can you hear me? . . . Look, as a colleague, I wonder if you could do me a favor. One of my men was on vacation on Sunshine, and he hasn't showed up here. We hope there hasn't been an accident. . . . Yes, an American. Name, Julio Gomez. No, I don't know where he was staying. He was down there for the game fishing.''

Chief Inspector Jones took this call seriously. His was a tiny force, and Metro-Dade's was enormous. But he would show the Americans that Chief Inspector Jones was not half-asleep. He decided to handle the case himself and summoned a constable and a Land-Rover.

Quite rightly, he started with the Quarter Deck Hotel, but there he drew a blank. He went on to the fishing quay and found Jimmy Dobbs working on his boat, having no charter that day. Dobbs related that Gomez had not shown up for their Friday charter, which was odd, and that he had been staying with Mrs. Macdonald.

The landlady reported that Julio Gomez had left in a hurry on Friday morning for the airport. Jones went there and spoke to the airport manager. He summoned the passport officer, who confirmed that Mr. Gomez had taken a lift with Mr. Klinger to Key West on Friday morning. He gave Inspector Jones the aircraft registration. Jones telephoned Broderick back at four P.M.

Lieutenant Broderick took time out to phone the Key West police, who checked with their own airport. The lieutenant summoned Eddie Favaro just after six. His face was grave.

"Eddie, I'm sorry. Julio made a sudden decision to come home Friday morning. There was no scheduled flight back, so he hitched a lift on a private plane for Key West. It never made it. The plane went down from fifteen thousand feet into the sea, fifty miles short of Key West. The Coast Guard says there were no survivors.''

Favaro sat down. He shook his head. "I don't believe it.''

"I hardly can myself. Look, I'm terribly sorry, Eddie. I know you were close.''

"Nine years,'' whispered Favaro. "Nine years he watched my back. What happens now?''

"The machine takes over,'' said Broderick. "I'll tell the Director myself. You know the procedure. If we can't have a funeral service, we'll have a memorial. Full departmental honors. I promise.''

*   *   *

The suspicions came later that night and the next morning.

On Sunday, a charter skipper named Joe Fanelli had taken two small English boys fishing out of Bud 'n' Mary's Marina on Islamorada, a resort in the Florida Keys well north of Key West. Six miles out beyond Alligator Reef, heading for the Hump and trolling as they went, one of the boys took a big bite on his line. Between them the brothers, Stuart and Shane, hauled in what they hoped was a big kingfish or wahoo or tuna. When the catch came up in the wake, Joe Fanelli leaned down and hauled it aboard. It turned out to be the remnants of a life-jacket, still bearing the stenciled number of the airplane to which it had once belonged, and some scorch marks.

The local police sent it up to Miami, where the forensic laboratory established that it had come from Barney Klinger's Navajo Chief, and that the scorch marks bore traces not of gasoline but of plastic explosive. It became a Homicide investigation.

The first thing Homicide did was check on the business affairs of Mr. Klinger. What they discovered caused them to think the case was a dead end. They had, after all, no mandate on the British territory of Sunshine, and little confidence that the local force would get to the bottom of what had to be a professional hit.

On Tuesday morning Sam McCready eased himself onto his poolside lounger at the Sonesta Beach Hotel on Key Biscayne, settled his second after-breakfast coffee on the table by his side, and opened the *Miami Herald*.

Without any particular interest, he scanned the paper for international news—there was precious little—and settled for local affairs. The second lead concerned fresh revelations in the disappearance of a light airplane over the sea southeast of Key West the previous Friday morning.

The news sleuths of the *Herald* had discovered not only that the plane might well have been destroyed by a bomb inside it, but that Mr. Barney Klinger was known as the uncrowned king of the illicit trade, theft, and laundering of spare aviation parts in South Florida.

After narcotics, this abstruse area of illegal behavior is probably the most lucrative. Florida bristles with airplanes—

airliners, cargo freighters, and private aircraft. It also contains some of the world's major legitimate companies in the provision of constantly needed new or reconditioned spare parts. AVIOL and the Instrument Locator Service supply replacement parts on a worldwide scale.

The illegitimate industry, on the other hand, specializes either in commissioning the theft of such parts for no-questions-asked sales to other (usually Third World) operators, or in the even more dangerous purveying of parts whose operational life is almost expended, selling them as reconditioned parts with most of their operational life still left. For the latter scam, the paperwork is forged. Since some of these parts sell for a quarter of a million dollars each, the profits for a ruthless operator can be huge.

Speculation was running high that someone had wanted to remove Mr. Klinger from the scene.

"In the midst of life," murmured McCready, and turned to the weather forecast. It was sunny.

Lieutenant Broderick summoned Eddie Favaro on that same Tuesday morning. He was even more grave than he had been the day before.

"Eddie, before we proceed with the memorial service with full honors for Julio, we have to consider a troubling new factor. What the hell was Julio doing sharing a plane with a sleazeball like Klinger?"

"He was trying to get back home," said Favaro.

"Was he? What was he doing down there?"

"Fishing."

"Was he? How come he was sharing the same week on Sunshine with Klinger? Did they have business to discuss?"

"Clay, listen to me. No way—no way in this world—was Julio Gomez corrupt. I won't believe it. He was trying to get home. He saw a plane, he asked for a ride, is all."

"I hope you're right," Broderick said soberly. "Why was he trying to get home two days ahead of schedule?

"That's what puzzles me," admitted Favaro. "He loved his fishing, looked forward to it all year. He would never have cut short two days of fishing without a reason. I want to go over there and find out why."

"You have three reasons for not going," said the lieutenant.

"This department is overworked, you are needed here, and any bomb—if bomb there was—was certainly aimed at Klinger. The girl and Julio were accidents. Sorry, Internal Affairs will have to check out Julio's financial situation. It can't be avoided. If he never met Klinger before Friday, it was just a tragic accident."

"I've got some leave time due me," said Favaro. "I want it, Clay. I want it now."

"Yes, you've got some leave time. And I can't deny it to you. But you go there and you're on your own, Eddie. That's British territory—we have no authority there. And I want your gun."

Favaro handed over his police automatic, left, and headed for the bank. At three that afternoon, he landed on Sunshine's airstrip, paid off his chartered four-seater, and watched it leave for Miami. Then he hitched a lift with one of the airstrip staff into Port Plaisance. Not knowing where else to go, he checked into the Quarter Deck.

Sir Marston Moberley sat in a comfortable chair in his walled garden and sipped a whiskey and soda. It was his favorite ritual of the day. The garden behind Government House was not large, but it was very private. A well-tended lawn covered most of the space, and bougainvillaea and jacaranda festooned the walls with their brilliant colors. The walls, which surrounded the garden on three sides—the fourth side was the house itself—were eight feet high and topped with shards of glass. In one wall was an old steel door, seven feet tall, but it was long out of use. Beyond it was a small lane that led into the heart of Port Plaisance. The steel door had been sealed years before, and on its outer side two semicircular steel hasps were secured by a padlock the size of a small dinner plate. All were long fused by rust.

Sir Marston enjoyed the cool of the evening. His adjutant was somewhere inside his own quarters at the other end of the house; his wife was out on an errand visiting the local hospital; Jefferson, his chef/steward/butler, would be preparing dinner in the kitchen. Sir Marston sipped his whiskey with appreciation, then almost choked when his ears were assailed by the scream of rending steel. He turned. He had time to say, "I say, what on earth—Now look here—"

The roar of the first bullet shocked and stunned him. The slug went through a fold of loose fabric in the sleeve of his cotton shirt. It hammered into the coral-block wall of the house behind him and fell back onto the path, misshapen and twisted. The second hit him full in the heart.

Chapter 2

Despite the twin booms of the handgun from the garden, there was no immediate reaction from inside the house. Only two people were there at that hour.

Jefferson was belowstairs preparing a fruit punch for the evening meal—Lady Moberley was a teetotaler. He would say later that when the blender was switched on the noise filled the kitchen, and it must have been on when the shooting took place.

The Governor's adjutant was Lieutenant Jeremy Haverstock, a downy-cheeked young subaltern seconded from the Queen's Dragoon Guards. He was in his room at the far end of Government House with the window closed and the air conditioning at full blast. He was also, so he would say, playing his radio and listening to music from Radio Nassau. He, too, heard nothing.

By the time Jefferson came out into the garden to consult Sir Marston over some point concerning the preparation of the lamb cutlets, the assassin had clearly withdrawn through the steel gate and had gone. Jefferson arrived at the top of the steps leading down to the garden and saw his employer lying flat on his back, arms wide, as the second shot had thrown him, a dark blotch still spreading across the front of his dark-blue-cotton shirt.

At first, Jefferson thought his master had fainted, and he ran down to help him up. When he saw the hole in the chest more clearly, he stood back, disbelieving for a moment, then ran panic-stricken to fetch Lieutenant Haverstock. The young army officer arrived seconds later, still in his boxer shorts.

Haverstock did not panic. He examined the body without touching it, established that Sir Marston was extremely dead, and sat down in the ex-Governor's chair to ponder what to do.

A previous commanding officer had written of Lieutenant Haverstock, "Wonderful breeding, not terribly bright," as if he were a Cavalry horse rather than a Cavalry officer. But in the Cavalry they tend to have their priorities about right: A good horse is irreplaceable, while a subaltern is not.

Haverstock sat in the chair a few feet from the body and thought the matter through, while a wide-eyed Jefferson watched from the top of the stairs that led to the verandah. The subaltern decided that (a) he had a dead Governor on his hands, (b) someone had shot him and escaped, and (c) he should inform a higher authority. The problem was, the Governor *was* the highest authority, or had been. At this point, Lady Moberley came home.

Jefferson heard the crunch of the wheels of the official Jaguar limousine on the gravel of the front drive and rushed out through the hallway to intercept her. His breaking of the news was lucid, if not very tactful. He confronted her in the hall and said, "Oh, Lady, de Governor been shot. He dead."

Lady Moberley hurried to the verandah to look down and was met by Haverstock coming up the steps. He assisted her to her bedroom and comforted her as she lay down. She seemed more bewildered than grief-stricken, as if worried lest the Foreign Office might now play merry hell with her husband's career.

Having got her settled, Lieutenant Haverstock dispatched Jefferson to summon the island's only doctor—who also happened to be the island's only coroner—and Chief Inspector Jones, who was the doctor/coroner's nephew. The lieutenant instructed the distraught butler to explain nothing to them, simply to ask each man to come urgently to Government House.

It was a fruitless request. Poor Jefferson told Inspector Jones the news in the hearing of three wide-eyed constables, and Dr. Caractacus Jones in front of his housekeeper. Like wildfire the news spread, even as the uncle and his nephew hurried to Government House.

While Jefferson was away, Lieutenant Haverstock pondered how to tell London. The residence had not been equipped with modern or secure communication systems. It had never been thought necessary to do so. Apart from the open phone line, the Governor's messages had always gone to London via the much more substantial British High Commission in Nassau, the Bahamas. For this, an elderly C2 system was used. It sat on a side table in the Governor's private office.

To look at, it was an ordinary Telex machine of the type known to, and dreaded by, foreign correspondents the world over. Connection was made to Nassau by tapping in the usual code and securing an acknowledgment from the other end. The Telex could then be switched to encrypted mode through a second box that sat beside the Telex machine. Any message sent would then appear "in clear" on the paper in front of the sender and would be automatically decoded at the Nassau end. In between the two points, it would be in code.

The trouble was, to operate the encoder, one had to insert corrugated disks according to the day of the month. These disks were kept in the Governor's safe, which was locked. The dead man's private secretary, Myrtle, had the combination of the safe, but she was away visiting her partents on Tortola in the Virgin Islands. During her absences, the Governor was wont to send his own messages. He too knew the safe's combination; Haverstock did not.

Eventually, Haverstock simply rang the High Commission in Nassau via the telephone exchange and told them verbally. After twenty minutes, an incandescent First Secretary called him back for confirmation, listened to his explanation, and told him crisply to seal Government House and hold the fort until backup could arrive from Nassau or London. The First Secretary then radioed a top-secret and coded message to the Foreign Office in London. It was already six P.M. and dark in the Caribbean. It was eleven P.M. in London, and the message went to the night duty officer. He called a senior official of the Caribbean desk at his home in Chobham, and the wheels began to roll.

On Sunshine, the news went through Port Plaisance within two hours, and on his regular evening call a radio ham told a fellow enthusiast in Chevy Chase, near Washington. The American ham, being a public-spirited fellow, called the Associated Press, which was dubious but finally emitted a dispatch that began, "The Governor of the British Caribbean Dependency known as the Barclay Islands may have been shot dead by an unknown assassin this evening, according to unconfirmed reports from the tiny group of islands."

The dispatch, written by a night duty subeditor who had consulted a large map with an even larger magnifying glass, went on to explain where and what the islands were.

In London, where by now it was the small hours of the morning, Reuters took the story off its rival's tape and tried to get confirmation from the Foreign Office. Just before dawn, the Foreign Office admitted it had received a report to that effect and that the appropriate steps were being taken.

The appropriate steps had involved the waking of a considerable number of people scattered in their various homes in and around London. Satellites operated by America's National Reconnaissance Office noted heavy radio traffic between London and its High Commission in Nassau, and the obedient machines reported down to the National Security Agency at Fort Meade. They told the CIA, which already knew because they read the Associated Press. About a billion dollars worth of technology worked it out three hours after a radio ham with a homemade set in a shack on the side of Spyglass Hill had told a pal in Chevy Chase.

In London, the Foreign Office alerted the Home Office, and they in turn raised Sir Peter Imbert, Commissioner of the Metropolitan Police, asking for a senior detective to be sent out immediately. The Commissioner woke Simon Crawshaw of the Specialist Operations Divison, who got on to the Commander controlling his Serious Crimes Branch.

Commander Braithwaite rang through to the twenty-four-hour Reserve Office and asked, "Who's in the frame?"

The Reserve Office duty sergeant consulted his roster in

New Scotland Yard. The RO at the Yard is a small office whose duty is to maintain a list of senior detectives available at short notice in the event of an urgent request to assist a police authority outside the metropolitan area. The detective at the top of the list has to be available to move at one hour's notice. The man next in line must move at six hours' notice, and the third one on twenty-four-hour notice.

"Detective Chief Superintendent Craddock, sir," said the duty sergeant. Then his eye caught a note pinned to the side of the roster. "No, sir, sorry. He has to be at the Old Bailey to give evidence at eleven this morning."

"Who's next?" growled the Commander from his home at West Drayton, out near Heathrow Airport.

"Mr. Hannah, sir."

"And who's his Detective Inspector?"

"Wetherall, sir."

"Ask Mr. Hannah to call me at home. Now," said the Commander.

Thus it was that just after four A.M., on a bitter, black December morning, the phone rang on a bedside table in Croydon and woke Detective Chief Superintendent Desmond Hannah. He listened to the instruction from the Reserve Office, and then, as bidden, he called a number in West Drayton.

"Bill? Des Hannah. What's up?"

He listened for five minutes, then asked, "Bill, where the hell is Sunshine?"

Back on the island, Dr. Caractacus Jones had examined the body and pronounced it very dead. Darkness had descended over the garden, and he worked by flashlight. Not that there was much he could do. He was a general practitioner, not a forensic pathologist. He looked after the islanders' general health as best he could, and he had a small surgery for the treatment of cuts and bruises. He had delivered more babies than he could recall, and he had removed ten times that number of fish hooks. As a doctor, he could issue a death certificate, and as a coroner, issue a burial certificate. But he had never cut up a dead Governor, and he did not intend to start now.

Serious injuries and maladies needing complex operations

were always flown to Nassau, where they had a fine modern hospital with all the facilities for operations and post-mortems. He did not even have a mortuary.

As Dr. Jones finished his examination, Lieutenant Haverstock returned from the private office.

"Our people in Nassau say that a senior officer will be sent from Scotland Yard," he announced. "Till then, we must keep everything just as it was."

Chief Inspector Jones had posted a constable on the front door to keep away the sightseers, whose faces had already begun to appear at the front gate. He had prowled the garden and discovered the steel door through which the assassin had apparently entered and left. It had been pulled closed by the departing killer, which was why Haverstock had not noticed it. Inspector Jones at once posted a second constable oustide the door and ordered him to keep everyone away from it. It might contain fingerprints that the man from Scotland Yard would need.

Outside in the darkness the constable sat down, leaned his back against the wall, and promptly fell asleep.

Inside the garden, Inspector Jones pronounced, "Everything must be left untouched until morning. The body must not be moved."

"Don't be a damned fool, boy," said his uncle, Dr. Jones. "It will go rotten. It is already."

He was right. In the heat of the Caribbean, bodies are normally interred within twenty-four hours. The alternative is unspeakable. A crowd of flies was already buzzing over the dead Governor's chest and eyes. The three men considered their problem, as Jefferson tended to Lady Moberley.

"It will have to be the ice house," said Dr. Jones at length. "There's nowhere else."

They had to agree he was right. The ice house, powered by the municipal generator, was down on the dock. Haverstock took the dead man's shoulders, and Chief Inspector Jones took his feet. With some difficulty they maneuverd the still-limp body up the stairs, across the sitting room, past the office, and out into the hall. Lady Moberley put her head around the corner of her bedroom door, glanced over the banisters as her late husband went across the hall, uttered a series of "oh-oh-oh-ohs," and retired again.

They realized in the hall that they could not carry Sir Marston all the way to the docks. The trunk of the Jaguar was considered for a moment, but it was rejected as being too small and not very seemly.

A police Land-Rover turned out to be the answer. Space was made in the back, and the former Governor was eased inside. Even with his shoulders against the rear of the front seats, his legs hung over the tailgate. Dr. Jones pushed them inside and closed the rear door. Sir Marston slumped, head forward, like someone returning from a very long and very liquid party.

With Inspector Jones at the wheel and Lieutenant Haverstock beside him, the Land-Rover drove down to the docks, followed by most of the population of Port Plaisance. There Sir Marston was laid out with greater ceremony in the ice house, where the temperature was well below zero.

Her Majesty's late Governor of the Barclay Islands spent his first night in the afterworld sandwiched between a large marlin and a very fine blackfin tuna. In the morning the expression on all three faces was much the same.

Dawn, of course, came five hours earlier in London than in Sunshine. At seven o'clock, when the first fingers of the new day were touching the roofs of Westminster Abbey, Detective Chief Superintendent Hannah was closeted with Commander Braithwaite in the latter's office in New Scotland Yard.

"You take off just before twelve on the scheduled BA flight from Heathrow for Nassau," said the Commander. "Tickets in first class are being arranged. The flight was full—it has meant easing another couple off the plane."

"And the team?" asked Hannah. "Will they be in club or economy?"

"Ah, the team, yes. Fact is, Des, they're being provided in Nassau. The Foreign Office is arranging it."

Desmond Hannah smelled a large rat. He was fifty-one, an old-fashioned thief-taker who had worked his way rung by rung up the ladder from bobby on the beat—testing door locks on the streets of London, helping old ladies cross the road, and directing tourists—to the rank of Chief Superintendent. He had one year to go before retirement from the Force and was probably destined like so many of his kind to accept a less stressful job as a senior security officer for a major corporation.

He knew he would never make Commander rank, not now, and four years earlier he had been seconded to the Murder Squad of the Serious Crimes Branch of the Specialist Operations Division, a slot known as the elephants' graveyard. You went in a hefty bull, and you came out a pile of bones.

But he liked things to be done right. On any assignment, even an overseas one, a Murder Squad detective could expect a backup team of at least four: a scene-of-crime officer, or SOCO, at least a sergeant; a lab liaison sergeant; a photographer; and a fingerprint man. The forensic aspect could be crucial, and usually was.

"I want them from here, Bill."

"Can't be done, Des. I'm afraid the Foreign Office is calling the shots on this one. They're paying for it all, according to the Home Office. And it seems they're penny-pinching. The High Commission in Nassau has arranged for the Bahamian Police to provide the forensic backup. I'm sure they're very good."

"Post-mortem? They doing that, too?"

"No," said Commander Braithwaite reassuringly, "we're sending Ian West out to Nassau for that. The body's still on the island. As soon as you've had a look, get it shipped back to Nassau in a stiff-bag. Ian will be following you twenty-four hours later. By the time he gets to Nassau, you should have got the body to Nassau in time for him to go to work."

Hannah grunted. He was slightly mollified. At least in Dr. Ian West, he would have one of the best forensic pathologists in the world.

"Why can't Ian come to this Sunshine place and do the PM there?" he asked.

"They don't have a mortuary on Sunshine," the Commander explained patiently.

"So where's the body?"

"I don't know."

"Hell, it'll be half decomposed by the time I get there," said Hannah. He could not have known that at that hour Sir Marston was not half decomposed. He was rock solid. Dr. West could not have gotten a chisel into him.

"I want ballistics done here," he said. "If I get the bullet or bullets back, I want Alan to have them. The bullets could tie up the whole thing.''

"All right," conceded the Commander. "Tell the High Commission people we need them back here in the diplomatic bag. Now, why don't you get a decent breakfast? The car will be here for you at nine. Your Detective Inspector will have the murder bag. He'll meet you at the car.

"What about the press?" asked Hannah as he left.

"Full cry, I'm afraid. It's not in the papers yet. The news only broke in the small hours. But all the wire services have run it. God knows where they got it so fast. There may be a few reptiles at the airport trying to get on the same flight."

Just before nine, Desmond Hannah appeared with his suitcase in the inner courtyard, where a Rover was waiting for him, a uniformed sergeant at the wheel. He looked around for Harry Wetherall, the Detective Inspector with whom he had worked for three years. He was nowhere to be seen. A pink-faced young man of about thirty came hurrying up. He carried a murder bag, a small suitcase that contained a variety of swabs, cloths, capsules, vials, plastic bags, scrapers, bottles, tweezers, and probes—the basic tools of the trade for discovering, removing, and retaining clues.

"Mr. Hannah?" said the young man.

"Who are you?"

"DI Parker, sir."

"Where's Wetherall?"

"He's ill, I'm afraid. Asian flu or something. The Reserve Office asked me to step in. Always keep my passport in my drawer just in case. It's awfully good to be working with you."

Blast Wetherall! thought Hannah. Damn his eyes!

They rode out to Heathrow largely in silence. At least, Hannah was silent. Parker ("It's Peter, really") expatiated on his knowledge of the Caribbean. He had been there twice, with Club Med.

"Have you ever been to the Caribbean, sir?" he asked.

"No," said Hannah, and lapsed back into silence.

At Heathrow, he and Parker were expected. Passport examination was a formality. The murder bag did not pass through the X-ray scanners, where it would have caused much

interest. Instead, an official led the pair around the formalities
and straight to the first class lounge.

The press was indeed in evidence, though Hannah did not
see them until he was aboard the aircraft. Two organizations
with money to spend had persuaded booked passengers to
vacate their seats and take a later flight. Others were trying to
get on the two Miami flights of the morning, while their head
offices arranged charter planes from Miami into Sunshine.
Camera teams from BBC TV, Independent TV News, and
British Satellite Broadcasting were heading for the Barclays,
spearheaded by their reporters. Reporter-photographer teams
from five major newspapers were also in the melee.

In the lounge, Hannah was approached by a panting young
sprog who introduced himself as being from the Foreign
Office. He had a large file.

"We've put together some background briefing for you,"
he said, handing over the file. "Geography, economy, population of the Barclays, that sort of thing. And, of course, a
background on the present political situation."

Hannah's heart sank. A nice domestic murder would probably have cleared itself up in a few days. But if this was
political . . . They were called for their flight.

After takeoff the irrepressible Parker took champagne from
the stewardess and answered questions about himself with
great pleasure. He was twenty-nine—young for a DI—and
was married to a real estate agent called Elaine. They lived in
the new and fashionable Dockland area, quite close to Canary
Wharf. His own passion was a Morgan 4+4 sports car, but
Elaine drove a Ford Escort GTI.

"Convertible, of course," said Parker.

"Of course," murmured Hannah. I've got a dinky on my
hands, he thought. Dual-income-no-kids. A high-flyer.

Parker had gone straight from school to a red-brick university and gotten a degree, starting with PPE (politics, philosophy, and economics) and switching to law. He had joined the
Metropolitan Police straight from there, and after the manda-
tory cadetship he had worked for a year in the outer suburbs
before going on the Bramshill Police College Special Course.
From there, he had spent four years in the Commissioner's
Force Planning Unit.

They were over County Cork when Hannah closed the

Foreign Office file and asked gently, "And how many murder investigations have you been on?"

"Well, this is my first, actually. That's why I was so pleased to be available this morning. But in my spare time I study criminology. I think it's so important to understand the criminal mind."

Desmond Hannah turned his face to the porthole in pure misery. He had a dead Governor, a pending election, a Bahamian forensic team, and a rookie DI who wanted to understand the criminal mind. After lunch, he dozed all the way to Nassau. He even managed to forget about the press. Until Nassau.

The Associated Press news bulletin of the previous evening had been too late to make the British newspapers in London, with their five-hour disadvantage, but it had been just in time to catch the *Miami Herald* before that paper was put to bed.

At seven in the morning, Sam McCready was sitting on his balcony sipping his first prebreakfast coffee of the day and gazing out over the azure sea when he heard the familiar rustle of the *Herald* coming under his door.

He padded across the room, took the paper, and returned to the balcony. The AP story was at the bottom of the front page, where a piece about a record-breaking lobster had been scrapped to make way for it. The story was just the AP dispatch, referring to unconfirmed reports. The headline said simply: BRITISH GOVERNOR SLAIN? McCready read it several times.

"How very naughty," he murmured, and withdrew to the bathroom to get washed, shaved, and dressed. At nine, he dismissed his cab outside the British Consulate in Miami, went in, and made himself known—as Mr. Frank Dillon of the Foreign Office. He had to wait half an hour for the arrival of the Consul, then he got his private meeting. By ten, he had what he had come for, a secure line to the embassy in Washington. He spoke for twenty minutes to the Head of the SIS Station, a colleague he knew well from London days and with whom he had stayed the previous week while attending the CIA seminar.

The Washington-based colleague confirmed the story and added a few more details that had just arrived from London.

"I thought I might pop over," said McCready.

"Not really our cup of tea, is it?" suggested the Head of Station.

"Probably not, but it might be worth a look. I'll need to draw some funds, and I'll need a communicator."

"I'll clear it with the Consul. Could you put him on the line?"

An hour later, McCready left the consulate with a wad of dollars, duly signed for, and an attaché case containing a portable telephone and an encrypter with a range that would enable him to make secure calls to the consulate in Miami and have them passed on to Washington.

He returned to the Sonesta Beach, packed, checked out, and called an air taxi company at the airport. They agreed on a two P.M. takeoff for the ninety-minute run to Sunshine.

Eddie Favaro was also up early. He had already decided there was only one place he could start—the game-fishing community down at the fishing quay. Wherever Julio Gomez had spent his vacation, a large part of it surely had been there.

Having no transport, he walked. It was not far. Almost every wall and tree he passed bore a poster urging the islanders to vote for one candidate or the other. The faces of both men—one big, round, and jolly, the other smooth, urbane, and paler in tone—beamed from the posters.

Some had been torn down or defaced, whether by children or by adherents to the other candidate, he could not tell. All had been professionally printed. On a warehouse wall near the docks was another message, crudely painted. It said, WE WANT REFERENDUM. As he passed, a black jeep carrying four men raced up.

The jeep screeched to a halt. The four men wore hard expressions, multicolored shirts, and wraparound black glasses that hid their eyes. Four black heads stared at the message, then swiveled toward Favaro as if he were responsible for it. Favaro shrugged as if to say, "Nothing to do with me." The four impassive faces stared at him until he rounded a corner. Then he heard the jeep, revving hard, drive away.

At the fishing quay, groups of men were discussing the same news that had occupied those in the hotel lobby. He interrupted one group to ask who took visitors fishing. One of the men pointed farther down the quay to a man working on a boat.

Favaro crouched on the quay and made his inquiry. He showed the fisherman a picture of Julio Gomez.

The man shook his head. "Sure, he was here last week. But he go out with Jimmy Dobbs. That's Jimmy's boat over there, the *Gulf Lady*."

There was nobody on the *Gulf Lady*. He leaned on a mooring post to wait. Like all cops, he knew the meaning of patience. Information gathered in a matter of seconds was for TV thrillers. In real life, you spent most of your time waiting. Jimmy Dobbs showed up at ten.

"Mr. Dobbs?"

"That's me."

"Hi—my name's Eddie. I'm from Florida. This your boat?"

"Sure is. You here for the fishing?"

"That's my game," said Favaro. "Friend of mine recommended you."

"That's nice."

"Julio Gomez. You remember him?"

The black man's open, honest face clouded. He reached into the *Gulf Lady* and took a rod from a holder. He examined the jig lure and the hook for several seconds, then handed the rod to Favaro.

"You like yellowtail snapper? They some good snapper right under the dock. Down at the far end."

Together they walked to the far end of the jetty, out of earshot of anyone else. Favaro wondered why.

Jimmy Dobbs took the rod back and cast expertly across the water. He reeled in slowly, letting the brightly colored jig wriggle and turn beneath the surface. A small blue runner made a dart for the lure and turned away.

"Julio Gomez dead," Jimmy Dobbs said gravely.

"I know," said Favaro. "I'd like to find out why. He fished with you a lot, I think."

"Every year. He good man, nice guy."

"He tell you what his job was in Miami?"

"Yep. Once."

"You ever tell anyone else?"

"Nope. You a friend or a colleague?"

"Both, Jimmy. Tell me, when did you last see Julio?"

"Right here, Thursday evening. We'd been out all day. He booked me for Friday morning. Never showed up."

"No," said Favaro. "He was at the airstrip, trying to get a flight to Miami. In a hurry. He picked the wrong plane—blew up over the sea. Why did we have to walk down here to talk?"

Jimmy Dobbs hooked a two-pound horse-eye jack and handed the shivering rod to Favaro. The American reeled in. He was inexpert. The jack took some slack line and jumped the hook.

"They some bad people on these islands," he said simply.

Favaro realized he could now identify an odor he had smelled in the town: It was fear. He knew about fear. No Miami cop is stranger to that unique aroma. Somehow, fear had now come to paradise.

"When he left you, he was a happy man?"

"Yep. One fine fish he was taking home for supper. He was happy. No problems."

"Where did he go from here?"

Jimmy Dobbs looked surprised. "To Mrs. Macdonald's, of course. He always stayed with her."

Mrs. Macdonald was not at home. She was out shopping. Favaro decided to come back later. First, he would try the airport. He returned to Parliament Square. There were two taxis, but both drivers were at lunch. There was nothing he could do about it; he crossed the square to the Quarter Deck to eat and wait for them to come back. He took a verandah seat from where he could watch for the taxis. All around him was the same excited buzz that had pervaded breakfast—the talk being only of the murder of the Governor the previous evening.

"They sending a senior detective from Scotland Yard," one of the group near Favaro announced.

Two men entered the bar. They were big, and they said not a word. The conversation died. The two men removed every poster proclaiming the candidacy of Marcus Johnson and put up different ones. The new posters said, VOTE LIVINGSTONE, THE PEOPLE'S CANDIDATE. When they had finished, they left.

The waiter came over and set down grilled fish and a beer.

"Who were they?" asked Favaro.

"Election helpers of Mr. Livingstone," the waiter said expressionlessly.

"People seem to be frightened of them."

"No, sah."

The waiter turned away, eyes blank. Favaro had seen that expression in interrogation rooms at the Metro-Dade headquarters. Shutters come down behind the eyes. The message is, "There's no one home."

The jumbo carrying Superintendent Hannah and DI Parker touched down at Nassau at three P.M., local time. A senior officer of the Bahamian Police boarded first, identified the two men from Scotland Yard, introduced himself, and welcomed them to Nassau. He escorted them out of the cabin before the other passengers, then down to a waiting Land-Rover. The first gust of warm, balmy air swept over Hannah. In his London clothes he felt sticky at once.

The Bahamian officer took their baggage checks and handed them to a constable, who would extract the two valises from the rest of the baggage. Hannah and Parker were driven straight to the VIP lounge. There they met the British Deputy High Commissioner, Mr. Longstreet, and a more junior staffer called Bannister.

"I'll be coming to Sunshine with you," said Bannister. "Some problem over there with the communications. It seems they can't get the Governor's safe open. I'll fix a new set, so you can talk to the High Commission here on a direct radio-telephone link. Secure, of course. And of course, we'll have to get the body back when the coroner releases it."

He sounded brisk and efficient. Hannah liked that. He met the four men from the forensic team provided by the Bahamian Police as a courtesy. The conference took an hour.

Hannah looked down from the windows to the airport apron below. Thirty yards away, a chartered ten-seater was waiting to take him and his now-expanded party to Sunshine. Between the building and the airplane, two camera teams had been set up to catch the moment. He sighed.

When the final details had been settled, the group left the VIP lounge and headed downstairs. Mircophones were thrust at him, notepads held ready.

"Mr. Hannah, are you confident of an early arrest?" "Will

this turn out to be a political murder?'' ''Is Sir Marston's death linked to the election campaign?''

He nodded and smiled but said nothing. Flanked by Bahamian constables, they all emerged from the building into the hot sunshine and headed for the aircraft. The TV cameras recorded it all. When the official party had boarded, the journalists raced away toward their own chartered planes, which had been obtained by the production of large wads of dollars or prechartered by the London offices. In an untidy gaggle the planes began to taxi for takeoff. It was four twenty-five.

At three-thirty, a small Cessna dropped its wings over Sunshine and turned for the final run-in to the grass airstrip.

"Pretty wild place!" the American pilot shouted to the man beside him. "Beautiful, but from way back! I mean, they don't have nothing here!"

"Short on technology," agreed Sam McCready. He looked through the prespex at the dusty strip coming towards them. To the left of the strip were three buildings: a corrugated-iron hangar, a low shed with a red tin roof (the reception building), and a white cube with the British flag flying above it—the police hut. Outside the reception shed, a figure in a short-sleeved beach shirt was talking to a man in boxer shorts and singlet. A car stood nearby. The palm trees rose on either side of the Cessna, and the small plane thumped onto the grit. The buildings flashed past as the pilot settled his nose-wheel and lifted his flaps. At the far end of the strip, he turned around and began to taxi back.

"Sure, I remember that plane. It was dreadful when I heard later that those poor people were dead."

Favaro found the baggage porter who had loaded the Navajo Chief the previous Friday morning. His name was Ben, and he always loaded the baggage. It was his job. Like most of the islanders, he was free-and-easy, honest, and prepared to talk.

Favaro produced a photograph. "Did you notice this man?"

"Sure. He was asking the owner of the plane for a lift to Key West."

"How do you know?"

"Standing right next to me," said Ben.

"Did he seem worried, anxious, in a hurry?"

"So would you be, man! He done told the owner his wife called him and their kid was sick. The girl, she say that was real bad, they should help him. So the owner said he could ride with them to Key West."

"Was there anyone else nearby?"

Ben thought for a while. "Only the other man helping load the luggage," he said. "Employed by the owner, I think."

"What did he look like, this other loader?"

"Never seen him before," said Ben. "Black man, not from Sunshine. Bright-colored shirt, dark glasses. Didn't say nothing."

The Cessna rumbled up to the customs shed. Ben and Favaro shielded their eyes from the flying dust. Favaro saw a rumpled-looking man of medium build get out, take a suitcase and attaché case from the locker, stand back, wave to the pilot, and go into the shed.

Favaro was pensive as he studied the scene. Julio Gomez did not tell lies. But he had no wife and child. He must have been desperate to get on that flight and home to Miami. But why? Knowing his partner, Favaro was convinced that he had been under threat. The bomb was not for Klinger. It was for Gomez.

He thanked Ben and wandered back to the taxi that waited for him. As he climbed in, a British voice at his elbow said, "I know it's a lot to ask, but could I hitch a ride into town? The cab rank seems to be empty."

It was the man who had just gotten off the Cessna. "Sure," said Favaro. "Be my guest."

"Awfully kind," said the Englishman as he put his gear in the trunk. On the five-minute ride into town, he introduced himself. "Frank Dillon," he said.

"Eddie Favaro," said the American. "You here for the fishing?"

"Alas, no. Not really my scene. Just here on vacation for a bit of piece and quiet."

"No chance," said Favaro. "There's chaos here. There's a whole crowd of London detectives due in soon, and a whole bunch of journalists. Last night someone shot the Governor in his garden."

"Good Lord!" said the Englishman. He seemed genuinely shocked.

Favaro dropped him on the steps of the Quarter Deck, dismissed the cab, and walked the few hundred yards through the back streets to Mrs. Macdonald's boarding house. Across Parliament Square, a big man was addressing a subdued crowd of citizens from the back of a flat truck. It was Mr. Livingstone himself. Favaro caught the booming roar of his oratory.

"And I say, brothers and sisters, you should share in the wealth of these islands! You should share in the fish caught from the sea, you should share the fine houses of the few rich who live up on the hill, you should share the . . ."

The crowd did not look very enthusiastic. The truck was flanked by the same two large men who had torn down the Johnson posters in the Quarter Deck Hotel in the lunch hour and put up their own. There were several similar men throughout the crowd seeking to start a cheering response. They cheered alone. Favaro walked on. This time Mrs. Macdonald was in.

Desmond Hannah touched down at twenty to six. It was almost dark. Four other, lighter aircraft had just made it in time and were able to depart back to Nassau before the light faded. Their cargoes were the BBC, ITV, the *Sunday Times* man sharing with the *Sunday Telegraph,* and Sabrina Tennant and her team from BSB, the British Satellite Broadcasting company.

Hannah, Parker, Bannister, and the four Bahamian officers were met by Lieutenant Haverstock and Inspector Jones, the former in a cream tropical suit and the latter immaculate in his uniform. On the off-chance of earning some dollars, both of Port Plaisance's taxis and two small vans had also appeared. All were snapped up.

By the time formalities were completed and the cavalcade had descended on the Quarter Deck Hotel, darkness had fallen. Hannah decreed there was no point in beginning investigations by flashlight, but he asked that the guard on Government House be continued through the night. Inspector Jones, much impressed to be working with a real Detective Chief Superintendent from Scotland Yard, barked out the orders.

Hannah was tired. It might be just after six in the islands, but it was eleven P.M. on his body clock, and he had been up since four A.M. He dined alone with Parker and Lieutenant Haverstock, which enabled him to get a firsthand account of what had actually happened the previous evening. Then he turned in.

The press found the bar with unerring and practiced speed. Rounds were ordered and consumed. The usual jocular banter of the press corps on a foreign assignment grew louder. No one noticed a man in a rumpled tropical suit drinking alone at the end of the bar and listening to their chatter.

"Where did he go after he left here?" Eddie Favaro asked Mrs. Macdonald. He was seated at her kitchen table while the good lady served up some of her conch chowder.

"He went over to the Quarter Deck for a beer," she said.

"Was he in a cheerful mood?"

Her lilting singsong voice filled the room. "Bless you, Mr. Favaro, he was a happy man. A fine fish for supper, I was preparing him. He said he would be back at eight o'clock. I told him not to be late, or the dorado spoil and go dry. He laughed and said he would be on time."

"And was he?"

"No, man. He was an hour and more late. The fish done spoil. And him talking nonsense."

"What did he say? This . . . nonsense."

"He didn't say much. Seemed worried bad. Then he said he seen a scorpion. Now you finish this soup up. That one bowl of God's goodness in there."

Favaro stiffened, his spoon halfway to his lips. "Did he say *a* scorpion, or *the* scorpion?"

She frowned at the effort of recollection.

"I thought he said *a*. But he mighta said *the*," she admitted.

Favaro finished his soup, thanked her, and went back to the hotel. The bar was rowdy. He found a place near the far end, away from the press crowd. The end stool was occupied by the Englishman from the airstrip, who raised his glass in salute but said nothing.

"Thank God for that," thought Favaro. The crumpled limey seemed at least to have the gift of silence.

Eddie Favaro needed to think. He knew how his friend and

partner had died, and he thought he knew why. In some mysterious manner, here in these paradise islands, Julio Gomez had seen—or thought he had seen—the coldest killer either of them had ever met.

Chapter 3

Desmond Hannah began work the following morning just after seven, while the cool of dawn still lay on the land. His starting place was Government House.

He had a long interview with the butler, Jefferson, who related to him the Governor's unswerving habit of retiring to his walled garden about five each afternoon, to take a whiskey and soda before the sun went down. He asked how many people would have known of this ritual. Jefferson frowned in concentration.

"Many people, sir. Lady Moberley, Lieutenant Haverstock, myself, Miss Myrtle the secretary—but she away with her parents on Tortola. Visitors to the house who had seen him there. Many people."

Jefferson described exactly where he had found the body, but he averred that he had not heard the shot. Later, this use of the word *shot* would convince Hannah that the butler was telling the truth. But he did not yet know how many shots there had been.

The forensic team from Nassau was working with Parker on the grass, looking for spent cartridges ejected from the killer's gun. They searched deep, for careless feet might have

trodden the small brass case or cases into the earth. The feet
of Lieutenant Haverstock, Inspector Jones, and his uncle Dr.
Jones had walked all over the grass on the night of the killing,
erasing all chances of useful footprints.

Hannah examined the steel gate in the garden wall as the
Bahamian fingerprint man dusted the steel for possible prints.
There were none. Hannah estimated that if the killer had
entered by the gate, as seemed to be the case, and fired
immediately, the Governor would have been standing between
the gate and the coral wall below the steps that led to his
reception area above. If any bullet had passed through him, it
should have hit that wall.

Hannah switched the attention of the team crawling about
the lawn to the path of crushed conch shells that ran along the
base of the wall. Then he went back to the house to talk to
Lady Moberley.

The Governor's widow awaited him in the drawing room
where Sir Marston had received the protest delegation from
the Committee for Concerned Citizens. She was a thin, pale
woman with mousy hair and skin that had been yellowed by
years in the tropics.

Jefferson appeared with a chilled lager beer on a tray.
Hannah hesitated, then took it. It was, after all, a very hot
morning.

Lady Moberley took a grapefruit juice. She looked at the
beer with raw hunger. Oh dear, thought Hannah.

There was nothing really that she could contribute. So far
as she knew, her husband had no enemies. Political crime was
unheard of in the islands. Yes, the election campaigns had
caused some small controversy, but all within the ambit of
the democratic process. She thought.

She herself had been five miles away at the time of the
shooting, visiting a small mission hospital on the slopes of
Spyglass Hill. It had been endowed by Mr. Marcus Johnson,
a very fine man and a great philanthropist, after his return to
his native Barclays six months ago. She had agreed to become
patroness of the facility. She had been in the official Jaguar,
being driven by the Governor's chauffeur, Stone.

Hannah thanked her and rose. Parker was outside tapping
at the window. Hannah went out to the terrace. Parker was in
a state of great excitement.

"You were right, sir! Here it is."

He held out his right hand. In the palm, badly distorted, was the flattened remnant of what had once been a lead bullet. Hannah stared at him bleakly.

"Thanks for handling it," he said. "Next time, shall we try tweezers and a plastic bag?"

Parker went pale, then scuttled down to the garden, put the bullet back on the conch-shell gravel, opened his murder bag, and took out a pair of tweezers. Several of the Bahamians grinned.

Parker laboriously lifted the crushed bullet with the tweezers and dropped it into a small clear bag.

"Now, wrap the bag in cotton wool and place it inside a glass jar with a screw top," said Hannah.

Parker did as he was told.

"Thank you. Now put it in the murder bag until we can send it to Ballistics," said Hannah. He sighed. This was going to be a hard slog. He was beginning to think he would have done better alone.

Dr. Caractacus Jones arrived, as requested. Hannah was glad to be able to talk to a fellow professional. Dr. Jones explained how he had been summoned from his home and surgery just after six the evening before last by Jefferson, who had been sent by Lieutenant Haverstock. Jefferson had told him he should come at once, as the Governor had been shot. The butler had not mentioned that the shooting was fatal, so Dr. Jones had brought his bag and driven over to see what he could do. As it turned out, the answer was, nothing.

Hannah led Dr. Jones into the late Sir Marston's office and asked him, in his capacity as the island's coroner, to sign a release for the body to be removed that afternoon to Nassau for a post-mortem.

In British jurisdiction, the court with the highest of all authorities is actually not the House of Lords but a coroner's court. It takes precedence over every other kind of court. To remove the body from the island of Sunshine to the territory of the Bahamas, a coroner's order was required. Dr. Jones signed without demur, and then it was legal. Bannister, the junior staffer from the Nassau High Commission who had accompanied them to Barclay's, typed the release on Govern-

ment House notepaper. He had just installed the new communications system and was prepared to transmit.

Hannah then asked Dr. Jones to show him the body. Down
at the dockside, the ice house was opened, and two of Inspector Jones's police constables slid the cadaver of their former
Governor, now like a frozen log, out from between the fish
and carried him to the shade of the nearby warehouse, where
they laid him on a door supported by two trestles.

For the press—now joined by a team from CNN out of
Atlanta who had tailed Hannah all morning—this was wonderful stuff. They photographed it all. Even the Governor's bed
companion of the previous thirty-six hours, the marlin, got a
spot on CNN's Headline News.

Hannah ordered the warehouse doors closed to keep them
out, and he made as thorough an examination of the rigid
body beneath the layer of ice as he could. Dr. Jones stood by
his side.

After peering at the frozen hole in the Governor's chest,
Hannah noticed a neat, circular tear in the sleeve of the left
arm. Slowly he kneaded the fabric between his finger and
thumb until his own hand's warmth made the material more
pliable. The frost melted. There were two such holes in the
shirt sleeve, one in and one out. But the skin was not marked.
He turned to Parker.

"Two bullets, minimum," he said quietly. "We are missing
a second bullet."

"Probably still in the body," said Dr. Jones.

"No doubt," said Hannah. "But damned if I can see any
sign of entry or exit holes. The flesh is too puckered up by
the cold. Still, Parker, I want the area behind where the
Governor was standing or sitting gone over again. And again.
Just in case it's there."

He ordered the dead Governor replaced in the ice house.
The cameras whirred again. The questions rained in. He
nodded and smiled and said, "All in good time, ladies and
gentlemen. It's the early days yet."

"But we've recovered a bullet," Parker said proudly. The
cameras all swiveled toward him.

Hannah began to think the assassin had shot the wrong
man. This was turning into a press conference. He did not

want one yet. "There'll be a full statement this evening," he said. "For the moment, it's back to work. Thank you."

He hustled Parker into the police Land-Rover, and they went back to Government House. Hannah asked Bannister to call Nassau over the new system and ask for a plane with stretcher, trolley, body bag, and two attendants by midafternoon. Then he accompanied Dr. Jones to his car. They were alone.

"Tell me, doctor, is there anyone on this island who really knows everything that goes on and everyone who lives here?"

Dr. Caractacus Jones grinned. "There's me," he said. "But no, I couldn't hazard a guess as to who did this. Anyway, I only returned from Barbados ten years ago. For the real history of these islands, you should visit Missy Coltrane. She's like . . . the grandmother of the Barclays. If you want someone to guess who done this, she might."

The doctor drove off in his battered Austin Mayflower. Hannah walked over to the doctor's nephew, Chief Inspector Jones, who stood beside the Land-Rover still.

"I'd like you to do something, Chief Inspector," Hannah said politely. "Would you go to the airstrip and check with the passport officer? Has anyone left the island since the killing? Anyone at all? Except the pilots of aircraft who arrived, turned around, and flew away without leaving the airstrip."

Inspector Jones threw up a salute and left.

The Governor's Jaguar was in the forecourt, and Oscar Stone, the chauffeur, was polishing it. Parker and the rest of the team were behind the house looking for the missing bullet.

"Oscar?" Hannah asked. "Do you know Missy Coltrane?"

"Oh yes, sah. She fine lady."

"Do you know where she lives?"

"Yessah. Flamingo House, top of Spyglass Hill."

Hannah checked his watch. It was half-past eleven, and the heat lay heavy. "Will she be in at this hour?" Oscar looked puzzled. "Of course, sah."

"Take me to see her, will you?"

The Jaguar wound its way out of town, then began to climb the lower slopes of Spyglass Hill, six miles west of Port Plaisance. It was an old Mark IX model, a classic by now, made the old-fashioned way, redolent of aromatic leather and burnished walnut. Hannah sat back and watched the landscape drift by.

The lowland scrub gave way to the greener vegetation of the upland slopes, and they passed small plots of maize, mangoes, and papayas. Wooden shacks stood back from the road, fronted by dusty yards where chickens scratched. Small brown children heard the car coming and scampered to the roadside to wave frantically. Hannah waved back.

They passed the neat white children's hospital that had been endowed by Marcus Johnson. Hannah glanced back and saw Port Plaisance sleeping in the heat. He could make out the red-roofed warehouse on the docks and the ice house next to it where the frozen Governor slept, the gritty sprawl of Parliament Square, the spire of the Anglican church, and the shingles of the Quarter Deck Hotel. Beyond, on the other side of town, shimmering in the haze, was the walled enclosure of Government House. Why on earth, he wondered, would anyone want to shoot the Governor?

They passed a neat bungalow that had once belonged to the late Mr. Barney Klinger, rounded two further curves, and emerged on the top of the hill. There stood a pink villa, Flamingo House.

Hannah pulled the wrought-iron bell chain by the door, and somewhere there was a low tinkle. A teenage girl answered the door, bare black legs emerging from a simple cotton frock.

"I'd like to see Missy Coltrane," said Hannah.

She nodded and admitted him, showing him into a large and airy sitting room. Open double doors led to a balcony with spectacular views over the island and the glittering blue sea that stretched away to Andros in the Bahamas, far off below the horizon.

The room was cool despite having no air conditioning. Hannah noticed it had no electricity at all. Three burnished brass oil lamps stood on low tables. Cooling breezes wafted from the open balcony doors through to the open windows on the other side. The array of memorabilia indicated it was the home of an elderly person. Hannah sauntered around the room as he waited.

There were pictures on the wall, scores of them, and all of birds of the Caribbean, skillfully painted in delicate watercolors. The only portrait that was not of a bird was of a man in the full white uniform of a British Colonial Governor. He stood staring out at the room, gray-haired and gray-moustached, with a tanned, lined, and kindly face. Two rows of miniature medals covered the left breast of his tunic. Hannah peered to see the small label beneath the oil painting. It said, SIR ROBERT COLTRANE, K.B.E., GOVERNOR OF THE BARCLAY ISLANDS, 1945–1953. He held his white helmet, adorned with white cockerel feathers, in the crook of his right arm; his left hand rested on the pommel of his sword.

Hannah smiled ruefully. "Missy" Coltrane must in fact be Lady Coltrane, the former Governor's widow. He moved farther round the wall to a display cabinet. Behind the glass, pinned to the hessian board, were the former Governor's military trophies, collected and displayed by his widow. There was the deep purple ribbon of the Victoria Cross, Britain's highest award for gallantry in the field, and the date of its award, 1917. It was flanked by the Distinguished Service Cross and the Military Cross. Other items the warrior had carried on his campaigns were pinned to the board around the medals.

"He was a very brave man," said a clear voice behind him.

Hannah spun around, embarrassed.

She had entered silently, the rubber tires of her wheelchair making no sound on the tiles. She was small and frail, with a cap of shining white curls and bright blue eyes.

Behind her stood the manservant who had pushed her in from the garden, a giant of awe-inspiring size. She turned to him.

"Thank you, Firestone. I'll be all right now."

He nodded and withdrew. She propelled herself a few feet farther into the room and gestured for Hannah to be seated. She smiled.

"The name? He was a foundling, discovered on a rubbish dump, in a Firestone tire. Now, you must be Detective Chief Superintendent Hannah from Scotland Yard. That's a very high rank for these poor islands. What can I do for you?"

"I must apologize for calling you Missy Coltrane to your housemaid," he said. "No one told me you were Lady Coltrane."

"No more," she said. "Here I am just Missy. They all call

me that. I prefer it that way. Old habits die hard. As you may
detect, I was not born British, but in South Carolina."

"Your late husband"—Hannah nodded toward the portrait—"was Governor here once."

"Yes. We met in the war. Robert had been through the First
War. He didn't have to come back for a second dose, but he
did. He got wounded again. I was a nurse. We fell in love,
married in 1943, and had ten glorious years until he died.
There were twenty-five years between our ages, but it didn't
matter a damn. After the war, the British Government made
him Governor here. After he died, I stayed on. He was only
fifty-six when he died. Delayed war wounds."

Hannah calculated. Sir Robert would have been born in
1897, got his Victoria Cross at twenty. She would be sixty-
eight, too young for a wheelchair. She seemed to read his
mind with those bright blue eyes.

"I slipped and fell," she said. "Ten years ago. Broke my
back. But you didn't come four thousand miles to discuss an
old woman in a wheelchair. How can I help you?"

Hannah explained.

"The fact is, I cannot perceive a motive. Whoever shot Sir
Marston must have hated him enough to do it. But among
these islanders, I cannot perceive a motive. You know these
people. Who would want to do it, and why?"

Lady Coltrane wheeled herself to the open window and
stared out for a while.

"Mr. Hannah, you are right. I do know these people. I have
lived here for forty-five years. I love these islands, and I love
their people. I hope I may think that they love me."

She turned around and gazed at him. "In the world scheme
of things, these islands matter for nothing. Yet these people
seem to have discovered something that has eluded the world
outside. They have found out how to be happy. Just that—not
rich, not powerful, but happy.

"Now London wants us to have independence. And two
candidates have appeared to compete for the power: Mr.
Johnson, who is very wealthy and has given large sums to the
islands, for whatever motive; and Mr. Livingstone, a socialist,
who wants to nationalize everything and divide it up among
the poor. Very noble, of course. Mr. Johnson, with his plans
for development and prosperity, and Mr. Livingstone, with

his plans for equality—I know them both. Knew them when they were boys. Knew them when they left in their teens to pursue careers elsewhere. And now they are back.''

"You suspect either of them?" asked Hannah.

"Mr. Hannah, it is the men they have brought with them. Look at the men who surround them. These are violent men, Mr. Hannah. The islanders know it. There have been threats, beatings. Perhaps you should look at the entourages of these two men, Mr. Hannah.''

On the drive back down the mountain, Desmond Hannah thought it over. A contract hit? The killing of Sir Marston had all the earmarks of one. After lunch he thought he would have a talk with the two candidates and take a look at their entourages.

As Hannah returned to the sitting room at Government House, a plump Englishman with several chins above his clerical collar jumped up from a chair. Parker was with him.

"Ah, Chief, this is the Reverend Simon Prince, the local Anglican vicar. He has some interesting information for us.''

Hannah wondered where Parker had got the word *Chief* from. He hated it. *Sir* would do nicely. *Desmond,* later— much later. Maybe.

"Any luck with that second bullet?"

"Er, no—not yet.''

"Better get on with it," said Hannah. Parker disappeared through the French windows. Hannah closed them.

"Well now, Mr. Prince. What would you like to tell me?"

"It's Quince," said the vicar. "Quince. This is all very distressing.''

"It is indeed. Especially for the Governor.''

"Oh, ah, yes. I meant really—well . . . my coming to you with information about a fellow of the cloth. I don't know whether I should, but I felt it might be germane.''

"Why don't you let me be the judge of that?" suggested Hannah mildly.

The reverend calmed down and sat.

"It all happened last Friday," he said. He told the story of the delegation from the Committee for Concerned Citizens and their rebuff by the Governor. When he had finished, Hannah frowned.

"What exactly did Reverend Drake say?" he asked.

"He said," repeated Quince, " 'We have to get rid of that Governor and get ourselves a new one.' "

Hannah rose. "Thank you very much, Mr. Quince. May I suggest you say no more about this, but leave it with me?"

After the grateful vicar scuttled out, Hannah thought it over. He did not particularly like stool pigeons, but he would now have to check out the fire-breathing Baptist, Walter Drake, as well.

At that point Jefferson appeared with a tray of cold lobster tails in mayonnaise. Hannah sighed. There were some compensations to being sent four thousand miles from home. And if the Foreign Office was paying . . . He poured himself a glass of chilled Chablis and started.

During Hannah's lunch, Chief Inspector Jones came back from the airport. "No one has left the island," he told Hannah, "not in the last forty hours."

"Not legally, at any rate," said Hannah. "Now, another chore, Mr. Jones. Do you keep a firearms register?"

"Of course."

"Fine. Would you check it through for me and visit everyone who has a listed firearm on the islands? We are looking for a large-caliber handgun. Particularly a handgun that cannot be produced, or one that has been recently cleaned and gleams with fresh oil."

"Fresh oil?"

"After being fired," said Hannah.

"Ah, yes, of course."

"One last thing, Chief Inspector. Does Reverend Drake have a registered firearm?"

"No. Of that I am certain."

When he had gone Hannah asked to see Lieutenant Haverstock. "Do you by any chance own a service revolver or automatic?" he asked.

"Oh, I say, look here. You don't really think . . ." expostulated the young subaltern.

"It occurred to me it might have been stolen, or misappropriated and replaced."

"Ah, yes. See your point, old boy. Actually, no. No gun.

Never brought one to the island. Got a ceremonial sword, though.''

"If Sir Marston had been stabbed, I might think of arresting you,'' Hannah said mildly. "Any guns in Government House at all?''

"No, not to my knowledge. Anyway, the killer came from outside, surely? Through the garden wall?''

Hannah had examined the wrenched-off lock on the steel gate in the garden wall at first light. From the angles of the two broken hasps and the torn-apart bar of the great padlock, there was a little question that someone had used a long and very strong crowbar to force the old steel to snap like that. But it also occurred to Hannah that the snapping of the lock might have been a ruse. It could have been done hours or even a couple of days earlier. No one had ever tested the gate; it was deemed to be rusted solid.

The killer could have torn off the lock and left the gate in the closed position in advance, then come through the house to kill the Governor and retreat back into the house afterward. What Hannah needed was that second bullet, hopefully intact, and the gun that had fired it. He looked out at the glittering blue sea. If it was down there, he'd never find it.

He rose, wiped his lips, and went out to find Oscar and the Jaguar. It was time he had a word with Reverend Drake.

Sam McCready also sat at lunch. When he entered the open-sided verandah dining room of the Quarter Deck, every table was full. Out on the square, men in bright beach shirts and wraparound dark glasses were positioning a flatbed truck decorated with bunting and daubed with posters from Marcus Johnson. The great man was due to speak at three.

Sam looked around the terrace and saw a single vacant chair. It was at a table that was occupied by one other luncher.

"We're a bit crowded today. Mind if I join you?'' he asked.

Eddie Favaro waved at the chair. "No problem.''

"You here for the fishing?'' asked McCready as he studied the brief menu.

"Yep.''

"Odd,'' said McCready after ordering Seviche, a dish of raw fish marinated in fresh lime juice. "If I didn't know better, I'd have said you were a cop.''

He did not mention the long-shot inquiry he had made the previous evening after studying Favaro at the bar—the call to a friend in the Miami office of the FBI—or the answer he had received that morning.

Favaro put down his beer and stared at him. "Who the hell are you?" he asked. "A British bobby?"

McCready waved his hand deprecatingly. "Oh no, nothing so glamorous. Just a civil servant trying to get a peaceful holiday away from the desk."

"So what's this about my being a cop?"

"Instinct. You carry yourself like a cop. Would you mind telling me why you're really here?"

"Why the hell should I?"

"Because," McCready suggested mildly, "you arrived just before the Governor was shot. And because of this."

He handed Favaro a sheet of paper. It was on Foreign Office–headed notepaper. It announced that Mr. Frank Dillon was an official of that office and begged "to whom it may concern" to be as helpful as possible.

Favaro handed it back and thought things over. Lieutenant Broderick had made it plain that he was on his own once he entered British territory.

"Officially, I'm on vacation," Favaro began. "No, I don't fish. Unofficially, I'm trying to find out why my partner was killed last week, and by whom."

"Tell me about it," suggested McCready. "I might be able to help."

Favaro told him how Julio Gomez had died. The Englishman chewed his raw fish and listened.

"I think he may have seen a man on Sunshine, and been seen himself. A man we used to know in Metro-Dade as Francisco Mendes, alias the Scorpion."

Eight years earlier, the drug-turf wars had started in South Florida, notably in the Metro-Dade area. Prior to that, the Colombians had shipped cocaine into the area, but the Cuban gangs had distributed it. Then the Colombians had decided they could cut out the Cuban middlemen and sell direct to the users. They began to move in on the Cubans' territory. The Cubans responded, and the turf wars broke out. The killings had continued ever since.

In the summer of 1984, a motorcyclist in red and white

leather, astride a Kawasaki, had drawn up outside a liquor store in the heart of the Dadeland Mall, produced an Uzi submachine carbine from a totebag, and calmly emptied the entire magazine into the busy store. Three people had died, fourteen were injured.

Normally, the killer would have gotten away, but a young motorcycle cop was giving a parking ticket two hundred yards away. When the killer threw down his empty Uzi and sped off, the policeman gave chase, broadcasting the description and direction as he went. Halfway down North Kendall Drive, the man on the Kawasaki slowed, pulled over, drew a nine-millimeter Sig Sauer automatic from his blouse front, took aim, and shot the oncoming policeman in the chest. As the young cop crashed over, the killer rode off at top speed, according to witnesses who gave a good description of the bike and the leather clothing. His helmet hid his face.

Although the Baptist Hospital was only four blocks away and the policeman was rushed into intensive care, he died before morning. He was twenty-three, and he left a widow and baby daughter.

His radio calls had alerted two prowl cars, which were closing on the area. A mile down the road, one of them saw the speeding motorcyclist and forced him into a turn so tight that he fell off. Before he could rise, he was under arrest.

By aspect, the man looked Hispanic. The case was given to Gomez and Favaro. For four days and nights they sat opposite the killer trying to get a single word out of him. He said nothing, absolutely nothing, in either Spanish or English. There were no powder traces on his hands, for he had worn gloves. But the gloves were gone, and despite searching every trash can in the area, the police never discovered them. They reckoned the killer had thrown them into the rear of a passing convertible. Public appeals turned up the Sig Sauer, tossed into a neighboring garden. It was the gun that had killed the policeman, but it bore no fingerprints.

Gomez believed the killer was Colombian—the liquor store had been a Cuban cocaine drop. After four days, he and Favaro nicknamed the suspect the Scorpion.

On the fourth day, a very high-priced lawyer turned up. He produced a Mexican passport in the name of Francisco Mendes. It was new and valid, but it bore no U.S. entry stamps. The lawyer conceded that his client might be an illegal immigrant and asked for bail. The police opposed it.

In front of the judge, a noted liberal, the lawyer protested that the police had only apprehended *a* man in red and white leather riding *a* Kawasaki, not *the* man on *the* Kawasaki who had killed the policeman and the others.

"That asshole of a judge granted bail," Favaro said to McCready now. "Half a million dollars. Within twenty-four hours, the Scorpion was gone. The bondsman handed over the half million with a grin. Chickenfeed."

"And you believe . . . ?" asked McCready.

"He wasn't just a mule. He was one of their top triggermen, or they'd never have gone to such trouble and expense to get him out. I think Julio saw him here, even found where he was living maybe. He left his fishing vacation early to try to get back so Uncle Sam would file an appeal for extradition from the British."

"Which we would have granted," said McCready. "I think we ought to inform the man from Scotland Yard. After all, the Governor was shot four days later. Even if the two cases turn out not to be linked, there's enough suspicion to comb the island for him. It's a small place."

"And if he's found? What offense has he committed on British territory?" Favaro asked.

"Well," said McCready, "for a start you could make a positive identification of him. That could constitute a holding charge. Detective Chief Superintendent Hannah may be from a different force, but no one likes a cop-killer. And if he produces a valid passport, as a Foreign Office official I could denounce it as a forgery. That makes a second holding charge."

Favaro grinned and held out his hand. "Frank Dillon, I like it. Let's go see your man from Scotland Yard."

Hannah stepped out of the Jaguar and walked toward the open doors of the plank-built Baptist chapel. From inside came the sound of song. He stepped through the doors and accustomed his eyes to the lower light inside. Leading the singing was the deep bass voice of Reverend Drake.

Rock of ages, cleft for me . . .

There was no musical accompaniment, just plainsong. The Baptist minister had left his pulpit and was striding up and down the aisle, his arms waving like the big black sails of a windmill as he encouraged his flock to give praise.

> *Let me hide myself in thee.*
> *Let the water and the blood . . .*

He caught sight of Hannah in the doorway, ceased singing, and waved his arms for quiet. The tremulous voices died away.

"Brothers and sisters!" roared the minister. "We are indeed privileged today. We are joined by Mr. Hannah, the man from Scotland Yard!"

The congregation turned in their pews and stared at the man in the door. Most were elderly men and women, with a scattering of young matrons and a gaggle of small children with huge saucer eyes.

"Join us, brother! Sing with us! Make room for Mr. Hannah."

Next to him, a vast matron in a flowered-print frock gave Hannah a wide smile and moved up, offering him her hymn book. Hannah needed it. He had forgotten the words, it had been so long. Together, they finished the rousing anthem. When the service was over, the congregation filed out, each member greeted by the perspiring Drake at the door.

As the last person left, Drake beckoned Hannah to follow him into his vestry, a small room attached to the side of the church.

"I cannot offer you beer, Mr. Hannah. But I'd be happy for you to share in my cold lemonade."

He took it from a Thermos flask and poured two glasses. It was lime-scented and delicious.

"And what can I do for the man from Scotland Yard?" inquired the pastor.

"Tell me where you were at five P.M. on Tuesday."

"Holding carol service practice here, in front of fifty good people," said Reverend Drake. "Why?"

Hannah put to him his remark of the previous Friday morning on the steps of Government House. Drake smiled at

Hannah. The detective was not a small man, but the preacher topped him by two inches.

"Ah, you have been talking with Mr. Quince." He pronounced the name as if he had sucked on a raw lime.

"I didn't say that," said Hannah.

"You didn't have to. Yes, I said those words. You think I killed Governor Moberley? No, sir, I am a man of peace. I do not use guns. I do not take life."

"Then what did you mean, Mr. Drake?"

"I meant that I did not believe the Governor would transmit our petition to London. I meant that we should pool our poor funds and send one person to London to ask for a new Governor, one who would understand us and propose what we ask."

"Which is?"

"A referendum, Mr. Hannah. Something bad is happening here. Strangers have come among us, ambitious men who want to rule our affairs. We are happy the way we are. Not rich, but content. If we had a referendum, the great majority would vote to stay British. Is that so wrong?"

"Not in my book," admitted Hannah, "but I don't make policy."

"Neither did the Governor. But he would carry a policy out, for his career, even if he knew it was wrong."

"He had no choice," said Hannah. "He was carrying out his orders."

Drake nodded into his lemonade. "That's what the men who put the nails into Christ said, Mr. Hannah."

Hannah did not want to be drawn into politics or theology. He had a murder to solve. "You didn't like Sir Marston, did you?"

"No, God forgive me."

"Any reason, apart from his duties here?"

"He was a hypocrite and a fornicator. But I did not kill him. The Lord giveth, and the Lord taketh away, Mr. Hannah. The Lord sees everything. On Tuesday evening the Lord summoned Sir Marston Moberley."

"The Lord seldom uses a large-caliber handgun," suggested Hannah. For a moment he thought he saw a hint of appreciation in Drake's glance. "You said 'fornicator.' What did that mean?"

Reverend Drake glanced at him sharply. "You don't know?"

"No."

"Myrtle, the missing secretary. You have not seen her?"

"No."

"She is a big girl, robust, lusty."

"No doubt. She is away with her parents in Tortola," said Hannah.

"No," said Drake gently, "she is in Antigua General Hospital, terminating a baby."

Oh dear, thought Hannah. He had only ever heard her referred to by name. He had not seen a picture of her. White parents live on Tortola, too.

"Is she . . . how shall I put it . . . ?"

"Black?" boomed Drake. "Yes, of course she's black. A big, bouncing black girl. The way Sir Marston liked them."

And Lady Moberley knew, thought Hannah. Poor washed-out Lady Moberley, driven to drink by all those years in the tropics and by all those native girls. She was resigned, no doubt. Or perhaps she was not. Perhaps she had been driven a bit too far, just this once.

"There is a hint of American in your accent," said Hannah as he left. "Can you tell me why?"

"There are many Baptist theological schools in America," replied Reverend Drake. "I studied for the ministry there."

Hannah drove back to Government House. On the way, he considered a list of possible suspects.

Lieutenant Jeremy Haverstock undoubtedly knew how to use a gun if he could get hold of one, but he had no apparent motive. Unless it was he who was the father of Myrtle's baby, and the Governor had threatened to break his career.

Lady Moberley, driven too far. She had plenty of motive, but she'd have needed an accomplice to rip off that steel gatelock. Unless it could have been done with a chain behind a Land-Rover.

The Reverend Drake, despite his protestations of being a man of peace. Even men of peace can be driven too far.

He recalled the advice of Lady Coltrane to look at the entourages of the two electoral candidates. Yes, he would do that, have a good look at these election helpers. But what was the motive there? Sir Marston had been playing their game for them, easing the islands into independence, with one of them as the new Prime Minister. Unless one of the groups had thought he was favoring the other.

When he got back to Government House, there was a spate of news waiting for him.

Chief Inspector Jones had checked his firearms register. There were only six workable guns on the island. Three were owned by expatriates—retired gentlemen, two British and one Canadian. They were twelve-bore shotguns, used for clay-pigeon shooting. The fourth was a rifle, owned by the fishing skipper Jimmy Dobbs, for use on sharks if ever a monster attacked his boat. The fifth gun was a presentation pistol, never fired, owned by another expatriate, an American who had settled on Sunshine. The gun was still in its glass-topped case, its seal unbroken. And the sixth gun was Jones's own, kept under lock and key at the police station.

"Damn," snorted Hannah. Whatever gun had been used, it was not kept legally.

Detective Parker, for his part, had a report on the garden. It had been searched from end to end and top to bottom. No second bullet. Either it had deflected off a bone in the Governor's body, come out at a different angle, and sped over the garden wall to be lost forever; or, more likely, it was still in the body.

Bannister had received news from Nassau. A plane would be landing at four, in one hour's time, to take the body to the Bahamas for post-mortem. Dr. West was due to touch down in a few minutes, and he would be waiting to take his charge to the mortuary at Nassau.

And there were two men waiting to see Hannah in the drawing room.

Hannah gave orders to have a van made ready to bring the body to the airstrip at four. Bannister, who would return to the High Commission there along with the body, left with Inspector Jones to supervise the arrangements. Then Hannah went to meet his new guests.

The man called Frank Dillon introduced himself and explained his chance vacation on the island and his equally chance meeting over lunch with the American. He produced his letter of introduction, and Hannah studied it with little pleasure. Bannister from the official High Commission in Nassau was one thing; a London-based official who happened to be taking an away-from-it-all holiday in the middle of a murder hunt was as likely as a vegetarian tiger. Then he met the American, who admitted that he was another detective.

Hannah's attitude changed, however, as Dillon narrated Favaro's story.

"You have a picture of this man Mendes?" he asked finally.

"No, not with me."

"Could one be obtained from police files in Miami?"

"Yes, sir. I could have it wired to your people in Nassau."

"You do that," said Hannah. He glanced at his watch. "I'll have a search of all passport records made, going back three months. See if there's a name of Mendes or any other Hispanic name entering the island. Now, you must excuse me—I have to see the body onto the plane for Nassau."

"Are you by any chance thinking of talking to the candidates?" asked McCready as they left.

"Yes," said Hannah, "first thing in the morning. While I'm waiting for the post-mortem report to come through."

"Would you mind if I came along?" asked McCready. "I promise not to say a thing. But after all, they are both . . . political, are they not?"

"All right," said Hannah reluctantly. He wondered whom this Frank Dillon really worked for.

On the way to the airstrip, Hannah noticed that the first of his posters were being affixed to spaces on walls where room could be found for them between the posters on behalf of the two candidates. There was so much paper being stuck over Port Plaisance, the place was getting plastered in it.

The official posters, prepared by the local printer under the auspices of Inspector Jones and paid for with Government House money, offered a reward of one thousand U.S. dollars to anyone reporting seeing someone in the alley behind the wall of the Government House garden at approximately five P.M. on Tuesday evening.

A thousand American dollars was a stunning sum for the ordinary people of Port Plaisance. It should bring someone out—someone who had seen something, or some person. And in Sunshine everybody knew everybody.

At the airstrip Hannah saw to the loading of the body, accompanied by Bannister and the four men of the Bahamian forensic team. Bannister would see that the entire volume of their scrapings and samples went on the evening flight to London, to be collected at dawn by a squad car from Scotland Yard and taken to the Home Office's forensic laboratory in Lambeth. He had few hopes it would turn up much; it was the second bullet he wanted, and Dr. West would retrieve that for him when he opened the body in Nassau that night.

Because he was at the airstrip, Hannah missed the Johnson rally in Parliament Square that afternoon. So did the press corps, who having covered the start of the rally, saw the police convoy driving past and followed it out to the airstrip.

McCready did not miss the rally. He was on the verandah of the Quarter Deck Hotel at the time.

A desultory crowd of about two hundred had gathered to hear their philanthropic benefactor address them. McCready noticed half a dozen men in brightly colored beach shirts and dark glasses mingling with the crowd, handing out small pieces of paper and flags on sticks. The flags were in the candidate's blue and white colors. The pieces of paper were dollar bills.

At precisely ten past three, a white Ford Fairlane—certainly the biggest car on the island—swept into the square and up to the speaking platform. Mr. Marcus Johnson leaped out and ascended the steps. He held up his hands in a boxer's victory salute. Led by the bright-shirted ones, there was a round of applause. Some flags waved. In minutes, Marcus Johnson was into his speech.

"And I promise you, my friends, and you are *all* my friends"—the dentifrice smile flashed from the bronze face—"when we are finally free, a wave of prosperity will come to these islands. There will be work—in the hotels, in the new marina, in the bars and cafés, in the new industries for the processing of fish from the sea for sale on the mainland—from all these things, prosperity will flow. And it will flow into *your* pockets, my friends, not into the hands of men far away in London—"

He was using a bullhorn to reach everyone in the square. The interruption came from a man who did not need a bullhorn. The deep bass came from the other side of the square, but it came over the sound of the politician.

"Johnson!" roared Walter Drake. "We do not want you here! Why don't you go back where you came from, and take your Yardies with you?"

Suddenly there was silence. The stunned crowd waited for the sky to fall. No one had ever interrupted Marcus Johnson before.

But the sky did not fall. Without a word, Johnson put down his megaphone and jumped into his car. At a word from him, it sped off, pursued by a second car containing his group of helpers.

"Who is that?" McCready asked the waiter on the verandah.

"Reverend Drake, sir," said the waiter. He seemed awestruck, even rather frightened.

McCready was thoughtful. He had heard a voice used like that somewhere before, and he tried to recall where. Then he placed it; during his National Service thirty years earlier, at Catterick Camp in Yorkshire. On a parade ground. He went to his room and made a secure call to Miami.

Reverend Walter Drake took his beating in silence. There were four of them, and they came for him that night as he left his church and walked home. They used baseball bats and their feet. They hit hard, whipping the wooden staves down onto the man on the ground. When they were finished, they left him. He might have been dead. They would not have minded. But he was not.

Half an hour later, he recovered consciousness and crawled to the nearest house. The frightened family called Dr. Caractacus Jones, who had the preacher brought to his clinic on a handcart, and he spent the rest of the night patching him up.

Desmond Hannah had a call that evening during supper. He had to leave the hotel to go to Government House to take it. It was from Dr. West in Nassau.

"Look, I know they're supposed to be preserved," said the forensic pathologist, "but this one's like a block of wood. Frozen solid."

"The locals did the best they could," said Hannah.

"So will I," said the doctor. "But it's going to take me twenty-four hours to thaw the bugger out."

"As fast as you can, please," said Hannah. "I need that damned bullet."

Chapter 4

Detective Chief Superintendent Hannah elected to interview Mr. Horatio Livingstone first. He rang him at his house in Shantytown just after sunrise, and the politician came to the phone after several minutes. Yes, he would be delighted to receive the man from Scotland Yard within the hour.

Oscar drove the Jaguar with Detective Parker beside him. Hannah was in the back with Dillon of the Foreign Office. Their route did not pass through the center of Port Plaisance, for Shantytown lay three miles down the coast, on the same side of the capital as Government House.

"Any progress with your inquiries, Mr. Hannah, or is that an unprofessional question?" Dillon asked politely.

Hannah never liked to discuss the state of an inquiry with anyone other than colleagues. Still, this Dillon was apparently from the Foreign Office.

"The Governor was killed by a single shot through the heart from a heavy-caliber handgun," he said. "There seem to have been two shots fired. One missed and hit the wall behind him. I recovered the slug and sent it to London."

"Badly distorted?" asked Dillon.

"I'm afraid so. The other bullet seems to be lodged in the

body. I'll know more when I get the results of the post-mortem from Nassau tonight.''

''And the killer?''

''Seems to have entered from the gate in the garden wall, which was torn off its locks. Fired from about a ten-foot range, then withdrew. Apparently.''

''Apparently?''

Hannah explained his idea that the torn-off lock might have been a ruse to distract attention from an assassin coming from the house itself.

Dillon was most admiring. ''I'd never have thought of that,'' he said.

The car entered Shantytown. As its name implied, it was a village of clustered homes made of wooden planks and galvanized sheet roofing, with some five thousand inhabitants.

Small shops selling an array of vegetables and T-shirts jostled for space with the houses and the bars. It was clearly Livingstone territory—no posters for Marcus Johnson were to be seen here, but those for Livingstone were everywhere.

In the center of Shantytown, reached by its widest (and only) street, stood a single walled compound. The walls were of coral blocks, and a single gate wide enough for a car admitted entry. Beyond the walls could be seen the roof of the house, the only two-story edifice in Shantytown. Hannah knew of the rumor that Mr. Livingstone owned many of the bars in the village and took tribute from those he did not.

The Jaguar halted at the gate, and Stone sounded the horn. All down the street, Barclayans were standing to stare at the gleaming limousine with the pennant fluttering from the front right wing. The Governor's car had never been into Shantytown before.

A small window in the gate opened, an eye surveyed the car, and the gate swung open. The Jaguar rolled forward into a dusty yard and stopped by the verandah to the house. Two men were in the yard, one by the gate and one waiting at the verandah. Both wore identical pale-gray safari suits. A third man in similar dress stood at an upstairs window. As the car halted, he withdrew.

Hannah, Parker, and Dillon were shown into the principal sitting room, cheaply but functionally furnished, and a few seconds later Horatio Livingstone appeared. He was a large fat man, and his jowly face was wreathed in smiles. He exuded bonhomie.

"Gentlemen, gentlemen, what an honor. Please, be seated."

He gestured for coffee and seated himself in a large chair. His small, button eyes flickered from one to the other of the three white faces before him. Two other men entered the room and seated themselves behind the candidate. Livingstone gestured to them.

"Two of my associates—Mr. Smith and Mr. Brown."

The two inclined their heads but said nothing.

"Now, Mr. Hannah, what can I do for you?"

"You will know, sir, that I am here to investigate the murder four days ago of Governor Sir Marston Moberley."

Livingstone's smile dropped, and he shook his head. "A dreadful thing," he rumbled. "We were all deeply shocked. A fine, fine man."

"I'm afraid I have to ask you what you were doing and where you were at five P.M. on Tuesday evening."

"I was here, Mr. Hannah, here among my friends, who will vouch for me. I was working on a speech to the Smallholders Association for the next day."

"And your associates, they were here? *All* here?"

"Every one of them. It was close to sundown. We had all retired for the day. Here, inside the compound."

"Your associates—are they Barclayans?" asked Dillon.

Hannah shot him a glance of irritation; the man had promised to say nothing.

Livingstone beamed. "Ah, no, I fear not. I and my fellow Barclayans have so little experience of organizing an election campaign, I felt I needed some administrative help." He gestured and beamed again, a reasonable man among reasonable men. "The preparing of speeches, posters, pamphlets, public meetings. My associates are from the Bahamas. You wish to see their passports? They were all examined when they arrived."

Hannah waved the necessity away. Behind Mr. Livingstone, Mr. Brown had lit a large cigar.

"Would you have any idea, Mr. Livingstone, who might have killed the Governor?" asked Hannah.

The fat man's smile dropped again, and he adopted a mien

of great seriousness. "Mr. Hannah, the Governor was helping us all on the road to our independence, to our final freedom from the British Empire. According to the policy of London. There was not the slightest motive for me or any of my associates to wish to harm him."

Behind him, Mr. Brown held his cigar to one side, and with the much-elongated nail of his little finger, he flicked an inch of ash from the tip so that the ash fell to the floor. The burning ember never touched the flesh of his finger.

McCready knew he had seen that gesture somewhere before. "Will you be holding any public meetings today?" he asked quietly.

Livingstone's small black eyes switched toward him. "Yes, at twelve I am addressing my brothers and sisters of the fishing community on the docks," he said.

"Yesterday there was a disturbance when Mr. Johnson addressed people in Parliament Square," said Dillon.

Livingstone showed no pleasure in the ruining of his rival's meeting. "A single heckler," he snapped.

"Heckling is also part of the democratic process," observed Dillon.

Livingstone stared at him, expressionless for once. Behind the creased jowls, he was angry. McCready realized he had seen that expression before; on the face of Idi Amin of Uganda, when he had been contradicted.

Hannah glowered at Dillon and rose. "I won't take up any more of your time, Mr. Livingstone," he said.

The politician, exuding jollity again, escorted them to the door. Two more gray safari suits saw them off the premises. Different men. That made seven of them, including the one at the upstairs window. All were pure Negroid except Mr. Brown, who was much paler, a quadroon, the only one who dared smoke without asking, the man in charge of the other six.

"I would be grateful," said Hannah in the car, "if you would leave the questioning to me."

"Sorry," said Dillon. "Strange man, didn't you think? I wonder where he spent the years between leaving here as a teenager and returning six months ago."

"No idea," said Hannah. It was only later, in London, when he was thinking things over, that he would wonder at

Dillon's remark about Livingstone leaving Sunshine as a teenager. It was Missy Coltrane who had told him, Desmond Hannah, that. Dillon had not been there.

At half-past nine, they arrived at the gates of Marcus Johnson's estate on the northern flank of Sawbones Hill.

Johnson's style was completely different from Livingstone's. He was clearly a wealthy man. An assistant in psychedelic beach shirt and black glasses opened the wrought-iron gates to the drive and let the Jaguar proceed up the raked gravel to the front door. Two gardeners were at work, tending the lawns, flower beds, and earthenware jars of bright geraniums.

The house was a spacious, two-story building with a roof of green glazed tiles, every block and stick of it imported. The three Englishmen alighted in front of a pillared Colonial portico and were led inside. They followed their guide, a second brightly shirted "assistant," across a reception area floored in marble slabs and furnished with European and Spanish-American antiques. Rugs from Bokhara and Kashan splashed the cream marble.

Marcus Johnson received them on a marble verandah scattered with white rattan chairs. Below the verandah lay the garden and tonsured lawns running to an eight-foot wall. Beyond the wall lay the coast road, which was one thing Johnson could not buy to give himself direct access to the sea. On the waters of Teach Bay, beyond the wall, was the stone jetty he had built. Next to it bobbed a Riva 40 speedboat. With long-range tanks, the Riva could reach the Bahamas at speed.

Where Horatio Livingstone was fat and creased, Marcus Johnson was slim and elegant. He wore an impeccable cream silk suit. The cast of his features indicated he was at least half white, and McCready wondered if he had known his father. Probably not. He had come from poverty in the Barclays as a boy, been brought up by his mother in a shack. His dark brown hair had been artifically straightened, from curly to wavy. Four heavy gold rings adorned his hands, and the teeth in the flashing smile were perfect.

He offered his guests a choice of Dom Perignon or Blue Mountain coffee. They chose coffee and sat down.

Desmond Hannah asked the same questions about the hour

of five P.M. the previous Tuesday evening. The reply was the same.

"Addressing an enthusiastic crowd of well over a hundred people outside the Anglican church in Parliament Square, Mr. Hannah. At five o'clock I was just finishing my address. From there I drove straight back here."

"And your . . . entourage?" asked Hannah, borrowing Missy Coltrane's word to describe the election campaign team in their bright shirts.

"All with me, to a man," said Johnson. He waved a hand, and one of the bright-shirts topped up the coffee. McCready wondered why he had no local serving staff inside the house, although he would have Barclayan gardeners. Despite the subdued light inside the verandah, the bright-shirts never removed their wraparound dark glasses.

From Hannah's point of view, the interlude was pleasant but fruitless. He had already been told by Chief Inspector Jones that the prosperity candidate had been on Parliament Square when the shots were fired at Government House. The Inspector himself had been on the steps of his own police station on the square, surveying the scene. He rose to leave.

"Do you have another public address scheduled for today?" asked Dillon.

"Yes, indeed. At two, on Parliament Square."

"You were there yesterday at three. There was a disturbance, I believe."

Marcus Johnson was a much smoother operator than Livingstone. No hint of temper. He shrugged.

"The Reverend Drake shouted some rude words. No matter. I had finished my speech. Poor Drake—well intentioned, no doubt, but foolish. He wishes the Barclays to remain in the last century. But progress must come, Mr. Dillon, and with it prosperity. I have the most substantial development plans in mind for our dear Barclays."

McCready nodded. Tourism, he thought, gambling, industry, pollution, a little prostitution—and what else?

"And now, if you will forgive me, I have a speech to prepare."

They were shown out, and they drove back to Government House.

"Thank you for your hospitality," said Dillon as he climbed

out. "Meeting the candidates was most instructive. I wonder where Johnson made all that money in the years he was away."

"No idea," said Hannah. "He's listed as a businessman. Do you want Oscar to run you back to the Quarter Deck?"

"No, thank you. I'll stroll."

In the bar the press corps was working its way through the beer supply. It was eleven o'clock. They were getting bored. Two full days had elapsed since they had been summoned to Heathrow to scramble to the Caribbean and cover a murder inquiry. All the previous day, Thursday, they had filmed what they could and interviewed whom they could. Pickings had been slim: a nice shot of the Governor coming out of the ice house from his bed between the fish; some long shots of Parker on his hands and knees in the Governor's garden; the dead Governor departing in a bag for Nassau; Parker's little gem about finding a single bullet. But nothing like a good, hard piece of news.

McCready mingled with them for the first time. No one asked who he was.

"Horatio Livingstone is speaking on the dock at twelve," he said. "Could be interesting."

They were suddenly alert. "Why?" asked someone.

McCready shrugged. "There was some savage heckling here on the square yesterday," he said. "You were at the airstrip."

They brightened up. A nice little riot would be the thing—failing that, some good heckling. The reporters began to run some imaginary headlines through their minds. "Election Violence Sweeps Sunshine Isle"—a couple of punches would justify that. Or if Livingstone got a hostile reception, "Paradise Vetoes Socialism."

The trouble was that so far, the population seemed to have no interest at all in the prospect of freedom from the Empire. Two news teams that had tried to put together a documentary on local reaction to independence had not been able to secure a single interviewee who would talk. People just walked away when the cameras, microphones, and notepads came out. Still, they picked up their gear and sauntered toward the docks.

McCready took time to make a single call to the British Consulate in Miami from the portable phone he kept in the attaché case under his bed. He asked for a seven-seater charter plane to land on Sunshine at four P.M. It was a long shot, but he hoped it would work.

Livingstone's cavalcade arrived from Shantytown at a quarter to twelve. One aide boomed through a megaphone, "Come and hear Horatio Livingstone, the people's candidate." Others erected two trestles and a stout plank to lift the people's candidate above the people.

At noon, Horatio Livingstone hoisted his bulk up the steps to the makeshift platform. He spoke into a megaphone on a stem in front of him, held up by one of the safari suits. Four TV cameras had secured elevated positions around the meeting, from which they could cover the candidate or, hopefully, the hecklers and the fighting.

The BSB cameraman had borrowed the cabin roof of the *Gulf Lady*. To back up his TV camera, he had a Nikon camera with a telephoto lens slung across his back. The reporter, Sabrina Tennant, stood beside him.

McCready climbed up to join them. "Hello," he said.

"Hi," said Sabrina Tennant. She took no notice of him.

"Tell me," he asked quietly. "Would you like a story that would blow your colleagues out of the water?"

Now she took notice. The cameraman looked across inquisitively.

"Can you use that Nikon to get in close, really close, on any face in that crowd?" asked McCready.

"Sure," said the cameraman. "I can get their tonsils if they open wide."

"Why not get full-face pictures of all the men in gray safari suits helping the candidate?" suggested McCready. The cameraman looked at Sabrina. She nodded. Why not?

The cameraman unhooked his Nikon and began to focus it. "Start with the pale-faced black standing along by the van," said McCready. "The one they call Mr. Brown."

"What have you got in mind?" asked Sabrina.

"Step into the cabin, and I'll tell you."

She did, and McCready talked for several minutes.

"You're joking," she said at length.

"No, I'm not, and I think I can prove it. But not here. The answers lie in Miami."

He talked to her again for a while. When he had finished, Sabrina Tennant went back to the roof. "Got them?" she asked.

The Londoner nodded. "A dozen close shots of every one, every angle. There are seven of them."

"Right, now let's shoot the entire meeting. Get me some footage for background and cutting."

She knew she already had eight magazines of footage, including shots of both candidates, the capital town, the beaches, the palm trees, and the airstrip—enough, skillfully cut, to make a great fifteen-minute story. What she needed now was a lead angle, and if the crumpled man with the apologetic air was right, she had it.

Her only problem was time. Her main feature spot was on *Countdown,* the flagship program of the BSB current affairs channel, which went out at noon on Sunday in England. She would need to send her material by satellite from Miami by no later than four P.M. on Saturday, the next day. So she had to be in Miami that night. It was nearly one o'clock now, extremely tight to get back to the hotel and book a Miami-based charter to be in Sunshine before sundown.

"Actually, I'm due to leave myself at four this afternoon," said McCready. "I've ordered my own plane from Miami. Happy to offer you a lift."

"Who the hell are you?" she asked.

"Just a holidaymaker. But I do know the islands. And their people. Trust me."

She had no bloody choice, thought Sabrina. If his story was true, this one was too good to miss. She went back to her cameraman to show him what she wanted. The telephoto lens of the camera lazed over the crowd, pausing there, there, and there. Against the van, Mr. Brown saw the lens pointing at him and climbed inside. The camera caught that too.

Inspector Jones reported to Desmond Hannah during the lunch hour. Every visitor to the islands for the past three months had been checked through passport records taken at the airstrip. No one answered either to the name of Francisco

Mendes or to the description of a Latin American. Hannah sighed.

If the dead American Gomez had not been mistaken—and he might well have been—the elusive Mendes could have slipped into the Barclays in a dozen ways. The weekly tramp steamer brought occasional passengers from "down island," and official coverage of the docks was sporadic. Yachts occasionally stopped by, mooring in bays and creeks around Sunshine and the other islands, their guests and crews disporting themselves in the crystal waters above the coral reefs until they hoisted sail and passed on. Anyone could slip ashore—or leave. Hannah suspected this Mendes, once he had been spotted and knew it, had flown the coop. If he had ever even been there.

Hannah rang Nassau, but Dr. West told him he could not start the autopsy until four that afternoon, when the body of the Governor would have finally returned to normal consistency.

"Call me as soon as you have that bullet," Hannah urged.

At two, an even more disgruntled press corps assembled in Parliament Square. From the point of view of sensations, the morning rally had been a flop. The speech had been the usual nationalize-everything rubbish that the British had discarded a decade earlier. The voters-to-be had been apathetic. As a world story, it was all cutting-room-floor material. If Hannah did not make an arrest soon, they thought, they might as well pack up and go home.

At ten past two, Marcus Johnson arrived in his long white convertible. He wore an ice-blue tropical suit and an open-neck Sea Island shirt as he mounted the back of the flatbed truck that served as his platform. More sophisticated than Livingstone, he had a microphone with two amplifiers strung from nearby palm trees.

As Johnson began speaking, McCready sidled up to Sean Whittaker, the free-lance stringer who covered the whole Caribbean from his Kingston, Jamaica, base for London's *Sunday Express*.

"Boring?" murmured McCready.

Whittaker gave him a glance. "Tripe," he agreed. "I think I'm going home tomorrow."

Whittaker reported stories and took his own pictures as well. A long-lens Yashica hung around his neck.

"Would you," asked McCready, "like a story that would blow your rivals out of the water?"

Whittaker turned and cocked an eyebrow. "What do you know that nobody else does?"

"Since the speech is a bore, why not come with me and find out?"

The two men proceeded across the square, into the hotel, and up to McCready's second-floor room. From the balcony, they could see the whole square below them.

"The minders, the men in multicolored beach shirts and dark glasses," said McCready. "Can you get full-face close-ups of them from here?"

"Sure," said Whittaker. "Why?"

"Do it, and I'll tell you."

Whittaker shrugged. He was an old hand; he had had tips in his time from the most unlikely sources. Some worked out, some did not. He adjusted his zoom lens and ran off two rolls of color prints and two of black-and-white.

McCready took him down to the bar, stood him a beer, and talked for thirty minutes.

Whittaker whistled. "Is this on the level?" he asked.

"Yes."

"Can you prove it?" Running this sort of story was going to need some hard-sourced quotes, or Robin Esser, the editor in London, would not use it.

"Not here," said McCready. "The proof lies in Kingston. You could get back tonight, finalize it tomorrow morning, and file by four P.M. Nine o'clock in London—just in time."

Whittaker shook his head. "Too late. The last Miami-Kingston flight is at seven-thirty. I'd need to be in Miami by six o'clock. Via Nassau, I'd never make it."

"As a matter of fact, I have my own plane leaving for Miami at four—in seventy minutes' time. I'd be happy to offer you a lift."

Whittaker rose to go and pack his suitcase. "Who the hell *are* you Mr. Dillon?" he asked.

"Oh, just someone who knows these islands, and this part of the world. Almost as well as you."

"Better," growled Whittaker, and left.

*   *   *

At four o'clock, Sabrina Tennant arrived at the airstrip with her cameraman. McCready and Whittaker were already there. The air taxi from Miami drifted down at ten past the hour.

When it was about to take off, McCready explained, "I'm afraid I can't make it. A last-minute phone call at the hotel. Such a pity, but the air taxi is paid for, and I can't get a rebate. It's too late. So please be my guests. Good-bye, and good luck."

Whittaker and Sabrina Tennant eyed each other suspiciously throughout the flight. Neither of them mentioned to the other what they had or where they were going. At Miami the television team headed into town; Whittaker transferred to the last flight to Kingston.

McCready returned to the Quarter Deck, extracted his portable phone, programmed it to a secure mode, and made a series of calls. One was to the British High Commission in Kingston, where he spoke to a colleague who promised to use his contacts to secure the appropriate interviews. Another was to the headquarters of the U.S. Drug Enforcement Administration, the DEA, in Miami, where he had a contact of long standing since the international drug trade has links with international terrorism. His third call was to the head of the CIA office in Miami. By the time he had finished, he had reason to hope his new-found friends of the press would be accorded every facility.

Just before six, the orange globe of the sun dropped toward the Dry Tortugas in the west, and darkness, as always in the tropics, came with remarkable speed. True dusk lasted only fifteen minutes. At six, Dr. West called from Nassau. Desmond Hannah took the call in the Governor's private office, where Bannister had set up the secure link to the High Commission across the water.

"You've got the bullet?" Hannah asked eagerly. Without forensic backup, his inquiry was running dry. He had several possible suspects but no eyewitnesses, no clearly guilty party, no confession.

"No bullet," said the distant voice from Nassau.

"What?"

"It went clean through him," said the forensic pathologist. He had finished his work at the mortuary half an hour earlier and had gone straight to the High Commission to make the call. "Do you want the medical jargon or the basics?"

"The basics will do," said Hannah. "What happened?"

"There was a single bullet. It entered between the second and third ribs, left-hand side, traveled through muscle and tissue, perforated the upper left ventricle of the heart, causing immediate death. It exited through the ribs at the back. I'm surprised you didn't see the exit hole."

"I didn't see either bloody hole," growled Hannah. "The flesh was so frozen, it had closed over both of them."

"Well," said Dr. West down the line, "the good news is, it touched no bone on the way through. A fluke, but that's the way it was. If you can find it, the slug should be intact—no distortion at all."

"No deflection off bone?"

"None."

"But that's impossible," protested Hannah. "The man had a wall behind him. We've searched the wall inch by inch. There's not a mark on it, except for the clearly visible dent made by the other bullet, the one that went through the sleeve. We've searched the gravel path beneath the wall. We've taken it up and sifted it. There is one bullet only, the second bullet, badly smashed up by the impact."

"Well, it came out all right," said the doctor. "The bullet that killed him, I mean. Someone must have stolen it."

"Could it have been slowed up to the point that it fell to the lawn between the Governor and the wall?" asked Hannah.

"How far behind the man was the wall situated?"

"No more than fifteen feet," said Hannah.

"Then, not in my view," said the pathologist. "I'm not into ballistics, but I believe the gun was a heavy-caliber handgun, fired at a range of more than five feet from the chest. There are no powder burns on the shirt, you see. But it was probably not more than twenty feet. The wound is neat and clean, and the slug would have been traveling fast. It would have been slowed by its passage through the body, but nowhere near enough to drop to the ground within fifteen feet. It must have hit the wall."

"But it didn't," Hannah protested. Unless, of course, someone had stolen it. If so, that someone had to be within the household. "Anything else?"

"Not a lot. The man was facing his assailant when he was shot. He didn't turn away."

Either he was a very brave man, thought Hannah, or more likely, he just couldn't believe his eyes.

"One last thing," said the doctor. "The bullet was traveling in an upward trajectory. The assassin must have been crouching or kneeling. If the ranges are right, the gun was fired about thirty inches off the ground."

Damn, thought Hannah. It must have gone clean over the wall. Or possibly it hit the house, but much higher up, near the guttering. In the morning Parker would have to start all over again, with ladders.

Hannah thanked the doctor and put the phone down. The full written report would reach him by the scheduled flight the next day.

Parker had now lost his four-man forensic team from the Bahamian Police, so he had to work alone the next day. Jefferson, the butler, aided by the gardener, held the ladder while the hapless Parker went up the house wall above the garden looking for the imprint of the second bullet. He went as high as the gutters, but he found nothing.

Hannah took his breakfast, served by Jefferson, in the sitting room. Lady Moberley drifted in now and again, arranged the flowers, smiled vaguely, and drifted back out again. She seemed blithely unconcerned whether her late husband's body, or what was left of it, was brought to Sunshine for burial or taken back to England. Hannah gained the impression that no one had cared much for Sir Marston Moberley, starting with his wife. Then he realized why she seemed so blithe. The vodka bottle was missing from the silver drinks tray. Lady Moberley was happy for the first time in years.

Desmond Hannah was not. He was puzzled. The more the hunt for the bullet went on in vain, the more it seemed his instinct had been right. It was an inside job, the torn-off lock on the steel gate a ruse. Someone had descended the steps from the sitting room where he now sat and had circled the sitting Governor, who had then seen the gun and risen to his feet. After the shots, the assailant had found one of his bullets in the gravel by the wall and taken it. He had failed to find the other in the dusk and had run off to hide the gun before any interruption came.

Hannah finished his breakfast, went outside, and glanced at Parker up near the gutter.

"Any luck?" he asked.

"Not a sign," Parker called down.

Hannah walked back to the wall and stood with his back to the steel gate. The previous evening he had stood on a trestle and stared over the gate at the alley behind it. Between five and six, the alley was constantly busy. People taking a short cut from Port Plaisance to Shantytown used it; smallholders returning from the town to their scattered homes behind the trees used it. Nearly thirty people had passed up and down it within the hour. At no time was the alley completely empty. At one time there had been seven people walking down it, one way or the other. The killer simply could not have come in that way without being spotted. Why should Tuesday evening have been so different from any other? Someone must have seen something.

Yet no one had come forward in response to the posters. What islander would forgo a thousand American dollars? It was a fortune. So . . . the killer had come from inside the house, as he had surmised.

The grilled front door to Government House had been closed that evening at that hour. It was self-locking from the inside. Jefferson would have answered if anyone rang the bell. No one could just walk through the gates, across the gravel forecourt, through the front door, across the hall, through the sitting room, and down the steps to the garden. It was no casual intruder; the front door would have blocked them. The ground-floor windows were grilled, Spanish style. There was no other way in—unless an athlete had vaulted the garden wall and dropped to the grass. . . . Possible.

But how to get out again? Through the house? Then there was a very good chance of being seen. Back over the wall? It had been minutely searched for scrape marks, as of someone climbing, and there were glass shards along the top. Out through the steel gate, previously opened? Another good chance of being seen.

No—it looked like an inside job. Oscar, the chauffeur, had vouched for Lady Moberley, who had been away at the children's hospital. That left harmless, bumbling old Jefferson, or young Haverstock of the Queen's Dragoon Guards.

Was this another white society scandal like the Kenyan affair before the war, or the killing of Sir Harry Oakes? Was it a one-killer affair, or were they all in on it? What was their motive—hate, lust, greed, revenge, political terror, or the threat of a ruined career? And what about the dead Julio Gomez? Had he really seen a South American contract killer on Sunshine? If so, where on earth did Mendes fit in?

Hannah stood with his back to the steel door, walked forward two paces, and dropped to his knees. He was still too high. He went on his stomach and propped his torso on his elbows, his eyes thirty inches above the grass. He stared at the point where Sir Marston would have been standing, having risen from his chair and taken one step forward. Then he was up and running.

"Parker!" he yelled. "Get off that ladder and come down here!"

Parker almost fell off, so loud was the shout. He had never seen the phlegmatic Hannah so disturbed. When he reached the terrace, he scampered down the steps to the garden.

"Stand there," said Hannah, pointing to a spot on the grass. "How tall are you?"

"Five foot ten, sir."

"Not tall enough. Go to the library and get me some books. The Governor was six foot two. Jefferson, get me a broom."

Jefferson shrugged. If the white policeman wanted to sweep the patio, that was his business. He went for a broom.

Hannah made Parker stand on four books on the spot where Sir Marston had stood. Crouching on the grass he aimed the broom handle like a rifle at Parker's chest. The broom sloped upward at twenty degrees.

"Step to one side."

Parker did so and fell off his books. Hannah stood up and walked to the steps that ran up the wall to the terrace, rising from left to right. It was still hanging on its wrought-iron bracket, as it had for three days and before that. The wire basket, packed with loam, cascaded brilliant geraniums. So thick were the clusters, one could hardly see the basket from which they came. As the forensic team worked on the wall, they had brushed the streaming flowers out of their faces.

"Bring that basket down," Hannah said to the gardener. "Parker, bring the murder bag. Jefferson get a bedsheet."

The gardener moaned as his work was strewn all over the bedsheet. One by one, Hannah extricated the flowers, tapping the loam clear of their roots before placing them on one side. When only the loam was left, he separated it into hand-size clods, using a spatula to break the clods into grains. And there it was.

Not only had the bullet passed through the Governor intact, it had not even touched the wire frame of the basket. It had gone between two strands of wire and stopped dead in the middle of the loam. It was in perfect condition. Hannah used tweezers to drop it into a plastic bag, wrapped the bag, and dropped it into a screw-top jar. He rocked back on his ankles and rose.

"Tonight, lad," he told Parker, "you are going back to London. With this. Alan Mitchell will work through Sunday for me. I've got the bullet. Soon I'll have the gun. Then I'll have the killer."

There was nothing more he could do at Government House. He asked that Oscar be summoned to drive him back to the hotel. As he waited for the chauffeur, he stood at the windows of the sitting room looking out over the garden wall toward Port Plaisance, the nodding palms and the shimmering sea beyond. The island slumbered in the heat of midmorning. Slumbered—or brooded?

This isn't paradise, he thought. It's a bloody powder keg.

Chapter 5

In the city of Kingston that morning, Sean Whittaker was having a remarkable reception. He had arrived late and gone straight to his apartment. Just after seven the next morning, the first call had come in. It was an American voice.

"Morning, Mr. Whittaker. Hope I didn't wake you."

"No, not at all. Who's that?"

"My name is Milton. Just Milton. I believe you have some photographs you might care to show me."

"That would depend on who I am showing them to," said Whittaker.

There was a low laugh down the line. "Why don't we meet?"

Milton arranged a rendezvous in a public place, and they met an hour later. The American did not look like the head of the DEA field station in Kingston, as Whittaker had expected. His casual air was more that of a young academic from the university.

"Forgive my saying so," said Whittaker, "but could you establish any bona fides at all?"

"Let's use my car," said Milton.

They drove to the American Embassy. Milton had a headquarters office outside the embassy, but he was persona grata inside it as well. He flashed his identity card to the Marine guard at the desk inside, then led the way to a spare office.

"All right," said Whittaker, "you're an American diplomat."

Milton did not correct him. He smiled and asked to see Whittaker's pictures. He surveyed them all, but one held his attention.

"Well, well," he said. "So that's where he is."

He opened his attaché case and produced a series of files, selecting one. The photograph on the first page of the dossier had been taken a few years earlier, with a long lens, apparently through an aperture in a curtain. But the man was the same as the man in the new photograph on his desk.

"Want to know who he is?" he asked Whittaker. It was an unnecessary question. The British reporter compared the two photographs and nodded.

"Okay, let's start at the beginning," said Milton, and he read out the contents of the file—not all of them, just enough. Whittaker took notes furiously.

The DEA man was thorough. There were details of a business career, meetings held, bank accounts opened, operations run, aliases used, cargoes delivered, profits laundered. When he had finished, Whittaker sat back.

"Phew," he said. "Can I source this on you?"

"I wouldn't specify Mr. Milton," said the American. "Highly placed sources within the DEA—that would do."

He escorted Whittaker back to the main entrance. On the steps he suggested, "Why don't you go down to Kingston police headquarters with the rest of the pictures? You may find you are expected."

At the police building, the bemused Whittaker was shown up to the office of Commissioner Foster, who sat along in his big air-conditioned room overlooking downtown Kingston. After greeting Whittaker, the Commissioner pressed his intercom and asked Commander Gray to step in. The head of the Criminal Investigation Division joined them a few minutes later. He brought a sheaf of files.

The two Jamaicans studied Whittaker's pictures of the eight bodyguards in bright beach shirts. Despite the wraparound dark glasses, Commander Gray did not hesitate. Opening a series of files, he identified the men one after the other. Whittaker noted everything.

"May I cite you two gentlemen as the source?" he asked.

"Certainly," said the Commissioner. "All have long criminal records. Three are wanted here as of now. You may quote me. We have nothing to hide. This meeting is on the record."

By midday, Whittaker had his story. He transmitted his pictures and text down the usual London link, took a long phone call from the news editor in London, and was assured of a good spread the following day. His expenses would not be queried—not for this one.

In Miami, Sabrina Tennant had checked into the Sonesta Beach Hotel, as she had been advised the previous evening, and took a call just before eight on Saturday morning. The appointment was set for an office building in central Miami. It was not the headquarters of the CIA in Miami, but it was a safe building.

She was shown to an office and met a man who led her to a TV screening room, where three of her videotapes were screened in front of two other men who sat in half darkness. They declined to introduce themselves and said nothing.

After the screening, she was led back to the first office, served coffee, and left alone for a while. When the first officer rejoined her, he suggested she call him Bill, and he asked her for the still photographs that had been taken at the dockside political rally of the previous day.

On the videos, the cameraman had not concentrated on the bodyguards of Horatio Livingstone, so they appeared only as peripheral figures. But in the stills they were in full-face shot. Bill opened a series of files and showed her other pictures of the same men.

"This one," he said, "the one by the van. What was he calling himself?"

"Mr. Brown," she said.

Bill laughed. "Do you know the Spanish word for 'brown?' " he asked.

"No."

"It's *moreno*—in this case, Hernan Moreno."

"Television is a visual medium," she said. "Pictures tell a

better story than words. Can I have these photos of yours for comparison with my own?"

"I'll have copies made for you," said Bill, "and we'll keep copies of yours."

Her cameraman had had to remain outside in the taxi. Covertly, he took a few pictures of the office building. It did not matter. He thought he was photographing CIA headquarters. He was not.

When they got back to the Sonesta Beach, Sabrina Tennant spread the photos—hers and those unusually provided from secret CIA files—on a large table in the borrowed banquet room, while the cameraman shot moving film of them all. She did a stand-up piece against a backdrop of the banquet room wall and a picture of President Bush, borrowed from the manager. It would suffice to give the impression of an inner CIA sanctum.

Later that morning, the pair found a deserted cove down a lane off U.S. Highway One and she did another piece, this time backed by white sand, waving palms, and a blue sea, a facsimile for a beach on Sunshine.

At midday she set up her satellite link with London and beamed all her material to the BSB in London. She had a long talk with her news editor as the cutting-room staff began to put the feature together. When they had finished it was a fifteen-minute news story that looked as if Sabrina Tennant had gone to the Caribbean with only one idea in mind—the exposé.

The editor rejigged the running order of the Sunday lunchtime edition of *Countdown* and called her back in Florida.

"It's a bloody cracker," he said. "Well done, love."

McCready had been busy, too. He spent part of the morning on his portable telephone to London and part talking to Washington.

In London he found the Director of the Special Air Service Regiment staying at the Duke of York's Barracks in King's Road, Chelsea. The leathery young general listened to McCready's request.

"As a matter of fact, I do," he said. "I've got two of them lecturing at Fort Bragg at the moment. I'll have to get clearance."

"No time," said McCready. "Look are they owed leave?"

"I suppose they are," said the Director.

"Fine. Then I'm offering them both three days of rest and recreation here in the sun. As my personal guests. What could be fairer than that?"

"Sam," said the Director, "you are a devious old bugger. I'll see what I can do. But they're on leave, Okay? Just sunbathing, nothing else."

"Perish the thought," said McCready.

With just seven days to go to Christmas, the citizens of Port Plaisance were preparing for the festive season that Saturday afternoon.

Despite the heat, many shop windows were being decorated with depictions of robins, holly, Yule logs, and polystyrene snow. Very few of the islanders had even seen a robin or a holly bush, let alone snow, but the British Victorian tradition had long suggested that Jesus had been born surrounded by them all, so they duly formed part of the Christmas decorations.

Outside the Anglican church, Mr. Quince, aided by a swarm of eager little girls, was decorating a tableau beneath a straw roof. A small plastic doll lay in the manger, and the children were placing figurines of oxen, sheep, donkeys, and shepherds.

On the outskirts of town, Reverend Drake was conducting choir practice for his carol service. His deep bass voice was not up to scratch. Beneath his black shirt, his torso was swathed in Dr. Jones's bandages to ease his sprung ribs, and his voice wheezed as if he were out of breath. His parishioners eyed each other meaningfully. Everyone knew what had happened to him on Thursday evening. Nothing remained a secret in Port Plaisance for long.

At three o'clock, a battered van drove into Parliament Square and stopped. From the driver's seat emerged the enormous figure of Firestone. He went around to the rear, opened the door, and lifted Missy Coltrane out, invalid chair and all. Slowly, he wheeled her down Main Street to do her shopping. There were no press about. Most of them, bored, had gone swimming off Conch Point.

Her progress was slow, being marked by innumerable greet-

ings. She responded to each, hailing shopkeepers and passersby with their names, never forgetting one.

"G'day, Missy Coltrane," "Good day, Jasper," "Good
day, Simon," "Good day, Emmanuel"—she asked after
wives and children, congratulated a beaming father-to-be on
his good fortune, sympathized with a case of a broken arm.
She made her usual purchases, and the shopkeepers brought
their wares to the door for her to examine.

She paid from a small purse she kept in her lap, while from
a larger handbag she dispensed a seemingly inexhaustible
supply of small candies to the crowd of children who offered
to carry her shopping bags in the hopes of a second ration.

She bought fresh fruit and vegetables; kerosene for her
lamps, matches, herbs, spices, meat, and oil. Her progress
brought her through the shopping area to the quay, where she
greeted the fishermen and bought two snapper and a wriggling
lobster that had been preordered by the Quarter Deck Hotel.
If Missy Coltrane wanted it, she got it. No argument. The
Quarter Deck would get the prawns and the conch.

As she returned to Parliament Square, she met Detective
Chief Supertindent Hannah descending from the hotel steps.
He was accompanied by Detective Parker and an American
called Favaro. They were off to the airstrip to meet the four
o'clock plane from Nassau.

She greeted them all, although she had never seen two of
them. Then Firestone lifted her up, placed her and her chair
beside the groceries in the rear of the van, and drove off.

"Who's that?" asked Favaro.

"An old lady who lives on a hill," said Hannah.

"Oh, I've heard of her," said Parker. "She's supposed to
know everything about this place."

Hannah frowned. Since his investigation had run out of
steam, the thought had occurred to him more than once that
Missy Coltrane might know more than she had let on about
who had fired those shots on Tuesday evening. Still, her
suggestion about the entourages of the two candidates had
been shrewd. He had seen them both, and his policeman's
instinct had told him he thought very little of them. If only
they had a motive.

The short-haul island-hopper from Nassau landed just after
four. The pilot had a package from the Metro-Dade Police

Department for a Mr. Favaro. The Miami detective identified himself and took the package. Parker, his sample bottle containing the vital bullet in his jacket pocket, boarded.

"There'll be a car for you at Heathrow tomorrow morning," said Hannah. "Straight to Lambeth. I want that bullet in the hands of Alan Mitchell as fast as possible."

On the ground, after the plane took off, Favaro showed the photos of Francisco Mendes, alias the Scorpion, to Hannah. The British detective studied them. There were ten in all, showing a lean, saturnine man with slicked-back black hair and a thin, expressionless mouth. The eyes, looking into the camera, were blank.

"Nasty-looking bastard," agreed Hannah. "Let's get them up to Chief Inspector Jones."

The head of the Barclayan Police was in his office on Parliament Square. The sound of carols came from the open doors of the Anglican church, and laughter came from the open bar of the Quarter Deck. The press was back.

Jones shook his head. "No, never seen him, man. Not in these islands."

"I don't think Julio would mistake his man," said Favaro. "We sat opposite him for four days."

Hannah was inclined to agree. Maybe he had been looking in the wrong place, inside Government House. Perhaps the killing *had* been a contract job. But why. . . ?

"Would you circulate these, Mr. Jones? Show them around. He was supposed to have been seen in the bar of the Quarter Deck last Thursday week. Maybe somebody else saw him. The barman, any other customers that night. Anyone who saw where he went when he left, anyone who saw him in any other bar—you know the score."

Inspector Jones nodded. He knew his patch. He would show the picture around.

At sundown, Hannah checked his watch. Parker would have arrived at Nassau an hour ago. He would be boarding the overnight plane to London about now. Eight hours' flying, add five hours for time zones, and he would touch down just after seven A.M. London time.

Alan Mitchell, the brilliant civilian scientist who headed the Home Office ballistics lab at Lambeth, had agreed to give up his Sunday to work on the bullet. He would subject it to every known test and phone Hannah by Sunday afternoon with his findings. Then Hannah would know exactly what weapon he was looking for. That would narrow the odds. Someone must have seen the weapon that was used. This was such a *small* community.

Hannah was interrupted over his supper by a call from Nassau.

"I'm afraid the plane's an hour delayed on takeoff," said Parker. "We're off in ten minutes. Thought you might like to alert London."

Hannah checked his watch. Half-past seven. He swore, put the phone down, and went back to his grilled grouper. It was cold.

He was taking his nightcap in the bar at ten when the bar phone rang.

"I'm awfully sorry about this," said Parker.

"Where the hell are you?" roared Hannah.

"In Nassau, Chief. You see, we took off at half-past seven, flew for forty-five minutes over the sea, developed a slight engine fault, and turned back. The engineers are working on it now. Shouldn't be long."

"Give me a call just before you take off," said Hannah. "I'll tell London of the new arrival time."

He was awakened at three in the morning.

"The engineers have fixed the fault," said Parker. "It was a warning light solenoid cut-out on the port outer engine."

"Parker," said Hannah slowly and carefully, "I don't care if it was the Chief Purser pissing in the fuel tank. Is it fixed?"

"Yes, sir."

"So you're taking off?"

"Well, not exactly. You see, by the time we make London, the crew will have exceeded their permitted hours without a rest. So they can't fly."

"Well, what about the slip crew? The ones who brought that plane in yesterday afternoon, twelve hours ago. They must have rested."

"Yes, well, they've been found, Chief. Only they thought they had a thirty-six-hour stopover. The First Officer went to a friend's stag night. He can't fly, either."

Hannah made a remark about the world's favorite airline to

which the chairman, Lord King, would have taken considerable exception, had he heard it.

"So what happens now?" he asked.

"We have to wait until the crew has rested. Then we fly," said the voice from Nassau.

Hannah rose and went out. There were no taxis, no Oscar. He walked all the way to Government House, raised Jefferson, and was let in. In the humid night he was soaked in sweat. He put through a long-distance call to Scotland Yard and got Mitchell's private number. He called that number to warn the scientists, but the man had left his home for Lambeth five minutes earlier. It was four A.M. in Sunshine, nine A.M. in London. He waited an hour until he could reach Mitchell at the laboratory to tell him Parker would not be there until early evening. Alan Mitchell was not pleased when he heard it. He had to drive all the way back to West Malling in Kent through a bitter December day.

Parker called again at midday on Sunday. Hannah was killing time in the bar at the Quarter Deck.

"Yes?" he said wearily.

"It's okay, Chief. The crew is rested. They're able to fly."

"Great," said Hannah. He checked his watch.

Eight hours' flying, add five for time zones—if Alan Mitchell would agree to work through the night, Hannah could have his answer in Sunshine by breakfast hour on Monday.

"So you're taking off now?" he asked.

"Well, not exactly," said Parker. "You see, if we did, we'd land after one A.M. at Heathrow. That's not allowed. Noise abatement, I'm afraid."

"So what the hell are you going to do?"

"Well, the usual takeoff time is just after six this afternoon here, landing just after seven A.M. at Heathrow. So they're going to revert to that timing."

"But that'll mean two jumbos taking off together," said Hannah.

"Yes, it does, Chief. But don't worry. Both will be full, so the airline won't take a loss."

"Thank God for that!" snapped Hannah, and put the phone down. Twenty-four hours, he thought, twenty-four bleeding hours. There are three things in this life about which one can do nothing: death, taxes, and airlines.

Then he spotted Dillon walking up the steps to the hotel with two fit-looking young men. Probably his taste, thought Hannah savagely, bloody Foreign Office. He was not in a good mood.

Across the square, a flock of Mr. Quince's parishioners— the men in neat dark suits, the women brightly caparisoned like birds of brilliant plumage—were streaming out of the church at the end of morning service, prayer books in white-gloved hands, wax fruit bobbing and nodding on straw hats. It was an (almost) normal Sunday morning on Sunshine Island.

In the home counties of England, things were not quite so peaceful. At Chequers, the country residence of the Prime Ministers of Great Britain, set amid twelve hundred rolling acres of Buckinghamshire, Mrs. Thatcher had been up early as usual and had plowed through four red dispatch boxes of state papers before joining Denis Thatcher for breakfast before a cheery log fire.

As she finished, there was a tap on the door, and her press secretary, Bernard Ingham, entered. He held the *Sunday Express* in his hand.

"Something I thought you might like to see, Prime Minister."

"So who's having a go at me now?" inquired the PM brightly.

"No," said the beetle-browed Yorkshireman. "It's about the Caribbean."

She read the large centerfold spread, and her brow furrowed. The pictures were there: of Marcus Johnson on the hustings in Port Plaisance, and again, a few years earlier, seen through a gap in a pair of curtains. There were photos of his eight bodyguards, all taken around Parliament Square on Friday, and matching pictures taken from Kingston Police files. Lengthy statements from "senior DEA sources in the Caribbean" and from Commissioner Foster of the Kingston Police occupied much of the accompanying text.

"But this is dreadful!" said the Prime Minister. "I must speak to Douglas."

She went straight to her private office and rang Douglas.

Her Majesty's Principal Secretary of State for Foreign

Affairs, Mr. Douglas Hurd, was with his family at his official
country residence—another mansion, called Chevening, set
in the county of Kent. He had perused the *Sunday Times,
Observer,* and *Sunday Telegraph,* but he had not yet reached
the *Sunday Express.*

"No, Margaret, I haven't seen it yet," he said. "But I have
it within arm's reach."

"I'll hold on," said the PM.

The Foreign Secretary, a former novelist of some note,
knew a good newspaper story when he saw one. This one
seemed to be extremely well sourced.

"Yes, I agree. It's disgraceful, if it's true. . . . Yes, yes,
Margaret, I'll get onto it in the morning and have the Caribbean desk check it out."

But civil servants are human beings too—a sentiment not
often echoed by the general public—and they have wives,
children, and homes. With six days to go to Christmas,
Parliament was in recess and even the ministries were thinly
staffed. Still, there had to be someone on duty the next
morning, Monday, and the matter of a new Governor could
be addressed then.

Mrs. Thatcher and her family went to Sunday-morning
service at Ellesborough and returned just after twelve. At one
they sat down for lunch with a few friends. These included
Bernard Ingham.

It was her political adviser Charles Powell who caught the
BSB program *Countdown* at twelve o'clock. He liked *Countdown.* It carried some good foreign news now and again, and
as an ex-diplomat that was his specialty. When he saw the
program's headlines and a reference to a later report on a
scandal in the Caribbean, he pressed the "record" button on
the VCR machine beneath the TV.

At two, Mrs. Thatcher was up again—she never saw much
point in spending a long time over food; it wasted part of a
busy day—and as she left the dining room a hovering Charles
Powell intercepted her. In her study he put the tape into her
VCR and ran it. She watched in silence. Then she rang
Chevening again.

Mr. Hurd, a devoted family man, had taken his small son
and daughter for a brisk walk across the fields. He had just

returned, hungry for his roast beef, when Mrs. Thatcher's second call came through.

"No, I missed that too, Margaret," he said.

"I have a tape," said the Prime Minister. "It is quite appalling. I'll send it straight to you. Please screen it when it arrives and call me back."

A dispatch rider roared through the gloom of a dismal December afternoon, skirted London via the M25 motorway, and was at Chevening by half-past four.

The Foreign Secretary called Chequers at five-fifteen and was put straight through. "I agree, Margaret, quite appalling," said Douglas Hurd.

"I suggest we need a new Governor out there," said the PM, "not in the new year, but now. We must show we are active, Douglas. You know who else will have seen these stories?"

The Foreign Secretary was well aware that Her Majesty was with her family at Sandringham but not cut off from world events. She was an avid newspaper reader, and she watched current affairs issues on television.

"I'll get on to it immediately," he said.

He did. The Permanent Under-Secretary was jerked out of his armchair in Sussex and began phoning around. At eight that evening the choice had fallen on Sir Crispian Rattray, a retired diplomat and former High Commissioner in Barbados, who was willing to go.

He agreed to report to the Foreign Office in the morning for formal appointment and a thorough briefing. He would fly on the late-morning plane from Heathrow, landing at Nassau on Monday afternoon. He would consult further with the High Commission there, spend the night, and arrive on Sunshine by chartered airplane on Tuesday morning to take the reins in hand.

"It shouldn't take long, my dear," he told Lady Rattray as he packed. "Mucks up the pheasant shooting, but there we are. Seems I'll have to withdraw the candidacy of these two rascals and see the elections through with two new candidates. Then they'll grant independence, I'll hoist the old flag down, London will send in a High Commissioner, the islanders will run their own affairs, and I can come home. Month or two, shouldn't doubt. Pity about the pheasants."

*   *   *

At nine o'clock on Sunday morning on Sunshine, McCready found Hannah having breakfast on the terrace at the hotel.

"Would you mind awfully if I used the new phone at Government House to call London?" he asked. "I ought to talk to my people about going back home."

"Be my guest," said Hannah. He looked tired and unshaved, as someone who had been up half the night.

At half-past nine, island time, McCready put his call through to Denis Gaunt. What his deputy told him about the *Sunday Express* and the *Countdown* program confirmed to McCready that what he had hoped would happen had indeed happened.

Since the small hours of the morning, a variety of news editors in London had been trying to call their correspondents in Port Plaisance with news of what the *Sunday Express* was carrying in its centerfold page spread and to ask for an urgent followup story. After lunch, London time, the calls redoubled—they had seen the *Countdown* story as well. None of the calls had come through.

McCready had briefed the switchboard operator at the Quarter Deck that all the gentlemen of the press were extremely tired and were not to be disturbed under any circumstances. He had himself been elected to take all their calls for them, and he would pass them on. A hundred-dollar bill had sealed the compact. The switchboard operator duly told every London caller that his party was "out" but that the message would reach him immediately. The messages were duly passed to McCready, who duly ignored them. The moment for further press coverage had not yet come.

At eleven A.M. he was at the airport to greet two young SAS sergeants flying in from Miami. They had been lecturing for the benefit of their colleagues in the American Green Berets at Fort Bragg, North Carolina, when alerted to take three days' furlough and report to their host on the island of Sunshine. They had flown south to Miami and chartered an air taxi to Port Plaisance.

Their baggage was meager, but it included one hold-all containing their toys, wrapped in beach towels. The CIA had been kind enough to ensure that bag cleared customs at

Miami, and McCready, waving his Foreign Office letter, claimed diplomatic immunity for it at Port Plaisance.

The Deceiver brought them back to the hotel and installed them in a room next to his own. They stashed their bag of "goodies" under the bed, locked the door, and went for a long swim. McCready had already told them when he would need them—at ten the next morning at Government House.

Having lunched on the terrace, McCready went to see the Reverend Walter Drake. He found the Baptist minister at his small house, resting his still bruised body. He introduced himself and asked how the pastor was feeling.

"Are you with Mr. Hannah?" asked Drake.

"Not exactly with him," said McCready. "More . . . keeping an eye on things while he gets on with his murder investigation. My concern is more the political side of things."

"You with the Foreign Office?" persisted Drake.

"In a way," said McCready. "Why do you ask?"

"I do not like your Foreign Office," said Drake. "You are selling my people down the river."

"Ah, now that might just be about to change," said McCready, and told the preacher what he wished of him.

Reverend Drake shook his head. "I am a man of God," he said. "You want different people for that sort of thing."

"Mr. Drake, yesterday I called Washington. Someone there told me that only seven Barclayans had ever served in the United States armed forces. One of them was listed as Drake W."

"Another man," growled Reverend Drake.

"This man said," pursued McCready quietly, "that the Drake W. they had listed had been a sergeant in the U.S. Marine Corps. Served two tours in Vietnam. Came back with a Bronze Star and two Purple Hearts. I wonder what happened to him?"

The big pastor lumbered to his feet, crossed the room, and stared out at the clapboard houses up and down the street where he lived.

"Another man," he growled, "another time, another place. I do only God's work now."

"Don't you think what I ask of you might qualify?"

The big man considered, then nodded. "Possibly."

"I think so, too," said McCready. "I hope I'll see you there. I need all the help I can get. Ten o'clock, tomorrow morning, Government House."

He left and strolled down through the town to the harbor. Jimmy Dobbs was working on the *Gulf Lady*. McCready spent thirty minutes with him, and they agreed on a charter voyage for the following day.

He was hot and sticky when he arrived at Government House just before five that afternoon. Jefferson served him an iced tea while he waited for Lieutenant Jeremy Haverstock to return. The young officer had been playing tennis with some other expatriates at a villa in the hills.

McCready's question to him was simple: "Will you be here at ten o'clock tomorrow morning?"

Haverstock thought it over. "Yes, I suppose so," he said.

"Good," said McCready. "Do you have your full tropical dress uniform with you?"

"Yes," said the cavalryman. "Only got to wear it once. A state ball in Nassau six months ago."

"Excellent," said McCready. "Ask Jefferson to press it and polish up the leather and brasses."

A mystified Haverstock escorted him to the front hall. "I suppose you've heard the good news?" he asked. "That detective chappie from Scotland Yard. Found the bullet yesterday in the garden. Absolutely intact. Parker's on his way to London with it."

"Good show," said McCready. "Spiffing news."

He had dinner with Eddie Favaro at the hotel at eight. Over coffee he asked, "What are you doing tomorrow?"

"Going home," said Favaro. "I only took a week off. Have to be back on the job Tuesday morning."

"Ah, yes. What time's your plane?"

"Booked an air taxi for midday."

"Couldn't delay it until four o'clock, could you?"

"I suppose so. Why?"

"Because I could do with your help. Say, Government House, ten o'clock? Thanks, see you then. Don't be late. Monday is going to be a very busy day."

McCready rose at six. A pink dawn, herald of another balmy day, was touching the tips of the palm trees out in Parliament

Square. It was delightfully cool. He washed and shaved and
went out into the square, where the taxi he had ordered
awaited him. His first duty was to say good-bye to an old
lady.

He spent an hour with her, between seven and eight, took
coffee and hot rolls, and made his farewells.

"Now, don't forget, Lady Coltrane," he said as he rose to
leave.

"Don't worry, I won't. And it's Missy."

She held out her hand. He stooped to take it.

At half-past eight, he was back in Parliament Square and
dropped in on Chief Inspector Jones. He showed the chief of
police his Foreign Office letter.

"Please be at Government House at ten o'clock," he said.
"Bring with you your two sergeants, four constables, your
personal Land-Rover, and two plain vans. Do you have a
service revolver?"

"Yes, sir."

"Please bring that too."

At the same moment, it was half-past one in London. But in
the Ballistics Department of the Home Office forensic laboratory in Lambeth, Mr. Alan Mitchell was not thinking of lunch.
He was staring into a microscope.

Beneath the lens, held at each end in a gentle clamp, was a
bullet. Mitchell stared at the striation marks that ran the
length of the lead slug, curving around the metal as they went.
They were the marks left by the rifling in the barrel that had
fired the bullet. For the fifth time that day, he gently turned
the bullet under the lens, picking out the other scratches—the
"lands"—that were as individual to a gun barrel as a fingerprint to a human hand.

Finally he was satisfied. He whistled in surprise and went
for one of his manuals. He had a whole library of them, for
Alan Mitchell was widely regarded as the most knowledgeable
weapons expert in Europe.

There were still other tests to be carried out. He knew that
somewhere four thousand miles across the sea, a detective
waited impatiently for his findings, but he would not be
hurried. He had to be sure, absolutely sure. Too many cases
in court had been lost because experts produced by the

defense had flawed the evidence presented by the forensic scientists for the prosecution.

There were tests to be carried out on the minuscule fragments of burnt powder that still adhered to the blunt end of the slug. Tests on the manufacture and composition of the lead, which he had already carried out on the twisted bullet he had had for two days, would have to be repeated on the newly arrived one. The spectroscope would plunge its rays deep into the metal itself, betraying the very molecular structure of the lead, identifying its approximate age and sometimes even the factory that had produced it. Alan Mitchell took the manual he sought from his shelves, sat down and began to read.

McCready dismissed his taxi at the gate of Government house and rang the bell. Jefferson recognized him and let him in. McCready explained he had to make another phone call on the international line that had been installed by Bannister, and that he had Mr. Hannah's permission. Jefferson showed him into the private study and left him.

McCready ignored the telephone and addressed himself to the desk. In the early stages of the investigation, Hannah had been through the drawers, using the dead Governor's keys, and after assuring himself there were no clues to the murder therein, he had relocked them all.

McCready had no keys, but he did not need them. He had picked the locks the previous day and found what he wanted. They were in the bottom left-hand drawer. There were two of them, but he needed only one.

It was an imposing sheet of paper, crisp to the touch and creamy like parchment. In the center at the top, raised and embossed in gold, was the royal coat-of-arms: the lion and the unicorn supporting the shield emblazoned in its four quarters with the heraldic emblems of England, Scotland, Wales, and Ireland.

Beneath, in bold black lettering, were the words:

WE, ELIZABETH THE SECOND, OF THE UNITED KING-
DOM OF GREAT BRITAIN AND NORTHERN IRELAND,
AND OF ALL HER TERRITORIES AND DEPENDENCIES
BEYOND THE SEAS, BY THE GRACE OF GOD QUEEN, DO

HEREBY APPOINT . . . (here there was a gap) TO BE
OUR . . . (another gap) IN THE TERRITORY OF . . . (a
third gap).

Beneath the text was a facsimile signature that read, "Elizabeth R."

It was a Royal Warrant. En blanc. McCready took a pen
from the inkstand of Sir Marston Moberley and filled it in,
using his best copperplate script. When he had finished, he
blew gently on the ink to dry it and used the gubernatorial
seal to stamp it.

Outside in the sitting room his guests were assembling. He
looked at the document again and shrugged. He had just
appointed himself Governor of the Barclays. For a day.

Chapter 6

There were six of them. Jefferson had served coffee and left. He did not inquire what they were doing there. It was not his business.

The two SAS sergeants, Newson and Sinclair, stood by the wall. They were in cream tracksuits and shod in cleated training shoes. Each had a pouch around the waist, held by a strap, the same as those favored by tourists for storing their cigarettes and sun oil on the beach. These pouches did not contain sun oil.

Lieutenant Haverstock had not changed into his dress uniform. He sat on one of the brocaded chairs, his long legs elegantly crossed. Reverend Drake was on the settee beside Eddie Favaro. Chief Inspector Jones, in his dark-blue tunic, silver buttons, and insignia, shorts, stockings, and shoes, stood by the door.

McCready took the warrant and offered it to Haverstock. "This arrived from London at dawn," he said. "Read, mark, learn, and inwardly digest."

Haverstock read the warrant.

"Well, that's all right then," he said, and passed it on. Inspector Jones read it, stiffened to attention, and said, "Yes, sir.'' He passed it to the sergeants. Newson said: ''All right by me,'' and Sinclair read it and said, ''No problem.''

He passed it to Favaro, who read it and muttered, ''Jeez,'' getting a warning glance from Reverend Drake, who took the document, read it, and growled, ''Lord be praised.''

''My first act,'' said McCready, ''is to empower you all— excepting Chief Inspector Jones, of course—with the authority of Special Constables. You are hereby deputized. Secondly, I'd better explain what we are going to do.''

He talked for thirty minutes. No one disagreed. Then he summoned Haverstock, and they left to change. Lady Moberley was still in bed enjoying a liquid breakfast. It made no matter. She and Sir Marston had had separate bedrooms, and the late Governor's dressing room was unoccupied. Haverstock showed McCready where it was and left. McCready found what he wanted right at the back of the wardrobe; the full dress uniform of a British colonial Governor, albeit two sizes too large.

When he re-entered the sitting room, the rumpled tourist in the creased jacket from the terrace bar of the Quarter Deck Hotel was gone. On his feet the George boots with their boxed spurs gleamed. The tight trousers were white, as was the tunic jacket, which buttoned to the throat. The gold buttons and gilt aiguillettes from the left breast pocket glittered in the sunlight, as did the slanting chain and spike on his Wolsey helmet. The sash around his waist was blue.

Haverstock was also in white, but his flat officer's cap was in dark blue with a black peak. The double-headed eagle of the Queen's Dragoon Guards was above the peak. His aiguillettes were also gilded, as were the patches of chain-mail covering each shoulder. A gleaming black leather strap lay slantwise across his chest and back, at the rear supporting a slim ammunition pouch, also in black leather. He wore his two service medals.

''Right, Mr. Jones. Let us go.'' said McCready. ''We must be about the Queen's business.''

Chief Inspector Jones swelled. No one had ever asked him to be about the Queen's business before. When the cavalcade left the front forecourt, it was led by the official Jaguar. Oscar drove, with a policeman beside him. McCready and Haverstock sat in the back, helmets on. Behind them came the

Land-Rover, driven by a second constable with Jones beside him. Favaro and Reverend Drake sat in the back.

Before leaving Government House, Sergeant Sinclair had quitely slipped Favaro a loaded Colt Cobra, which now nestled in the American detective's waistband beneath his loose shirt. The sergeant had also offered one to Reverend Drake, who had shaken his head.

The two vans were driven by the remaining two constables. Newson and Sinclair crouched by their open side doors. The police sergeants were in the last van.

At a sedate pace, the Jaguar rolled into Shantytown. Down the long main street people stopped and stared. The two figures in the back sat up straight and looked ahead.

At the gates to the walled compound of Mr. Horatio Livingstone, McCready ordered the car to stop. He descended. So did Lieutenant Haverstock. A crowd of several hundred Barclayans emerged from the surrounding alleys and watched them, mouths agape. McCready did not ask for admission; he just stood in front of the double gate.

Sergeants Newson and Sinclair jogged up to the wall. Newson cupped his hands, Sinclair put a heel in them, and Newson heaved. The lighter man went over the wall without touching the shards of glass along its top. The gates were unlocked from the inside. Sinclair stood back as McCready entered with Haverstock at his side. The vehicles rolled after them at a walking pace.

Three men in gray safari suits were halfway across the compound, running for the gate, when McCready appeared. They stopped and stared at the two white-uniformed figures walking purposefully toward the front door. Sinclair disappeared. Newson darted through the open gates and did the same.

McCready walked up the steps of the verandah and into the house. Behind him, Haverstock stood on the verandah and stared at the three gray safari suits. They kept their distance. Favaro and Drake, Jones, the two police sergeants, and three constables left their vehicles and came after them. One constable remained with the cars and vans. Haverstock then joined the group inside. There were now ten of them and one outside.

In the big reception room the policemen took positions by

the doors and windows. A door opened, and Horatio Livingstone emerged. He surveyed the invasion with ill-concealed
rage.

"You can't come in here! What is the meaning of this?" he
shouted.

McCready held out his warrant. "Would you please read
this?" he said.

Livingstone read it and tossed it contemptuously to the
floor. Jones retrieved it and handed it back to McCready, who
restored it to his pocket.

"I would like you to summon all your Bahamian staff
here—all seven of them—with their passports, if you please,
Mr. Livingstone."

"By whose authority?" snapped Livingstone.

"I *am* the supreme authority," said McCready.

"Imperialist!" shouted Livingstone. "In fifteen days I will
be the authority here, and then—"

"If you decline," said McCready calmly, "I will ask Chief
Inspector Jones here to arrest you for attempting to subvert
the course of justice. Mr. Jones, are you ready to carry out
your duty?"

"Yes, sir."

Livingstone glowered at them all. He called one of his aides
from a side room and gave the order. One by one the men in
safari suits appeared. Favaro circulated, collecting their Bahamian passports. He handed them to McCready.

McCready went through them one by one, handing each to
Haverstock. The lieutenant glanced at them and tut-tutted.

"These passports are all false," said McCready. "They are
good, but they are forgeries."

"That's not true!" screamed Livingstone. "They are perfectly valid!"

He was right. They were not forged. They had been pur-
chased with a very substantial bribe.

"No," said McCready, "these men are not Bahamians.
Nor are you a democratic socialist. You are, in fact, a dedicated Communist who has worked for years for Fidel Castro,
and these men around you are Cuban officers. Mr. Brown
over there is, in fact, Captain Hernan Moreno of the Direccion
General de Informacion, the Cuban equivalent of the KGB.
The others, picked for their pure Negroid appearance and

fluent English, are also Cubans from the DGI. I am arresting them all for illegal entry into the Barclays, and you for aiding and abetting.''

It was Moreno who went for his gun first. It was tucked in his waistband at the back, hidden by the safari jacket, as were all the guns. He was very fast, and his hand was behind his back reaching for the Makarov before anyone in the reception area could move.

The Cuban was stopped by a sharp shout from the top of the stairs that led to the upper flors: *"Fuera la mano, o seras fiambre."*

Hernan Moreno got the message just in time. His hand stopped moving. He froze. So did the six others, who were in the act of following his example.

Sinclair's Spanish was fluent and colloquial. *Fiambre* is a collation of cold meats, and in Spanish slang, a stiff, or corpse.

The two sergeants were at the top of the stairs, side by side, having entered through upper windows. Their touristic pouches were empty, but their hands were not. Each held a small but reliable Heckler and Koch MP5 machine pistol.

"These men," said McCready mildly, "are not accustomed to missing. Now, please ask your men to put their hands above their heads.''

Livingstone remained silent.

Favaro slipped up behind him, slid his arm around the man's chest, and eased the barrel of his Colt Cobra into his right nostril. "Three seconds," he whispered. "Then I have an awful accident.''

"Do it," rasped Livingstone.

Fourteen hands went upward and stayed there. The three police constables went around collecting the seven handguns.

"Frisk," said McCready. The police sergeants frisked each Cuban. Two knives in calf-sheaths were discovered.

"Search the house," said McCready.

The seven Cubans were lined up, facing the sitting-room wall, hands on top of heads. Livingstone sat in his club chair, covered by Favaro. The SAS men stayed on the stairs in case of an attempt at mass breakout. There was none. The five local police officers searched the house.

They discovered a variety of extra weapons, a large sum of

American dollars, further sums of Barclayan pounds, and a powerful short-wave radio with encrypter.

"Mr. Livingstone," said McCready, "I could ask Mr. Jones to charge your associates with a variety of offenses under British law—false passports, illegal entry, carrying of unlicensed guns—it's a long list. Instead, I am going to expel them all as undesirable aliens. Now—within the hour. You may, if you wish, stay on here alone. You are, after all, a Barclayan by birth. But you would still be open to charges of aiding and abetting, and frankly you might feel safer back where you belong, on Cuba."

"I'll second that," growled Reverend Drake.

Livingstone nodded.

In single file, the Cubans were marched out to the second of the two vans waiting in the courtyard. Only one tried violence. Attempting to run, he was blocked by a local constable and threw the officer to the ground.

Inspector Jones acted with remarkable speed. He produced from his belt the short holly-wood truncheon known to generations of British policeman as "the holly." There was a loud *pok* as the timber bounced off the Cuban's head. The man sank to his knees, feeling quite unwell.

"Don't do that," Chief Inspector Jones advised him.

The Cubans and Horatio Livingstone sat on the floor of the van, hands on heads, while Sergeant Newson leaned over from the front seat, covering them with his machine pistol. The cavalcade formed up again and trundled slowly out of Shantytown to the fishing quay in Port Plaisance. McCready kept the pace slow so that hundreds of Barclayans could see what was going on.

At the fishing quay, the *Gulf Lady* waited, her engine idling. Behind her, she towed a garbage scow newly fitted with two pairs of oars.

"Mr. Dobbs," said McCready, "please tow these gentleman as far as the start of Cuban territorial waters, or until a Cuban patrol boat starts to cruise in your direction. Then cast them loose. They can be pulled home by their fellow countrymen, or row home with the onshore breeze."

Jimmy Dobbs looked askance at the Cubans. There were seven of them, plus Livingstone.

"Lieutenant Haverstock here will accompany you," said McCready. "He will, of course, be armed."

Sergeant Sinclair gave Haverstock the Colt Cobra that the Reverend Drake had declined to use. Haverstock stepped onto the *Gulf Lady* and took position sitting on the cabin roof, facing aft.

"Don't worry, old boy," he said to Dobbs. "If one of them moves, I'll just blow his nuts off."

"Mr. Livingstone," said McCready, looking down at the eight men in the scow, "one last thing. When you reach Cuba, you may tell Señor Castro that taking over the Barclays through a stooge candidate in the elections, and then perhaps annexing the islands to Cuba, or turning them into an international revolutionary training camp, was a wonderful idea. But you might also tell him that it ain't going to work. Not now, not ever. He'll have to salvage his political career some other way. Good-bye, Mr. Livingstone. Don't come back."

More than a thousand Barclayans thronged the quay as the *Gulf Lady* turned away from the jetty and headed for the open sea.

"One more chore, I believe, gentlemen," said McCready, and strode back down the jetty toward the Jaguar, his gleaming white uniform cutting a swath through the crowd of onlookers.

The wrought-iron gates to the estate of Marcus Johnson were locked. Newson and Sinclair stepped out of the side door of their van and went straight over the wall without touching the top. Minutes later, from inside the estate, there came a soft *thunk*, as of the edge of a hard hand coming into contact with the human frame. The electric motor hummed, and the gates swung open.

Inside, and to the right, was a small hut with a control panel and telephone. Slumped on the floor was a man in bright beach shirt, his dark glasses crushed on the floor beside him. He was thrown into the last van with the two police sergeants. Newson and Sinclair slipped away across the lawns and were lost to view among the bushes.

Marcus Johnson was descending the tiled staircase toward the open-plan reception area when McCready strode in. He was pulling a silk bathrobe around himself.

"May I ask what the hell this means?" he demanded.

"Certainly," said McCready. "Please read this."

Johnson handed the warrant back.

"So? I have committed no offense. You break into my house—London will hear of this, Mr. Dillon. You will regret this morning's work. I have lawyers."

"Good," said McCready. "You may well need them. Now, I want to interview your staff, Mr. Johnson—your election assistants, your associates. One has been kind enough to escort us to the door. Please bring him in."

The two police sergeants picked up the gatekeeper, whom they had been supporting between them, and dropped him on a sofa.

"The other seven, if you please, Mr. Johnson, with their passports."

Johnson crossed to an onyx telephone and picked it up. The line was dead. He put it down.

"I intend to summon the police," he said.

"I am the police," retorted Chief Inspector Jones. "Please do as the Governor asks."

Johnson thought it over, then called upstairs. A head appeared at the upper banister. Johnson gave the order.

Two men in bright shirts emerged from the verandah and stood beside their master. Five more came down from the upper rooms. Several muffled female squeals were heard. There had apparently been a party going on.

Inspector Jones went around collecting their passports. The man on the sofa had his own removed from his back pocket.

McCready examined them all, one by one, shaking his head as he did so.

"They are not forgeries," Johnson said with quiet assurance, "and as you see, all my associates entered Sunshine Island legally. The fact that they are of Jamaican nationality is irrelevant."

"Not quite," said McCready, "since all of them failed to declare that they have criminal records, contrary to Section Four, Subsection B-1, of the Immigration Act."

Johnson looked dumbfounded, as well he might. McCready had just invented the whole thing.

"In fact," he said evenly, "all these men are members of a criminal conspiracy known as the Yardbirds."

The Yardbirds had started as street gangs in the slums of

Kingston, taking their name from the backyard where they held sway. They began in protection racketeering and earned a reputation for vicious violence. Later, they developed into purveyors of hemp and the cocaine-derivative crack and went international. For short, they are known as Yardies.

One of the Jamaicans was standing near a wall against which a baseball bat was leaning. His hand slowly crept nearer to the bat.

Reverend Drake caught the movement. "Hallelujah, brother," he said quietly, and hit him. Just once. Very hard. They teach many things in Baptist colleges, but the short-arm jab as a means of converting the ungodly is not one of them. The Jamaican rolled up his eyes and slid to the floor.

The incident acted as a signal. Four of the six remaining Yardies went for their waistbands beneath their beach shirts.

"Freeze! Hold it!"

Newson and Sinclair had waited until the upper floor was vacated, except for the girls, before coming in through the windows. Now they were on the upper landing, machine pistols covering the open area below. Hands froze in mid-movement.

"They daren't fire," snarled Johnson. "They'd hit you all."

Favaro came across the marble floor in a roll and rose behind Marcus Johnson. He slid his left hand under the man's throat and dug the barrel of the Colt into his kidneys.

"Maybe," he said, "but you go first."

"Your hands above your heads, if you please," said Mc-Cready.

Johnson swallowed and nodded. The six Yardies raised their hands. They were ordered to walk to the wall and lean against it, hands high. The two police sergeants relieved them of their guns.

"I suppose," snapped Johnson, "you will be calling me a Yardbird. I am a citizen of these islands, a respectable businessman."

"No," said McCready reasonably, "you're not. You're a cocaine dealer. That's how you made your fortune. Running dope for the Medellín cartel. Since leaving these islands as a poor teenager, you've spent most of your time in Colombia, or setting up dummy companies in Europe and North America to launder cocaine money. And now, if you please, I would like to meet your Colombian chief executive, Señor Mendes.''

"Never heard of him. No such man," said Johnson.

McCready thrust a photograph under his nose.

Johnson's eyes flickered.

"This Señor Mendes, or whatever he is calling himself now."

Johnson remained silent. McCready looked up and nodded to Newson and Sinclair. They had already seen the photograph. The soldiers disappeared. Minutes later, there were two short, rapid bursts of fire from the upper floor and a series of female screams.

Three Latin-looking women appeared at the top of the stairs and ran down. McCready ordered two of the constables to take them out to the lawn and guard them. Sinclair and Newson appeared, pushing a man in front of them. He was thin and sallow, with straight black hair. The sergeants pushed him down the stairs but stayed at the top.

"I could charge your Jamaicans with a variety of offenses under the law here," McCready said to Johnson, "but in fact I have reserved nine seats on the afternoon plane to Nassau. I think you will find the Bahamian Police more than happy to escort you all to the Kingston flight. In Kingston you are expected. Search the house.''

The remaining local police did the search. They found two more prostitutes hiding under beds, further weapons, and a large amount of American dollars in an attaché case. In Johnson's bedroom were a few ounces of white powder.

"Half a million dollars," hissed Johnson to McCready. "Let me go, and it's yours.''

McCready handed the attaché case to Reverend Drake. "Distribute it among the island's charities," he said. Drake nodded. "Burn the cocaine.''

One of the policemen took the packets and went outside to start a bonfire.

"Let's go," said McCready.

At four that afternoon the short-haul carrier from Nassau stood on the grass strip, its propellers whirling. The eight Yardbirds, all cuffed, were escorted aboard by two Bahamian Police sergeants, who had come to collect them. Marcus Johnson, his hands cuffed behind him, stood waiting to board.

"You may, after Kingston has extradited you to Miami, be able to get a message to Señor Ochoa, or Señor Escobar, or whoever it is for whom you work," said McCready.

"Tell him that the taking-over of the Barclays through a proxy was a brilliant idea. To own the coast guards, customs, and police of the new state, to issue diplomatic passports at will, to have diplomatic luggage sent to the States, to build refineries and store depots here in complete freedom, to set up laundering banks with impunity—all extremely ingenious. And profitable, with the casinos for the high rollers, the bordellos . . .

"But if you can get the message through, tell him from me, it ain't going to work. Not in these islands."

Five minutes later, the boxlike frame of the short-haul lifted off, tilted its wings, and headed away toward the coast of Andros.

McCready walked over to a six-seat Cessna parked behind the hangar. Sergeants Newson and Sinclair were aboard, in the back row, their bag of "goodies" stashed by their feet, on their way back to Fort Bragg. In front of them sat Francisco Mendes, whose real Colombian name had turned out to be something else. His wrists were tied to the frame of his seat. He leaned out of the open door and spat onto the ground.

"You cannot extradite me," he said in very good English. "You can arrest me and wait for the Americans to ask for extradition. That is all."

"And that would take months," said McCready. "My dear chap, you're not being arrested, just expelled." He turned to Eddie Favaro. "I hope you don't mind giving his fellow a lift to Miami," he said. "Of course, it could be that as you touch down, you will suddenly recognize him as someone wanted by the Metro-Dade force. After that, it's up to Uncle Sam."

They shook hands, and the Cessna ran up the grass strip, turned, paused, and put on full power. Seconds later it was out over the sea, turning northwest toward Florida.

McCready walked slowly back to the Jaguar, where Oscar waited. Time to go back to Government House, change, and hang the white uniform of Governor back in the wardrobe.

When he arrived, Detective Chief Superintendent Hannah was in Sir Marston Moberley's office taking a call from

London. McCready slipped upstairs and came down in his rumpled tropical suit. Hannah was hurrying out of the office, calling for Oscar and the Jaguar.

Alan Mitchell had worked until nine that Monday evening before he put through the call to Sunshine Island, where it was only four in the afternoon. Hannah took the call eagerly. He had spent the whole afternoon in the office waiting for the call.

"It's remarkable," said the ballistics expert. "One of the most extraordinary bullets I've ever examined. Certainly never seen one like it used in a murder before."

"What's odd about it?" asked Hannah.

"Well, the lead, to start with. It's extremely old. Seventy years, at least. They haven't made lead of that molecular consistency since the early 1920s. The same applies to the powder. Some tiny traces of it remained on the bullet. It was a chemical type introduced in 1912 and discontinued in the early 1920s."

"But what about the gun?" insisted Hannah.

"That's the point," said the scientist in London. "The gun matches the ammunition used. The bullet has an absolutely unmistakable signature, like a fingerprint. Unique. It has exactly seven grooves, with a right-hand twist, left by the barrel of the revolver. No other handgun ever left those seven right-hand grooves. Remarkable, what?"

"Wonderful," said Hannah. "Just one gun could have fired that shot? Excellent. Now, Alan, which gun?"

"Why, the Webley 4.55, of course. Nothing like it."

Hannah was not an expert in handguns. He would not have known, at a glance, a Webley 4.55 from a Colt .44 Magnum. Not to look at, that is.

"Fine, Alan. Now tell me, what is so special about the Webley 4.55?"

"Its age. It's a bloody antique. It was first issued in 1912, discontinued about 1920. It's a revolver with an extremely long barrel, quite distinctive. They were never very popular because that extralong barrel kept getting in the way. Accurate though, for the same reason. They were issued as service revolvers to British officers in the trenches in the First World War. Have you ever seen one?"

Hannah thanked him and replaced the receiver.

"Oh yes," he breathed, "I've seen one."

He was rushing across the hall when he saw that strange man Dillon from the Foreign Office.

"Use the phone if you like. It's free," he called, and climbed into the Jaguar.

When he was shown in, Missy Coltrane was in her wheelchair in the sitting room. She greeted him with a welcoming smile.

"Why, Mr. Hannah, how nice to see you again," she said. "Won't you sit down and take some tea?"

"Thank you, Lady Coltrane, I think I prefer to stand. I'm afraid I have some questions to ask you. Have you ever seen a handgun known as a Webley 4.55?"

"Why now, I don't think I have," she said meekly.

"I take leave to doubt that, ma'am. You have in fact got one. Your late husband's old service revolver. In that trophy case over there. And I'm afraid I must take possession of it as vital evidence."

He turned and walked to the glass-fronted trophy case. They were all there—the medals, the insignia, the citations, the cap badges. But they were rearranged. Behind some of them could be dimly discerned some oil smudges on the hessian, where another trophy had once hung.

Hannah turned back. "Where has it gone, Lady Coltrane?" he asked tightly.

"Dear Mr. Hannah, I'm sure I don't know what you are talking about."

He hated to lose a case, but he could feel this one slipping slowly away. The gun or a witness—he needed one or the other. Beyond the windows the blue sea was darkling in the fading light. Somewhere out there, deep in its unquestioning embrace, he knew lay a Webley 4.55. Oil smudges do not make a court case.

"It was there, Lady Coltrane. On Thursday, when I came to see you. It was there in the cabinet."

"Why, Mr. Hannah, you must be mistaken. I have never seen any . . . Wembley."

"Webley, Lady Coltrane. Wembley is where they play football." He felt he was losing this match six-nil.

"Mr. Hannah, what exactly is it you suspect of me?" she asked.

"I don't suspect, ma'am, I know. I know what happened. Proof is another matter. Last Tuesday, at about this hour, Firestone picked you and your chair up with those huge arms of his and placed you in the back of your van, as he did on Saturday for your shopping expedition. I had thought perhaps you never left this house, but with his help, of course, you can.

"He drove you down to the alley behind the Governor's residence, set you down, and with his own hands tore the lock off the steel gate. I thought it might take a Land-Rover and chain to pull that lock off, but of course he could do it. I should have seen that when I met him. I missed it. Mea culpa.

"He pushed you through the open gate and left you. I believe you had the Webley in your lap. Antique it may have been, but it had been kept oiled over the years, and the ammunition was still inside it. With a short barrel you'd never have hit Sir Moberley, not even firing two-handed. But this Webley had a very long barrel, very accurate.

"And you were not quite new to guns. You met your husband in the war, as you said. He was wounded, and you nursed him. But it was in a *maquis* hospital in Nazi-occupied France. He was with the British Special Operations Executive, and you, I believe, were with the American equivalent, the Office of Strategic Services.

"The first shot missed and hit the wall. The second did the job and lodged in a flower-basket full of loam. That's where I found it. London identified it today. It's quite distinctive. No gun ever fired that bullet but a Webley 4.55, such as you had in that case."

"Oh dear, poor Mr. Hannah. It's a wonderful story, but can you prove it?"

"No, Lady Coltrane, I can't. I needed the gun, or a witness. I'll bet a dozen people saw you and Firestone in that alley, but none of them will ever testify. Not against Missy Coltrane. Not on Sunshine. But there are two things that puzzle me. Why? Why kill that unlovable Governor? Did you *want* the police here?"

She smiled and shook her head. "The press, Mr. Hannah. Always snooping about, always asking questions, always investigating backgrounds. Always so suspicious of everyone in politics."

"Yes, of course. The ferrets of the press."

"And the other puzzle, Mr. Hannah?"

"Who warned you, Lady Coltrane? On Tuesday evening you put the gun back in the case. It was there on Thursday. Now it is gone. Who warned you?"

"Mr. Hannah, give my love to London when you get back. I haven't seen it since the Blitz, you know. And now I never shall."

Desmond Hannah had Oscar drive him back to Parliament Square. He dismissed Oscar by the police station; Oscar would have to polish up the Jaguar in time for the new Governor's arrival the next day. It was about time Whitehall reacted, he thought. He began to cross the square to the hotel.

"Evening, Mistah Hannah."

He turned. A complete stranger, smiling and greeting him.

"Er . . . good evening."

Two youths in front of the hotel were dancing in the dust. One had a cassette player around his neck. The tape was playing a calypso number. Hannah did not recognize it. It was "Freedom Come, Freedom Go." He recognized "Yellow Bird," however—it was coming from the Quarter Deck bar. He recalled that in five days he had not heard a steel band or a calypso.

The doors of the Anglican church were open; Reverend Quince was giving forth on his small organ. He was playing "Gaudeamus Igitur."

By the time Hannah strode up the steps of the hotel, he realized there was an air of levity about the streets. It did not match his own mood. He had some serious report-writing to do. After a late-night call to London, he would go home in the morning. There was nothing more he could do. He hated to lose a case, but he knew this one would remain on the file. He could return to Nassau on the plane that brought in the new Governor, and fly on to London.

He crossed the terrace bar toward the staircase. There was that man Dillon again, sitting on a stool nursing a beer. Strange fellow, he thought as he went up the stairs. Always sitting around waiting for something. Never actually seemed to *do* anything.

*   *   *

On Tuesday morning, a de Havilland Devon droned in toward Sunshine from Nassau and deposited the new Governor, Sir Crispian Rattray. From the shade of the hangar McCready watched the elderly diplomat, crisp in cream linen with wings of silver hair flying from beneath his white panama hat, descend from the aircraft to meet the welcoming committee.

Lieutenant Haverstock, back from his marine odyssey, introduced him to various notables from the town, including Dr. Caractacus Jones and his nephew, Chief Inspector Jones. Oscar was there with the newly polished Jaguar, and after the introductions the small cavalcade drove off toward Port Plaisance.

Sir Rattray would discover that he had little to do. The two candidates appeared to have withdrawn their candidacies and gone on vacation. He would appeal for other candidates. None would come forward—Reverend Drake would see to that.

With the January elections postponed, the British Parliament would reconvene and, under pressure from the opposition, the government would concede that a referendum in March might well be appropriate. But that was all in the future.

Desmond Hannah boarded the empty Devon for the journey to Nassau. From the top of the steps he had a last look around. That strange fellow Dillon seemed to be sitting with his suitcase and attaché case again, waiting for something. Hannah did not wave. He intended to mention Mr. Dillon when he got back to London.

Ten minutes after the Devon left, McCready's air taxi from Miami arrived. He had to return his portable telephone to the Miami CIA office and say a few thank-yous to friends in Florida before flying on to London. He would be home in time for Christmas. He would spend it alone in his flat in Kensington. Perhaps he would go down to the Special Forces Club for a drink with some old mates.

The Piper took off, and McCready had a last look at the drowsy town of Port Plaisance, going about its business in the morning sun. He saw Spyglass Hill drift by, and a pink villa on its peak.

The pilot turned once more for his course to Miami. The wing dipped, and McCready looked down at the interior of the island. On a dusty track a small brown child looked up and waved. McCready waved back. With luck, and for the moment, he thought, the boy could grow up without ever having to live under the red flag or to sniff cocaine.

Epilogue

"I am sure we are all deeply grateful," said Timothy Edwards, "to Denis for his excellent presentation. I would suggest that as the hour is late, my colleagues and I mull the matter over between ourselves, to see if there is room for a variation of the Service policy in this matter, and deliver our view in the morning."

Denis Gaunt had to return his file to the clerk from Records. When he turned around, Sam McCready was gone. He had slipped away almost as Edwards finished speaking. Gaunt traced him ten minutes later to his office.

McCready was still in shirt-sleeves, his creased cotton jacket over a chair, puttering about. Two cardboard wine crates stood on the floor.

"What are you doing?" asked Gaunt.

"Clearing out my bits and bobs."

There were only two photographs, and he kept them in a drawer, not ostentatiously propped on the desk. One was of May, the other of his son on his graduation day, smiling diffidently in a black academic's gown. McCready put them into one of the boxes.

"You're crazy," said Gaunt. "I think we may have cracked

it. Not Edwards, of course, but the two Controllers. I think
they may change their minds. We know they both like you,
want you to stay.''

McCready took his compact disk player and put it in the
other box. Sometimes he liked to play soft classical music
when he was deep in thought. There was hardly enough bric-
a-brac to fill both the boxes, though. Certainly there were no
me-shaking-hands-with-a-celebrity photos on his walls; the
few Impressionist prints were service-issue. He straightened
up and looked at the two boxes.

"Not a lot, really, for thirty years," he murmured.

"Sam, for God's sake, it's not over yet. They could change
their minds.''

McCready turned and gripped Gaunt by his upper arms.
"Denis, you're a great guy. You did a good job in there. You
gave it your best shot. And I'm going to ask the Chief to let
you take over the desk. But you have to learn on which side
of the sky the sun rises. It's over. Verdict and sentence were
handed down weeks ago, in another office, by another man.''

Denis Gaunt sat down miserably in his boss's chair. "Then
what the hell was it all for?''

"The hell it was for was this: Because I care about this
fucking Service, and because they're getting it wrong. Because there's a bloody dangerous world out there, and it's not
getting less dangerous, but more so. And because dickheads
like Edwards are going to be left looking after the security of
this old country that I happen to love, and that frightens the
shit out of me. I knew I couldn't change anything in that
hearing, but I wanted to make the bastards squirm. Sorry,
Denis, I should have told you. Will you have my boxes run
over to my flat sometime?''

"You could still take one of the jobs they've offered you.
Just to spite them," suggested Gaunt.

"Denis, as the poet said, 'One wild, sweet hour of glorious
life is worth a world without a name.' For me, sitting down
there in the archive library or approving expense accounts
would be a world without a name. I've had my hour, done my
best—it's over. I'm off. There's a whole sunny world out
there, Denis. I'm going out there, and I'm going to enjoy
myself.''

Denis Gaunt looked as if he were attending a funeral. "They'll see you again around here," he said.

"No, they won't."

"The Chief will give you a farewell party."

"No party. I can't stand cheap sparkling wine. Plays merry hell with my gut. So does Edwards being nice to me. Walk me down to the main door?"

Century House is a village, a tiny parish. Down the corridor to the lift, on the ride to the ground floor, across the tiled lobby, colleagues and secretaries called, "Hi, Sam—hallo, Sam." They did not say, "Bye-bye, Sam," but it was what they meant. A few of the secretaries paused as if they would like to straighten his tie one last time. He nodded and smiled and walked on.

The main door stood at the end of the tiled hall, beyond it the street. McCready wondered whether he should use his compensation to buy a cottage in the country, grow roses and marrows, attend church on Sunday mornings, become a pillar of the community. But how to fill the days?

He regretted that he had never developed any absorbing hobbies, like his colleagues who bred tropical fish or collected stamps or walked up and down mountains in Wales. And what could he say to the neighbors? "Good morning, my name's Sam, I've retired from the Foreign Office, and no, I can't tell you a damned thing I did there." Old soldiers are allowed to write their memoirs and bore tourists in the snug bar. But not those who have spent their lives in the shadowed places. They must remain silent forever.

Mrs. Foy from Travel Documents was crossing the lobby, her high heels clacking on the tiles, a statuesque widow in her late thirties. Quite a number of denizens of Century House had tried their luck with Suzanne Foy, but she was not known as the Fortress for nothing.

Their paths crossed. She stopped and turned. Somehow, McCready's tie-knot had arrived at the area of the middle of his chest. She reached out, tightened it, and slid it back toward the top shirt button. Gaunt watched. He was too young to remember Jane Russell, so he could not make the obvious comparison.

"Sam, you should have someone take you home for something nourishing," she said.

Denis Gaunt watched her hips sway across the lobby to the lift doors. He wondered what it would be like to be given something nourishing by Mrs. Foy. Or vice versa.

Sam McCready pushed open the plate-glass door to the street. A wave of hot summer air blew in. He turned, reached into his breast pocket, and brought out an envelope.

"Give it to them, Denis. Tomorrow morning. It's what they want, after all."

Denis took it and stared at it.

"You had it all the time," he said. "You wrote it days ago. You cunning old bastard!"

But he was talking to the closing door.

McCready turned right and ambled toward Westminster Bridge half a mile away, his jacket over his shoulder. He loosened his tie back down to the third shirt button. It was a hot June afternoon, one of those that made up the great heat wave of the summer of 1990. The early commuter traffic poured past him toward the Old Kent Road.

It would be nice out at sea today, he thought, with the Channel bobbing bright and blue under the sun. Perhaps he should take that cottage in Devon, with his own boat in the harbor, after all. He could even invite Mrs. Foy down there. For something nourishing.

Westminster Bridge rose before him. Across it the House of Parliament, whose freedoms and occasional foolishness he had spent thirty years trying to protect, towered against the blue sky. The newly cleaned tower of Big Ben glowed gold in the sunlight beside the sluggish Thames.

Halfway across the bridge, a news vendor stood beside his stand with a pile of copies of the *Evening Standard*. At his feet stood a placard. It bore the words; BUSH-GORBY—COLD WAR OVER—OFFICIAL. McCready stopped to buy a paper.

"Thank you, guv," said the news vendor. He gestured toward his placard. "All over, then, eh?"

"Over?" asked McCready.

"Yeah. All them international crises. Thing of the past."

"What a lovely idea," agreed McCready, and strolled on.

Four weeks later, Saddam Hussein invaded Kuwait. Sam McCready heard the radio bulletin while fishing two miles off the Devon coast. He considered the newsflash, then decided it was time to change his bait.

About the Author

Frederick Forsyth, who lives outside London, is the author of six best-selling novels: *The Day of the Jackal, The Devil's Alternative, The Dogs of War, The Fourth Protocol, The Odessa File,* and *The Negotiator.* His other works include *The Biafra Story, The Shepherd,* and a collection of stories, *No Comebacks.*